MF Lot 1
SC
29May07
44.10
44.10

# The
# Thirteenth
# Tale

**Center Point
Large Print**

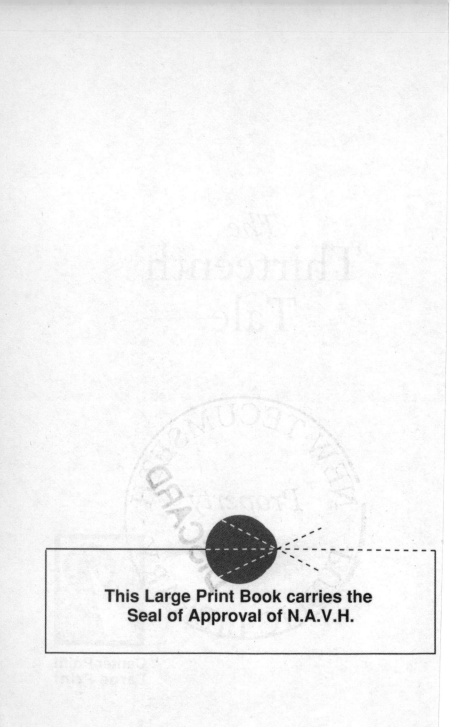

**This Large Print Book carries the
Seal of Approval of N.A.V.H.**

*The*
# Thirteenth
# Tale

## DIANE SETTERFIELD

CENTER POINT PUBLISHING
THORNDIKE, MAINE

This Center Point Large Print edition
is published in the year 2007 by arrangement with
Atria Books, a division of Simon & Schuster, Inc.

The text of this Large Print edition is unabridged. In other
aspects, this book may vary from the original edition. Printed in
Thailand. Set in 16-point Times New Roman type.

ISBN: 1-58547-892-X
ISBN 13: 978-1-58547-892-7

Library of Congress Cataloging-in-Publication Data

Setterfield, Diane.
 The thirteenth tale / Diane Setterfield.--Center Point large print ed.
  p. cm.
 ISBN-13: 978-1-58547-892-7 (lib. bdg. : alk. paper)
  1. Recluses as authors--Fiction. 2. Women authors--Fiction. 3. Family--Fiction.
 4. Female friendship--Fiction. 5. Large type books.  I. Title.

PS3619.E86T48 2007
813'.6--dc22

2006023236

*In memory*

*Ivy Dora and Fred Harold Morris*
*Corina Ethel and Ambrose Charles Setterfield*

All children mythologize their birth. It is a universal trait. You want to know someone? Heart, mind and soul? Ask him to tell you about when he was born. What you get won't be the truth; it will be a story. And nothing is more telling than a story.

—VIDA WINTER, *TALES OF CHANGE AND DESPERATION*

—DIANE SETTERFIELD, *The Thirteenth Tale*

# *Beginnings*

## THE LETTER

It was November. Although it was not yet late, the sky was dark when I turned into Laundress Passage. Father had finished for the day, switched off the shop lights and closed the shutters; but so I would not come home to darkness he had left on the light over the stairs to the flat. Through the glass in the door it cast a foolscap rectangle of paleness onto the wet pavement, and it was while I was standing in that rectangle, about to turn my key in the door, that I first saw the letter. Another white rectangle, it was on the fifth step from the bottom, where I couldn't miss it.

I closed the door and put the shop key in its usual place behind Bailey's *Advanced Principles of Geometry*. Poor Bailey. No one has wanted his fat gray book for thirty years. Sometimes I wonder what he makes of his role as guardian of the bookshop keys. I don't suppose it's the destiny he had in mind for the masterwork that he spent two decades writing.

A letter. For me. That was something of an event. The crisp-cornered envelope, puffed up with its thickly folded contents, was addressed in a hand that must have given the postman a certain amount of trouble. Although the style of the writing was old-fashioned, with its heavily embellished capitals and curly flourishes, my first impression was that it had been written by a child. The letters seemed untrained. Their uneven strokes either faded into nothing or were heavily etched into the paper. There was no sense of flow in the letters that spelled out my name. Each had been undertaken separately—M A R G A R E T L E A—as a new and daunting enterprise. But I knew no children. That is when I thought, It is the hand of an invalid.

It gave me a queer feeling. Yesterday or the day before, while I had been going about my business, quietly and in private, some unknown person—some *stranger*—had gone to the trouble of marking my name onto this envelope. Who was it who had had his mind's eye on me while I hadn't suspected a thing?

Still in my coat and hat, I sank onto the stair to read the letter. (I never read without making sure I am in a secure position. I have been like this ever since the age of seven when, sitting on a high wall and reading *The Water Babies,* I was so seduced by the descriptions of underwater life that I unconsciously relaxed my muscles. Instead of being held buoyant by the water that so vividly surrounded me in my mind, I plummeted to the ground and knocked myself out. I can still feel the scar under my fringe now. Reading can be dangerous.)

I opened the letter and pulled out a sheaf of half a dozen pages, all written in the same laborious script. Thanks to my work, I am experienced in the reading of difficult manuscripts. There is no great secret to it.

Patience and practice are all that is required. That and the willingness to cultivate an inner eye. When you read a manuscript that has been damaged by water, fire, light or just the passing of the years, your eye needs to study not just the shape of the letters but other marks of production. The speed of the pen. The pressure of the hand on the page. Breaks and releases in the flow. You must relax. Think of nothing. Until you wake into a dream where you are at once a pen flying over vellum and the vellum itself with the touch of ink tickling your surface. Then you can read it. The intention of the writer, his thoughts, his hesitations, his longings and his meaning. You can read as clearly as if you were the very candlelight illuminating the page as the pen speeds over it.

Not that this letter was anything like as challenging as some. It began with a curt "Miss Lea"; thereafter the hieroglyphs resolved themselves quickly into characters, then words, then sentences.

This is what I read:

*I once did an interview for the* Banbury Herald. *I must look it out one of these days, for the biography. Strange chap they sent me. A boy, really. As tall as a man, but with the puppy fat of youth. Awkward in his new suit. The suit was brown and ugly and meant for a much older man. The collar, the cut, the fabric, all wrong. It was the kind of thing a mother might buy for a boy leaving school for his first job, imagining that her child will somehow grow into it. But boys do not leave their boyhood behind when*

11

*they leave off their school uniform.*

*There was something in his manner. An intensity. The moment I set eyes on him, I thought, "Aha, what's he after?"*

*I've nothing against people who love truth. Apart from the fact that they make dull companions. Just so long as they don't start on about storytelling and honesty, the way some of them do. Naturally that annoys me. But provided they leave me alone, I won't hurt them.*

*My gripe is not with lovers of the truth but with truth herself. What succor, what consolation is there in truth, compared to a story? What good is truth, at midnight, in the dark, when the wind is roaring like a bear in the chimney? When the lightning strikes shadows on the bedroom wall and the rain taps at the window with its long fingernails? No. When fear and cold make a statue of you in your bed, don't expect hard-boned and fleshless truth to come running to your aid. What you need are the plump comforts of a story. The soothing, rocking safety of a lie.*

*Some writers don't like interviews of course. They get cross about it. "Same old questions," they complain. Well, what do they expect? Reporters are hacks. We writers are the real thing. Just because they always ask the same questions, it doesn't mean we have to give them the same old answers, does it? I mean, making things up, it's what we do for a living. So I give dozens of interviews a year. Hun-*

12

dreds over the course of a lifetime. For I have never believed that genius needs to be locked away out of sight to thrive. My genius is not so frail a thing that it cowers from the dirty fingers of the newspapermen.

In the early years they used to try to catch me out. They would do research, come along with a little piece of truth concealed in their pocket, draw it out at an opportune moment and hope to startle me into revealing more. I had to be careful. Inch them in the direction I wanted them to take, use my bait to draw them gently, imperceptibly, toward a prettier story than the one they had their eye on. A delicate operation. Their eyes would start to shine, and their grasp on the little chip of truth would loosen, until it dropped from their hand and fell, disregarded, by the wayside. It never failed. A good story is always more dazzling than a broken piece of truth.

Afterward, once I became famous, the Vida Winter interview became a sort of rite of passage for journalists. They knew roughly what to expect, would have been disappointed to leave without the story. A quick run through the normal questions (Where do you get your inspiration? Are your characters based on real people? How much of your main character is you?) and the shorter my answers the better they liked it. (Inside my head. No. None.) Then, the bit they were waiting for, the thing they had really come for. A dreamy, expectant look stole across their faces. They were like little *children at bedtime. And you, Miss Winter, they said. Tell me about yourself.*

*And I told. Simple little stories really, not much to them. Just a few strands, woven together in a pretty pattern, a memorable motif here, a couple of sequins there. Mere scraps from the bottom of my ragbag. Hundreds more where they came from. Offcuts from novels and stories, plots that never got finished, stillborn characters, picturesque locations I never found a use for. Odds and ends that fell out in the editing. Then it's just a matter of neatening the edges, stitching in the ends, and it's done. Another brand-new biography.*

*They went away happy, clutching their notebooks in their paws like children with sweets at the end of a birthday party. It would be something to tell their grandchildren. "One day I met Vida Winter, and she told me a story."*

*Anyway, the boy from the* Banbury Herald. *He said, "Miss Winter, tell me the truth." Now, what kind of appeal is that? I've had people devise all kinds of stratagems to trick me into telling, and I can spot them a mile off, but that? Laughable. I mean, whatever did he expect?*

*A good question. What did he expect? His eyes were glistening with an intent fever. He watched me so closely. Seeking. Probing. He was after something quite specific, I was sure of it. His forehead was damp with perspiration. Perhaps he was sickening for something. Tell me the truth, he said.*

14

*I felt a strange sensation inside. Like the past coming to life. The watery stirring of a previous life turning in my belly, creating a tide that rose in my veins and sent cool wavelets to lap at my temples. The ghastly excitement of it. Tell me the truth.*

*I considered his request. I turned it over in my mind, weighed up the likely consequences. He disturbed me, this boy, with his pale face and his burning eyes.*

*"All right," I said.*

*An hour later he was gone. A faint, absentminded good-bye and no backward glance.*

*I didn't tell him the truth. How could I? I told him a story. An impoverished, malnourished little thing. No sparkle, no sequins, just a few dull and faded patches, roughly tacked together with the edges left frayed. The kind of story that looks like real life. Or what people imagine real life to be, which is something rather different. It's not easy for someone of my talent to produce a story like that.*

*I watched him from the window. He shuffled away up the street, shoulders drooping, head bowed, each step a weary effort. All that energy, the charge, the verve, gone. I had killed it. Not that I take all the blame. He should have known better than to believe me.*

*I never saw him again.*

*That feeling I had, the current in my stomach, my temples, my fingertips—it remained with me for quite a while. It rose and fell, with the memory of* the boy's words. *Tell me the truth.* "No," I said. Over and over again. "No." But it wouldn't be still. It was a distraction. More than that, it was a danger. In the end I did a deal. "Not yet." It sighed, it fidgeted, but eventually it fell quiet. So quiet that I as good as forgot about it.

What a long time ago that was. Thirty years? Forty? More, perhaps. Time passes more quickly than you think.

The boy has been on my mind lately. *Tell me the truth.* And lately I have felt again that strange inner stirring. There is something growing inside me, dividing and multiplying. I can feel it, in my stomach, round and hard, about the size of a grapefruit. It sucks the air out of my lungs and gnaws the marrow from my bones. The long dormancy has changed it. From being a meek and biddable thing, it has become a bully. It refuses all negotiation, blocks discussion, insists on its rights. It won't take no for an answer. *The truth,* it echoes, calling after the boy, watching his departing back. And then it turns to me, tightens its grip on my innards, gives a twist. *We made a deal, remember?*

It is time.

Come on Monday. I will send a car to meet you from the half past four arrival at Harrogate Station.

*Vida Winter*

How long did I sit on the stairs after reading the letter? I don't know. For I was spellbound. There is

16

something about words. In expert hands, manipulated deftly, they take you prisoner. Wind themselves around your limbs like spider silk, and when you are so enthralled you cannot move, they pierce your skin, enter your blood, numb your thoughts. Inside you they work their magic. When I at last woke up to myself, I could only guess what had been going on in the darkness of my unconsciousness. What had the letter done to me?

I knew very little about Vida Winter. I was aware naturally of the various epithets that usually came attached to her name: England's best-loved writer; our century's Dickens; the world's most famous living author; and so on. I knew of course that she was popular, though the figures, when I later researched them, still came as a surprise. Fifty-six books published in fifty-six years; they are translated into forty-nine languages; Miss Winter has been named twenty-seven times the most borrowed author from English libraries; nineteen feature films have been based on her novels. In terms of statistics, the most disputed question is this: Has she or has she not sold more books than the Bible? The difficulty comes less from working out how many books she has sold (an ever-changing figure in the millions) than in obtaining solid figures for the Bible—whatever one thinks of the word of God, his sales data are notoriously unreliable. The figure that might have interested me the most, as I sat there at the bottom of the stairs, was twenty-two. This was the number of biographers who, for want of information, or lack of encouragement, or after inducements or threats from Miss Winter herself, had been persuaded to give up trying to discover the truth about her. But I knew none of this then. I knew only one statistic, and it was one that seemed relevant: How many books by Vida Winter had I, Margaret Lea, read? None.

I shivered on the stairs, yawned and stretched. Returning to myself, I found that my thoughts had been rearranged in my absence. Two items in particular had been selected out of the unheeded detritus that is my memory and placed for my attention.

The first was a little scene involving my father. A box of books we are unpacking from a private library clearance includes a number of Vida Winters. At the shop we don't deal in contemporary fiction. "I'll take them to the charity shop in my lunch hour," I say, and leave them on the side of the desk. But before the morning is out, three of the four books are gone. Sold. One to a priest, one to a cartographer, one to a military historian. Our clients' faces, with the customary outward paleness and inner glow of the book lover, seem to light up when they spot the rich colors of the paperback covers. After lunch, when we have finished the unpacking and the cataloging and the shelving and we have no customers, we sit reading as usual. It is late autumn, it is raining and the windows have misted up. In the background is the hiss of the gas heater; we hear the sound without hearing it for, side by side, together and miles apart, we are deep in our books.

"Shall I make tea?" I ask, surfacing.

No answer.

I make tea all the same and put a cup next to him on the desk.

An hour later the untouched tea is cold. I make a fresh pot and put another steaming cup beside him on the desk. He is oblivious to my every movement.

Gently I tilt the volume in his hands so that I can see the cover. It is the fourth Vida Winter. I return the book to its original position and study my father's face. He cannot hear me. He cannot see me. He is in another world, and I am a ghost.

That was the first memory.

The second is an image. In three-quarter profile, carved massively out of light and shade, a face towers over the commuters who wait, stunted, beneath. It is only an advertising photograph pasted on a billboard in a railway station, but to my mind's eye it has the impassive grandeur of long-forgotten queens and deities carved into rock faces by ancient civilizations. To contemplate the exquisite arc of the eye; the broad, smooth sweep of the cheekbones; the impeccable line and proportions of the nose, is to marvel that the randomness of human variation can produce something so supernaturally perfect as this. Such bones, discovered by the archaeologists of the future, would seem an artifact, a product not of blunt-tooled nature but of the very peak of artistic endeavor. The skin that embellishes these remarkable bones has the opaque luminosity of alabaster; it appears paler still by contrast with the elaborate twists and coils of copper hair that are arranged with such precision about the fine temples and down the strong, elegant neck.

As if this extravagant beauty were not enough, there are the eyes. Intensified by some photographic sleight of hand to an inhuman green, the green of glass in a church window, or of emeralds or of boiled sweets, they gaze out over the heads of the commuters with perfect inexpression. I can't say whether the other travelers that day felt the same way as I about the picture; they had read the books, so they may have had a different perspective on things. But for me, looking into the large green eyes, I could not help being reminded of that commonplace expression about the eyes being the gateway to the soul. This woman, I remember thinking, as I gazed at her green, unseeing eyes, does not have a soul.

Such was, on the night of the letter, the extent of my knowledge about Vida Winter. It was not much. Though on reflection perhaps it was as much as anyone else might know. For although everyone knew Vida Winter—knew her name, knew her face, knew her books—at the same time nobody knew her. As famous for her secrets as for her stories, she was a perfect mystery.

Now, if the letter was to be believed, Vida Winter wanted to tell the truth about herself. This was curious enough in itself, but curiouser still was my next thought: Why should she want to tell it to *me?*

Rising from the stairs, I stepped into the darkness of the shop. I didn't need the light switch to find my way. I know the shop the way you know the places of your childhood. Instantly the smell of leather and old paper was soothing. I ran my fingertips along the spines, like a pianist along his keyboard. Each book has its own individual note: the grainy, linen-covered spine of Daniels's *History of Map Making*, the cracked leather of Lakunin's minutes from the meetings of the St. Petersburg Cartographic Academy; a well-worn folder that contains his maps, hand-drawn, hand-colored. You could blindfold me and position me anywhere on the three floors of this shop, and I could tell you from the books under my fingertips where I was.

We see few customers in Lea's Antiquarian Booksellers, a scant half-dozen a day on average. There is a flurry of activity in September when the students come to buy copies of the new year's set texts; another in May when they bring them back after the exams. These books my father calls migratory. At other times of the year we can go days without seeing a client. Every summer brings the odd tourist who, having wandered off the beaten track, is prompted by curiosity to step out of the sunshine and into the shop, where he pauses for an instant, blinking as his eyes adjust. Depending on how weary he is of eating ice cream and watching the punts on the river, he might stay for a bit of shade and tranquillity or he might not. More commonly visitors to the shop are people who, having heard about us from a friend of a friend, and finding themselves near Cambridge, have made a special detour. They have anticipation on their faces as they step into the shop, and not infrequently apologize for disturbing us. They are nice people, as quiet and as amiable as the books themselves. But mostly it is just Father, me and the books.

How do they make ends meet? you might think, if you saw how few customers come and go. But you see, the shop is, in financial terms, just a sideline. The proper business takes place elsewhere. We make our living on the basis of perhaps half a dozen transactions a year. This is how it works: Father knows all the world's great collectors, and he knows the world's great collections. If you were to watch him at the auctions or book fairs that he attends frequently, you would notice how often he is approached by quietly spoken, quietly dressed individuals, who draw him aside for a quiet word. Their eyes are anything but quiet. *Does he know of* . . . they ask him, and *Has he ever heard whether* . . . A book will be mentioned. Father answers vaguely. It doesn't do to build up hope. These things usually lead nowhere. But on the other hand, if he were to hear anything . . . And if he doesn't already have it, he makes a note of the person's address in a little green notebook. Then nothing happens for quite some time. But later— a few months or many months, there is no knowing— at another auction or book fair, seeing a certain other person, he will inquire, very tentatively, whether . . . and again the book is mentioned. More often than not, it ends there. But sometimes, following the conversations, there may be an exchange of letters. Father spends a great deal of time composing letters. In French, German, Italian, even occasionally Latin. Nine times out of ten the answer is a courteous two-line refusal. But sometimes—half a dozen times a year—the reply is the prelude to a journey. A journey in which Father collects a book here, and delivers it there. He is rarely gone for more than forty-eight hours. Six times a year. *This* is our livelihood.

The shop itself makes next to no money. It is a place to write and receive letters. A place to while away the hours waiting for the next international bookfair. In the opinion of our bank manager, it is an indulgence, one that my father's success entitles him to. Yet in reality—my father's reality and mine; I don't pretend reality is the same for everyone—the shop is the very heart of the affair. It is a repository of books, a place of safety for all the volumes, once so lovingly written, that at present no one seems to want.

And it is a place to read.

A is for Austen, B is for Brontë, C is for Charles and D is for Dickens. I learned my alphabet in this shop. My father walking along the shelves, me in his arms, explaining alphabetization at the same time as he taught me to spell. I learned to write there, too: copying out names and titles onto index cards that are still there in our filing box, thirty years later. The shop was both my home and my job. It was a better school for me than school ever was, and afterward it was my own private university. It was my life.

My father never put a book into my hands and never forbade a book. Instead, he let me roam and graze, making my own more and less appropriate selections. I read gory tales of historic heroism that nineteenth-century parents thought were suitable for children, and gothic ghost stories that were surely not; I read accounts of arduous travel through treacherous lands undertaken by spinsters in crinolines, and I read hand-books on decorum and etiquette intended for young ladies of good family; I read books with pictures and books without; books in English, books in French, books in languages I didn't understand, where I could make up stories in my head on the basis of a handful of guessed-at words. Books. Books. And books.

At school I kept all this shop reading to myself. The bits of archaic French I knew from old grammars found their way into my essays, but my teachers took them for spelling mistakes, though they were never able to eradicate them. Sometimes a history lesson would touch upon one of the deep but random seams of knowledge I had accumulated by my haphazard reading in the shop. *Charlemagne?* I would think. What, *my* Charlemagne? From the shop? At these times I stayed mum, dumbstruck by the momentary collision of two worlds that were otherwise so entirely apart.

In between reading, I helped my father in his work. At nine I was allowed to wrap books in brown paper and address them to our more distant clients. At ten I was permitted to walk these parcels to the post office. At eleven I relieved my mother of her only job in the shop: the cleaning. Armored in a headscarf and housecoat against the grime, germs and general malignity inherent in "old books," she used to walk the shelves with her fastidious feather duster, her lips pressed tight and trying not to inhale. From time to time the feathers would stir up a cloud of imaginary dust, and she recoiled, coughing. Inevitably she snagged her stockings on the crate that, with the predictable malevolence of books, would just happen to be positioned behind her. I offered to do the dusting. It was a job she was glad to be rid of; she didn't need to come out to the bookshop after that.

When I was twelve, Father set me looking for lost books. We designated items lost when they were in stock according to the records but missing from their rightful position on the shelves. They might have been stolen but, more likely, they had been left in the wrong place by an absentminded browser. There were seven rooms in the shop, lined floor to ceiling with books, thousands of volumes.

"And while you're at it, check the alphabetization," Father said.

It was a job that would take forever; I wonder now whether he was entirely serious in entrusting it to me. To tell the truth it hardly mattered, for in undertaking it *I* was serious.

It took me a whole summer of mornings, but at the

beginning of September, when school started, every lost book had been found, every misplaced volume returned to its home. Not only that, but—and in retrospect, this is the thing that seems important—my fingers had made contact, albeit briefly, with every book in the shop.

By the time I was in my teens, I was giving my father so much assistance that on quiet afternoons we had little real work to do. Once the morning's work was done, the new stock shelved, the letters written, once we had eaten our sandwiches by the river and fed the ducks, it was back to the shop to read.

Gradually my reading grew less random. More and more often I found myself meandering on the second floor. Nineteenth-century literature, biography, autobiography, memoirs, diaries and letters.

My father noticed the direction of my reading. He came home from fairs and sales with books he thought might be interesting for me. Shabby little books, in manuscript mostly, yellowed pages tied with ribbon or string, sometimes handbound. The ordinary lives of ordinary people. I did not simply read them. I devoured them. Though my appetite for food grew frail, my hunger for books was constant. It was the beginning of my vocation.

I am not a proper biographer. In fact I am hardly a biographer at all. For my own pleasure mainly, I have written a number of short biographical studies of insignificant personages from literary history. My interest has always been in writing biographies of the also-rans: people who lived in the shadow of fame in their own lifetime and who, since their death, have sunk into profound obscurity. I like to disinter lives that have been buried in unopened diaries on archive shelves for a hundred years or more. Rekindling breath from memoirs that have been out of print for decades pleases me more than almost anything else.

From time to time one of my subjects is just significant enough to arouse the interest of a local academic publisher, and so I have a small number of publications to my name. Not books. Nothing so grand. Just essays really, a few flimsy pages stapled in a paper cover. One of my essays—"The Fraternal Muse," a piece on the Landier brothers, Jules and Edmond, and the diary that they wrote in tandem—caught the eye of a history editor and was included in a hardback collection of essays on writing and the family in the nineteenth century. It must have been this essay that captured the attention of Vida Winter, but its presence in the collection is quite misleading. It sits surrounded by the work of academics and professional writers, just as though I were a proper biographer, when in fact I am only a dilettante, a talented amateur.

Lives—dead ones—are just a hobby of mine. My real work is in the bookshop. My job is not to sell the books—my father does that—but to *look after* them. Every so often I take out a volume and read a page or two. After all, reading is looking after in a manner of speaking. Though they're not old enough to be valuable for their age alone, nor important enough to be sought after by collectors, my charges are dear to me, even if, as often as not, they are as dull on the inside as on the outside. No matter how banal the contents, there is always something that touches me. For someone now dead once thought these words significant enough to write them down.

People disappear when they die. Their voice, their laughter, the warmth of their breath. Their flesh. Eventually their bones. All living memory of them ceases. This is both dreadful and natural. Yet for some there is an exception to this annihilation. For in the books they write they continue to exist. We can rediscover them. Their humor, their tone of voice, their moods. Through the written word they can anger you or make you happy. They can comfort you. They can perplex you. They can alter you. All this, even though they are dead. Like flies in amber, like corpses frozen in ice, that which according to the laws of nature should pass away is, by the miracle of ink on paper, preserved. It is a kind of magic.

As one tends the graves of the dead, so I tend the books. I clean them, do minor repairs, keep them in good order. And every day I open a volume or two, read a few lines or pages, allow the voices of the forgotten dead to resonate inside my head. Do they sense it, these dead writers, when their books are read? Does a pinprick of light appear in their darkness? Is their soul stirred by the feather touch of another mind reading theirs? I do hope so. For it must be very lonely being dead.

Although I have touched here on my very private pre-occupations, I can see nonetheless that I have been putting off the essential. I am not given to acts of self-revelation; it rather looks as though in forcing myself to overcome my habitual reticence, I have written anything and everything in order to avoid writing the one thing that matters.

And yet I *will* write it. "Silence is not a natural environment for stories," Miss Winter told me once. "They need words. Without them they grow pale, sicken and die. And then they haunt you."

Quite right, too. So here is my story.

I was ten when I discovered the secret my mother was keeping. The reason it matters is that it wasn't her secret to keep. It was mine.

My parents were out that evening. They didn't go out often, and when they did, I was sent next door to sit in Mrs. Robb's kitchen. The next-door house was exactly like ours but reversed, and the backwardness of it all made me feel seasick, so when parents' evening out rolled around, I argued once again that I was old enough and sensible enough to be left at home without a babysitter. I had no great hope of success, yet this time my father agreed. Mother allowed herself to be persuaded with only the proviso that Mrs. Robb would look in at half past eight.

They left the house at seven o'clock, and I celebrated by pouring a glass of milk and drinking it on the sofa, full of admiration at my own grandness. Margaret Lea, old enough to stay home without a sitter. After the milk I felt unexpectedly bored. What to do with this freedom? I set off on a wander, marking the territory of my new freedom: the dining room, the hall, the down-stairs toilet. Everything was just as it had always been. For no particular reason, I was reminded of one of my baby fears, about the wolf and the three pigs. *I'll huff and I'll puff and I'll blow your house down!* He wouldn't have had any trouble blowing my parents' house down. The pale, airy rooms were too insubstan-tial to resist, and the furniture, with its brittle delicacy, would collapse like a pile of matchsticks if a wolf so much as looked at it. Yes, that wolf would have the house down with a mere whistle, and the three of us would be breakfast in no time. I began to wish I was in the shop, where I was never afraid. The wolf could huff and puff all he liked; with all those books doubling the thickness of the walls Father and I would be as safe as in a fortress.

Upstairs I peered into the bathroom mirror. It was for reassurance, to see what I looked like as a grown-up girl. Head tilted to the left, then to the right, I studied my reflection from all angles, willing myself to see someone different. But it was only me looking back at myself.

My own room held no promise. I knew every inch of it and it knew me; we were dull companions now. Instead, I pushed open the door of the guest room. The blank-faced wardrobe and bare dressing table paid lip service to the idea that you could brush your hair and get dressed here, but somehow you knew that behind their doors and drawer fronts they were empty. The bed, its sheets and blankets tightly tucked in and smoothed down, was uninviting. The thin pillows looked as though they had had the life drained out of them. It was always called the guest room, but we never had guests. It was where my mother slept.

Perplexed, I backed out of the room and stood on the landing.

This was it. The rite of passage. Staying home alone. I was joining the ranks of the grown-up children: Tomorrow I would be able to say, in the playground, "Last night I didn't go to a sitter. I stayed home by myself." The other girls would be wide-eyed. For so long I had wanted this, and now that it was here, I didn't know what to make of it. I'd expected that I would expand to fit the experience automatically, that I would get my first glimpse of the person I was destined to be. I'd expected the world to give up its childlike and familiar appearance to show me its secret, adult side. Instead, cloaked in my new independence, I felt younger than ever. Was there something wrong with me? Would I ever find out how to grow up?

I toyed with the idea of going round to Mrs. Robb's. But no. There was a better place. I crawled under my father's bed.

The space between the floor and the bed frame had shrunk since I was last there. Hard against one shoulder was the holiday suitcase, as gray in daylight as it was here in the dark. It held all our summer paraphernalia:

31

sunglasses, spare film for the camera, the swimming costume that my mother never wore but never threw away. On the other side was a cardboard box. My fingers fumbled with the corrugated flaps, found a way in, and rummaged. The tangled skein of Christmas-tree lights. Feathers covering the skirt of the tree angel. The last time I was under this bed I had believed in Father Christmas. Now I didn't. Was that a kind of growing up?

Wriggling out from under the bed, I dislodged an old biscuit tin. There it was, half sticking out from under the frill of the valance. I remembered the tin—it had been there forever. A picture of Scottish crags and firs on a lid too tight to open. Absently I tried the lid. It gave way so easily under my older, stronger fingers that I felt a pang of shock. Inside was Father's passport and various, differently sized pieces of paper. Forms, part printed, part handwritten. Here and there a signature.

For me, to see is to read. It has always been that way. I flicked through the documents. My parents' marriage certificate. Their birth certificates. My own birth certificate. Red print on cream paper. My father's signature. I refolded it carefully, put it with the other forms I'd already read, and passed on to the next. It was identical. I was puzzled. Why would I have two birth certificates?

Then I saw it. Same father, same mother, same date of birth, same place of birth, *different name.*

What happened to me in that moment? Inside my head everything came to pieces and came back together differently, in one of those kaleidoscopic reorganizations the brain is capable of.

I had a twin.

Ignoring the tumult in my head, my curious fingers unfolded a second piece of paper.

A death certificate.

My twin was dead.

Now I knew what it was that had stained me.

Though I was stupefied by the discovery, I was not surprised. For there had always been a feeling. The knowledge, too familiar to have ever needed words, that there was *something*. An altered quality in the air to my right. A coagulation of light. Something peculiar to me that set empty space vibrating. My pale shadow.

Pressing my hands to my right side, I bowed my head, nose almost to shoulder. It was an old gesture, one that had always come to me in pain, in perplexity, under duress of any kind. Too familiar to be pondered until now, my discovery revealed its meaning. I was looking for my twin. Where she should have been. By my side.

When I saw the two pieces of paper, and when the world had recovered itself enough to start turning again on its slow axis, I thought, So that's it. Loss. Sorrow. Loneliness. There was a feeling that had kept me apart from other people—and kept me company—all my life, and now that I had found the certificates, I knew what the feeling was. My sister.

After a long time there came the sound of the kitchen door opening downstairs. Pins and needles in my calves, I went as far as the landing, and Mrs. Robb appeared at the bottom of the stairs.

"Is everything all right, Margaret?"

"Yes."

"Have you got everything you need?"

"Yes."

"Well, come round if you need to."

"All right."

"They won't be long now, your mum and dad."

She left.

I returned the documents to the tin and put the tin back under the bed. I left the bedroom, closing the door behind me. In front of the bathroom mirror I felt the shock of contact as my eyes locked together with the eyes of another. My face tingled under her gaze. I could feel the bones under my skin.

Later, my parents' steps on the stairs.

I opened the door, and on the landing Father gave me a hug.

"Well done," he said. "Good marks all round."

Mother looked pale and tired. Going out would have started one of her headaches.

"Yes," she said. "Good girl."

"And so, how was it, sweetheart? Being home on your own?"

"It was fine."

"Thought it would be," he said. And then, unable to stop himself, he gave me another hug, a happy, two-armed affair, and kissed the top of my head. "Time for bed. And don't read too long."

"I won't."

Later I heard my parents going about the business of getting ready for bed. Father opening the medicine cupboard to find Mother's pills, filling a glass with water. His voice saying, as it so frequently did, "You'll feel better after a good night's sleep." Then the door of the guest room closed. A few moments later the bed creaked in the other room, and I heard my father's light click off.

I knew about twins. A cell that should ordinarily become one person inexplicably becomes two identical people instead.

I was a twin.

My twin was dead.

What did that make me now?

Under the covers I pressed my hand against the silver-pink crescent on my torso. The shadow my sister had left behind. Like an archaeologist of the flesh, I explored my body for evidence of its ancient history. I was as cold as a corpse.

With the letter still in my hand, I left the shop and went upstairs to my flat. The staircase narrowed at each of the three stories of books. As I went, turning out lights behind me, I began to prepare phrases for a polite letter of refusal. I was, I could tell Miss Winter, the wrong kind of biographer. I had no interest in contemporary writing. I had read none of Miss Winter's books. I was at home in libraries and archives and had never interviewed a living writer in my life. I was more at ease

35

with dead people and was, if the truth be told, nervous of the living.

It probably wasn't necessary to put that last bit in the letter.

I couldn't be bothered to make a meal. A cup of cocoa would do.

Waiting for the milk to heat, I looked out of the window. In the night glass was a face so pale you could see the blackness of the sky through it. We pressed cheek to cold, glassy cheek. If you had seen us, you would have known that were it not for this glass, there was really nothing to tell us apart.

## THIRTEEN TALES

*Tell me the truth.* The words from the letter were trapped in my head, trapped, it seemed, beneath the sloping ceiling of my attic flat, like a bird that has got in down the chimney. It was natural that the boy's plea should have affected me; I who had never been told the truth, but left to discover it alone and in secret. *Tell me the truth.* Quite.

But I resolved to put the words and the letter out of my head.

It was nearly time. I moved swiftly. In the bathroom I soaped my face and brushed my teeth. By three minutes to eight I was in my nightdress and slippers, waiting for the kettle to boil. Quickly, quickly. A minute to eight. My hot-water bottle was ready, and I filled a glass with water from the tap. Time was of the essence. For at eight o'clock the world came to an end. It was reading time.

The hours between eight in the evening and one or two in the morning have always been my magic hours. Against the blue candlewick bedspread the white pages of my open book, illuminated by a circle of lamplight, were the gateway to another world. But that night the magic failed. The threads of plot that had been left in suspense overnight had somehow gone flaccid during the day, and I found that I could not care about how they would eventually weave together. I made an effort to secure myself to a strand of the plot, but as soon as I had managed it, a voice intervened—*Tell me the truth*—that unpicked the knot and left it flopping loose again.

My hand hovered instead over the old favorites: *The Woman in White, Wuthering Heights, Jane Eyre* . . .

But it was no good. *Tell me the truth.* . . .

Reading had never let me down before. It had always been the one sure thing. Turning out the light, I rested my head on the pillow and tried to sleep.

Echoes of a voice. Fragments of a story. In the dark I heard them louder. *Tell me the truth.* . . .

At two in the morning I got out of bed, pulled on some socks, unlocked the flat door and, wrapped in my dressing gown, crept down the narrow staircase and into the shop.

At the back there is a tiny room, not much bigger than a cupboard, that we use when we need to pack a book for the post. It contains a table and, on a shelf, sheets of brown paper, scissors and a ball of string. As well as these items there is also a plain wooden cabinet that holds a dozen or so books.

The contents of the cabinet rarely change. If you were to look into it today you would see what I saw that night: a book without a cover resting on its side, and next to it an ugly tooled leather volume. A pair of books in Latin standing upright. An old Bible. Three volumes of botany, two of history and a single tatty book of astronomy. A book in Japanese, another in Polish and some poems in Old English. Why do we keep these books apart? Why are they not kept with their natural companions on our neatly labeled shelves? The cabinet is where we keep the esoteric, the valuable, the rare. These volumes are worth as much as the contents of the entire rest of the shop, more even.

The book that I was after—a small hardback, about four inches by six, only fifty or so years old—was out of place next to all these antiquities. It had appeared a couple of months ago, placed there I imagined by Father's inadvertence, and one of these days I meant to ask him about it and shelve it somewhere. But just in case, I put on the white gloves. We keep them in the cabinet to wear when we handle the books because, by a curious paradox, just as the books come to life when we read them, so the oils from our fingertips destroy them as we turn the pages. Anyway, with its paper cover intact and its corners unblunted, the book was in fine condition, one of a popular series produced to quite a high standard by a publishing house that no longer exists. A charming volume, and a first edition, but not the kind of thing that you would expect to find among the Treasures. At jumble sales and village fêtes, other volumes in the series sell for a few pence.

The paper cover was cream and green: a regular motif of shapes like fish scales formed the background, and two rectangles were left plain, one for the line drawing of a mermaid, the other for the title and author's name. *Thirteen Tales of Change and Desperation* by Vida Winter.

I locked the cabinet, returned the key and flashlight to their places and climbed the stairs back to bed, book in gloved hand.

I didn't intend to read. Not as such. A few phrases were all I wanted. Something bold enough, strong enough, to still the words from the letter that kept going around in my head. Fight fire with fire, people say. A couple of sentences, a page maybe, and then I would be able to sleep.

I removed the dust jacket and placed it for safety in the special drawer I keep for the purpose. Even with gloves you can't be too careful. Opening the book, I inhaled. The smell of old books, so sharp, so dry you can taste it.

The prologue. Just a few words.

But my eyes, brushing the first line, were snared.

All children mythologize their birth. It is a universal trait. You want to know someone? Heart, mind and soul? Ask him to tell you about when he was born. What you get won't be the truth; it will be a story. And nothing is more telling than a story.

It was like falling into water.

Peasants and princes, bailiffs and bakers' boys, merchants and mermaids, the figures were all immediately familiar. I had read these stories a hundred, a thousand, times before. They were stories everyone knew. But gradually, as I read, their familiarity fell away from them. They became strange. They became new. These characters were not the colored manikins I remembered from my childhood picture books, mechanically acting out the story one more time. They were *people*. The blood that fell from the princess's finger when she touched the spinning wheel was wet, and it left the tang of metal on her tongue when she licked her finger before falling asleep. When his comatose daughter was brought to him, the king's tears left salt burns on his face. The stories were shot through with an unfamiliar mood. Everyone achieved their heart's desire—the king had his daughter restored to life by a stranger's kiss, the beast was divested of his fur and left naked as a man, the mermaid walked—but only when it was too late did they realize the price they must pay for escaping their destiny. Every Happy Ever After was tainted. Fate, at first so amenable, so reasonable, so open to negotiation, ends up by exacting a cruel revenge for happiness.

The tales were brutal and sharp and heartbreaking. I loved them.

It was while I was reading "The Mermaid's Tale"—the twelfth tale—that I began to feel stirrings of an anxiety that was unconnected to the story itself. I was distracted: my thumb and right index finger were sending me a message: *Not many pages left.* The knowledge nagged more insistently until I tilted the book to check. It was true. The thirteenth tale must be a very short one.

I continued my reading, finished tale twelve and turned the page.

Blank.

I flicked back, forward again. Nothing.

*There was no thirteenth tale.*

There was a sudden rush in my head, I felt the sick dizziness of the deep-sea diver come too fast to the surface.

Aspects of my room came back into view, one by one. My bedspread, the book in my hand, the lamp still shining palely in the daylight that was beginning to creep in through the thin curtains.

It was morning.

I had read the night away.

There was no thirteenth tale.

In the shop my father was sitting at the desk with his head in his hands. He heard me come down the stairs and looked up, white-faced.

"Whatever is it?" I darted forward.

He was too shocked to speak; his hands roused themselves to a mute gesture of desperation before slowly replacing themselves over his horrified eyes. He groaned.

My hand hovered over his shoulder, but I am not in the habit of touching people, so it fell instead to the cardigan that he had draped over the back of his chair.

"Is there anything I can do?" I asked.

When he spoke, his voice was weary and shaken. "We'll have to phone the police. In a minute. In a minute . . ."

"The police? Father, what's happened?"

"A break-in." He made it sound like the end of the world.

I looked around the shop, bewildered. Everything was neat and in order. The desk drawers had not been forced, the shelves not ransacked, the window not broken.

"The cabinet," he said, and I began to understand.

"The *Thirteen Tales.*" I spoke firmly. "Upstairs in my flat. I borrowed it."

Father looked up at me. His expression combined relief with utter astonishment. "You *borrowed* it?"

"Yes."

"*You* borrowed it?"

"Yes." I was puzzled. I was always borrowing things from the shop, as he knew.

"But *Vida Winter* . . . ?"

And I realized that some kind of explanation was called for.

I read *old* novels. The reason is simple: I prefer proper endings. Marriages and deaths, noble sacrifices and miraculous restorations, tragic separations and unhoped-for reunions, great falls and dreams fulfilled; these, in my view, constitute an ending worth the wait. They should come after adventures, perils, dangers and dilemmas, and wind everything up nice and neatly. Endings like this are to be found more commonly in old novels than new ones, so I read old novels.

Contemporary literature is a world I know little of. My father had taken me to task on this topic many times during our daily talks about books. He reads as much as I do, but more widely, and I have great respect for his opinions. He has described in precise, measured words the beautiful desolation he feels at the close of novels where the message is that there is no end to human suffering, only endurance. He has spoken of endings that are muted, but which echo longer in the memory than louder, more explosive denouements. He has explained why it is that ambiguity touches his heart more nearly than the death and marriage style of finish that I prefer.

During these talks, I listen with the gravest attention and nod my head, but I always end up continuing in my old habits. Not that he blames me for it. There is one thing on which we are agreed: There are too many books in the world to read in a single lifetime; you have to draw the line somewhere.

Once Father even told me about Vida Winter. "Now, there's a living writer who would suit you."

But I had never read any Vida Winter. Why should I when there were so many dead writers I had still not discovered?

Except that now I had come down in the middle of the night to take the *Thirteen Tales* from the cabinet. My father, with good reason, was wondering why.

"I got a letter yesterday," I began.

He nodded.

"It was from Vida Winter."

Father raised his eyebrows but waited for me to go on.

"It seems to be an invitation for me to visit her. With a view to writing her biography."

His eyebrows lifted by another few millimeters.

"I couldn't sleep, so I came down to get the book."

I waited for Father to speak, but he didn't. He was thinking, a small frown creasing his brow. After a time I spoke again. "Why is it kept in the cabinet? What makes it so valuable?"

Father pulled himself away from his train of thought to answer. "Partly because it's the first edition of the first book by the most famous living writer in the English language. But mostly because it's flawed. Every following edition is called *Tales of Change and Desperation*. No mention of thirteen. You'll have noticed there are only twelve stories?"

I nodded.

"Presumably there were originally supposed to be thirteen, then only twelve were submitted. But there was a mixup with the jacket design and the book was printed with the original title and only twelve stories. They had to be recalled."

"But your copy . . ."

44

"Slipped through the net. One of a batch sent out by mistake to a shop in Dorset, where one customer bought a copy before the shop got the message to pack them up and send them back. Thirty years ago he realized what the value might be and sold it to a collector. The collector's estate was auctioned in September and I bought it. With the proceeds from the Avignon deal."

"The Avignon deal?" It had taken two years to negotiate the Avignon deal. It was one of Father's most lucrative successes.

"You wore the gloves, of course?" he asked sheepishly.

"Who do you take me for?"

He smiled before continuing. "All that effort for nothing."

"What do you mean?"

"Recalling all those books because the title was wrong. Yet people still call it the *Thirteen Tales*, even though it's been published as *Tales of Change and Desperation* for half a century."

"Why is that?"

"It's what a combination of fame and secrecy does. With real knowledge about her so scant, fragments of information like the story of the recalled first edition take on an importance beyond their weight. It has become part of her mythology. The mystery of the thirteenth tale. It gives people something to speculate about."

There is a short silence. Then, directing his gaze vaguely into the middle distance, and speaking lightly

45

so that I could pick up his words or let them go, as I chose, he murmured, "And now a biography . . . How unexpected."

I remembered the letter, my fear that its writer was not to be trusted. I remembered the insistence of the young man's words, "Tell me the truth." I remembered the *Thirteen Tales* that took possession of me with its first words and held me captive all night. I wanted to be held hostage again.

"I don't know what to do," I told my father.

"It is different from what you have done before. Vida Winter is a living subject. Interviews instead of archives."

I nodded.

"But you want to know the person who wrote the *Thirteen Tales*."

I nodded again.

My father put his hands on his knees and sighed. He knows what reading is. How it takes you.

"When does she want you to go?"

"Monday," I told him.

"I'll run you to the station, shall I?"

"Thank you. And—"

"Yes?"

"Can I have some time off? I ought to do some more reading before I go up there."

"Yes," he said, with a smile that didn't hide his worry. "Yes, of course."

There followed one of the most glorious times of my

46

adult life. For the first time ever I had on my bedside
table a pile of brand-new, glossy paperbacks, purchased
from a regular bookshop. *Betwixt and Between* by Vida
Winter; *Twice Is Forever* by Vida Winter; *Hauntings* by
Vida Winter; *Out of the Arc* by Vida Winter; *Rules of
Affliction* by Vida Winter; *The Birthday Girl* by Vida
Winter; *The Puppet Show* by Vida Winter. The covers,
all by the same artist, glowed with heat and power:
amber and scarlet, gold and deep purple. I even bought
a copy of *Tales of Change and Desperation*; its title
looked bare without the *Thirteen* that makes my
father's copy so valuable. His own copy I had returned
to the cabinet.

Of course one always hopes for something special
when one reads an author one hasn't read before, and
Miss Winter's books gave me the same thrill I had
when I discovered the Landier diaries, for instance.
But it was more than that. I have always been a reader;
I have read at every stage of my life, and there has
never been a time when reading was not my greatest
joy. And yet I cannot pretend that the reading I have
done in my adult years matches in its impact on my
soul the reading I did as a child. I still believe in stories. I still forget myself when I am in the middle of a
good book. Yet it is not the same. Books are, for me,
it must be said, the most important thing; what I
cannot forget is that there was a time when they were
at once more banal and more essential than that. When
I was a child, books were *everything*. And so there is
in me, always, a nostalgic yearning for the *lost* plea-

sure of books. It is not a yearning that one ever expects to be fulfilled. And during this time, these days when I read all day and half the night, when I slept under a counterpane strewn with books, when my sleep was black and dreamless and passed in a flash and I woke to read again—the lost joys of reading returned to me. Miss Winter restored to me the virginal qualities of the novice reader, and then with her stories she ravished me.

From time to time my father would knock at the door at the top of the stairs. He stared at me. I must have had that dazed look intense reading gives you. "You won't forget to eat, will you?" he said, as he handed me a bag of groceries or a pint of milk.

I would have liked to stay in my flat forever with those books. But if I was to go to Yorkshire to meet Miss Winter, then there was other work to be done. I took a day off from reading and went to the library. In the newspaper room, I looked at the books pages of the national newspapers for pieces on Miss Winter's recent novels. For every new book that came out, she summoned a number of journalists to a hotel in Harrogate, where she met them one by one and gave them, separately, what she termed her life story. There must have been dozens of these stories in existence, hundreds perhaps. I found almost twenty without looking very hard.

After the publication of *Betwixt and Between*, she was the secret daughter of a priest and a

48

schoolmistress; a year later in the same newspaper she got publicity for *Hauntings* by telling how she was the runaway child of a Parisian courtesan. For *The Puppet Show*, she was, in various newspapers, an orphan raised in a Swiss convent, a street child from the backstreets of the East End and the stifled only girl in a family of ten boisterous boys. I particularly liked the one in which, becoming accidentally separated in India from her Scottish missionary parents, she scraped out an existence for herself in the streets of Bombay, making a living as a storyteller. She told stories about pine trees that smelled like the freshest coriander, mountains as beautiful as the Taj Mahal, haggis more delicious than any street-corner pakora and bagpipes. Oh, the sound of the bagpipes! So beautiful it defied description. When many years later she was able to return to Scotland—a country she had left as a tiny baby—she was gravely disappointed. The pine trees smelled nothing like coriander. Snow was *cold*. Haggis tasted flat. As for the bagpipes . . .

Wry and sentimental, tragic and astringent, comic and sly, each and every one of these stories was a masterpiece in miniature. For a different kind of writer, they might be the pinnacle of her achievement; for Vida Winter they were mere throwaways. No one, I think, would have mistaken them for the truth.

The day before my departure was Sunday and I spent the afternoon at my parents' house. It never changes; a single lupine exhalation could reduce it to rubble.

49

My mother smiled a small, taut smile and talked brightly while we had tea. The neighbor's garden, road-works in town, a new perfume that had brought her up in a rash. Light, empty chat, produced to keep silence at bay, silence in which her demons lived. It was a good performance: nothing to reveal that she could hardly bear to leave the house, that the most minor unexpected event gave her a migraine, that she could not read a book for fear of the feelings she might find in it.

Father and I waited until Mother went to make fresh tea before talking about Miss Winter.

"It's not her real name," I told him. "If it was her real name, it would be easy to trace her. And everyone who has tried has given up for want of information. No one knows even the simplest fact about her."

"How curious."

"It's as if she came from nowhere. As if before being a writer she didn't exist at all. As if she invented herself at the same time as her book."

"We know what she chose for a pen name. That must reveal something, surely," my father suggested.

"Vida. From *vita,* Latin, meaning life. Though I can't help thinking of French, too."

*Vide* in French means empty. The void. Nothingness. But we don't use words like this in my parents' house, so I left it for him to infer.

"Quite." He nodded. "And what about Winter?"

Winter. I looked out of the window for inspiration. Behind my sister's ghost, dark branches stretched naked across the darkening sky, and the flower beds

50

were bare black soil. The glass was no protection against the chill; despite the gas fire, the room seemed filled with bleak despair. What did winter mean to me? One thing only: death.

There was a silence. When it became necessary to say something so as not to burden the previous exchange with an intolerable weight, I said, "It's a spiky name. V and W. Vida Winter. Very spiky."

My mother came back. Placing cups on saucers, pouring tea, she talked on, her voice moving as freely in her tightly policed plot of life as though it were seven acres.

My attention wandered. On the mantel over the fireplace was the one object in the room that might be considered decorative. A photograph. Every so often my mother talks about putting it away in a drawer, where it will be safe from dust. But my father likes to see it, and since he so rarely opposes her, on this she cedes to him. In the picture are a youthful bride and groom. Father looks the same as ever: quietly handsome, with dark, thoughtful eyes; the years do not change him. The woman is scarcely recognizable. A spontaneous smile, laughter in her eyes, warmth in her gaze as she looks at my father. She looks happy.

Tragedy alters everything.

I was born, and the woman in the wedding photo disappeared.

I looked out into the dead garden. Against the fading light, my shadow hovered in the glass, looking into the dead room. What did she make of us? I wondered.

What did she think of our attempts to persuade ourselves that this was life and that we were really living
it?

ARRIVAL

I left home on an ordinary winter day, and for miles
my train ran under a gauzy white sky. Then I
changed trains, and the clouds massed. They grew
thicker and darker, more and more bloated, as I traveled
north. At any moment I expected to hear the first scattering of drops on the windowpane. Yet the rain did not
come.

At Harrogate, Miss Winter's driver, a dark-haired,
bearded man, was disinclined to talk. I was glad, for his
lack of conversation left me free to study the unfamiliar
views that unfolded as soon as we left the town behind.
I had never been north before. My researches had taken
me to London and, once or twice, across the channel to
libraries and archives in Paris. Yorkshire was a county
I knew only from novels, and novels from another century at that. Once we left the town behind, there were
few signs of the contemporary world, and it was possible to believe I was traveling into the past at the same
time as into the countryside. The villages were quaint,
with their churches and pubs and stone cottages; then,
the farther we went, the smaller the villages became
and the greater the distance between them until isolated
farmhouses were the only interruptions to the naked

winter fields. At last we left even the farmhouses behind and it grew dark. The car's headlamps showed me swathes of a colorless, undefined landscape: no fences, no walls, no hedges, no buildings. Just a vergeless road and each side of it, vague undulations of darkness.

"Is this the moors?" I asked.

"It is," the driver said, and I leaned closer to the window, but all I could make out was the waterlogged sky that pressed down claustrophobically on the land, on the road, on the car. Beyond a certain distance even the light from our headlamps was extinguished.

At an unmarked junction we turned off the road and bumped along for a couple of miles on a stony track. We stopped twice for the driver to open a gate and close it behind us, then on we went, jolting and shaking for another mile.

Miss Winter's house lay between two slow rises in the darkness, almost-hills that seemed to merge into each other and that revealed the presence of a valley and a house only at the last turn of the drive. The sky by now was blooming shades of purple, indigo and gunpowder, and the house beneath it crouched long and low and very dark. The driver opened the car door for me, and I stepped out to see that he had already unloaded my case and was ready to pull away, leaving me alone in front of an unlit porch. Barred shutters blacked out the windows and there was not a single sign of human habitation. Closed in upon itself, the place seemed to shun visitors.

I rang the bell. Its clang was oddly muted in the damp air. While I waited I watched the sky. Cold crept through the soles of my shoes, and I rang the bell again. Still no one came to the door.

About to ring for a third time, I was caught by surprise when with no sound at all the door was opened.

The woman in the doorway smiled professionally and apologized for keeping me waiting. At first sight she seemed very ordinary. Her short, neat hair was the same palish shade as her skin, and her eyes were neither blue nor gray nor green. Yet it was less the absence of color than a lack of expression that made her plain. With some warmth of emotion in them, her eyes could, I suspected, have gleamed with life; and it seemed to me, as she matched my scrutiny glance for glance, that she maintained her inexpressivity only by deliberate effort.

"Good evening," I said. "I am Margaret Lea."

"The biographer. We've been expecting you."

What is it that allows human beings to see through each other's pretendings? For I understood quite clearly in that moment that she was anxious. Perhaps emotions have a smell or a taste; perhaps we transmit them unknowingly by vibrations in the air. Whatever the means, I knew just as surely that it was nothing about me in particular that alarmed her, but only the fact that I had come and was a stranger.

She ushered me in and closed the door behind me. The key turned in the lock without a sound and there was not a squeak as the well-oiled bolts were slid noiselessly into place.

Standing there in my coat in the hallway, I experienced for the first time the most profound oddity of the place. Miss Winter's house was entirely silent.

The woman told me her name was Judith, and that she was the housekeeper. She asked about my journey and mentioned the hours of meals and the best times to get hot water. Her mouth opened and closed; as soon as her words fell from her lips they were smothered by the blanket of silence that descended and extinguished them. The same silence swallowed our footfalls, and muffled the opening and closing of doors as she showed me, one after another, the dining room, the drawing room, the music room.

There was no magic behind the silence—it was the soft-furnishings that did it. Overstuffed sofas were piled with velvet cushions; there were upholstered footstools, chaise longues and armchairs; tapestries hung on the walls and were used as throws over upholstered furniture. Every floor was carpeted, every carpet overlaid with rugs. The damask that draped the windows also baffled the walls. Just as blotting paper absorbs ink, so all this wool and velvet absorbed sound, with one difference: Where blotting paper takes up only excess ink, the fabric of the house seemed to suck in the very essence of the words we spoke.

I followed the housekeeper. We turned left and right, and right and left, went up and down stairs until I was thoroughly confused. I quickly lost all sense of how the convoluted interior of the house corresponded with its outer plainness. The house had been altered over time,

I supposed, added to here and there; probably we were in some wing or extension invisible from the front. "You'll get the hang of it," the housekeeper mouthed, seeing my face, and I understood her as if I were lip-reading. Finally we turned from a half-landing and came to a halt. She unlocked a door that opened into a sitting room. There were three more doors leading off it. "Bathroom," she said, opening one of the doors, "bedroom," opening another, "and study." The rooms were as padded with cushions and curtains and hangings as the rest of the house.

"Will you take your meals in the dining room, or here?" she asked, indicating the small table and a single chair by the window.

I did not know whether meals in the dining room meant eating with my hostess, and unsure of my status in the house (was I a guest or an employee?), I hesitated, wondering whether it was politer to accept or to refuse. Divining the cause of my uncertainty, the house-keeper added, as though having to overcome a habit of reticence, "Miss Winter always eats alone."

"Then if it's all the same to you, I'll eat here."

"I'll bring you soup and sandwiches straightaway, shall I? You must be hungry after the train. You've things to make your tea and coffee just here." She opened a cupboard in the corner of the bedroom to reveal a kettle, the other paraphernalia for drinks making and even a tiny fridge. "It will save you from running up and down to the kitchen," she added, and threw in an abashed smile, by way of apology, I thought, for not wanting me in her kitchen.

She left me to my unpacking.

In the bedroom it was the work of a minute to unpack my few clothes, my books and my toiletries. I pushed the tea and coffee things to one side and replaced them with the packet of cocoa I had brought from home. Then I had just enough time to test the high antique bed—it was so lavishly covered with cushions that there could be any number of peas under the mattress and I would not know it—before the housekeeper returned with a tray.

"Miss Winter invites you to meet her in the library at eight o'clock."

She did her best to make it sound like an invitation, but I understood, as I was no doubt meant to, that it was a command.

## MEETING MISS WINTER

Whether by luck or accident I cannot say, but I found my way to the library a full twenty minutes earlier than I had been commanded to attend. It was not a problem. What better place to kill time than a library? And for me, what better way to get to know someone than through her choice and treatment of books?

My first impression was of the room as a whole, and it struck me by its marked difference from the rest of the house. The other rooms were thick with the corpses

57

of suffocated words; here in the library you could breathe. Instead of being shrouded in fabric, it was a room made of wood. There were floorboards underfoot, shutters at the tall windows and the walls were lined with solid oak shelves.

It was a high room, much longer than it was wide. On one side five arched windows reached from ceiling almost to floor; at their base window seats had been installed. Facing them were five similarly shaped mirrors, positioned to reflect the view outside, but tonight echoing the carved panels of the shutters. The bookshelves extended from the walls into the rooms, forming bays; in each recess an amber-shaded lamp was placed on a small table. Apart from the fire at the far end of the room, this was the only lighting, and it created soft, warm pools of illumination at the edge of which rows of books melted into darkness.

Slowly I made my way down the center of the room, taking a look into the bays on my right and left. After my first glances I found myself nodding. It was a proper, well-maintained library. Categorized, alphabetized and clean, it was just as I would have done it myself. All my favorites were there, with a great number of rare and valuable volumes as well as more ordinary, well-thumbed copies. Not only *Jane Eyre, Wuthering Heights, The Woman in White,* but *The Castle of Otranto, Lady Audley's Secret, The Spectre Bride.* I was thrilled to come across a *Dr. Jekyll and Mr. Hyde* so rare that my father had given up believing in its existence.

Marveling at the rich selection of volumes on Miss Winter's shelves, I browsed my way toward the fireplace at the far end of the room. In the final bay on the right, one particular set of shelves stood out even from some distance: Instead of displaying the mellow, predominantly brown stripes that were the spines of the older books, this stack showed the silvery blues, sage greens and pink-beiges of more recent decades. They were the only modern books in the room. Miss Winter's own works. With her earliest titles at the top of the stack and recent novels at the bottom, each work was represented in its many different editions and even in different languages. I saw no *Thirteen Tales*, the mistitled book I had read at the bookshop, but in its other guise as *Tales of Change and Desperation* there were more than a dozen different editions.

I selected a copy of Miss Winter's most recent book. On page one an elderly nun arrives at a small house in the backstreets of an unnamed town that seems to be in Italy; she is shown into a room where a pompous young man, whom we take to be English or American, greets her in some surprise. (I turned the page. The first paragraphs had drawn me in, just as I had been drawn in every time I had opened one of her books, and without meaning to, I began to read in earnest.) The young man does not at first appreciate what the reader already understands: that his visitor has come on a grave mission, one that will alter his life in ways he cannot be expected to foresee. She begins her explanation and bears it patiently (I turned the page; I had forgotten the library, forgotten Miss Winter, forgotten myself) when he treats her with the levity of indulged youth . . .

And then something penetrated through my reading and drew me out of the book. A prickling sensation at the back of the neck.

*Someone was watching me.*

I know the back-of-the-neck experience is not an uncommon phenomenon; it was, however, the first time it had happened to *me*. Like those of a great many solitary people, my senses are acutely attuned to the presence of others, and I am more used to being the invisible spy in a room than to being spied upon. Now someone was watching me, and not only that, but whoever it was had been watching me for some time. How long had that unmistakable sensation been tickling me? I thought back over the past minutes, trying to retrace the memory of the body behind my memory of the book. Was it since the nun began to speak to the young man? Since she was shown into the house? Or earlier? Without moving a muscle, head bent over the page as though I had noticed nothing, I tried to remember.

Then I realized.

I had felt it even before I picked up the book.

Needing a moment to recover myself, I turned the page, continuing the pretense of reading.

"You can't fool me."

Imperious, declamatory, magisterial.

There was nothing to be done but turn and face her.

Vida Winter's appearance was not calculated for concealment. She was an ancient queen, sorceress or goddess. Her stiff figure rose regally out of a profusion of fat purple and red cushions. Draped around her shoulders, the folds of the turquoise-and-green cloth that cloaked her body did not soften the rigidity of her frame. Her bright copper hair had been arranged into an elaborate confection of twists, curls and coils. Her face, as intricately lined as a map, was powdered white and finished with bold scarlet lipstick. In her lap, her hands were a cluster of rubies, emeralds and white, bony knuckles; only her nails, unvarnished, cut short and square like my own, struck an incongruous note.

What unnerved me more than all the rest were her sunglasses. I could not see her eyes but, as I remembered the inhuman green irises from the poster, her dark lenses seemed to develop the force of a searchlight; I had the impression that from behind them she was looking through my skin and into my very soul.

I drew a veil over myself, masked myself in neutrality, hid behind my appearance.

For an instant I think she was surprised that I was not transparent, that she could not see straight through me, but she recovered quickly, more quickly than I had.

"Very well," she said tartly, and her smile was for herself more than for me. "To business. Your letter gives me to understand that you have reservations about the commission I am offering you."

"Well, yes, that is—"

The voice ran on as if it had not registered the interruption. "I could suggest increasing the monthly stipend and the final fee."

I licked my lips, sought the right words. Before I could speak, Miss Winter's dark shades had bobbed up and down, taking in my flat brown bangs, my straight skirt and navy cardigan. She smiled a small, pitying smile and overrode my intention to speak. "But pecuniary interest is clearly not in your nature. How quaint." Her tone was dry. "I have written about people who don't care for money, but I never expected to meet one." She leaned back against the cushions. "Therefore I conclude that the difficulty concerns integrity. People whose lives are not balanced by a healthy love of money suffer from an appalling obsession with personal integrity."

She waved a hand, dismissing my words before they were out of my mouth. "You are afraid of undertaking an authorized biography in case your independence is compromised. You suspect that I want to exert control over the content of the finished book. You know that I have resisted biographers in the past and are wondering what my agenda is in changing my mind now. Above all"—that dark gaze of her sunglasses again—"you are afraid I mean to lie to you."

I opened my mouth to protest but found nothing to say. She was right.

"You see, you don't know what to say, do you? Are you embarrassed to accuse me of wanting to lie to you? People don't like to accuse each other of lying. And for heaven's sake, sit down."

I sat down. "I don't accuse you of anything," I began mildly, but immediately she interrupted me.

"Don't be so polite. If there's one thing I can't abide, it's politeness."

Her forehead twitched, and an eyebrow rose over the top of the sunglasses. A strong black arch that bore no relation to any natural brow.

"Politeness. Now, there's a poor man's virtue if ever there was one. What's so admirable about inoffensiveness, I should like to know. After all, it's easily achieved. One needs no particular talent to be polite. On the contrary, being nice is what's left when you've failed at everything else. People with ambition don't give a damn what other people think about them. I hardly suppose Wagner lost sleep worrying whether he'd hurt someone's feelings. But then he was a genius."

Her voice flowed relentlessly on, recalling instance after instance of genius and its bedfellow selfishness, and the folds of her shawl never moved as she spoke. She must be made of steel, I thought.

Eventually she drew her lecture to a close with the words: "Politeness is a virtue I neither possess nor esteem in others. We need not concern ourselves with it." And with the air of having had the final word on the subject, she stopped.

"You raised the topic of lying," I said. "That is something we might concern ourselves with."

"In what respect?" Through the dark lenses, I could just see the movements of Miss Winter's lashes. They crouched and quivered around the eye, like the long legs of a spider around its body.

"You have given nineteen different versions of your life story to journalists in the last two years alone. That's just the ones I found on a quick search. There are many more. Hundreds, probably."

She shrugged. "It's my profession. I'm a storyteller."

"I am a biographer. I work with facts."

She tossed her head and her stiff curls moved as one. "How horribly dull. I could never have been a biographer. Don't you think one can tell the truth much better with a story?"

"Not in the stories you have told the world so far."

Miss Winter conceded a nod. "Miss Lea," she began. Her voice was slower. "I had my reasons for creating a smoke screen around my past. Those reasons, I assure you, are no longer valid."

"What reasons?"

"Life is compost."

I blinked.

"You think that a strange thing to say, but it's true. All my life and all my experience, the events that have befallen me, the people I have known, all my memories, dreams, fantasies, everything I have ever read, all of that has been chucked onto the compost heap, where over time it has rotted down to a dark, rich, organic mulch. The process of cellular breakdown makes it unrecognizable. Other people call it the imagination. I think of it as a compost heap. Every so often I take an idea, plant it in the compost, and wait. It feeds on that black stuff that used to be a life, takes its energy for its own. It germinates. Takes root. Produces shoots. And so

64

on and so forth, until one fine day I have a story, or a novel."

I nodded, liking the analogy.

"Readers," continued Miss Winter, "are fools. They believe all writing is autobiographical. And so it is, but not in the way they think. The writer's life needs time to rot away before it can be used to nourish a work of fiction. It must be allowed to decay. That's why I couldn't have journalists and biographers rummaging around in my past, retrieving bits and pieces of it, preserving it in their words. To write my books I needed my past left in peace, for time to do its work."

I considered her answer, then asked, "And what has happened to change things now?"

"I am old. I am ill. Put those two facts together, biographer, and what do you get? The end of the story, I think."

I bit my lip. "And why not write the book yourself?"

"I have left it too late. Besides, who would believe me? I have cried wolf too often."

"Do you intend to tell me the truth?" I asked.

"Yes," she said, but I had heard the hesitation even though it lasted only a fraction of a second.

"And why do you want to tell it to *me?*"

She paused. "Do you know, I have been asking myself the very same question for the last quarter of an hour. Just what kind of a person *are* you, Miss Lea?"

I fixed my mask in place before replying. "I am a shop assistant. I work in an antiquarian bookshop. I am an amateur biographer. Presumably you have read

65

my work on the Landier brothers?"

"It's not much to go on, is it? If we are to work together, I shall need to know a little more about who you are. I can hardly spill the secrets of a lifetime to a person of whom I know nothing. So, tell me about yourself. What are your favorite books? What do you dream about? Whom do you love?"

On the instant I was too affronted to reply.

"Well, answer me! For goodness' sake! Am I to have a stranger living under my roof? A stranger working for me? It is not reasonable. Tell me this, do you believe in ghosts?"

Governed by something stronger than reason, I rose from my chair.

"Whatever are you doing? Where are you going? Wait!"

I took one step after another, trying not to run, conscious of the rhythm of my feet rapping out on the wooden boards, while she called to me in a voice that contained an edge of panic.

"Come back!" she cried. "I am going to tell you a story—a marvelous story!"

I did not stop.

"Once upon a time there was a haunted house—"

I reached the door. My fingers closed on the handle.

"Once upon a time there was a library—"

I opened the door and was about to step into its emptiness when, in a voice hoarse with something like fear, she launched the words that stopped me in my tracks.

"Once upon a time there were *twins*—"

66

I waited until the words stopped their ringing in the air and then, despite myself, I looked back. I saw the back of a head, and hands that rose, trembling, to the averted face.

Tentatively I took a step back into the room. At the sound of my feet, the copper curls turned.

I was stunned. The glasses were gone. Green eyes, bright as glass and as real, looked to me with something like a plea. For a moment I simply stared back. Then, "Miss Lea, won't you please sit down," said a voice shakily, a voice that was and was not Vida Winter's.

Drawn by something beyond my control, I moved toward the chair and sat down.

"I'm not making any promises," I said wearily.

"I'm not in a position to exact any," came the answer in a small voice.

Truce.

"Why did you choose me?" I asked again, and this time she answered.

"Because of your work on the Landier brothers. Because you know about siblings."

"And will you tell me the truth?"

"I will tell you the truth."

The words were unambiguous enough, but I heard the tremor that undermined them. She meant to tell me the truth, I did not doubt it. She had decided to tell. Perhaps she even wanted to tell. Only she did not quite believe that she would. Her promise of honesty was spoken as much to convince herself as to persuade me, and she heard the lack of conviction at its heart as clearly as I did.

And so I made a suggestion. "I will ask you three things. Things that are a matter of public record. When I leave here, I will be able to check what you tell me. If I find you have told me the truth about them, I will accept the commission."

"Ah, the rule of three . . . The magic number. Three trials before the prince wins the hand of the fair princess. Three wishes granted to the fisherman by the magic talking fish. Three bears for Goldilocks and Three Billy Goats Gruff. Miss Lea, if you had asked me two questions or four I might have been able to lie, but three . . ."

I slid my pencil from the ring binding of my pad and opened the cover.

"What is your real name?"

She swallowed. "Are you quite sure this is the best way to proceed? I could tell you a ghost story—a rather good one, even if I do say so myself. It might be a better way of getting to the heart of things . . ."

I shook my head. "Tell me your name."

The jumble of knuckles and rubies shifted in her lap; the stones glowed in the firelight.

"My name *is* Vida Winter. I went through the necessary legal procedures in order to be able to call myself by that name legally and honestly. What you want to know is the name by which I was known prior to the change. That name was—"

She paused, needing to overcome some obstacle within herself, and when she pronounced the name it was with a noticeable neutrality, an utter absence of intonation, as though it were a word in some foreign language she had never applied herself to learning: "That name was Adeline March."

As though to cut short even the minimal vibration the name carried in the air, she continued rather tartly, "I hope you're not going to ask my date of birth. I am of an age at which it is de rigueur to have forgotten it."

"I can manage without, if you give me your place of birth."

She released an irritated sigh. "I could tell you much better, if you would only allow me to tell it my way . . ."

"This is what we have agreed. Three facts on public record."

She pursed her lips. "You will find it is a matter of record that Adeline March was born in Saint Bartholomew's Hospital, London. I can hardly be expected to offer any personal guarantee of the veracity of that detail. Though I am an exceptional person, I am not so exceptional that I can remember my own birth."

I noted it down.

Now the third question. I had, it must be admitted, no particular third question prepared. She did not want to tell me her age, and I hardly needed her date of birth. With her long publishing history and the date of her first book, she could not be less than seventy-three or -four, and to judge by her appearance, altered though it was by illness and makeup, she could be no

69

more than eighty. But the uncertainty didn't matter; with her name and her place of birth, I could find the date out for myself anyway. From my first two questions, I already had the information I needed in order to ascertain that a person by the name of Adeline March actually existed. What to ask, then? Perhaps it was my desire to hear Miss Winter tell a story, but when the occasion arose to play my third question as a wild card, I seized it.

"Tell me," I began slowly, carefully. In the stories with the wizards, it is always with the third wish that everything so dangerously won is disastrously snatched away. "Tell me something that happened to you in the days before you changed your name, for which there exists a public record." Educational successes, I was thinking. School sporting achievements. Those minor triumphs that are recorded for proud parents and for posterity.

In the hush that followed, Miss Winter seemed to draw all of her external self into her core; under my very eyes she managed to absent herself from herself, and I began to understand how it was that earlier I had failed to see her. I watched the shell of her, marveled at the impossibility of knowing what was going on beneath the surface.

And then she emerged.

"Do you know why my books are so successful?"

"For a great many reasons, I believe."

"Possibly. Largely it is because they have a beginning, a middle and an end. In the right order. Of course all stories have beginnings, middles and endings; it is having them in the right order that matters. That is why people like my books."

She sighed and fidgeted with her hands. "I am going to answer your question. I am going to tell you something about myself, which happened before I became a writer and changed my name, and it is something for which there exists a public record. It is the most important thing that has ever happened to me. But I did not expect to find myself telling it to you so soon. I shall have to break one of my rules to do it. I shall have to tell you the end of my story before I tell you the beginning."

"The *end* of your story? How can that be, if it happened before you started writing?"

"Quite simply because my story—my own personal story—ended before my writing began. Storytelling has only ever been a way of filling in the time since everything finished."

I waited, and she drew in her breath like a chess player who finds his key piece cornered.

"I would sooner not tell you. But I have promised, haven't I? The rule of three. It's unavoidable. The wizard might beg the boy not to make a third wish, because he knows it will end in disaster, but the boy *will* make a third wish and the wizard is bound to grant it because it is in the rules of the story. You asked me to tell you the truth about three things, and I must, because of the rule of three. But let me first ask you something in return."

"What?"

"After this, no more jumping about in the story. From tomorrow, I will tell you my story, beginning at the beginning, continuing with the middle, and with the end at the end. Everything in its proper place. No cheating. No looking ahead. No questions. No sneaky glances at the last page."

Did she have the right to place conditions on our deal, having already accepted it? Not really. Still, I nodded.

"I agree."

She could not quite look at me as she spoke.

"I lived at Angelfield."

Her voice trembled over the place name, and she scratched nervously at her palm in an unconscious gesture.

"I was sixteen."

Her voice grew stilted; fluency deserted her.

"There was a fire."

The words were expelled from her throat hard and dry, like stones.

"I lost everything."

And then, the cry breaking from her lips before she could stop it, "Oh, Emmeline!"

There are cultures in which it is believed that a name contains all a person's mystical power. That a name should be known only to God and to the person who holds it and to very few privileged others. To pronounce such a name, either one's own or someone else's, is to invite jeopardy. This, it seemed, was such a name.

72

Miss Winter pressed her lips together, too late. A tremor ran through the muscles under the skin.

Now I knew I was tied to the story. I had stumbled upon the heart of the tale that I had been commissioned to tell. It was love. And loss. For what else could the sorrow of that exclamation be but bereavement? In a flash I saw beyond the mask of white makeup and the exotic draperies. For a few seconds it seemed to me that I could see right into Miss Winter's heart, right into her thoughts. I recognized the very essence of her—how could I fail to, for was it not the essence of me? We were both lone twins. With this realization, the leash of the story tightened around my wrists, and my excitement was suddenly cut through with fear.

"Where can I find a public record of this fire?" I asked, trying not to let my perturbed feelings show in my voice.

"The local newspaper. The *Banbury Herald*."

I nodded, made a note in my pad and flipped the cover closed.

"Although," she added, "there is a record of a different kind that I can show you now."

I raised an eyebrow.

"Come nearer."

I rose from my chair and took a step, halving the distance between us.

Slowly she raised her right arm, and held out to me a closed fist that seemed three-quarters precious stones in their clawlike settings. In a movement that spoke of great effort, she turned her hand and opened it, as though she had some surprise gift concealed and was about to offer it to me.

But there was no gift. The surprise was the hand itself.

The flesh of her palm was like no flesh I had seen before. Its whitened ridges and purple furrows bore no relation to the pink mound at the base of my fingers, the pale valley of my palm. Melted by fire, her flesh had cooled into an entirely unrecognizable landscape, like a scene left permanently altered by the passage of a flow of lava. Her fingers did not lie open but were drawn into a claw by the shrunken tightness of the scar tissue. In the heart of her palm, scar within a scar, burn inside burn, was a grotesque mark. It was set very deep in her clutch, so deep that with a sudden nausea I wondered what had happened to the bone that should be there. It made sense of the odd set of the hand at the wrist, the way it seemed to weigh upon her arm as though it had no life of its own. The mark was a circle embedded in her palm, and extending from it, in the direction of the thumb, a short line.

Thinking about it now, I realize that the mark had more or less the form of a $Q$, but at the time, in the shock of this unexpected and painful act of revealment, it had no such clarity, and it disturbed me the way I would be disturbed by the appearance on a page of English of an unfamiliar symbol from a lost and unreadable language.

A sudden vertigo took hold of me and I reached behind me for my chair.

"I'm sorry," I heard her say. "One gets so used to one's own horrors, one forgets how they must seem to other people."

I sat down and gradually the blackness at the edge of my vision receded.

Miss Winter closed her fingers into her damaged palm, swiveled her wrist and drew the jewel-encrusted fist back into her lap. In a protective gesture she curled the fingers of her other hand around it.

"I'm sorry you didn't want to hear my ghost story, Miss Lea."

"I'll hear it another time."

Our interview was over.

On my way back to my quarters I thought of the letter she had sent me. The strained and painstaking hand that I had never seen the like of before. I had put it down to illness. Arthritis perhaps. Now I understood. From the very first book and through her entire career, Miss Winter had written her masterpieces with her left hand.

In my study the velvet curtains were green, and a pale gold watermark satin covered the walls. Despite the woolly hush, I was pleased with the room, for the overall effect was relieved by the broad wooden desk and the plain upright chair that stood under the window. I switched on the desk lamp and laid out the ream of paper I had brought with me, and my twelve pencils. They were brand-new: unsharpened columns of red, just what I like to start a new project with. The last thing I took from my bag was my pencil sharpener. I screwed it like a vise to the edge of the desk and set the paper basket directly underneath.

On impulse I climbed onto the desk and reached behind the elaborate valance to the curtain pole. My fingers groped for the tops of the curtains, and I felt for the hooks and stitches that attached them. It was hardly a job for one person; the curtains were floor length, lined and interlined, and their weight, flung over my shoulder, was crushing. But after a few minutes, first one then the other curtain was folded and in a cupboard. I stood in the center of the floor and surveyed the result of my work.

The window was a large expanse of dark glass, and in the center of it, my ghost, darkly transparent, was staring in at me. Her world was not unlike my own: the pale outline of a desk on the other side of the glass, and farther back a deeply buttoned armchair placed inside the circle of light cast by a standard lamp. But where my chair was red, hers was gray; and where my chair stood on an Indian rug, surrounded by light gold walls, her chair hovered spectrally in an undefined, endless plane of darkness in which vague forms, like waves, seemed to shift and breathe.

Together we began the little ritual of preparing our desks. We divided a ream of paper into smaller piles and flicked through each one, to let the air in. One by one we sharpened our pencils, turning the handle and watching the long shavings curl and dangle their way to the paper bin below. When the last pencil had been shaved to a fine point, we did not put it down with the others, but kept hold of it.

"There," I said to her. "Ready for work."

She opened her mouth, seemed to speak to me. I couldn't hear what she was saying.

I have no shorthand. During the interview I had simply jotted down lists of keywords, and my hope was that if I wrote up our interviews immediately afterward, these words would be enough to jog my memory. And from that first meeting, it worked well. Glancing at my notebook from time to time, I filled the center of my sheets of foolscap with Miss Winter's words, conjuring her image in my mind, hearing her voice, seeing her mannerisms. Soon I was hardly aware of my notebook but was taking dictation from the Miss Winter in my head.

I left wide margins. In the left-hand one I noted any mannerisms, expressions and gestures that seemed to add something to her meaning. The right-hand margin I left blank. Later, rereading, it was here that I would enter my own thoughts, comments, questions.

I felt as though I had worked for hours. I emerged to make myself a cup of cocoa, but it was time suspended and did not disturb the flow of my recreation; I returned to my work and picked up the thread as though there had been no interruption.

"One gets so used to one's own horrors, one forgets how they must seem to other people," I wrote at last in the middle column, and in the left I added a note describing the way she closed the fingers of her good hand over the closed fist of the damaged one.

I drew a double line under the last line of script, and stretched. In the window the other me stretched as well. She took the pencils whose points she had worn and sharpened them one by one.

She was mid-yawn when something began to happen to her face. First it was a sudden blurring in the center of her forehead, like a blister. Another mark appeared on her cheek, then beneath her eye, on her nose, on her lips. Each new blemish was accompanied by a dull thud, a percussion that grew faster and faster. In a few seconds her entire face, it seemed, had decomposed.

But it was not the work of death. It was only rain. The long-awaited rain.

I opened the window, let my hand be drenched, then wiped the water over my eyes and face. I shivered. Time for bed.

I left the window ajar so that I could listen to the rain as it continued to fall with an even, muffled softness. I heard it while I was undressing, while I was reading and while I slept. It accompanied my dreams like a poorly tuned radio left on through the night, broadcasting a fuzzy white noise beneath which were the barely audible whispers of foreign languages and snatches of unfamiliar tunes.

A t nine o'clock the next morning Miss Winter sent for me and I went to her in the library.

By daylight the room was quite different. With the shutters folded back, the full-height windows let the light flood in from the pale sky. The garden, still wet from the night's downpour, gleamed in the morning sun. The exotic plants by the window seats seemed to touch leaf with their hardier, damper cousins beyond the glass, and the delicate framework that held the panes in place seemed no more solid than the glimmering threads of a spider's web stretched across a garden path from branch to branch. The library itself, slighter, narrower seemingly than the night before, appeared as a mirage of books in the wet winter garden.

In contrast to the palely blue sky and the milk-white sun, Miss Winter was all heat and fire, an exotic hothouse flower in a northern winter garden. She wore no sunglasses today, but her eyelids were colored purple, lined Cleopatra-style with kohl and fringed with the same heavy black lashes as yesterday. In the clear daylight I saw what I had not seen the night before: along the ruler-straight parting in Miss Winter's copper curls was a narrow margin of pure white.

"You remember our agreement," she began, as I sat down in the chair on the other side of the fire. "Beginnings, middles and endings, all in the correct order. No cheating. No looking ahead. No questions."

I was tired. A strange bed in a strange place, and I had woken with a dull, atonic tune ringing in my head. "Start where you like," I said.

"I shall start at the beginning. Though of course the beginning is never where you think it is. Our lives are so important to us that we tend to think the story of them begins with our birth. First there was nothing, then *I* was born. . . . Yet that is not so. Human lives are not pieces of string that can be separated out from a knot of others and laid out straight. Families are webs. Impossible to touch one part of it without setting the rest vibrating. Impossible to understand one part without having a sense of the whole.

"My story is not only mine; it is the story of Angelfield. Angelfield the village. Angelfield the house. And the Angelfield family itself. George and Mathilde; their children, Charlie and Isabelle; Isabelle's children, Emmeline and Adeline. Their house, their fortunes, their fears. And their ghost. One should always pay attention to ghosts, shouldn't one, Miss Lea?"

She gave me a sharp look; I pretended not to see it.

"A birth is not really a beginning. Our lives at the start are not really our own but only the continuation of someone else's story. Take me, for instance. To look at me now, you would think my birth must have been something special, wouldn't you? Accompanied by strange portents, and attended by witches and fairy godmothers. But no. Not a bit of it. In fact, when I was born I was no more than a subplot.

"But how do I know this story that precedes my birth,

I hear you thinking. What are the sources? Where does the information come from? Well, where does any information come from in a house like Angelfield? The servants, of course. The Missus, in particular. Not that I learned it all directly from her lips. Sometimes, it is true, she would reminisce about the past while she sat cleaning the silverware, and seem to forget my presence as she spoke. She frowned as she remembered village rumors and local gossip. Events and conversations and scenes rose to her lips and played themselves out afresh over the kitchen table. But sooner or later the story would lead her into areas unsuitable for a child—unsuitable in particular for *me*—then suddenly she would remember I was there, break off her account mid-sentence and start rubbing the cutlery vigorously, as if to erase the past altogether. But there can be no secrets in a house where there are children. I pieced the story together another way. When the Missus talked with the gardener over their morning tea, I learned to interpret the sudden silences that punctuated seemingly innocent conversations. Without appearing to notice anything, I saw the silent glances that certain words provoked between them. And when they thought they were alone and could talk privately . . . they were not in fact alone. In this way I understood the story of my origins. And later, when the Missus was no longer the woman she used to be, when age confused her and released her tongue, then her meanderings confirmed the story I had spent years divining. It is this story—the one that came to me in hints, glances and silences—I am going to translate into words for you now."

Miss Winter cleared her throat, preparing to start. "Isabelle Angelfield was odd."

Her voice seemed to slip away from her, and she stopped, surprised. When she spoke again, her tone was cautious.

"Isabelle Angelfield was born during a rainstorm."

It came again, the abrupt loss of voice.

So used was she to hiding the truth that it had become atrophied in her. She made one false start, then another. But, like a gifted musician who, after years without playing, takes up her instrument again, she finally found her way.

She told me the story of Isabelle and Charlie.

☙❦❧

Isabelle Angelfield was odd.

Isabelle Angelfield was born during a rainstorm.

It is impossible to know whether or not these facts are connected. But when, two and a half decades later, Isabelle left home for the second time, people in the village looked back and remembered the endlessness of the rain on the day of her birth. Some remembered as if it was yesterday that the doctor was late, delayed by the floods caused by the river having burst its banks. Others recalled beyond the shadow of a doubt that the cord had been wrapped round the baby's neck, almost strangling her before she could be born. Yes, it was a difficult birth, all right, for on the stroke of six, just as the baby was born and the doctor rang the bell, hadn't the mother passed away, out of this world and into the next? So if the weather had been fine, and the doctor had been earlier, and if the cord had not deprived the child of oxygen, and if the mother had not died . . .

And if, and if, and if. Such thinking is pointless. Isabelle was as Isabelle was, and that is all there is to say about the matter.

The infant, a white scrap of fury, was motherless. And at the beginning, to all intents and purposes, it looked like she'd be fatherless, too. For her father, George Angelfield, fell into a decline. He locked himself in the library and refused point-blank to come out. This might seem excessive; ten years of marriage is usually enough to cure marital affection, but Angelfield was an odd fellow, and there it was. He had loved his wife—his ill-tempered, lazy, selfish and pretty Mathilde. He had loved her more than he loved his horses, more even than his dog. As for their son, Charlie, a boy of nine, it never entered George's head to wonder whether he loved him more or less than Mathilde, for the fact was, he never thought of Charlie at all.

Bereaved, driven half mad with grief, George Angelfield sat all day in the library, eating nothing, seeing no one. And he spent his nights there, too, on the daybed, not sleeping but staring red-eyed at the moon. This went on for months. His pale cheeks became paler; he grew thin; he stopped speaking. Specialists were called from London. The vicar came and left again. The dog pined away from want of affection, and when it died, George Angelfield barely noticed.

In the end the Missus got fed up with it all. She

picked up baby Isabelle from the crib in the nursery and took her downstairs. She strode past the butler, ignoring his protestations, and went into the library without knocking. Up to the desk she marched, and she plumped the baby down in George Angelfield's arms without a word. Then she turned her back and walked out, slamming the door behind her.

The butler made to go in, thinking to retrieve the infant, but the Missus raised her finger and hissed, "Don't you dare!" He was so startled that he obeyed. The household servants gathered outside the library door, looking at one another, not knowing what to do. But the force of the Missus's conviction held them paralyzed, and they did nothing.

It was a long afternoon, and at the end of it one of the underhouse maids ran to the nursery. "He's come out! The master's come out!"

At her normal pace and in her normal manner, the Missus came downstairs to hear what had happened.

The servants had stood about in the hall for hours, listening at the door and peeking through the keyhole. At first their master just sat there, looking at the baby, with a dull and perplexed expression on his face. The baby wriggled and gurgled. When George Angelfield was heard cooing and chuckling in response, the servants exchanged looks of astonishment, but they were more astonished later to hear lullabies. The baby slept and there was silence. Her father, the servants reported, did not once take his eyes from his daughter's face. Then she awoke, hungry, and set to crying. Her shrieks rose in intensity and pitch until finally the door was flung open.

There stood my grandfather with his baby in his arms.

Seeing his servants standing idly about, he glared at them and his voice boomed out: "Is a baby left to starve in this house?"

From that day on George Angelfield took personal charge of his daughter. He fed her, bathed her and the rest, moved her cot into his room in case she cried of loneliness in the night, fashioned a papoose so that he could take her riding, read to her (business letters, the sports pages and romantic novels), and shared all his thoughts and plans with her. He behaved, in short, as though Isabelle was a sensible, pleasant companion and not a wild and ignorant child.

Perhaps it was her looks that made her father love her. Charlie, the neglected older child, nine years Isabelle's senior, was his father's son: a lumpen, pasty, carrot-topped boy, with heavy feet and a slow expression. But Isabelle inherited her looks from both her parents. The ginger hair shared by her father and brother was burnished in the girl child to a rich, glossy auburn. In her, the pale Angelfield complexion was stretched over fine French bones. She had the better chin from the father's side, and the better mouth from the mother's. She had Mathilde's slanting eyes and long lashes, but when they lifted, it was to reveal the astonishing emerald irises that were the emblem of the Angelfields. She was, physically at least, perfection itself.

The household adapted to the unusual state of affairs.

They lived with the unspoken agreement to behave as though it were entirely normal for a father to dote on his baby daughter. It was not to be considered unmanly, ungentlemanly or ridiculous that he kept her constantly by him.

But what about Charlie, the baby's brother? He was a slow-witted boy whose mind turned in circles around his few obsessions and preoccupations, but who could not be prevailed upon to learn new ideas or think logically. He ignored the baby and welcomed the changes her arrival introduced to the household. Before Isabelle there had been two parents to whom the Missus might report instances of bad behavior, two parents whose reactions were impossible to foresee. His mother had been an inconsistent disciplinarian; sometimes having him spanked for bad behavior, at other times merely laughing. His father, although stern, was distracted, and the punishments he intended were frequently forgotten. Catching sight of the boy, though, he would have the vague sense that there might be some misdemeanor to correct, and he would spank the child, thinking that if it wasn't actually owed it would do in advance for next time. This taught the boy a good lesson: He stayed out of the way of his father.

With the coming of the baby Isabelle, all this changed. Mamma was gone, and Papa as good as, too busy with his little Isabelle to concern himself with hysterical reports from housemaids about mice roasted with the Sunday joint or pins pressed by malicious hands deep into the soap. Charlie was free to do as he pleased, and what pleased him was removing floor-boards at the top of the attic stairs and watching the housemaids tumble down and sprain their ankles.

The Missus could scold, but then she was only the Missus, and in this new, free life he could maim and wound to his heart's content, in the certain knowledge that he would get away with it. Consistent adult behavior is said to be good for children, and consistent neglect certainly suited this child, for in these early years of his semi-orphanhood Charlie Angelfield was as happy as the day is long.

George Angelfield's adoration of his daughter per-sisted through all the trials a child can inflict on a parent. When she started to talk, he discovered her to be preternaturally gifted, a veritable oracle, and he began to consult her on everything, until the household came to be run according to the caprices of a three-year-old child.

Visitors were rare, and as the household descended from eccentricity into chaos, they became rarer. Then the servants began to complain among themselves. The butler had left before the child was two. Cook put up for a year longer with the irregular mealtimes that the child demanded, then the day came when she, too, handed in her notice. When she left she took the kitchen girl with her, and in the end it was left to the Missus to ensure the provision of cake and jelly at odd hours. The house-maids felt under no obligation to occupy themselves with chores: Not unreasonably they believed that their small salaries barely compensated them for the cuts and bruises, sprained ankles and stomach upsets they incurred owing to Charlie's sadistic experiments. They left and were replaced by a succession of temporary help, none of whom lasted long. Finally even the temporary help was dispensed with.

By the time Isabelle was five the household had shrunk to George Angelfield, the two children, the Missus, the gardener and the gamekeeper. The dog was dead, and the cats, fearful of Charlie, kept outdoors, taking refuge in the garden shed when the weather turned cold.

If George Angelfield noticed their isolation, their domestic squalor, he did not regret it. He had Isabelle; he was happy.

If anyone missed the servants it was Charlie. Without them he was lost for subjects for his experiments. When he was scouting around for someone to hurt, his eye fell, as it was bound sooner or later to do, on his sister.

He couldn't afford to make her cry in the presence of his father, and since she rarely left her father's side, Charlie was faced with a difficulty. How to get her away?

By enticement. Whispering promises of magic and surprise, Charlie led Isabelle out of the side door, along one end of the knot garden, between the long borders, out through the topiary garden and along the beech avenue to the woods. There was a place Charlie knew. An old hovel, dank and windowless, a good place for secrets.

What Charlie was after was a victim, and his sister,

walking behind him, smaller, younger and weaker, must have seemed ideal. But she was odd and she was clever, and things did not turn out exactly as he expected.

Charlie pulled his sister's sleeve up and drew a piece of wire, orange with rust, along the white inside of her forearm. She stared at the red beads of blood that were welling up along the livid line, then turned her gaze upon him. Her green eyes were wide with surprise and something like pleasure. When she put out her hand for the wire he gave it to her automatically. She pulled up her other sleeve, punctured the skin and with application drew the wire down almost to her wrist. Her cut was deeper than the one he had given her, and the blood rose up at once and trickled. She gave a sigh of satisfaction as she looked at it and then licked the blood away. Then she offered the wire back to him and motioned to him to pull up his sleeve.

Charlie was bewildered. But he dug the wire into his arm because she wanted it, and he laughed through the pain.

Instead of a victim Charlie had found himself the strangest of conspirators.

Life went on for the Angelfields, sans parties, sans hunt meetings, sans housemaids and sans most of the things that people of their class took for granted in those days. They turned their backs on their neighbors, allowed their estate to be managed by the tenants, and depended on the goodwill and honesty of the Missus and the gardener for those day-to-day transactions with the world that were necessary for survival.

George Angelfield forgot about the world, and for a time the world forgot about him. And then they remembered him. It was to do with money.

There were other large houses in the vicinity. Other more or less aristocratic families. Among them was a man who took great care of his money. He sought out the best advice, invested large sums where wisdom dictated and speculated small sums where the risk of loss was greater but the profit, in the case of success, high. The large sums he lost completely. The small ones went up—moderately. He found himself in a pickle. In addition he had a lazy, spendthrift son and a goggle-eyed, thick-ankled daughter. Something had to be done.

George Angelfield never saw anyone, hence he was never offered financial tips. When his lawyer sent him recommendations, he ignored them, and when his bank sent him letters, he did not write back. As a consequence of this, the Angelfield money, instead of expending itself chasing one deal after another, lounged in its bank vault and grew fat.

Money talks. Word got out.

"Doesn't George Angelfield have a son?" asked the wife of the near-bankrupt. "How old would he be now? Twenty-six?"

And if not the son for their Sybilla, then why not the girl for Roland? thought the wife. She must be reaching a marriageable age by now. And the father was known to dote on her: She would not come empty-handed.

"Nice weather for a picnic," she said, and her husband, in the way of husbands, did not see the connection.

The invitation languished for a fortnight on the drawing room windowsill, and it might have remained there until the sun bleached the color out of the ink, had it not been for Isabelle. One afternoon, at a loss for something to do, she came down the stairs, puffed out her cheeks in boredom, picked the letter up and opened it.

"What's that?" said Charlie.

"Invitation," she said. "To a picnic."

A picnic? Charlie's mind turned it over. It seemed strange. But he shrugged and forgot it.

Isabelle stood up and went to the door.

"Where are you going?"

"To my room."

Charlie made to follow her, but she stopped him. "Leave me alone," she said. "I'm not in the mood."

He complained, took a handful of her hair and ran his fingers over the nape of her neck, finding the bruises he had made last time. But she twisted away from him, ran upstairs and locked the door.

An hour later, hearing her come down the stairs, he went to the doorway. "Come to the library with me," he asked her.

"No."

"Then come to the deer park."

"No."

He noticed that she had changed her clothes. "What

do you look like that for?" he said. "You look stupid."

She was wearing a summer dress that had belonged to their mother, made of a flimsy white material and trimmed with green. Instead of her usual tennis shoes with their frayed laces, she had put on a pair of green satin sandals a size too big—also their mother's—and had attached a flower in her hair with a comb. She had lipstick on.

His heart darkened. "Where are you going?" he asked.

"To the picnic."

He grabbed her by the arm, dug his fingers in and pulled her toward the library.

"No!"

He pulled her harder.

She hissed at him, "Charlie, I said no!"

He let her go. When she said no like that, he knew it meant no. He had found that out in the past. She could be in a bad temper for days.

She turned her back on him and opened the front door.

Full of anger, Charlie looked for something to hit. But he had already broken everything that was breakable. The things that were left would do more harm to his knuckles than he could do to them. His fists slackened; he followed Isabelle out of the door and to the picnic.

The young people at the lakeside made a pretty picture from a distance, in their summer frocks and white shirts. The glasses they held were filled with a liquid that sparkled in the sunlight, and the grass at their feet looked soft enough to go barefoot. In reality, the picnickers were sweltering beneath their clothes, the champagne was warm, and if anyone had thought to take their shoes off they would have had to walk through goose droppings. Still, they were willing to feign jollity, in the hope that their pretense would encourage the real thing.

A young man at the edge of the crowd caught sight of movement up near the house. A girl in a strange outfit accompanied by a lump of a man. There was something about her.

He failed to respond to his companion's joke; the companion looked to see what had caught his attention and fell silent in turn. A group of young women, eternally alert to the doings of young men even when the young men are behind their backs, turned to see what had caused the sudden silence. And there followed a sort of ripple effect, whereby the entire party turned to face the newcomers, and seeing them, were struck dumb.

Across the wide lawn walked Isabelle.

She neared the group. It parted for her as the sea parted for Moses, and she walked straight through it to the lake edge. She stood on a flat rock that jutted out over the water. Someone came toward her with a glass and a bottle, but she waved them away. The sun was bright, it had been a long walk and it would take more than champagne to cool her down.

She took off her shoes, hung them in a tree and, arms

outstretched, let herself fall into the water.

The crowd gasped, and when she rose to the surface, water streaming from her form in ways that recalled the birth of Venus, they gasped again.

This plunge into the water was another thing people remembered years later, after she left home for the second time. They remembered, and shook their heads in a mix of pity and condemnation. The girl had had it in her all that time. But on the day it was put down to sheer high spirits, and people were grateful to her. Single-handedly Isabelle brought the whole party to life.

One of the young men, the boldest, with fair hair and a loud laugh, kicked off his shoes, removed his tie and leapt into the lake with her. A trio of his friends followed. In no time at all, the young men were all in the water, diving, calling, shouting and outdoing one another in athleticism and splash.

Thinking quickly, the girls saw there was only one way to go. They hung their sandals in the branches, put on their most excited faces and splashed into the water, uttering cries that they hoped would sound abandoned, while doing their utmost to prevent any excessive dampening of their hair.

Their efforts were in vain. The men had eyes only for Isabelle.

Charlie did not follow his sister into the water. He stood, a little farther off, and watched. With his red hair and his pallor, he was a man made for rain and indoor pursuits. His face had gone pink in the sun, and his eyes stung as the sweat from his brow ran into them. But he hardly blinked. He could not bear to take his eyes off Isabelle.

How many hours later was it that he found himself with her again? It seemed an eternity. Enlivened by Isabelle's presence the picnic went on much longer than anybody had expected, and yet it seemed to the other guests to have passed in a flash, and they would all have stayed longer if they could. The party broke up with consoling thoughts of other picnics to come, a round of promised invitations and damp kisses.

When Charlie approached her, Isabelle had a young man's jacket arranged around her shoulders and the young man himself in the palm of her hand. Not far off a girl loitered, uncertain whether her presence was wanted. Though she was plump, plain and female, the resemblance she nonetheless bore to the young man made it clear she was his sister.

"Come on," Charlie said roughly to his sister.

"So soon? I thought we might go for a walk. With Roland and Sybilla." She smiled graciously at Roland's sister, and Sybilla, surprised at the unexpected kindness, beamed back.

Charlie could get his own way with Isabelle at home—sometimes—by hurting her, but in public he didn't dare, and so he buckled under.

What happened during that walk? There were no witnesses to the events that took place in the forest. For want of witnesses there was no gossip. At least not at first. But one does not have to be a genius to deduce

95

from later events what took place under the canopy of summer foliage that evening.

It would have been something like this:

Isabelle would have found some pretext for sending the men away.

"My shoes! I left them in the tree!" And she'd have sent Roland to fetch them, and Charlie, too, for a shawl of Sybilla's or some other item.

The girls settled themselves on a patch of soft ground. In the men's absence they waited in the growing darkness, drowsy from champagne, breathing in the remains of the sun's heat and with it the beginning of something darker, the forest and the night. The warmth of their bodies began to drive the moisture from their dresses, and as the folds of fabric dried, they detached themselves from the flesh beneath and tickled.

Isabelle knew what she wanted. Time alone with Roland. But to get it, she had to be rid of her brother.

She began to talk while they lolled back against a tree. "So which is your beau, then?"

"I don't really have a beau," Sybilla admitted.

"But you should." Isabelle rolled on her side, took the feathery leaf of a fern and let it run over her lips. Then she let it run over the lips of her companion.

"That tickles," Sybilla murmured.

Isabelle did it again. Sybilla smiled, eyes half shut, and did not stop her when Isabelle ran the soft leaf down her neck and around the neckline of her dress, paying special attention to the swell of the breasts. Sybilla emitted a semi-nasal giggle.

96

When the leaf ran down to her waist and beyond, Sybilla opened her eyes.

"You've stopped," she complained.

"I haven't," said Isabelle. "It's just that you can't feel it through your dress." And she pulled up the hem of Sybilla's dress and played the fronds along her ankles. "Better?"

Sybilla reclosed her eyes.

From the somewhat thick ankle the green plume found its way to a distinctly chunky knee. An adenoidal murmur escaped from between Sybilla's lips, though she did not stir until the fronds came to the very top of her legs, and she did not sigh until Isabelle replaced the greenery with her own tender fingers.

Isabelle's sharp eyes did not once leave the face of the older girl, and the moment the girl's eyelids gave the first hint of a flicker, she drew her hand away.

"Of course," she said, very matter-of-fact, "it's a beau you need really."

Sybilla, roused unwillingly from her incomplete rapture, was slow to catch on. "For the tickling," Isabelle had to explain. "It's much better with a beau."

And when Sybilla asked her newfound friend, "How do you know?" Isabelle had the answer all ready: "Charlie."

By the time the boys returned, shoes and shawl in hand, Isabelle had achieved her purpose. Sybilla, a certain dishevelment apparent in her skirt and petticoat, regarded Charlie with an expression of warm interest.

97

Charlie, indifferent to the scrutiny, was looking at Isabelle.

"Have you thought how similar Isabelle and Sybilla are?" Isabelle said carelessly. Charlie glared. "The sounds of the names, I mean. Almost interchangeable, wouldn't you say?" She sent a sharp glance at her brother, forcing him to understand. "Roland and I are going to walk a bit farther. But Sybilla's tired. You stay with her." Isabelle took Roland's arm.

Charlie looked coldly at Sybilla, registered the disarrangement of her dress. She stared back at him, eyes wide, mouth slightly open.

When he turned back to where Isabelle had been, she was already gone. Only her laughter came back to him from the darkness, her laughter and the low rumble of Roland's voice. He would get his own back later. He would. Time and time again she would pay for this.

In the meantime he had to vent his feelings somehow.

He turned to Sybilla.

The summer was full of picnics. And for Charlie, it was full of Sybillas. But for Isabelle there was only one Roland. Every day she slipped out of Charlie's sight, escaped his grasp and disappeared on her bicycle. Charlie could never find out where the pair met, was too slow to follow her as she took flight, the bicycle wheels spinning beneath her, hair flying behind. Sometimes she would not return until darkness had fallen, sometimes not even then. When he scolded her, she laughed at him and turned her back as though he simply wasn't there. He tried to hurt her, to maim her, but as she eluded him time after time, slipping through his fingers like water, he realized how much their games had been dependent on her willingness. However great his strength, her quickness and cleverness meant she got away from him every time. Like a boar enraged by a bee, he was powerless.

Once in a while, placatory, she gave in to his entreaties. For an hour or two she lent herself to his will, allowing him to enjoy the illusion that she was back for good and that everything between them was as it always had been. But it *was* an illusion, as Charlie soon learned, and her renewed absence after these interludes was all the more agonizing.

Charlie forgot his pain only momentarily with the Sybillas. For a time his sister prepared the way for him, then as she became more and more delighted with Roland, Charlie was left to make his own arrangements. He lacked his sister's subtlety; there was an incident that could have been a scandal, and a vexed Isabelle told him that if that was how he intended to go about things then he would have to choose a different sort of woman. He turned from the daughters of minor aristocrats to those of farriers, farmers and foresters. Personally he couldn't tell the difference, yet the world seemed to mind less.

Frequent though they were, these instances of forgetfulness were fleeting. The shocked eyes, the bruised arms, the bloodied thighs were erased from memory the moment he turned away from them. Nothing could touch the great passion in his life: his feelings for Isabelle.

One morning toward the end of the summer, Isabelle turned the blank pages in her diary and counted the days. She closed the book and replaced it in the drawer thoughtfully. When she had decided, she went downstairs to her father's study.

Her father looked up. "Isabelle!" He was pleased to see her. Since she had taken to going out more he was especially gratified when she came to seek him out like this.

"Darling Pa!" She smiled at him.

He caught a glint of something in her eye. "Is there something afoot?"

Her eyes traveled to a corner of the ceiling and she smiled. Without shifting her gaze from the dark corner, she told him she was leaving.

At first he hardly understood what she had said. He felt a pulse beat in his ears. His vision blurred. He closed his eyes, but inside his head there were volcanoes, meteorite strikes and explosions. When the flames died down and there was nothing left in his inner world but a silent, devastated landscape, he opened his eyes.

What had he done?

In his hand was a lock of hair, with a bloodied clod of skin attached at one end. Isabelle was there, her back to the door, her hands behind her. One beautiful green eye was bloodshot; one cheek looked red and slightly swollen. A trickle of blood crept from her scalp, reached her eyebrow and was diverted away from her eye.

He was aghast at himself and at her. He turned away from her in silence and she left the room.

Afterward he sat for hours, twisting the auburn hair that he had found in his hand, twisting and twisting, tighter and tighter around his finger, until it dug deep into his skin, until it was so matted that it could not be unwound. And finally, when the sensation of pain had at last completed its slow journey from his finger to his consciousness, he cried.

Charlie was absent that day and did not return home until midnight. Finding Isabelle's room empty he wandered through the house, knowing by some sixth sense that disaster had struck. Not finding his sister, he went to his father's study. One look at the gray-faced man told him everything. Father and son regarded each other for a moment, but the fact that their loss was shared did not unite them. There was nothing they could do for each other.

In his room Charlie sat on the chair next to the window, sat there for hours, a silhouette against a rectangle of moonlight. At some point he opened a drawer and removed the gun he had obtained by extortion from a local poacher, and two or three times he raised it to his temple. Each time the force of gravity soon returned it to his lap.

At four o'clock in the morning he put the gun away, and took up instead the long needle that he had pilfered from the Missus's sewing box a decade before and which had since seen much use. He pulled up his trouser leg, pushed his sock down and made a new puncture mark in his skin. His shoulders shook, but his hand was steady as on his shinbone he scored a single word: *Isabelle*.

Isabelle by this time was long gone. She had returned to her room for a few minutes and then left it again, taking the back stairs to the kitchen. Here she had given the Missus a strange, hard hug, which was quite unlike her, and then she slipped out of the side door and darted through the kitchen garden toward the garden door, set in a stone wall. The Missus's sight had been fading for a very long time, but she had developed the ability to judge people's movements by sensing vibrations in the air, and she had the impression that Isabelle hesitated, for the briefest of moments, before she closed the garden door behind her.

When it became apparent to George Angelfield that Isabelle was gone, he went into his library and locked the door. He refused food, he refused visitors. There were only the vicar and the doctor to come calling now, and both of them got short shrift. "Tell your God he can go to hell!" and "Let a wounded animal die in peace, won't you!" was the limit of their welcome.

A few days later they returned and called the gardener to break the door down. George Angelfield was dead. A brief examination was enough to establish that the man had died from septicemia, caused by the circle of human hair that was deeply embedded in the flesh of his ring finger.

Charlie did not die, though he didn't understand why not. He wandered about the house. He made a trail of footprints in the dust and followed it every day, starting at the top of the house and working down. Attic bedrooms not used for years, servants' rooms, family rooms, the study, the library, the music room, the drawing room, the kitchens. It was a restless, endless, hopeless search. At night he went out to roam the estate, his legs carrying him tirelessly forward, forward, forward. All the while he fingered the Missus's needle in his pocket. His fingertips were a bloody, scabby mess. He missed Isabelle.

Charlie lived like this through September, October, November, December, January and February, and at the beginning of March, Isabelle returned.

Charlie was in the kitchen, tracing his footsteps, when he heard the sound of hooves and wheels approaching the house. Scowling, he went to the window. He wanted no visitors.

A familiar figure stepped down from the car—and his heart stood still.

He was at the door, on the steps, beside the car all in one moment, and *Isabelle was there.*

He stared at her.

Isabelle laughed. "Here," she said, "take this." And she handed him a heavy parcel wrapped up in cloth.

103

She reached into the back of the carriage and took something out. "And this one." He tucked it obediently under his arm. "Now, what I'd like most in the world is a very large brandy."

Stunned, Charlie followed Isabelle into the house and to the study. She made straight for the drinks cupboard and took out glasses and a bottle. She poured a generous slug into a glass and drank it in one go, showing the whiteness of her throat, then she refilled her own glass and the second, which she held out to her brother. He stood there, paralyzed and speechless, his hands full with the tightly wrapped bundles. Isabelle's laughter resounded about his ears again and it was like being too close to an enormous church bell. His head started to spin and tears sprang to his eyes. "Put them down," Isabelle instructed. "We'll drink a toast." He took the glass and inhaled the spirit fumes. "To the future!" He swallowed the brandy in one gulp and coughed at its unfamiliar burn.

"You haven't even seen them, have you?" she asked.

He frowned.

"Look." Isabelle turned to the parcels he had placed on the study desk, pulled the soft wrapping away, and stood back so that he could see. Slowly he turned his head and looked. The parcels were babies. Two babies. Twins. He blinked. Registered dimly that some kind of response was called for, but didn't know what he was supposed to say or do.

"Oh, Charlie, *wake up,* for goodness' sake!" and his sister took both his hands in hers and dragged him into a madcap dance around the room. She swirled him around and around and around, until the dizziness started to clear his head, and when they came to a halt she took his face in her hands and spoke to him. "Roland's dead, Charlie. It's you and me now. Do you understand?"

He nodded.

"Good. Now, where's Pa?"

When he told her, she was quite hysterical. The Missus, roused from the kitchen by the shrill cries, put her to bed in her old room, and when at last she was quiet again, asked, "These babies . . . what are they called?"

"March," Isabelle responded.

But the Missus knew that. Word of the marriage had reached her some months before, and news of the birth (she'd not needed to count the months on her fingers, but she did it anyway and pursed her lips). She knew of Roland's death from pneumonia a few weeks ago; knew too how old Mr. and Mrs. March, devastated by the death of their only son and repelled by the fey insouciance of their new daughter-in-law, now quietly shunned Isabelle and her children, wishing only to grieve.

"What about Christian names?"

"Adeline and Emmeline," said Isabelle sleepily.

"And how do you tell them apart?"

But the child-widow was sleeping already. And as she dreamed in her old bed, her escapade and her husband already forgotten, her virgin's name was restored to her.

When she woke in the morning it would be as if her marriage had never been, and the babies themselves would appear to her not as her own children—she had not a single maternal bone in her body—but as mere spirits of the house.

The babies slept, too. In the kitchen, the Missus and the gardener bent over their smooth, pale faces and talked in low voices.

"Which one is which?" he asked.

"I don't know."

One each side of the old crib, they watched. Two half-moon sets of lashes, two puckered mouths, two downy scalps. Then one of the babies gave a little flutter of the eyelids and half opened one eye. The gardener and the Missus held their breath. But the eye closed again and the baby lapsed into sleep.

"That one can be Adeline," the Missus whispered. She took a striped tea towel from a drawer and cut strips from it. She plaited the strips into two lengths, tied the red one around the wrist of the baby who had stirred, the white one around the wrist of the baby who had not.

Housekeeper and gardener, each with a hand on the crib, watched, until the Missus turned a glad and tender face to the gardener and spoke again.

"Two babies. Honestly, Dig. At our age!"

When he raised his eyes from the babies, he saw the tears that misted her round brown eyes.

His rough hand reached out across the crib. She wiped her foolishness away and, smiling, put her small, plump hand in his. He felt the wetness of her tears pressed against his own fingers.

Beneath the arch of their clasped hands, beneath the trembling line of their gaze, the babies were dreaming.

❦

It was late when I finished transcribing the story of Isabelle and Charlie. The sky was dark and the house was asleep. All of the afternoon and evening and for part of the night I had been bent over my desk, with the story retelling itself in my ears while my pencil scratched line after line, obeying its dictation. My pages were densely packed with script: Miss Winter's own flood of words. From time to time my hand moved to the left and I scribbled a note in the left-hand margin, when her tone of voice or a gesture seemed to be part of the narrative itself.

Now I pushed the last sheet of paper from me, set down my pencil and clenched and stretched my aching fingers. For hours Miss Winter's voice had conjured another world, raising the dead for me, and I had seen nothing but the puppet show her words had made. But when her voice fell still in my head, her image remained and I remembered the gray cat that had appeared, as if by magic, on her lap. Silently he had sat under her stroking hand, regarding me fixedly with his round yellow eyes. If he saw my ghosts, if he saw my secrets, he did not seem the least perturbed, but only blinked and continued to stare indifferently.

"What's his name?" I had asked.

"Shadow," she absently replied.

107

At last in bed, I turned out the light and closed my eyes. I could still feel the place on the pad of my finger where the pencil had made a groove in my skin. In my right shoulder, a knot from writing was not yet ready to untie itself. Though it was dark, and though my eyes were closed, all I could see was a sheet of paper, lines of my own handwriting with wide margins. The right-hand margin drew my attention. Unmarked, pristine, it glowed white, made my eyes sting. It was the column I reserved for my own comments, notes and questions.

In the dark, my fingers closed around a ghost pencil and twitched in response to the questions that penetrated my drowsiness. I wondered about the secret tattoo Charlie bore inside his body, his sister's name etched onto his bone. How long would the inscription have remained? Could a living bone mend itself? Or was it with him till he died? In his coffin, underground, as his flesh rotted away from the bone, was the name Isabelle revealed to the darkness? Roland March, the dead husband, so soon forgotten. . . . Isabelle and Charlie. Charlie and Isabelle. Who was the twins' father? And behind my thoughts, the scar on Miss Winter's palm rose into view. The letter *Q* for *question*, seared into human flesh.

As I started to sleepwrite my questions, the margin seemed to expand. The paper throbbed with light. Swelling, it engulfed me, until I realized with a mixture of trepidation and wonderment that I was enclosed in the grain of the paper, embedded in the white interior of the story itself. Weightless, I wandered all night long in

Miss Winter's story, plotting its landscape, measuring its contours and, on tiptoe at its borders, peering at the mysteries beyond its bounds.

## GARDENS

I woke early. Too early. The monotonous fragment of a tune was scratching at my brain. With more than an hour to wait before Judith's knock at the door with breakfast, I made myself a cup of cocoa, drank it scaldingly hot and went outdoors.

Miss Winter's garden was something of a puzzle. The sheer size of it was overwhelming for a start. What I had taken at first sight to be the border of the garden—the hedge of yew on the other side of the formal beds—was only a kind of inner wall that divided one part of the garden from another. And the garden was full of such divisions. There were hedges of hawthorne and privet and copper beech, stone walls covered with ivy, winter clematis and the bare, scrambling stems of rambling roses, and fences, neatly paneled or woven in willow.

Following the paths, I wandered from one section to another, but I could not fathom the layout. Hedges that looked solid viewed straight on, sometimes revealed a diagonal passageway when viewed obliquely. Shrubberies were easy to wander into and near-impossible to escape from. Fountains and statues that I thought I had left well behind me reappeared. I spent a lot of time stock-still, looking around me in perplexity and shaking my head. Nature had made a maze of itself and was setting out deliberately to thwart me.

Turning a corner, I came across the reticent, bearded man who had driven me from the station. "Maurice is what they call me," he said, reluctantly introducing himself.

"How do you manage not to get lost?" I wanted to know. "Is there a trick to it?"

"Only time," he said, without looking up from his work. He was kneeling over an area of churned-up soil, leveling it and pressing the earth around the roots of the plants.

Maurice, I could tell, did not welcome my presence in the garden. I didn't mind, being of a solitary nature myself. After that I made a point, whenever I saw him, of taking a path in the opposite direction, and I think he shared my discretion, for once or twice, catching a glimpse of movement out of the corner of my eye, I glanced up to see Maurice backing out of an entrance or making a sudden, divergent turn. In this way we successfully left each other in peace. There was ample room for us to avoid each other without any sense of constraint.

Later that day I went to Miss Winter and she told me more about the household at Angelfield.

The name of the Missus was Mrs. Dunne, but to the children of the family she had always been the Missus, and she had been in the house it seemed forever. This was a rarity: Staff came and went quickly at Angelfield, and since departures were slightly more frequent than arrivals, the day came when she was the only indoors servant remaining. Technically the housekeeper, in reality she did everything. She scrubbed pots and laid fires like an underhousemaid; when it was time to make a meal she was cook and when it was time to serve it she was butler. Yet by the time the twins were born she was growing old. Her hearing was poor, her sight poorer, and although she didn't like to admit it, there was much she couldn't manage.

The Missus knew how children ought to be brought up: regular mealtimes, regular bedtimes, regular baths. Isabelle and Charlie had grown up over-indulged and neglected at the same time, and it broke her heart to see how they turned out. Their neglect of the twins was her chance, she hoped, to break the pattern. She had a plan. Under their noses, in the heart of all their chaos, she meant to raise two normal, ordinary little girls. Three square meals a day, bedtime at six, church on Sunday.

But it was harder than she thought.

For a start there was the fighting. Adeline would fly at her sister, fists and feet flailing, yanking at hair and landing blows wherever she could. She chased her sister wielding red-hot coals in the fire tongs. The Missus hardly knew what worried her more: Adeline's persistent and merciless aggression, or Emmeline's constant, ungrudging acceptance of it. For Emmeline, though she pleaded with her sister to stop tormenting her, never once retaliated. Instead, she bowed her head passively and waited for the blows that rained down on her shoulders and back to stop. The Missus had never once known Emmeline to raise a hand against Adeline. She had the goodness of two children in her, and Adeline the wickedness of two. In a way, the Missus thought, it made sense.

Then there was the vexed issue of food. At mealtimes, more often than not, the children simply could not be found. Emmeline adored eating, but her love of food never translated itself into the discipline of meals. Her hunger could not be accommodated by three meals a day; it was a ravenous, capricious thing. Ten, twenty, fifty times a day, it struck, making urgent demands for food, and when it had been satisfied with a few mouthfuls of something, it departed and food became an irrelevance again. Emmeline's plumpness was maintained by a pocket constantly full of bread and raisins, a portable feast that she would take a bite from whenever and wherever she fancied. She came to the table only to replenish these pockets before wandering off to loll by the fire or lie in a field somewhere.

Her sister was quite different. Adeline was made like a piece of wire with knots for knees and elbows. Her fuel was not the same as that of other mortals. Meals were not for her. No one ever saw her eat; like the wheel of perpetual motion she was a closed circuit, running on energy provided from some miraculous inner source. But the wheel that spins eternally is a myth, and when the Missus noticed in the morning an empty plate where there had been a slice of gammon the night before, or a loaf of bread with a chunk missing, she guessed where they had gone and sighed. Why wouldn't her girls eat food off a plate, like normal children?

Perhaps she might have managed better if she'd been younger. Or if the girls had been one instead of two. But the Angelfield blood carried a code that no amount of nursery food and strict routine could rewrite. She didn't want to see it; she tried not to see it for a long time, but in the end she realized. The twins were odd, there were no two ways about it. They were strange all through, right into their very hearts.

The way they talked, for instance. She would see them through the kitchen window, a blurred pair of forms whose mouths appeared to be moving nineteen to the dozen. As they approached the house, she caught fragments of the buzz of speech. And then they came in. Silent. "Speak up!" she was always telling them. But she was going deaf and they were shy; their chat was for themselves, not for others. "Don't be silly," she told Dig when he told her the girls couldn't speak properly. "There's no stopping them, when they get going."

The realization came to her one day in winter. For once both girls were indoors; Adeline had been induced by Emmeline to stay in the warmth, by the fire, out of the rain. Ordinarily the Missus lived in a blur of fog; on this day she was blessed by an unexpected clearing in her vision, a new sharpness of hearing, and as she passed the door of the drawing room she caught a fragment of their noise and stopped. Sounds flew backward and forward between them, like tennis balls in some game; sounds that made them smile or laugh or send each other malicious glances. Their voices rose in squeals and swooped down in whispers. From any distance you'd have thought it the lively, free-flowing chatter of ordinary children. But her heart sank. It was no language she had ever heard. Not English, and not the French that she had got used to when George's Mathilde was alive and that Charlie still used with Isabelle. John was right. They didn't talk properly.

The shock of understanding froze her there in the doorway. And as sometimes happens, one illumination opened the door to another. The clock on the mantelpiece chimed and, as always, the mechanism under glass sent a little bird out of a cage to flap a mechanical circuit before reentering the cage on the other side. As soon as the girls heard the first chime, they looked up at the clock. Two pairs of wide green eyes watched, unblinking, as the bird labored around the inside of the bell, wings up, wings down, wings up, wings down.

There was nothing particularly cold, particularly inhuman about their gaze. It was just the way children look at inanimate moving objects. But it froze the Missus to the core. For it was exactly the same as the way they looked at her, when she scolded, chided or exhorted.

They don't realize that I am alive, she thought. They don't know that anyone is alive but themselves.

It is a tribute to her goodness that she didn't find them monstrous. Instead, she felt sorry for them.

How lonely they must be. How very lonely.

And she turned from the doorway and shuffled away.

From that day on the Missus revised her expectations. Regular mealtimes and bathtimes, church on Sunday, two nice, normal children—all these dreams went out of the window. She had just one job now. To keep the girls safe.

Turning it over in her head, she thought she understood why it was. Twins, always together, always two. If it was normal in their world to be two, what would other people, who came not in twos but ones, seem like to them? We must seem like halves, the Missus mused. And she remembered a word, a strange word it had seemed at the time, that meant people who had lost parts of themselves. Amputees. That's what we are to them. Amputees.

Normal? No. The girls were not and would never be normal. But, she reassured herself, things being as they were, the twins being twins, perhaps their strangeness was only *natural*.

Of course all amputees hanker after the state of twinness. Ordinary people, untwins, seek their soul mate, take lovers, marry. Tormented by their incompleteness they strive to be part of a pair. The Missus was no different from anyone else in this respect. And she had her other half: John-the-dig.

They were not a couple in the traditional sense. They

were not married; they were not even lovers. A dozen or fifteen years older than he, she was not old enough to be his mother, quite, but was older than he would have expected for a wife. At the time they met, she was of an age when she no longer expected to marry anyone. While he, a man in his prime, expected to marry, but somehow never did. Besides, once he was working with the Missus, drinking tea with her every morning and sitting at the kitchen table to eat her food every evening, he fell out of the habit of seeking the company of young women. With a bit more imagination they might have been able to leap the bounds of their own expectations; they might have recognized their feelings for what they were: love of the deepest and most respectful kind. In another day, another culture, he might have asked her to be his wife and she might have said yes. At the very least, one can imagine that some Friday night after their fish and mash, after their fruit pie and custard, he might have taken her hand—or she his—and they might have led each other in bashful silence to one or other of their beds. But the thought never entered their heads. So they became friends, the way old married couples often do, and enjoyed the tender loyalty that awaits the lucky on the other side of passion, without ever living the passion itself.

His name was John-the-dig, John Digence to those who didn't know him. Never a great one for writing, once the school years were past (and they were soon past, for there were not many of them), he took to leaving off the last letters of his surname to save time. The first three letters seemed more than adequate: Did they not say who he was, what he did, more succinctly, more accurately, even, than his full name? And so he used to sign himself John Dig, and to the children he became John-the-dig.

He was a colorful man. Blue eyes like pieces of blue glass with the sun behind. White hair that grew straight up on top of his head, like plants reaching for the sun. And cheeks that went bright pink with exertion when he was digging. No one could dig like him. He had a special way of gardening, with the phases of the moon: planting when the moon was waxing, measuring time by its cycles. In the evening, he pored over tables of figures, calculating the best time for everything. His great-grandfather gardened like that, and his grandfather and his father. They maintained the knowledge.

John-the-dig's family had always been gardeners at Angelfield. In the old days, when the house had a head gardener and seven hands, his great-grandfather had rooted out a box hedge under a window and, so as not to be wasteful, he'd taken hundreds of cuttings a few inches long. He grew them on in a nursery bed, and when they reached ten inches, he planted them in the garden. He clipped some into low, sharp-edged hedges, let others grow shaggy, and when they were broad enough, took his shears to them and made spheres. Some, he could see, wanted to be pyramids, cones, top hats. To shape his green material, this man with the large, rough hands learned the patient, meticulous delicacy of a lacemaker. He created no animals, no human figures. Not for him the peacocks, lions, life-size men on bicycles that you saw in other gardens. The shapes that pleased him were either strictly geometric or bafflingly, bulgingly abstract.

By the time of his last years, the topiary garden was the only thing that mattered. He was always eager to be finished with his other work of the day; all he wanted was to be in "his" garden, running his hands over the surfaces of the shapes he had made, as he imagined the time, fifty, a hundred years hence, when his garden would have grown to maturity.

At his death, his shears passed into the hands of his son and, decades later, his grandson. Then, when this grandson died, it was John-the-dig, who had finished his apprenticeship at a large garden some thirty miles away, who came home to take on the job that had to be his. Although he was only the undergardener, the topiary had been his responsibility from the very beginning. How could it be otherwise? He picked up the shears, their wooden handles worn to shape by his father's hand, and felt his fingers fit the grooves. He was home.

In the years after George Angelfield lost his wife, when the number of staff diminished so dramatically, John-the-dig stayed on. Gardeners left and were not replaced. When he was still a young man he became, by default, head gardener, though he was also the only gardener. The workload was enormous; his employer took no interest; he worked without thanks. There were other jobs, other gardens. He would have been offered any job he had applied for—you only had to see him to trust him. But he never left Angelfield. How could he? Working in the topiary garden, putting his shears into their leather sheath when the light began to fade, he didn't need to reflect that the trees he was pruning were the very same trees that his great-grandfather had planted, that the routines and motions of his work were the same ones that three generations of his family had done before him. All this was too deeply known to require thought. He could take it for granted. Like his trees, he was rooted to Angelfield.

What were his feelings that day, when he went into his garden and found it ravaged? Great gashes in the sides of the yews, exposing the brown wood of their hearts. The mop-heads decapitated, their spherical tops lying at their feet. The perfect balance of the pyramids now lop-sided, the cones hacked about, the top hats chopped into and left in tatters. He stared at the long branches, still green, still fresh, that were strewn on the lawn. Their slow shriveling, their curling desiccation, their dying was yet to come.

Stunned, with a trembling that seemed to pass from his heart to his legs and into the ground beneath his feet, he tried to understand what had happened. Was it some bolt from the sky that had picked out his garden for destruction? But what freak storm is it that strikes in silence?

No. Someone had done this.

Turning a corner he found the proof: abandoned on the dewy grass, blades agape, the large shears and next to them the saw.

When he didn't come in for lunch, the Missus, worried, went to find him. Reaching the topiary garden she raised a hand to her mouth in horror, then, gripping her apron, walked on with a new urgency.

When she found him, she raised him from the ground. He leaned heavily on her as she led him with tender care to the kitchen and sat him in a chair. She made tea, sweet and hot, and he stared, unseeing, into space. Without a word, holding the cup to his lips, she tilted sips of the scalding liquid into his mouth. At last his eyes sought hers, and when she saw the loss in them, she felt her own tears spring up.

"Oh Dig! I know. I know."

His hands grasped her shoulders and the shaking of his body was the shaking of her body.

The twins did not appear that afternoon, and the Missus did not go to find them. When they turned up in the evening, John was still in his chair, white and haggard. He flinched at the sight of them. Curious and indifferent, their green eyes passed over his face just as they had passed over the drawing room clock.

Before she put the twins to bed the Missus dressed the cuts on their hands from the saw and the shears. "Don't touch the things in John's shed," she grumbled. "They're sharp; they'll hurt you."

And then, still not expecting to be heeded, "Why did

you do it? Oh, why did you do it? You have broken his heart."

She felt the touch of a child's hand on hers. "Missus sad," the girl said. It was Emmeline.

Startled, the Missus blinked away the fog of her tears and stared.

The child spoke again. "John-the-dig sad."

"Yes," the Missus whispered. "We are sad."

The girl smiled. It was a smile without malice. Without guilt. It was simply a smile of satisfaction at having noted something and correctly identified it. She had seen tears. She had been puzzled. But now she had found the answer to the puzzle. It was sadness.

The Missus closed the door and went downstairs. This was a breakthrough. It was communication, and it was the beginning, perhaps, of something greater than that. Was it possible that one day the girl might *understand?*

She opened the door to the kitchen and went in to rejoin John in his despair.

❧

That night I had a dream.

Walking in Miss Winter's garden, I met my sister.

Radiant, she unfolded her vast golden wings, as though to embrace me, and I was filled with joy. But when I approached I saw her eyes were blind and she could not see me. Then despair filled my heart.

Waking, I curled into a ball until the stinging heat on my torso had subsided.

M iss Winter's house was so isolated, and the life of its inhabitants so solitary, that I was surprised during my first week there to hear a vehicle arriving on the gravel at the front of the house. Peering from the library window, I saw the door of a large black car swing open and caught a glimpse of a tall, dark-haired man. He disappeared into the porch and I heard the brief ring of the bell.

I saw him again the next day. I was in the garden, perhaps ten feet from the front porch, when I heard the crackle of tires on gravel. I stood still, retreated inside myself. To anyone who took the trouble to look, I was plainly visible, but when people are expecting to see nothing, that is usually what they see. The man did not see me.

His face was grave. The heavy line of his brow cast his eyes into shadow, while the rest of his face was distinguished by a numb stillness. He reached into his car for his case, slammed the door and went up the steps to ring the bell.

I heard the door open. Neither he nor Judith spoke a word, and he disappeared inside the house.

Later that day, Miss Winter told me the story of Merrily and the perambulator.

꙰

As the twins grew older, they explored farther and farther afield and soon knew all the farms and all the gardens on the estate. They had no sense of boundaries, no understanding of property, and so they went where they wished. They opened gates and didn't always close them. They climbed over fences when they got in their way. They tried kitchen doors, and when they opened— usually they did, people didn't lock doors much in Angelfield—they went inside. They helped themselves to anything tasty in the pantry, slept for an hour on the beds upstairs if they felt weary, took saucepans and spoons away with them to scare birds in the fields.

The local families got upset about it. For every accusation made, there was someone who had seen the twins at the relevant time in another distant place; at least they had seen one of them; at least they thought they had. And then it came about that all the old ghost stories were remembered. No old house is without its stories; no old house is without its ghosts. And the very twinness of the girls had a spookiness about it. There was something *not right* about them, everyone agreed, and whether it was because of the girls themselves or for some other reason, there came to be a disinclination to approach the old house, as much among the adults as the children, for fear of what might be seen there.

But eventually the inconvenience of the incursions won ground over the thrill of ghost talk, and the women grew angry. On several occasions they cornered the girls red-handed and shouted. Anger pulled their faces all out of shape, and their mouths opened and closed so quickly, it made the girls laugh. The women didn't understand why the girls were laughing. They didn't know it was the speed and jumble of the words pouring from their own mouths that had bewildered the twins. They thought it was pure devilment and shouted even more. For a time the twins stayed to watch the spectacle of the villagers' anger, then they turned their backs and walked off.

When their husbands came home from the fields, the women would complain, say something had to be done, and the men would say, "You're forgetting they're the children of the big house." And the women said in return, "Big house or no, children didn't ought to be allowed to run riot the way them two girls do. It's not right. Something's got to be done." And the men would sit quiet over their plates of potato and meat and shake their heads and nothing would be done.

Until the incident of the perambulator.

There was a woman in the village called Mary Jameson. She was the wife of Fred Jameson, one of the farm laborers, and she lived with her husband and his parents in one of the cottages. The couple were newly-weds, and before her marriage the woman had been called Mary Leigh, which explains the name the twins invented for her in their own language: They called her Merrily, and it was a good name for her. Sometimes she would go and meet her husband from the fields and they would sit in the shelter of a hedge at the end of the day, while he had a cigarette. He was a tall brown man with big feet and he used to put his arm around her waist and tickle her and blow down the front of her dress to make her laugh. She tried not to laugh, to tease him, but she wanted to laugh really, and eventually she always did.

She'd have been a plain woman if it wasn't for that laugh of hers. Her hair was a dirty color that was too dark to be blond, her chin was big and her eyes were small. But she had that laugh, and the sound of it was so beautiful that when you heard it, it was as if your eyes saw her through your ears and she was transformed. Her eyes disappeared altogether above her fat moon cheeks, and suddenly, in their absence, you noticed her mouth. Plump cherry-colored lips and even white teeth—no one else in Angelfield had teeth to match hers—and a little pink tongue that was like a kitten's. And the sound. That beautiful, rippling, unstoppable music that came gurgling out of her throat like spring-water from an underground stream. It was the sound of joy. He married her for it. And when she laughed his voice went soft, and he put his lips against her neck and said her name, Mary, over and over again. And the vibration of his voice on her skin tickled her and made her laugh, and laugh, and laugh.

Anyway, during the winter, while the twins kept to the gardens and the park, Merrily had a baby. The first warm days of spring found her in the garden, hanging out little clothes on a line. Behind her was a black perambulator. Heaven knows where it had come from; it wasn't the usual kind of thing for a village girl to have; no doubt it was some second- or thirdhand thing, bought cheap by the family (though no doubt seeming very dear) in order to mark the importance of this first child and grandchild. In any case, as Merrily bent for another little vest, another little chemise, and pegged them on the line, she was singing, like one of the birds that were singing, too, and her song seemed destined for the beautiful black perambulator. Its wheels were silver and very high, so although the carriage was large and black and rounded, the impression was of speed and weightlessness.

The garden gave onto fields at the back; a hedge divided the two spaces. Merrily did not know that from behind the hedge two pairs of green eyes were fixed on the perambulator.

Babies make a lot of washing, and Merrily was a hardworking and devoted mother. Every day she was out in the garden, putting the washing out and taking it in. From the kitchen window, as she washed napkins and vests in the sink, she kept an eye on the fine perambulator outdoors in the sun. Every five minutes it seemed she was nipping outdoors to adjust the hood, tuck in an extra blanket or simply sing.

Merrily was not the only one who was devoted to the perambulator. Emmeline and Adeline were besotted.

Merrily emerged one day from under the back porch with a basket of washing under one arm, and the perambulator wasn't there. She halted abruptly. Her mouth opened and her hands came up to her cheeks; the basket tumbled into the flower bed, tipping collars and socks onto the wallflowers. Merrily never looked once toward the fence and the brambles. She turned her head left and right as if she couldn't believe her eyes, left and right, left and right, left and right, all the time with the panic building up inside her, and in the end she let out a shriek, a high-pitched noise that rose into the blue sky as if it could rend it in two.

Mr. Griffin looked up from his vegetable plot and came to the fence, three doors down. Next door old Granny Stokes frowned at the kitchen sink and came out onto her porch. Astounded, they looked at Merrily, wondering whether their laughing neighbor was really capable of making such a sound, and she looked wildly back at them, dumbstruck, as though her cry had used up a lifetime's supply of words.

Eventually she said it. "My baby's gone."

And once the words were out they sprang into action. Mr. Griffin jumped over three fences in a flash, took Merrily by the arm and led her around to the front of her house, saying, "Gone? Where's he gone?" Granny Stokes disappeared from her back porch and a second later her voice floated in the air from the front garden, calling out for help.

And then a growing hubbub: "What is it? What's happened?"

"Taken! From the garden! In the perambulator!"

"You two go that way, and you others go that way."

"Run and fetch her husband, somebody."

All the noise, all the commotion at the front of the house.

At the back everything was quiet. Merrily's washing bobbed about in the lazy sunshine, Mr. Griffin's spade rested tranquilly in the well-turned soil, Emmeline caressed the silver spokes in blind, quiet ecstasy and Adeline kicked her out of the way so that they could get the thing moving.

They had a name for it. It was the voom.

They dragged the perambulator along the backs of the houses. It was harder than they had thought. For a start the pram was heavier than it appeared, and also they were pulling it along very uneven ground. The edge of the field was slightly banked, which tilted the pram at an angle. They could have put all four wheels on the level, but the newly turned earth was softer there, and the wheels sank into the clods of soil. Thistles and brambles snagged in the spokes and slowed them down, and it was a miracle that they kept going after the first twenty yards. But they were in their element. They pushed with all their might to get that pram home, gave it all their strength, and hardly seemed to feel the effort at all. They made their fingers bleed tearing the thistles away from the wheels, but on they went, Emmeline still crooning her love song to it, giving it a surreptitious stroke with her fingers from time to time, kissing it.

At last they came to the end of the fields and the house was in sight. But instead of making directly for it they turned toward the slopes of the deer park. They wanted to play. When they had pushed the pram to the top of the longest slope with their indefatigable energy, they set it in position. They lifted out the baby and put it on the ground, and Adeline heaved herself into the carriage. Chin on knees, holding on to the sides, she was white-faced. At a signal from her eyes, Emmeline gave the pram the most powerful push she could manage.

At first the pram went slowly. The ground was rough, and the slope, up here, was slight. But then the pram picked up speed. The black carriage flashed in the late sun as the wheels turned. Faster and faster, until the spokes became a blur and then not even a blur. The incline became steeper, and the bumps in the ground caused the pram to shake from side to side and threaten to take off.

A noise filled the air.

"Aaaaaaaaaaaaaaaaaaaaaa!"

Adeline, shrieking with pleasure as the pram hurtled downhill, shaking her bones and rattling her senses.

Suddenly it was clear what was going to happen.

One of the wheels struck against a piece of rock sticking out from the soil. There was a spark as metal screeched against stone, and the pram suddenly was speeding not downhill but through the air, flying into the sun, wheels upward. It traced a serene curve against the blue of the sky, until the moment when the ground heaved up violently to snatch it, and there came the sickening sound of something breaking. After the echo of Adeline's exhilaration reverberating in the sky, everything was suddenly very quiet.

Emmeline ran down the hill. The wheel facing the sky was buckled and half wrenched off; the other was still turning, slowly, all its urgency lost.

A white arm extended from the crushed cavity of the

black carriage and rested at a strange angle on the stony ground. On the hand were purple bramble stains and thistle scratches.

Emmeline knelt. Inside the crushed cavity of the carriage, all was dark.

But there was movement. A pair of green eyes staring back.

"Voom!" she said, and she smiled.

The game was over. It was time to go home.

～※～

Aside from the story itself, Miss Winter spoke little in our meetings. In the early days I used to say "How are you?" on arriving in the library, but she said only, "Ill. How are you?" with a bad-tempered edge to her voice as though I was a fool for asking. I never answered her question, and she didn't expect me to, so the exchanges soon came to an end. I would sidle in, exactly a minute early, take my place in the chair on the other side of the fire and take my notebook out of my bag. Then, with no preamble at all, she would pick up her story wherever she had left off. The end of these sessions was not governed by the clock. Sometimes Miss Winter would speak until she reached a natural break at the end of an episode. She would pronounce the last words, and the cessation of her voice had a finality about it that was unmistakable. It was followed by a silence as unambiguous as the white space at the end of a chapter. I would make a last note in my book, close the cover, gather my things together and take my leave. At other times, though, she would break off unexpectedly, in the middle of a scene, sometimes in the middle of a sentence, and I would look up to see her white face tightly drawn into a mask of endurance. "Is there anything I can do?" I asked, the first time I saw her like this. But she just closed her eyes and gestured for me to go.

When she finished telling me the story of Merrily and the perambulator, I put my pencil and notebook into my bag and, standing up, said, "I shall be going away for a few days."

"No." She was severe.

"I'm afraid I must. I was only expecting to be here for a few days initially, and I've been here for over a week. I don't have enough things with me for a prolonged stay."

"Maurice can take you to town to buy whatever you need."

"I need my books. . . ."

She gestured at her library shelves.

I shook my head. "I'm sorry, but I really have to go."

"Miss Lea, you seem to think that we have all the time in the world. Perhaps *you* do, but let me remind you, I am a busy woman. I do not want to hear any more talk of going away. Let that be the end of it."

I bit my lip and for a moment felt cowed. But I rallied. "Remember our agreement? Three true things? I need to do some checking."

She hesitated. "You don't believe me?"

I ignored her question. "Three true things that I could check. You gave me your word."

Her lips tightened in anger, but she concurred.

"You may leave on Monday. Three days. No more. Maurice will take you to the station."

I was in the middle of writing up the story of Merrily and the perambulator when there came a knock at my door. It was not time for dinner, so I was surprised; Judith had never interrupted my work before.

"Would you come to the drawing room?" she asked. "Dr. Clifton is here. He would like a word with you."

As I entered the room, the man I had already seen arriving at the house rose to his feet. I am no good at shaking hands, so I was glad when he seemed to decide not to offer me his, but it left us at a loss to find some other way to start.

"You are Miss Winter's biographer, I understand?"

"I'm not sure."

"Not sure?"

"If she is telling me the truth, then I am her biographer. Otherwise I am just an amanuensis."

"Hmm." He paused. "Does it matter?"

"To whom?"

"To you."

I didn't know, but I knew his question was impertinent, so I didn't answer it.

"You are Miss Winter's doctor, I suppose?"

"I am."

"Why have you asked to see me?"

"It is Miss Winter, actually, who has asked me to see you. She wants me to make sure you are fully aware of her state of health."

132

"I see."

With unflinching, scientific clarity, he proceeded to his explanation. In a few words he told me the name of the illness that was killing her, the symptoms she suffered, the degree of her pain and the hours of the day at which it was most and least effectively masked by the drugs. He mentioned a number of other conditions she suffered from, serious enough in themselves to kill her, except that the other disease was going to get there first. And he set out, as far as he was able, the likely progression of the illness, the need to ration the increases in dosage in order to have something in reserve for later, when, as he put it, she would really need it.

"How long?" I asked, when his explanation came to an end.

"I can't tell you. Another person would have succumbed already. Miss Winter is made of strong stuff. And since you have been here—" He broke off with the air of someone who finds himself inadvertently on the brink of breaking a confidence.

"Since *I* have been here . . . ?"

He looked at me and seemed to wonder, then made up his mind. "Since you have been here, she seems to be managing a little better. She says it is the anesthetic qualities of storytelling."

I was not sure what to make of this. Before I could examine my thoughts, the doctor was continuing. "I understand you are going away . . ."

"Is that why she has asked you to speak to me?"

"It is only that she wants you to understand that time is of the essence."

"You can let her know that I understand."

Our interview over, he held the door as I left, and as I passed him, he addressed me once more, in an unexpected whisper. "The thirteenth tale . . . ? I don't suppose . . ."

In his otherwise impassive face I caught a flash of the feverish impatience of the reader.

"She has said nothing about it," I said. "Though even if she had, I would not be at liberty to tell you."

His eyes cooled and a tremor ran from his mouth to the corner of his nose.

"Good day, Miss Lea."

"Good day, Doctor."

## DR. AND MRS. MAUDSLEY

On my last day Miss Winter told me about Dr. and Mrs. Maudsley.

Leaving gates open and wandering into other people's houses was one thing, walking off with a baby in its pram was quite another. The fact that the baby, when it was found, was discovered to be none the worse for its temporary disappearance was beside the point. Things had got out of hand; action was called for.

The villagers didn't feel able to approach Charlie directly about it. They understood that things were strange at the house, and they were half afraid to go there. Whether it was Charlie or Isabelle or the ghost that encouraged them to keep their distance is hard to say. Instead, they approached Dr. Maudsley. This was not the doctor whose failure to arrive promptly may or may not have caused the death in childbirth of Isabelle's mother, but a new man who had served the village for eight or nine years at this time.

Dr. Maudsley was not young, yet though he was in his middle forties he gave the impression of youth. He was not tall, nor really very muscular, but he had an air of vitality, of vigor about him. His legs were long for his body and he used to stride along at a great pace, with no apparent effort. He could walk faster than anyone, had grown used to finding himself talking into thin air and turning to find his walking companion scurrying along a few yards behind his back, panting with the effort of keeping up. This physical energy was matched by a great mental liveliness. You could hear the power of his brain in his voice, which was quiet but quick, with a facility for finding the right words for the right person at the right time. You could see it in his eyes: dark brown and very shiny, like a bird's eyes, observant, intent, with strong, neat eyebrows above.

Maudsley had a knack of spreading his energy around him—that's no bad thing for a doctor. His step on the path, his knock at the door, and his patients would start feeling better already. And not least, they liked him. He was a tonic in himself, that's what people said. It made a difference to him whether his patients lived or died, and when they lived, which was nearly always, it mattered how well they lived.

Dr. Maudsley had a great love of intellectual activity. Illness was a kind of puzzle to him, and he couldn't rest until he'd solved it. Patients got used to him turning up at their houses first thing in the morning when he'd spent the night puzzling over their symptoms, to ask one more question. And once he'd worked out a diagnosis, then there was the treatment to resolve. He consulted the books, of course, was fully cognizant of all the usual treatments, but he had an original mind that kept coming back to something as simple as a sore throat from a different angle, constantly casting about for the tiny fragment of knowledge that would enable him not only to get rid of the sore throat but to understand the phenomenon of the sore throat in an entirely new light. Energetic, intelligent and amiable, he was an exceptionally good doctor and a better than average man. Though, like all men, he had his blind spot.

The delegation of village men included the baby's father, his grandfather and the publican, a weary-looking fellow who didn't like to be left out of anything. Dr. Maudsley welcomed the trio and listened attentively as two of the three men recounted their tale. They began with the gates left open, went on to the vexed issue of the missing saucepans and arrived after some minutes at the climax of their story: the kidnapping of the infant in the perambulator.

"They're running wild," the younger Fred Jameson said finally.

"Out of control," added the older Fred Jameson.

"And what do you say?" asked Dr. Maudsley of the third man. Wilfred Bonner, standing to one side, had, until now, remained silent.

Mr. Bonner took his cap off and drew in a slow, whistling breath. "Well, I'm no medical man, but it seems to me them girls is *not right*." He accompanied his words with a look full of significance, then, in case he hadn't got his message across, tapped his bald head, once, twice, three times.

All three men looked gravely at their shoes.

"Leave it with me," said the doctor. "I'll speak to the family."

And the men left. They had done their bit. It was up to the doctor, the village elder, now.

Though he'd said he would speak to the family, what the doctor actually did was speak to his wife.

"I doubt they meant any harm by it," she said, when he had finished telling the story. "You know what girls are. A baby is so much more fun to play with than a doll. They wouldn't have hurt him. Still, they must be told not to do it again. Poor Mary." And she lifted her eyes from her sewing and turned her face to her husband.

Mrs. Maudsley was an exceedingly attractive woman. She had large brown eyes with long lashes that curled prettily, and her dark hair that had not a trace of gray in it was pulled back in a style of such simplicity that only a true beauty would not be made plain by it. When she moved, her form had a rounded, womanly grace.

The doctor knew his wife was beautiful, but they had been married too long for it to make any difference to him.

"They think in the village that the girls are mentally retarded."

"Surely not!"

"It's what Wilfred Bonner thinks, at least."

She shook her head in wonderment. "He is afraid of them because they are twins. Poor Wilfred. It is just old-fashioned ignorance. Thank goodness the younger generation is more understanding."

The doctor was a man of science. Though he knew it was statistically unlikely that there was any mental abnormality in the twins, he would not rule it out until he had seen them. It did not surprise him, though, that his wife, whose religion forbade her to believe ill of anyone, would take for granted that the rumor was ill-founded gossip.

"I'm sure you are right," he murmured with a vagueness that meant he was sure she was wrong. He had given up trying to get her to believe only what was *true;* she had been raised to the kind of religion that could admit no difference between what was true and what was *good.*

"What will you do, then?" she asked him.

"Go and see the family. Charles Angelfield is a bit of a hermit, but he'll have to see me if I go."

Mrs. Maudsley nodded, which was her way of disagreeing with her husband, though he didn't know it. "What about the mother? What do you know of her?"

"Very little."

And the doctor continued to think in silence, and Mrs. Maudsley continued her sewing, and after a quarter of an hour had passed, the doctor said, "Perhaps you might go, Theodora? The mother might sooner see another woman than a man. What do you say?"

And so three days later Mrs. Maudsley arrived at the house and knocked at the front door. Astonished to get no answer, she frowned—after all, she had sent a note to say she was coming—and walked round to the back. The kitchen door was ajar, so with a quick knock she went in. No one was there. Mrs. Maudsley looked around. Three apples on the table, brown and wrinkled and starting to collapse upon themselves, a black dish-cloth next to a sink piled high with dirty plates, and the window so filthy that inside you could hardly tell day from night. Her dainty white nose sniffed the air. It told her everything she needed to know. She pursed her lips, set her shoulders, took a tight grip on the tortoiseshell handle of her bag and set off on her crusade. She went from room to room looking for Isabelle, but on the way taking in the squalor, the mess, the unkemptness that lurked everywhere.

The Missus tired easily, and she couldn't manage the stairs very well, and her sight was going, and she often thought she had cleaned things when she hadn't, or meant to clean them and then forgot, and to be honest, she knew nobody really cared, so she mostly concentrated on feeding the girls, and they were lucky she managed that much. So the house was dirty, and it was dusty, and when a picture was knocked wonky it stayed wonky for a decade, and when one day Charlie couldn't find the paper bin in his study, he just dropped the paper onto the floor in the place where the paper bin used to be, and it soon occurred to him that it was less fuss to chuck it out once a year than to do it once a week.

Mrs. Maudsley didn't like what she saw at all. She frowned at the half-closed curtains, and sighed at the tarnished silver, and shook her head in amazement at the saucepans on the stairs and the sheet music that was scattered all over the floor of the hallway. In the drawing room, she bent down automatically to retrieve a playing card, the three of spades, that was lying dropped or discarded in the middle of the floor, but when she looked around the room for the rest of the pack, she was at a loss, so great was the disorder. Glancing helplessly back at the card she became aware of the dust covering it and, being a fastidious, white-gloved woman, was overwhelmed with the desire to put it down, only where? For a few seconds she was para-lyzed with anxiety, torn between the desire to end the contact between her pristine glove and the dusty, faintly sticky playing card, and her own unwillingness to put the card down in a place that wasn't the right one. Eventually, with a perceptible shudder of the shoulders, she placed it on the arm of the leather armchair and walked with relief out of the room.

The library seemed better. It was dusty, certainly, and the carpet was threadbare, but the books themselves were in their places, which was something. Yet even in the library, just when she was preparing herself to believe that there remained some small feeling for order buried in this filthy, chaotic family, she came across a makeshift bed. Tucked into a dark corner between two sets of shelves, it was just a flea-ridden blanket and a filthy pillow, and at first she took it for a cat's bed. Then, looking again, she spotted the corner of a book visible beneath the pillow. She drew it out. It was *Jane Eyre*.

From the library she passed to the music room, where she found the same disorder she had seen elsewhere. The furniture was arranged bizarrely, as though to facilitate the playing of hide-and-seek. A chaise longue was turned to face a wall, a chair was half hidden by a chest that had been dragged from its place under the window—there was a broad sweep of carpet behind it where the dust was less thick and the green color showed through more distinctly. On the piano, a vase contained blackened, brittle stems, and around it a neat circle of papery petals like ashes. Mrs. Maudsley reached her hand toward one and picked it up; it crumbled, leaving a nasty yellow-gray stain between her white-gloved fingers.

Mrs. Maudsley seemed to slump down onto the piano stool.

The doctor's wife wasn't a bad woman. She was sufficiently convinced of her own importance to believe that God actually did watch everything she did and listen to everything she said, and she was too taken up

141

with rooting out the pride she was prone to feeling in her own holiness to notice any other failings she might have had. She was a do-gooder, which means that all the ill she did, she did without realizing it.

What was going on in her mind as she sat there on the piano stool, staring into space? These were people who couldn't keep their flower vases topped up. No wonder their children were misbehaving! The extent of the problem seemed suddenly to have been revealed to her through the dead flowers, and it was in a distracted, absent fashion that she pulled off her gloves and spread her fingers on the black and gray keys of the piano.

The sound that resounded in the room was the harshest, most unpianolike noise imaginable. This was in part because the piano had been neglected, unplayed and untuned, for many years. It was also because the vibration of the instrument's strings was instantly accompanied by another noise, equally unmelodic. It was a kind of a howling hiss, an irritated, wild sort of a screech, like that of a cat whose tail has got under your feet.

Mrs. Maudsley was shaken entirely out of her reverie by it. On hearing the yowl, she stared at the piano in disbelief and stood up, her hands to her cheeks. In her bewilderment she had only the barest moment to register that she was not alone.

There, rising from the chaise longue, a slight figure in white—

Poor Mrs. Maudsley.

She had not the time to appreciate that the white-robed figure was brandishing a violin, and that the violin was descending very quickly and with great force toward her own head. Before she could take in any of this, the violin made contact with her skull, blackness overwhelmed her and she fell, unconscious, to the floor.

With her arms sprawled any old how, and her neat white handkerchief still tucked inside her watch strap, she looked as though there wasn't a drop of life left in her. Little puffs of dust that had come up from the carpet when she landed fell gently back down.

There she lay for a good half hour, until the Missus, back from the farm where she had been to collect eggs, happened to glance in at the door and see a dark shape where she hadn't seen a dark shape before.

There was no sign of a figure in white.

⁂

As I transcribed from memory, Miss Winter's voice seemed to fill my room with the same degree of reality with which it had filled the library. She had a way of speaking that engraved itself on my memory and was as reliable as a phonograph recording. But at this point, where she said, "There was no sign of a figure in white," she had paused, and so now I paused, pencil hovering above the page, as I considered what had happened next.

I had been engrossed in the story, and so it took me a moment to refocus my eye from the prone figure of the doctor's wife in the story to the storyteller herself. When I did I was dismayed. Miss Winter's normal

143

pallor had given way to an ugly yellow-gray tint, and her frame, always rigid it must be said, seemed at present to be girding itself against some invisible assault. There was a trembling around her mouth, and I guessed that she was on the point of losing the struggle to hold her lips in a firm line and that a repressed grimace was close to winning the day.

I rose from my chair in alarm but had no idea what I ought to do.

"Miss Winter," I exclaimed helplessly, "whatever is it?"

"My wolf," I thought I heard her say, but the effort to speak was enough to send her lips into a quiver. She closed her eyes, seemed to struggle to measure her breathing. Just as I was on the point of running to find Judith, Miss Winter regained control. The rise and fall of her chest slowed, the tremors in her face ceased, and though she was still pale as death, she opened her eyes and looked at me.

"Better. . . ." she said weakly.

Slowly I returned to my chair.

"I thought you said something about a wolf," I began.

"Yes. That black beast that gnaws at my bones whenever he gets a chance. He loiters in corners and behind doors most of the time, because he's afraid of these." She indicated the white pills on the table beside her. "But they don't last forever. It's nearly twelve and they are wearing off. He is sniffing at my neck. By half past he will be digging his teeth and claws in. Until one, when I can take another tablet and he will have to return to his corner. We are always clockwatching, he and I. He pounces five minutes earlier every day. But I cannot take my tablets five minutes earlier. That stays the same."

"But surely the doctor—"

"Of course. Once a week, or once every ten days, he adjusts the dose. Only never quite enough. He does not want to be the one to kill me, you see. And so when it comes, it must be the wolf that finishes me off."

She looked at me, very matter-of-fact, then relented.

"The pills are here, look. And the glass of water. If I wanted to, I could put an end to it myself. Whenever I chose. So do not feel sorry for me. I have chosen this way because I have things to do."

I nodded. "All right."

"So. Let's get on and do them, shall we? Where were we?"

"The doctor's wife. In the music room. With the violin."

And we continued our work.

❀

Charlie wasn't used to dealing with problems.

He *had* problems. Plenty of them—holes in the roof, cracked windowpanes, pigeons moldering away in the attic rooms—but he ignored them. Or perhaps was so far removed from the world that he just didn't notice them. When the water penetration got too bad he just closed up a room and started using another one. The house was big enough, after all. One wonders whether in his slow-moving mind he realized that other people actively maintained their homes. But then, dilapidation was his natural environment. He felt at home in it.

Still, a doctor's wife apparently dead in the music room was a problem he couldn't ignore. If it had been one of us . . . But an *outsider.* That was another matter. Something had to be done, although he had no notion of what that something might be, and he stared, stricken, at the doctor's wife as she put her hand to her throbbing head and moaned. He might be stupid, but he knew what this meant. Calamity was coming.

The Missus sent John-the-dig for the doctor and in due course the doctor arrived. And it seemed for a while that premonitions of disaster were ill-founded, for it was found that the doctor's wife was not badly hurt at all, barely even concussed. She refused a tot of brandy, accepted tea and after a short while was as right as rain. "It was a woman," she said. "A woman in white."

"Nonsense," said the Missus, at once reassuring and dismissive. "There is no woman in white in the house."

Tears glittered in Mrs. Maudsley's brown eyes, but she was adamant. "Yes, a woman, slightly built, there on the chaise longue. She heard the piano and rose up and—"

"Did you see her for long?" Dr. Maudsley asked.

"No, it was just for a moment."

"Well then, you see? It cannot be," the Missus interrupted her, and though her voice was sympathetic it was also firm. "There is no woman in white. You must have seen a ghost."

And then for the first time, John-the-dig's voice was heard. "They do say that the house is haunted."

For a moment the assembled group looked at the broken violin abandoned on the floor, and considered the lump that was forming on Mrs. Maudsley's temple, but before anyone had time to respond to the theory, Isabelle appeared in the doorway. Slim and willowy, she was wearing a pale lemon dress; her haphazard top-knot was unkempt and her eyes, though beautiful, were wild.

"Could this be the person you saw?" the doctor asked his wife.

Mrs. Maudsley measured Isabelle against the picture in her mind. How many shades separate white from pale yellow? Where exactly is the borderline between slight and slim? How might a blow to the head affect a person's memory? She wavered, then, seeing the emerald eyes and finding an exact match in her memory, decided.

"Yes. This is the person."

The Missus and John-the-dig avoided exchanging a glance.

From that moment, forgetting his wife, it was Isabelle the doctor attended to. He looked at her closely, kindly, with worry in the back of his eyes while he asked her question after question. When she refused to answer he was unrattled, but when she was bothered to reply—by turns arch, impatient, nonsensical—he listened carefully, nodding as he made notes in his doctor's pad. Taking her wrist to measure her pulse, he noted with alarm the cuts and scars that marked the inside of her forearm.

"Does she do this herself?"

Reluctantly honest, the Missus murmured, "Yes," and the doctor pressed his lips into a worried line.

"May I have a word with you, sir?" he asked, turning to Charlie. Charlie looked blankly at him, but the doctor took him by the elbow—"The library, perhaps?"—and led him firmly out of the room.

In the drawing room the Missus and the doctor's wife waited and pretended not to pay any attention to the sounds that came from the library. There was the hum not of voices but of a single voice, calm and measured. When it stopped, we heard "No" and again "No!" in Charlie's raised voice, and then again the low tones of the doctor. They were gone for some time, and we heard Charlie's protestations over and over before the door opened and the doctor came out, looking serious and shaken. Behind him, there was a great howl of despair and impotence, but the doctor only winced and pulled the door closed behind him.

"I'll make the arrangements with the asylum," he told the Missus. "Leave the transport to me. Will two o'clock be all right?"

Baffled, she nodded her head, and the doctor's wife rose to leave.

At two o'clock three men came to the house, and they led Isabelle out to a brougham in the drive. She submitted herself to them like a lamb, settled obediently in the seat, never even looked out as the horses trotted slowly down the drive, toward the lodge gates.

The twins, unconcerned, were drawing circles with their toes in the gravel of the drive.

Charlie stood on the steps watching the brougham as it grew smaller and smaller. He had the air of a child whose favorite toy is being taken away, and who cannot believe—not quite, not yet—that it is really happening.

From the hall the Missus and John-the-dig watched him anxiously, waiting for the realization to dawn.

The car reached the lodge gates and disappeared through them. Charlie continued to stare at the open gates for three, four, five seconds. Then his mouth opened. A wide circle, twitching and trembling, that revealed his quivering tongue, the fleshy redness of his throat, strings of spittle across a dark cavity. Mesmerized we watched, waiting for the awful noise to emerge from the gaping, juddering mouth, but the sound was not ready to come. For long seconds it built up, accumulating inside him until his whole body seemed full of pent-up sound. At long last he fell to his knees on the steps and the cry emerged from him. It was not the elephantine bellow we were expecting, but a damp, nasal snort.

The girls looked up from their toe circles for a moment, then returned impassively to them. John-the-dig tightened his lips and turned away, heading back to the garden and work. There was nothing for him to do here. The Missus went to Charlie, placed a consoling hand on his shoulder and attempted to persuade him into the house, but he was deaf to her words and only snuffled and squeaked like a thwarted schoolboy.

And that was that.

☙❧

That was that? The words were a curiously understated endnote to the disappearance of Miss Winter's mother. It was clear that Miss Winter didn't think much of Isabelle's abilities as a parent; indeed the word *mother* seemed absent from her lexicon. Perhaps it was understandable; from what I could see, Isabelle was the least maternal of women. But who was I to judge other people's relations with their mothers?

I closed my book, slid my pencil into the spiral and stood up.

"I'll be away for three days," I reminded her. "I'll be back on Thursday."

And I left her alone with her wolf.

## DICKENS'S STUDY

I finished writing up that day's notes. All dozen pencils were blunt now; I had some serious sharpening to do. One by one, I inserted the lead ends into the sharpener. If you turn the handle slowly and evenly you can sometimes get the coil of lead-edged wood to twist and dangle in a single drop all the way to the paper bin, but tonight I was tired, and they kept breaking under their own weight.

I thought about the story. I had warmed to the Missus and John-the-dig. Charlie and Isabelle made me nervous. The doctor and his wife had the best of motives, but I suspected their intervention in the lives of the twins would come to no good.

The twins themselves puzzled me. I knew what other people thought of them. John-the-dig thought they couldn't speak properly; the Missus believed they didn't understand other people were alive; the villagers thought they were wrong in the head. What I didn't know—and this was more than curious—was what the storyteller thought. In telling her tale, Miss Winter was like the light that illuminates everything but itself. She was the disappearing point at the heart of the narrative. She spoke of *they*; more recently she had spoken of *we*; the absence that perplexed me was *I*. What could it be that had caused her to distance herself from her story in this way?

If I were to ask her about it, I knew what she would say. "Miss Lea, we made an agreement." Already I had asked her questions about one or two details of the story, and though from time to time she would answer, when she didn't want to, she would remind me of our first meeting. "No cheating. No looking ahead. No questions."

I reconciled myself to remaining curious for a long time, and yet, as it happened, something happened that very evening that cast a certain illumination on the matter.

I had tidied my desk and was setting about my

packing when there came a tap on my door. I opened it to find Judith in the corridor.

"Miss Winter wonders whether you have time to see her for a moment."

This was Judith's polite translation of a more abrupt *Fetch Miss Lea,* I was in no doubt.

I finished folding a blouse and went down to the library.

Miss Winter was seated in her usual position and the fire was blazing, but otherwise the room was in darkness.

"Would you like me to put some lights on?" I asked from the doorway.

"No." Her answer came distantly to my ears, and so I walked down the aisle toward her. The shutters were open, and the dark sky, pricked all over with stars, was reflected in the mirrors.

When I arrived beside her, the dancing light from the fire showed me that Miss Winter was distracted. In silence I sat in my place, lulled by the warmth of the fire, staring into the night sky reflected in the library mirrors. A quarter of an hour passed while she ruminated, and I waited.

Then she spoke.

"Have you ever seen that picture of Dickens in his study? It's by a man called Buss, I believe. I've a reproduction of it somewhere, I'll look it out for you. Anyway, in the picture, he has pushed his chair back from his desk and is drowsing, eyes closed, bearded chin on chest. He is wearing his slippers. Around his head, characters from his books are drifting in the air like cigar smoke; some throng above the papers on the desk, others have drifted behind him, or floated downward as though they believe themselves capable of walking on their own two feet on the floor. And why not? They are presented with the same firm lines as the writer himself, so why should they not be as real as him? They are *more* real than the books on the shelves, books that are sketched with the barest hint of a line here and there, fading in places to a ghostly nothingness.

"Why recall the picture now, you must be wondering. The reason I remember it so well is that it seems to be an image of the way I have lived my own life. I have closed my study door on the world and shut myself away with people of my imagination. For nearly sixty years I have eavesdropped with impunity on the lives of people who do not exist. I have peeped shamelessly into hearts and bathroom closets. I have leaned over shoulders to follow the movements of quills as they write love letters, wills and confessions. I have watched as lovers love, murderers murder and children play their make-believe. Prisons and brothels have opened their doors to me; galleons and camel trains have transported me across sea and sand; centuries and continents have fallen away at my bidding. I have spied upon the misdeeds of the mighty and witnessed the nobility of the meek. I have bent so low over sleepers in their beds that they might have felt my breath on their faces. I have seen their dreams.

"My study throngs with characters waiting to be written. Imaginary people, anxious for a life, who tug at my sleeve, crying, 'Me next! Go on! My turn!' I have to select. And once I have chosen, the others lie quiet for ten months or a year, until I come to the end of the story, and the clamor starts up again.

"And every so often, through all these writing years, I have lifted my head from my page—at the end of a chapter, or in the quiet pause for thought after a death scene, or sometimes just searching for the right word—and have seen a face at the back of the crowd. A familiar face. Pale skin, red hair, a steady green-eyed gaze. I know exactly who she is, yet am always surprised to see her. Every time she manages to catch me off my guard. Often she has opened her mouth to speak to me, but for decades she was too far away to be heard, and besides, as soon as I became aware of her presence I would avert my gaze and pretend I hadn't seen her. She was not, I think, taken in.

"People wonder what makes me so prolific. Well, it's because of her. If I have started a new book five minutes after finishing the last, it is because to look up from my desk would mean meeting her eye.

"The years have passed; the number of my books on the bookshop shelves has grown, and consequently the crowd of personages floating in the air of my study has thinned. With every book that I have written, the babble of voices has grown quieter, the sense of bustle in my head reduced. The faces pressing for attention have diminished, and always, at the back of the group but nearer with every book, there she was. The green-eyed girl. Waiting.

"The day came when I finished the final draft of my final book. I wrote the last sentence, placed the last full stop. I knew what was coming. The pen slipped from my hand and I closed my eyes. 'So,' I heard her say, or perhaps it was me, 'it's just the two of us now.'

"I argued with her for a bit. 'It will never work,' I told her. 'It was too long ago, I was only a child, I've forgotten.' Though I was only going through the motions.

"'But *I* haven't forgotten,' she says. 'Remember when . . .'

"Even I know the inevitable when I see it. I *do* remember."

The faint vibration in the air fell still. I turned from my stargazing to Miss Winter. Her green eyes were staring at a spot in the room as though they were at that very moment seeing the green-eyed child with the copper hair.

"The girl is you."

"Me?" Miss Winter's eyes turned slowly away from the ghost child and in my direction. "No, she is not me. She is—" She hesitated. "She is someone I used to be. That child ceased existing a long, long time ago. Her life came to an end the night of the fire as surely as though she had perished in the flames. The person you see before you now is nothing."

"But your career . . . the stories . . ."

"When one is nothing, one invents. It fills a void."

Then we sat in silence and watched the fire. From time to time Miss Winter rubbed absently at her palm.

"Your essay on Jules and Edmond Landier," she began after a time.

I turned reluctantly to her.

"What made you choose them as a subject? You must have had some particular interest? Some personal attraction?"

I shook my head. "Nothing special, no."

And then there was just the stillness of the stars and the crackling of the fire.

It must have been an hour or so later, when the flames were lower, that she spoke a third time.

"Margaret." I believe it was the first time she had called me by my first name. "When you leave here tomorrow . . ."

"Yes?"

"You will come back, won't you?"

It was hard to judge her expression in the flickering, dying light of the fire, and it was hard to tell how far the trembling in her voice was the effect of fatigue or illness, but it seemed to me, in the moment before I answered—"Yes. Of course I will come back"—that Miss Winter was afraid.

The next morning Maurice drove me to the station and I took the train south.

Where else to begin my research but at home, in the shop?

I was fascinated by the old almanacs. Since I was a child, any moment of boredom or anxiety or fear would send me to these shelves to flick through the pages of names and dates and annotations. Between these covers, past lives were summarized in a few brutally neutral lines. It was a world where men were baronets and bishops and ministers of parliament, and women were wives and daughters. There was nothing to tell you whether these men liked kidneys for breakfast, nothing to tell you whom they loved or what form their fear gave to the shapes in the dark after they blew the candle out at night. There was nothing personal at all. What was it, then, that moved me so in these sparse annotations of the lives of dead men? Only that they *were* men, that they *had* lived, that now they were dead.

Reading them, I felt a stirring in me. In me, but not *of* me. Reading the lists, the part of me that was already on the other side woke and caressed me.

I never explained to anyone why the almanacs meant so much to me; I never even said I liked them. But my father took note of my preference, and whenever volumes of the sort came up at auction, he made sure to get them. And so it was that all the illustrious dead of the country, going back many generations, were spending their after-life tranquilly on the shelves of our second floor. With me for company.

It was on the second floor, crouched in the window seat, that I turned the pages of names. I had found Miss Winter's grandfather George Angelfield. He was not a baronet, nor a minister, nor a bishop, but still, here he was. The family had aristocratic origins—there had once been a title, but a few generations earlier there had been a split in the family: the title had gone one way, the money and the property another. He was on the property side. The almanacs tended to follow the titles, but still, the connection was close enough to merit an entry, so here he was: Angelfield, George; his date of birth; residing at Angelfield House in Oxfordshire; married to Mathilde Monnier of Reims, France; one son, Charles. Tracing him through the almanacs for later years, I found an amendment a decade later: one son, Charles; one daughter, Isabelle. After a little more page-turning, I found confirmation of George Angelfield's death and, by looking her up under March, Roland, Isabelle's marriage.

For a moment it amused me to think that I had gone all the way to Yorkshire to hear Miss Winter's story, when all the time it was here, in the almanacs, a few feet under my bed. But then I started thinking properly. What did it prove, this paper trail? Only that such people as George and Mathilde and their children, Charles and Isabelle, existed. There was nothing to say that Miss Winter had not found them the same way I had, by flicking through a book. These almanacs could be found in libraries all over the place. Anyone who wanted could look through them. Might she not have found a set of names and dates and embroidered a story around them to entertain herself?

Alongside these misgivings I had another problem. Roland March had died, and with his death the paper trail for Isabelle came to an end. The world of the almanac was a queer one. In the real world, families branched like trees, blood mixed by marriage passed from one generation to the next, making an ever-wider net of connections. Titles, on the other hand, passed from one man to one man, and it was this narrow, linear progression that the almanac liked to highlight. On each side of the title line were a few younger brothers, nephews, cousins, who came close enough to fall within the span of the almanac's illumination. The men who might have been lord or baronet. And, though it was not said, the men who still might, if the right string of tragedies were to occur. But after a certain number of branchings in the family tree, the names fell out of the margins and into the ether. No combination of ship-wreck, plague and earthquake would be powerful enough to restore these third cousins to prominence. The almanac had its limits. So it was with Isabelle. She was a woman; her babies were girls; her husband (not a lord) was dead; her father (not a lord) was dead. The almanac cut her and her babies adrift; she and they fell into the vast ocean of ordinary people, whose births and deaths and marriages are, like their loves and fears and breakfast preferences, too insignificant to be worth recording for posterity.

Charlie, though, was a male. The almanac could stretch itself—just—to include him, though the dimness of insignificance was already casting its shadow. Information was scant. His name was Charles Angelfield. He had been born. He lived at Angelfield. He was not married. He was not dead. As far as the almanac was concerned, this information was sufficient.

I took out one volume after another, found again and again the same sketchy half-life. With every new tome I thought, This will be the year they leave him out. But each year, there he was, still Charles Angelfield, still of Angelfield, still unmarried. I thought again about what Miss Winter had told me about Charlie and his sister, and bit my lip thinking about what his long bachelorhood signified.

And then, when he would have been in his late forties, I found a surprise. His name, his date of birth, his place of residence and a strange abbreviation—*ldd*—that I had never noticed before.

I turned to the table of abbreviations.

*Ldd: legal decree of decease.*

Turning back to Charlie's entry, I stared at it for a long time, frowning, as though if I looked hard enough, there would be revealed in the grain or the watermark of the paper itself the elucidation of the mystery.

In this year he had been legally decreed to be dead. As far as I understood, a legal decree of decease was what happened when a person disappeared and after a certain time his family, for reasons of inheritance, was allowed

160

to assume that he was dead, though there was no proof and no body. I had a feeling that a person had to be lost without trace for seven years before he could be decreed dead. He might have died at any time in that period. He might not even be dead at all, but only gone, lost or wandering, far from everyone who had ever known him. Dead in law, but that didn't necessarily mean dead in person. What kind of life was it, I wondered, that could end in this vague, unsatisfactory way? *Ldd.*

I closed the almanac, put it back in its position on the shelf and went down to the shop to make cocoa.

"What do you know about the legal procedures you have to take to have someone declared dead?" I called to my father while I stood over the pan of milk on the stove.

"No more than you do, I should think," came the answer.

Then he appeared in the doorway and handed me one of our dog-eared customer cards. "This is the man to ask. Retired professor of law. Lives in Wales now, but he comes here every summer for a browse and a walk by the river. Nice fellow. Why don't you write? You might ask whether he wants me to hold that *Justitiae Naturalis Principia* for him at the same time."

When I'd finished my cocoa, I went back to the almanac to find out what else I could about Roland March and his family. His uncle had dabbled in art and when I went to the art history section to follow this up, I learned that his portraits, while now acknowledged to

161

be mediocre, had been for a short period the height of fashion. Mortimer's *English Provincial Portraiture* contained the reproduction of an early portrait by Lewis Anthony March, entitled *Roland, nephew of the artist.* It is an odd thing to look into the face of a boy who is not quite yet a man, in search of the features of an old woman, his daughter. For some minutes I studied his fleshy, sensual features, his glossy blond hair, the lazy set of his head.

Then I closed the book. I was wasting my time. Were I to look all day and all night, I knew I would not find a trace of the twins he was supposed to have fathered.

## IN THE ARCHIVES OF THE *BANBURY HERALD*

The next day I took the train to Banbury, to the offices of the *Banbury Herald.*

It was a young man who showed me the archives. The word *archive* might sound rather impressive to someone who has not had much to do with them, but to me, who has spent her holidays for years in such places, it came as no surprise to be shown into what was essentially a large, windowless basement cupboard.

"A house fire at Angelfield," I explained briefly, "about sixty years ago."

The boy showed me the shelf where the holdings for the relevant period were shelved.

"I'll lift the boxes for you, shall I?"

"And the books pages, too, from about forty years ago, but I'm not sure which year."

"Books pages? Didn't know the *Herald* ever had books pages." And he moved his ladder, retrieved another set of boxes and placed them beside the first one on a long table under a bright light.

"There you are then," he said cheerily, and he left me to it.

The Angelfield fire, I learned, was probably caused by an accident. It was not uncommon for people to stockpile fuel at the time, and it was this that had caused the fire to take hold so fiercely. There had been no one in the house but the two nieces of the owner, both of whom escaped and were in hospital. The owner himself was believed to be abroad. (*Believed to be . . .* I wondered. I made a quick note of the dates—another six years were to elapse before the ldd.) The column ended with some comments on the architectural significance of the house, and it was noted that it was uninhabitable in its current state.

I copied out the story and scanned headlines in the following issues in case there were updates but, finding nothing, I put the papers away and turned to the other boxes.

"Tell me the truth," he had said. The young man in the old-fashioned suit who had interviewed Vida Winter for the *Banbury Herald* forty years ago. And she had never forgotten his words.

There was no trace of the interview. There was nothing even that could properly be called a books page. The only literary items at all were occasional book reviews under the heading "You might like to read . . ." by a reviewer called Miss Jenkinsop. Twice my eye came to rest on Miss Winter's name in these paragraphs. Miss Jenkinsop had clearly read and enjoyed Miss Winter's novels; her praise was enthusiastic and just, if unscholarly in expression, but it was plain she had never met their author and equally plain that she was not the man in the brown suit.

I closed the last newspaper and folded it neatly in its box.

The man in the brown suit was a fiction. A device to snare me. The fly with which a fisherman baits his line to draw the fish in. It was only to be expected. Perhaps it was the confirmation of the existence of George and Mathilde, Charlie and Isabelle that had raised my hopes. They at least were real people; the man in the brown suit was not.

Putting my hat and gloves on, I left the offices of the *Banbury Herald* and stepped out into the street.

As I walked along the winter streets looking for a café, I remembered the letter Miss Winter had sent me. I remembered the words of the man in the brown suit, and how they had echoed around the rafters of my rooms under the eaves. Yet the man in the brown suit was a figment of her imagination. I should have expected it. She was a spinner of yarns, wasn't she? A storyteller. A fabulist. A liar. And the plea that had so moved me—*Tell me the truth*—had been uttered by a man who was not even real.

I was at a loss to explain to myself the bitterness of my disappointment.

## RUIN

From Banbury I took a bus.

"Angelfield?" said the bus driver. "No, there's no service to Angelfield. Not yet, anyhow. Might be different when the hotel's built."

"Are they building there, then?"

"Some old ruin they're pulling down. Going to be a fancy hotel. They might run a bus then, for the staff, but for now the best you can do is get off at the Hare and Hounds on the Cheneys Road and walk from there. 'Bout a mile, I reckon."

There wasn't much in Angelfield. A single street whose wooden sign read, with logical simplicity, The Street. I walked past a dozen cottages, built in pairs. Here and there a distinctive feature stood out—a large yew tree, a children's swing, a wooden bench—but for the most part each dwelling, with its neatly embroidered thatch, its white gables and the restrained artistry in its brickwork, resembled its neighbor like a mirror image.

The cottage windows looked out onto fields that were neatly defined with hedges and studded here and there with trees. Farther away sheep and cows were visible, and then a densely wooded area, beyond which, according to my map, was the deer park. There was no pavement as such, but that hardly mattered for there was no traffic, either. In fact I saw no sign of human life at all until I passed the last cottage and came to a combined post office and general store.

Two children in yellow mackintoshes came out of the shop and ran down to the road ahead of their mother, who had stopped at the postbox. Small and fair, she was struggling to stick stamps onto envelopes without dropping the newspaper tucked under her arm. The older child, a boy, reached up to put his sweet wrapper in the bin attached to a post at the roadside. He went to take his sister's wrapper, but she resisted. "I can do it! I can do it!" She stood on tiptoe and stretched up her arm, ignoring her brother's protestations, then tossed the paper toward the mouth of the bin. A breeze caught it and carried it across the road.

"I told you so!"

Both children turned and launched themselves into a dash—then jolted to a halt when they saw me. Two blond fringes flopped down over pairs of identically shaped brown eyes. Two mouths fell into the same expression of surprise. Not twins, no, but so close. I stooped to pick up the wrapper and held it out toward them. The girl, willing to take it, went to step forward. Her brother, more cautious, stuck his arm out to bar her way and called, "Mum!"

The fair-haired woman watching from the postbox had seen what had happened. "All right, Tom. Let her take it." The girl took the paper from my hand without looking at me. "Say thank you," the mother called. The children did so in restrained voices, then turned their backs from me and leaped thankfully away. This time the woman lifted her daughter up to reach the bin, and in doing so looked at me again, eyeing my camera with veiled curiosity.

Angelfield was not a place where I could be invisible.

She offered a reserved smile. "Enjoy your walk," she said, and then she turned to follow her children, who were already running back along the street toward the cottages.

I watched them go.

The children ran, swooping and diving around each other, as though attached by an invisible cord. They switched direction at random, made unpredictable changes of speed, with telepathic synchronicity. They were two dancers, moving to the same inner music, two leaves caught up in the same breeze. It was uncanny and perfectly familiar. I'd have liked to watch them longer, but, fearful that they might turn and catch me staring, I pulled myself away.

After a few hundred yards the lodge gates came into view. The gates themselves were not only closed but welded to the ground and each other by writhing twists of ivy that wove in and out of the elaborate metalwork. Over the gates, a pale stone arch sat high above the road, its sides extending into two small single-room buildings with windows. In one window a piece of paper was displayed. Inveterate reader that I am, I couldn't resist; I clambered through the long wet grass to read it. But it was a ghost notice. The colored logo of a construction company had survived, but beneath it, two pale gray stains the shape of paragraphs and, slightly darker but not much, the shadow of a signature. It had the shape of writing, but the meaning had been bleached out by months of sunshine.

Preparing to walk a long way around the boundary to find a way in, I had taken only a few steps when I came to a small wooden gate set in a wall with nothing but a latch to fasten it. In an instant I was inside.

The drive had once been graveled, but now the pebbles underfoot were interspersed with bare earth and scrubby grass. It led in a long curve to a small stone and flint church with a lych-gate, then curved the other way, behind a sweep of trees and shrubs that obscured the view. On each side the borders were overgrown; branches of different bushes were fighting for space and at their feet grass and weeds were creeping into whatever spaces they could find.

I walked toward the church. Rebuilt in Victorian times, it retained the modesty of its medieval origins. Small and neat, its spire indicated the direction of heaven without trying to pierce a hole in it. The church was positioned at the apex of the gravel curve; as I drew closer my eye veered away from the lych-gate and toward the vista that was opening up on the other side of me. With each step, the view widened and widened, until at last the pale mass of stone that was Angelfield House appeared and I stopped dead in my tracks.

The house sat at an awkward angle. Arriving from

the drive, you came upon a corner, and it was not at all clear which side of the house was the front. It was as though the house knew it ought to meet its arriving visitors face-on, but at the last minute couldn't repress the impulse to turn back and gaze upon the deer park and the woodlands at the end of the terraces. The visitor was met not by a welcoming smile but by a cold shoulder.

This sense of awkwardness was only increased by the other aspects of its appearance. The house was of asymmetrical construction. Three great bays, each one four stories high, stood out from the body of the house, their twelve tall and wide windows offering the only order and harmony the facade could muster. In the rest of the house, the windows were a higgledy-piggledy arrangement, no two alike, none level with its neighbor whether left and right or up and down. Above the third floor, a balustrade tried to hold the disparate architecture together in a single embrace, but here and there a jutting stone, a partial bay, an awkward window, were too much for it; it disappeared only to start up again the other side of the obstacle. Above this balustrade there rose an uneven roofline of towers, turrets and chimney stacks, the color of honey.

A ruin? Most of the golden stone looked as clean and as fresh as the day it had been quarried. Of course the elaborate stonework of the turrets looked a little worn, the balustrading was crumbling in places, but all the same, it was hardly a ruin. To see it then, with the blue sky behind it, birds flying around its towers and the grass green round about, I had no difficulty at all in imagining the place inhabited.

Then I put my glasses on, and realized.

The windows were empty of glass and the frames had rotted or burned away. What I had taken for shadows over the windows on the right-hand side were fire stains. And the birds swooping in the sky above the house were not diving down behind the building but inside it. There was no roof. It was not a house but only a shell.

I took my glasses off again and the scene reverted to an intact Elizabethan house. Might one get a sense of brooding menace if the sky were painted indigo and the moon suddenly clouded over? Perhaps. But against today's cloudless blue the scene was innocence itself.

A barrier stretched across the drive. Attached to it was a notice. *Danger. Keep Out.* Noticing a join in the fence where the sections were just lodged together, I shifted a panel, slipped inside and pulled it to behind me.

Skirting the cold shoulder I came to the front of the house. Between the first and second bays, six broad, low steps led up to a paneled double door. The steps were flanked by a pair of low pedestals, on which were mounted two giant cats carved out of some dark, polished material. The undulations of their anatomy were so persuasively carved that, running my fingers over one, I half expected fur, was startled by the cool hardness of the stone.

It was the ground-floor window of the third bay that was marked by the darkest fire-staining. Perched on a chunk of fallen masonry, I was tall enough to peer inside. What I saw caused a deep disquiet to bloom in my chest. There is something universal, something familiar to all, in the concept of a room. Though my bedroom over the shop and my childhood bedroom at my parents' house and my bedroom at Miss Winter's are all very different, they nonetheless share certain elements, elements that remain constant in all places and for all people. Even a temporary encampment has something overhead to protect it from the elements, space for a person to enter, move about, and leave, and something that permits you to distinguish between inside and outside. Here there was none of that.

Beams had fallen, some at one end only so that they cut the space diagonally, coming to rest on the heaps of masonry, woodwork and other indistinguishable material that filled the room to the level of the window. Old birds' nests were wedged in various nooks and angles. The birds must have brought seeds; snow and rain had flooded in with the sunlight, and somehow, in this wreck of a place, plants were growing: I saw the brown winter branches of buddleia, and elders grown spindly reaching for the light. Like a pattern on wallpaper, ivy scrambled up the walls. Craning my neck, I looked up, as into a dark tunnel. Four tall walls were still intact, but instead of seeing a ceiling, I saw only four thick beams, irregularly spaced, and beyond them more empty space before another few beams, then the same again and again. At the end of the tunnel was light. The sky.

Not even a ghost could survive here.

It was almost impossible to think that once there had been draperies, furnishings, paintings. Chandeliers had lit up what was now illuminated by the sun. What had it been, this room? A drawing room, a music room, a dining room?

I squinted at the mass of stuff heaped in the room. Out of the jumble of unrecognizable stuff that had once been a home, something caught my eye. I had taken it at first for a half-fallen beam, but it wasn't thick enough. And it appeared to have been attached to the wall. There was another. Then another. At regular intervals, these lengths of wood seemed to have joints in them, as if other pieces of wood had once been attached at right angles. In fact, there, in a corner, was one where these other sections were still present.

Knowledge tingled in my spine.

These beams were *shelves*. This jumble of nature and wrecked architecture was a *library*.

In a moment I had clambered through the glassless window.

Carefully I made my way around, testing my footing at every step. I peered into corners and dark crevices, but there were no books. Not that I had expected any— they would never survive the conditions. But I hadn't been able to help looking.

For a few minutes I concentrated on my photographs. I took shots of the glassless window frames, the timber planks that used to hold books, the heavy oak door in its massive frame.

Trying to get the best picture of the great stone fire-place, I was bending from the waist, leaning slightly sideways, when I paused. I swallowed, noted my slightly raised heartbeat. Was it something I had heard? Or felt? Had something shifted deep in the arrangement of rubble beneath my feet? But no. It was nothing. All the same, I picked my way carefully to the edge of the room, where there was a hole in the masonry large enough to step through.

I was in the main hallway. Here were the high double doors I had seen from outside. The staircase, being made of stone, had survived the fire intact. A broad sweep upward, the handrail and balustrades now ivy clad, the solid lines of its architecture were nonetheless clear: a graceful curve widening into a shell-like curl at its base. A kind of fancy upside-down apostrophe.

The staircase led to a gallery that must once have run the entire width of the entrance hall. To one side there was only a jagged edge of floorboards and a drop to the stone floor below. The other side was almost complete. The vestiges of a handrail along the gallery, and then a corridor. A ceiling, stained but intact; a floor; doors even. It was the first part of the house I had seen that appeared to have escaped the general destruction. It looked like somewhere you could live.

I took a few quick pictures and then, testing each new board beneath my feet before shifting my weight, moved warily into the corridor.

The handle of the first door opened onto a sheer drop, branches and blue sky. No walls, no ceiling, no floor, just fresh outdoors air.

I pulled the door closed again and edged along the corridor, determined not to be unnerved by the dangers of the place. Watching my feet all the time, I came to the second door.

I turned the handle and let the door swing open.

There was movement!

*My sister!*

Almost I took a step toward her.

Almost.

Then I realized. A mirror. Shadowy with dirt and tarnished with dark spots that looked like ink.

I looked down to the floor I had been about to step onto. There were no boards, only a drop of twenty feet onto hard stone flags.

I knew now what I had seen, yet still my heart continued its frenzy. I raised my eyes again, and there she was. A white-faced waif with dark eyes, a hazy, uncertain figure trembling inside the old frame.

She had seen me. She stood, hand raised toward me longingly, as though all I had to do was step forward to take it. And would it not be the simplest solution, all told, to do that and at last rejoin her?

How long did I stand there, watching her wait for me?

"No," I whispered, but still her arm beckoned me. "I'm sorry." Her arm slowly fell.

Then she raised a camera and took a photograph of me.

I was sorry for her. Pictures through glass never come out. I know. I've tried.

I stood with my hand on the handle of the third door. The rule of three, Miss Winter had said. But I wasn't in the mood for her story anymore. Her dangerous house with its indoor rain and trick mirror had lost its interest for me.

I would go. To take photographs of the church? Not even that. I would go to the village store. I would telephone a taxi. Go to the station and from there home.

All this I would do, in a minute. For the time being, I wanted to stay like this, head leaning against the door, fingers on the handle, indifferent to whatever was beyond, and waiting for the tears to pass and my heart to calm itself.

I waited.

Then, beneath my fingers, the handle to the third room began to turn *of its own accord.*

## THE FRIENDLY GIANT

I ran.

I jumped over the holes in the floorboards, leaped down the stairs three at a time, lost my footing and lunged at the handrail for support. I grasped at a handful of ivy, stumbled, saved myself and lurched forward again. The library? No. The other way. Through an archway. Branches of elder and buddleia caught at my clothes, and I half fell several times as my feet scrabbled through the detritus of the broken house.

At last, inevitably, I crashed to the ground, and a wild cry escaped my lips.

"Oh dear, oh dear. Did I startle you? Oh dear."

I stared back through the archway.

Leaning over the gallery landing was not the skeleton or monster of my imaginings, but a giant. He moved smoothly down the stairs, stepped daintily and unconcernedly through the debris on the floor and came to stand over me with an expression of the utmost concern on his face.

"Oh my goodness."

He must have been six-foot-four or -five, and was broad, so broad that the house seemed to shrink around him.

"I never meant . . . You see, I only thought . . . Because you'd been there some time, and . . . But that doesn't matter now, because the thing is, my dear, are you hurt?"

I felt reduced to the size of a child. But for all his great dimensions, this man, too, had something of a child about him. Too plump for wrinkles, he had a round, cherubic face, and a halo of silver-blond curls sat neatly around his balding head. His eyes were round like the frames of his spectacles. They were kind and had a blue transparency.

I must have been looking dazed, and pale, too, perhaps. He knelt by my side and took my wrist.

"My, my, that was quite a tumble you took. If only I'd . . . I should never have . . . Pulse a bit high. Hmm."

176

My shin was stinging. I reached to investigate a tear in the knee of my trousers, and my fingers came away bloodied.

"Dear, oh dear. It's the leg, is it? Is it broken? Can you move it?" I wriggled my foot, and the man's face was a picture of relief.

"Thank goodness. I should never have forgiven myself. Now, you stay there while I . . . I'll just get the . . . Back in a minute." And off he went. His feet danced delicately in and out of the jagged edges of wood, then skipped swiftly up the stairs, while the upper half of his body sailed serenely above, as if unconnected to the elaborate footwork going on below.

I took a deep breath and waited.

"I've put the kettle on," he announced as he returned. It was a proper first-aid kit he had with him, white with a red cross on it, and he took out an antiseptic lotion and some gauze.

"I always said, someone will get hurt in that old place one of these days. I've had the kit for years. Better safe than sorry, eh? Oh dear, oh dear!" He winced with empathy as he pressed the stinging pad against my cut shin. "Let's be brave, shall we?"

"Do you have electricity here?" I asked. I was feeling bewildered.

"Electricity? But it's a ruin." He stared at me, astonished by my question, as though I might have suffered a concussion in the fall and lost my reason.

"It's just that I thought you said you'd put the kettle on."

"Oh, I see! No! I have a camping stove. I used to have a Thermos flask, but"—he turned his nose up—"tea from a Thermos is not very nice, is it? Now, does it sting very badly?"

"Only a bit."

"Good girl. Quite a tumble that was. Now tea— lemon and sugar all right? No milk, I'm afraid. No fridge."

"Lemon will be lovely."

"Right. Well, let's make you comfortable. The rain has stopped, so tea outdoors?" He went to the grand old double door at the front of the house and unlatched it. With a creak smaller than one expected, the doors swung open, and I began to get to my feet.

"Don't move!"

The giant danced back toward me, bent down and picked me up. I felt myself being raised into the air and carried smoothly outside. He sat me sideways on the back of one of the black cats I had admired an hour earlier.

"You wait there, and when I come back, you and I will have a lovely tea!" and he went back into the house. His huge back glided up the stairs and disappeared into the entrance of the corridor and the third room.

"Comfy?"

I nodded.

"Marvelous." He smiled as though it were indeed marvelous. "Now, let us introduce ourselves. My name

is Love. Aurelius Alphonse Love. Do call me Aurelius."
He looked at me expectantly.

"Margaret Lea."

"Margaret." He beamed. "Splendid. Quite splendid.
Now, eat."

Between the ears of the big black cat he had unfolded
a napkin, corner by corner. Inside was a dark and sticky
slice of cake, cut generously. I bit into it. It was the perfect cake for a cold day: spiced with ginger, sweet but
hot. The stranger strained the tea into dainty china cups.
He offered me a bowl of sugar lumps, then took a blue
velvet pouch from his breast pocket, which he opened.
Resting on the velvet was a silver spoon with an elongated *A* in the form of a stylized angel ornamenting the
handle. I took it, stirred my tea and passed it back to
him.

While I ate and drank, my host sat on the second cat,
which took on an unexpected kittenish appearance
beneath his great girth. He ate in silence, neatly and
with concentration. He watched me eat, too, anxious
that I should appreciate the food.

"That was lovely," I said. "Homemade, I think?"

The gap between the two cats was about ten feet,
and to converse we had to raise our voices slightly,
giving the conversation a somewhat theatrical air, as
though it were some performance. And indeed we had
an audience. In the rain-washed light, close to the
edge of the woods, a deer, stock-still, regarded us curiously. Unblinking, alert, nostrils twitching. Seeing I
had spotted it, it made no attempt to run but decided,

on the contrary, not to be afraid.

My companion wiped his fingers on his napkin, then shook it out and folded it into four. "You liked it then? The recipe was given to me by Mrs. Love. I've been making this cake since I was a child. Mrs. Love was a wonderful cook. A marvelous woman all round. Of course, she is departed now. A good age. Though one might have hoped— But it was not to be."

"I see." Though I wasn't sure I did see. Was Mrs. Love his wife? Though he'd said he'd been making her cake since he was a child. Surely he couldn't mean his mother? Why would he call his mother Mrs. Love? Two things were clear, though: He had loved her and she was dead. "I'm sorry," I said.

He accepted my condolences with a sad expression, then brightened. "But it's a fitting memorial, don't you think? The cake, I mean?"

"Certainly. Was it long ago? That you lost her?"

He thought. "Nearly twenty years. Though it seems more. Or less. Depending on how one looks at it."

I nodded. I was none the wiser.

For a few moments we sat in silence. I looked out to the deer park. At the cusp of the wood, more deer were emerging. They moved with the sunlight across the grassy park.

The stinging in my leg had diminished. I was feeling better.

"Tell me . . ." the stranger began, and I suspected he had needed to pluck up the courage to ask his question. "Do you have a mother?"

I felt a start of surprise. People hardly ever notice me for long enough to ask me personal questions.

"Do you mind? Forgive me for asking, but— How can I put it? Families are a matter of . . . of . . . But if you'd rather not— I am sorry."

"It's all right," I said slowly. "I don't mind." And actually I didn't. Perhaps it was the series of shocks I'd had, or else the influence of this queer setting, but it seemed that anything I might say about myself here, to this man, would remain forever in this place, with him, and have no currency anywhere else in the world. Whatever I said to him would have no consequences. So I answered his question. "Yes, I do have a mother."

"A mother! How— Oh, how—" A curiously intense expression came into his eyes, a sadness or a longing. "What could be pleasanter than to have a mother!" he finally exclaimed. It was clearly an invitation to say more.

"You don't have a mother, then?" I asked.

Aurelius's face twisted momentarily. "Sadly—I have always wanted— Or a father, come to that. Even brothers or sisters. Anyone who actually belonged to me. As a child I used to pretend. I made up an entire family. Generations of it! You'd have laughed!" There was nothing to laugh at in his face as he spoke. "But as to an actual mother . . . a factual, known mother . . . Of course, everybody has a mother, don't they? I know that. It's a question of knowing who that mother is. And I have always hoped that one day— For it's not out of the question, is it? And so I have never given up hope."

"Ah."

"It's a very sorry thing." He gave a shrug that he wanted to be casual, but wasn't. "I should have liked to have a mother."

"Mr. Love—"

"Aurelius, please."

"Aurelius. You know, with mothers, things aren't always as pleasant as you might suppose."

"Ah?" It seemed to have the force of a great revelation to him. He peered closely at me. "Squabbles?"

"Not exactly."

He frowned. "Misunderstandings?"

I shook my head.

"Worse?" He was stupefied. He sought what the problem might be in the sky, in the woods and finally, in my eyes.

"Secrets," I told him.

"Secrets!" His eyes widened to perfect circles. Baffled, he shook his head, making an impossible attempt to fathom my meaning. "Forgive me," he said at last. "I don't know how to help. I know so very little about families. My ignorance is vaster than the sea. I'm sorry about the secrets. I'm sure you are right to feel as you do."

Compassion warmed his eyes and he handed me a neatly folded white handkerchief.

"I'm sorry," I said. "It must be delayed shock."

"I expect so."

While I dried my eyes he looked away from me toward the deer park. The sky was darkening by slow degrees. Now I followed his gaze to see a shimmer of white: the pale coat of the deer as it leaped lightly into the cover of the trees.

"I thought you were a ghost," I told him. "When I felt the door handle move. Or a skeleton."

"A skeleton! Me! A skeleton!" He chuckled, delighted, and his entire body seemed to shake with mirth.

"But you turned out to be a giant."

"Quite so! A giant." He wiped the laughter from his eyes and said, "There is a ghost, you know—or so they say."

*I know,* I almost said, *I saw her,* but of course it wasn't my ghost he was talking about.

"Have you seen the ghost?"

"No," he sighed. "Not even the shadow of a ghost."

We sat in silence for a moment, each of us contemplating ghosts of our own.

"It's getting chilly," I remarked.

"Leg feeling all right?"

"I think so." I slid off the cat's back and tried my weight on it. "Yes. It's much better now."

"Wonderful. Wonderful."

Our voices were murmurs in the softening light.

"Who exactly was Mrs. Love?"

"The lady who took me in. She gave me her name. She gave me her recipe book. She gave me everything, really."

I nodded.

Then I picked up my camera. "I think I should be

183

going, actually. I ought to try for some photos at the church before the light quite disappears. Thank you so much for the tea."

"I must be off in a few minutes myself. It has been so nice to meet you, Margaret. Will you come again?"

"You don't actually live here, do you?" I asked doubtfully.

He laughed. It was a dark, rich sweetness, like the cake.

"Bless me, no. I have a house over there." He gestured toward the woods. "I just come here in the afternoons. For, well, let's say for contemplation, shall we?"

"They're knocking it down soon. I suppose you know?"

"I know." He stroked the cat, absently, fondly. "It's a shame, isn't it? I shall miss the old place. Actually I thought you were one of their people when I heard you. A surveyor or something. But you're not."

"No, I'm not a surveyor. I'm writing a book about someone who used to live here."

"The Angelfield girls?"

"Yes."

Aurelius nodded ruminatively. "They were twins, you know. Imagine that." For a moment his eyes were far away.

"Will you come again, Margaret?" he asked as I picked up my bag.

"I'm bound to."

He reached into his pocket and drew out a card. Aurelius Love, Traditional English Catering for Weddings,

Christenings and Parties. He pointed to the address and telephone number. "Do telephone me when you come again. You must come to the cottage and I'll make you a proper tea."

Before we parted, Aurelius took my hand and patted it in an easy, old-fashioned manner. Then his massive frame glided gracefully up the wide sweep of steps and he closed the heavy doors behind him.

Slowly I walked down the drive to the church, my mind full of the stranger I had just met—met and befriended. It was most unlike me. And as I passed through the lych-gate, I reflected that perhaps *I* was the stranger. Was it just my imagination, or since meeting Miss Winter was I not quite myself?

## GRAVES

I had left it too late for the light, and photographs were out of the question. So I took my notebook out for my walk in the churchyard. Angelfield was an old community but a small one, and there were not so very many graves. I found John Digence, *Gathered to the Garden of the Lord*, and a woman, Martha Dunne, *Loyal Servant of our Lord*, whose dates corresponded closely enough with what I expected for the Missus. I copied the names, dates and inscriptions into my notebook. One of the graves had fresh flowers on it, a gay bunch of orange chrysanthemums, and I went closer to see who it was who was remembered so warmly. It was

*Joan Mary Love, Never Forgotten.*

Though I looked, I could not see the Angelfield name anywhere. But it did not puzzle me for more than a minute. The family of the house would not have ordinary graves in the churchyard. Their tombs would be grander affairs, marked by effigies and with long histories carved into their marble slabs. And they would be inside, in the chapel.

The church was gloomy. The ancient windows, narrow pieces of greenish glass held in a thick stone framework of arches, let in a sepulchral light that weakly illuminated the pale stone arches and columns, the whitened vaults between the black roof timbers and the smooth polished wood of the pews. When my eyes had adjusted, I peered at the memorial stones and monuments in the tiny chapel. Angelfields dead for centuries all had their epitaphs here, line after loquacious line of encomium, expensively carved into costly marble. Another day I would come back to decipher the engravings of these earlier generations; for today it was only a handful of names I was looking for.

With the death of George Angelfield, the family's loquacity came to an end. Charlie and Isabelle—for presumably it was they who decided—seemed not to have gone to any great lengths in summing up their father's life and death for generations to come. *Released from earthly sorrows, he is with his Savior now,* was the stone's laconic message. Isabelle's role in this world and her departure from it were summed up in the most conventional terms: *Much loved mother and sister, she is gone to a better place.* But I copied it into my notebook all the same and did a quick calculation. Younger than me! Not so tragically young as her husband, but still, not an age to die.

I almost missed Charlie's. Having eliminated every other stone in the chapel, I was about to give up, when my eye finally made out a small, dark stone. So small was it, and so black, that it seemed designed for invisibility, or at least insignificance. There was no gold leaf to give relief to the letters so, unable to make them out by eye, I raised my hand and felt the carving, Braille style, with my fingertips, one word at a time.

CHARLIE ANGELFIELD
HE IS GONE INTO THE DARK NIGHT.
WE SHALL NEVER SEE HIM MORE.

There were no dates.

I felt a sudden chill. Who had selected these words, I wondered? Was it Vida Winter? And what was the mood behind them? It seemed to me that there was room for a certain ambiguity in the expression. Was it the sorrow of bereavement? Or the triumphant farewell of the survivors to a bad lot?

Leaving the church and walking slowly down the gravel drive to the lodge gates, I felt a light, almost weightless scrutiny on my back. Aurelius was gone, so what was it? The Angelfield ghost, perhaps? Or the burned-out eyes of the house itself? Most probably it was just a deer, watching me invisibly from the shadow of the woods.

"It's a shame," said my father in the shop that evening, "that you can't come home for a few hours."

"I *am* home," I protested, feigning ignorance. But I knew it was my mother he was talking about. The truth was that I couldn't bear her tinny brightness, nor the pristine paleness of her house. I lived in shadows, had made friends with my grief, but in my mother's house I knew my sorrow was unwelcome. She might have loved a cheerful, chatty daughter, whose brightness would have helped banish her own fears. As it was, she was afraid of my silences. I preferred to stay away. "I have so little time," I explained. "Miss Winter is anxious that we should press on with the work. And it's only a few weeks till Christmas, after all. I'll be back again then."

"Yes," he said. "It will be Christmas soon."

He seemed sad and worried. I knew I was the cause, and I was sorry I couldn't do anything about it.

"I've packed a few books to take back to Miss Winter's with me. I've put a note on the cards in the index."

"That's fine. No problem."

❧❧

That night, drawing me out of sleep, a pressure on the edge of my bed. The angularity of bone pressing against my flesh through the bedclothes.

It is her! Come for me at last!

All I have to do is open my eyes and look at her. But fear paralyzes me. What will she be like? Like me? Tall and thin with dark eyes? Or—it is this I fear—has she come direct from the grave? What terrible thing is it that I am about to join myself—*rejoin* myself—to?

The fear dissolves.

I have woken up.

The pressure through the blankets is gone, a figment of sleep. I do not know whether I am relieved or disappointed.

I got up, repacked my things, and in the bleakness of the winter dawn walked to the station for the first train north.

# *Middles*

### HESTER ARRIVES

When I left Yorkshire, November was going strong; by the time I returned it was in its dying days, about to tilt into December.

December gives me headaches and diminishes my already small appetite. It makes me restless in my reading. It keeps me awake at night with its damp, chilly darkness. There is a clock inside me that starts to tick on the first of December, measuring the days, the hours and the minutes, counting down to a certain day, the anniversary of the day my life was made and then unmade: my birthday. I do not like December.

This year the sense of foreboding was made worse by the weather. A heavy sky hovered repressively over the house, casting us into an eternal dim twilight. I arrived back to find Judith scurrying from room to room, collecting desk lamps and standard lamps and reading lamps from guest rooms that were never used, and arranging them in the library, the drawing room, my own rooms. Anything to keep at bay the murky grayness that lurked in every corner, under every chair, in the folds of the curtains and the pleats of the upholstery.

Miss Winter asked no questions about my absence,

nor did she tell me anything about the progression of her illness, but even after so short an absence, her decline was clear to see. The cashmere wraps fell in apparently empty folds around her diminished frame, and on her fingers the rubies and emeralds seemed to have expanded, so thin had her hands become. The fine white line that had been visible in her parting before I left had broadened; it crept along each hair, diluting the metallic tones to a weaker shade of orange. But despite her physical frailty, she seemed full of some force, some energy, that overrode both illness and age and made her powerful. As soon as I presented myself in the room, almost before I had sat down and taken out my notebook, she began to speak, picking up the story where she had left off, as though it were brimful in her and could not be contained a moment longer.

※※

With Isabelle gone, it was felt in the village that something should be done for the children. They were thirteen; it was not an age to be left unattended; they needed a woman's influence. Should they not be sent to school somewhere? Though what school would accept children such as these? When a school was found to be out of the question, it was decided that a governess should be employed.

A governess was found. Her name was Hester. Hester Barrow. It was not a pretty name, but then she was not a pretty girl.

Dr. Maudsley organized it all. Charlie, locked in his

grief, was scarcely aware of what was going on, and John-the-dig and the Missus, mere servants in the house, were not consulted. The doctor approached Mr. Lomax, the family solicitor, and between the two of them and with a hand from the bank manager, all the arrangements were made. Then it was done.

Helpless, passive, we all shared in the anticipation, each with our particular mix of emotion. The Missus was divided. She felt an instinctive suspicion of this stranger who was to come into her domain, and connected with this suspicion was the fear of being found wanting—for she had been in charge for years and knew her limitations. She also felt hope. Hope that the new arrival would instill a sense of discipline in the children and restore manners and sanity to the house. In fact, so great was her desire for a settled and well-run domestic life that in the advent of the governess's arrival she took to issuing orders, as though we were the sort of children who might comply. Needless to say, we took no notice.

John-the-dig's feelings were less divided, were in fact entirely hostile. He would not be drawn into the Missus's long wonderings about how things would be, and refused by stony silence to encourage the optimism that was ready to take root in her heart. "If she's the right kind of person . . ." she would say, or "There's no knowing how much better things could be . . . ," but he stared out of the kitchen window and would not be drawn. When the doctor suggested that he take the brougham to meet the governess at the station he was downright rude. "I've not got the time to be traipsing across the county after damned schoolmistresses," he replied, and the doctor was obliged to make arrangements to collect her himself. Since the incident with the topiary garden, John had not been the same, and now, with the coming of this new change, he spent hours alone, brooding over his own fears and concerns for the future. This incomer meant a fresh pair of eyes, a fresh pair of ears, in a house where no one had looked or listened properly for years. John-the-dig, habituated to secrecy, foresaw trouble.

In our separate ways we all felt daunted. All except Charlie, that is. When the day came, only Charlie was his usual self. Though he was locked away and out of sight, his presence was nonetheless made known by the thundering and clattering that shook the house from time to time, a din to which we'd all become so accustomed that we scarcely even noticed. In his vigil for Isabelle, the man had no notion of day or time, and the arrival of a governess meant nothing to him.

We were idling that morning in one of the front rooms on the first floor. A bedroom, you'd have called it, if the bed had been visible under the pile of junk that had accumulated there the way junk does over the decades. Emmeline was working away with her nails at the silver embroidery threads that ran through the pattern of the curtains. When she succeeded in freeing one, she surreptitiously put it in her pocket, ready to add later to the magpie stash under her bed. But her concentration was broken. Someone was coming, and whether she knew what that meant or not, she had been contaminated by the sense of expectation that hung about the house.

It was Emmeline who first heard the brougham. From the window we watched the new arrival alight, brush the creases out of her skirt with two brisk strokes of her palms and look about her. She looked at the front door, to her left, to her right, and then—I leaped back—up. Perhaps she took us for a trick of the light or a window drape lifted by the breeze from a broken windowpane. Whatever she saw, it can't have been us.

But we saw her. Through Emmeline's new hole in the curtain we stared. We didn't know what to think. Hester was of average height. Average build. She had hair that was neither yellow nor brown. Skin the same color. Coat, shoes, dress, hat: all in the same indistinct tint. Her face was devoid of any distinguishing feature. And yet we *stared.* We stared at her until our eyes ached. Every pore in her plain little face was illuminated. Something shone in her clothes and in her hair. Something radiated from her luggage. Something cast a glow around her person, like a lightbulb. Something made her exotic.

We had no idea what it was. We'd never imagined the like of it before.

We found out later, though.

Hester was clean. Scrubbed and soaped and rinsed and buffed and polished all over.

You can imagine what she thought of Angelfield.

When she'd been in the house about a quarter of an

hour she had the Missus call us. We ignored it and waited to see what happened next. We waited. And waited. Nothing happened. That was where she wrong-footed us for the first time, had we only known it. All our expertise in hiding was useless if she wasn't going to come looking for us. And she did not come. We hung about in the room, growing bored, then vexed by the curiosity that seeded itself in us despite our resistance. We became attentive to the sounds from downstairs: John-the-dig's voice, the dragging of furniture, some banging and knocking. Then it fell quiet. At lunchtime we were called and did not go. At six the Missus called us again, "Come and have supper with your new governess, children." We stayed on in the room. No one came. There was the beginning of a sense that the new-comer was a force to be reckoned with.

Later came the sound of the household getting ready for bed. Footsteps on the stairs, the Missus, saying, "I hope you'll be comfortable, Miss," and the voice of the governess, steel in velvet, "I'm sure I will, Mrs. Dunne. Thank you for all your trouble."

"About the girls, Miss Barrow—"

"Don't you worry about them, Mrs. Dunne. They'll be all right. Good night."

And after the sound of the Missus's feet shuffling cautiously down the stairs, all was quiet.

Night fell and the house slept. Except us. The Missus's attempts to teach us that nighttime was for sleeping had failed as all her lessons had failed, and we had no fear of the dark. Outside the governess's door we listened and heard nothing but the faint scratch scratch of a mouse under the boards, so we went on downstairs, to the larder.

The door would not open. The lock had never been used in our lifetime, but tonight it betrayed itself with a trace of fresh oil.

Emmeline waited patiently, blankly, for the door to open, as she had always waited before. Confident that in a moment there would be bread and butter and jam for the taking.

But there was no need to panic. The Missus's apron pocket. That's where the key would be. That's where the keys always were: a ring of rusted keys, unused, for doors and locks and cupboards all over the house, and any amount of fiddling to know which key matched which lock.

The pocket was empty.

Emmeline stirred, wondered distantly at the delay.

The governess was shaping up into a real challenge. But she wouldn't catch us that way. We would go out. You could always get into one of the cottages for a snack.

The handle of the kitchen door turned, then stopped. No amount of tugging and jiggling could free it. It was padlocked.

The broken window in the drawing room had been boarded up, and the shutters secured in the dining room. There was only one other chance. To the hall and the great double doors we went. Emmeline, bewildered, padded along behind. She was hungry. Why all this fuss with doors and windows? How long before she could fill her tummy with food? A shaft of moonlight, tinted blue by the colored glass in the hall windows, was enough to highlight the huge bolts, heavy and out of reach, that had been oiled and slid into place at the top of the double doors.

We were imprisoned.

Emmeline spoke. "Yum yum," she said. She was hungry. And when Emmeline was hungry, Emmeline had to be fed. It was as simple as that. We were in a fix. It was a long time coming, but eventually Emmeline's poor little brain realized that the food she longed for could not be had. A look of bewilderment came into her eyes, and she opened her mouth and wailed.

The sound of her cry carried up the stone staircase, turned into the corridor to the left, rose up another flight of stairs and slipped under the door of the new governess's bedroom.

Soon another noise was added to it. Not the blind shuffle of the Missus, but the smart, metronomic step of Hester Barrow's feet. A brisk, unhurried click, click, click. Down a set of stairs, along a corridor, to the gallery.

I took refuge in the folds of the long curtains just before she emerged onto the galleried landing. It was midnight. At the top of the stairs she stood, a compact little figure, neither fat nor thin, set on a sturdy pair of legs, the whole topped by that calm and determined countenance. In her firmly belted blue dressing gown and with her hair neatly brushed, she looked for all the world as though she slept sitting up and ready for morning. Her hair was thin and stuck flat to her head, her face was lumpen and her nose was pudgy. She was plain, if not worse than plain, but plainness on Hester had not remotely the same effect that it might on any other woman. She drew the eye.

Emmeline, at the foot of the stairs, had been sobbing with hunger a moment ago, yet the instant Hester appeared in all her glory, she stopped crying and stared, apparently placated, as though it were a cakestand piled high with cake that had appeared before her.

"How nice to see you," said Hester, coming down the stairs. "Now, who are you? Adeline or Emmeline?"

Emmeline, openmouthed, was silent.

"No matter," the governess said. "Would you like some supper? And where is your sister? Would she like some, too?"

"Yum," said Emmeline, and I didn't know if it was the word *supper* or Hester herself who had provoked it.

Hester looked around, seeking the other twin. The curtain appeared to her as just a curtain, for after a cursory glance she turned all her attention to Emmeline. "Come with me." She smiled. She drew a key out of her blue pocket. It was a clean blue-silver, buffed to a high shine, and it glinted tantalizingly in the blue light.

It did the trick. "Shiny," Emmeline pronounced and, without knowing what it was or the magic it could work, she followed the key—and Hester with it—back through the cold corridors to the kitchen.

In the folds of the curtain my hunger pangs gave way

to anger. Hester and her key! Emmeline! It was like the perambulator all over again. It was *love*.

That was the first night and it was Hester's victory.

The grubbiness of the house did not transfer itself to our pristine governess the way one might have expected. Instead it was the other way around. The few rays of light, drained and dusty, that managed to penetrate the uncleaned windows and the heavy curtains seemed always to fall on Hester. She gathered them to herself and reflected them back into the gloom, refreshed and vitalized by their contact with her. Little by little the gleam extended from Hester herself to the house. On the first full day it was just her own room that was affected. She took the curtains down and plunged them into a tub of soapy water. She pegged them on the line where the sun and wind woke up the unsuspected pattern of pink and yellow roses. While they were drying, she cleaned the window with newspaper and vinegar to let the light in, and when she could see what she was doing, she scrubbed the room from floor to ceiling. By nightfall she had created a little haven of cleanliness within those four walls. And that was just the beginning.

With soap and with bleach, with energy and with determination, she imposed hygiene on that house. Where for generations the inhabitants had lumbered half-seeing and purposeless, circling after nothing but their own squalid obsessions, Hester came as a spring-cleaning miracle. For thirty years the pace of life indoors had been measured by the slow movement of the motes of dust caught in an occasional ray of weary sunlight. Now Hester's little feet paced out the minutes and the seconds, and with a vigorous swish of a duster, the motes were gone.

After cleanliness came order, and the house was first to feel the changes. Our new governess did a very thorough tour. She went from bottom to top, tutting and frowning on every floor. There was not a single cupboard or alcove that escaped her attention; with pencil and notebook in hand, she scrutinized every room, noting damp patches and rattling windows, testing doors and floorboards for squeaks, trying old keys in old locks, and labeling them. She left doors locked behind her. Though it was only a first "going over," a preparatory stage to the main restoration, nevertheless she made a change in every room she entered: a pile of blankets in a corner folded and left tidily on a chair; a book picked up and tucked under her arm to be returned later to the library; the line of a curtain set straight. All this done with noticeable haste but without the slightest impression of hurry. It seemed she had only to cast her eye about a room for the darkness in it to recede, for the chaos to begin shamefacedly to put itself in order, for the ghosts to beat a retreat. In this manner, every room was Hestered.

The attic, it is true, did stop her in her tracks. Her jaw dropped and she looked aghast at the state of the roof cavity. But even in this chaos she was invincible. She gathered herself together, tightening her lips, and scratched and scribbled away at her page with even greater vigor. The very next day, a builder came. We knew him from the village—an unhurried man with a strolling pace. In speech he stretched out his vowel sounds to give his mouth a rest before the next consonant. He kept six or seven jobs going at once and rarely finished any of them; he spent his working days smoking cigarettes and eyeing the job in hand with a fatalistic shake of the head. He climbed our stairs in his typical lazy fashion, but after he'd been five minutes with Hester we heard his hammer going nineteen to the dozen. She had galvanized him.

Within a few days there were mealtimes, bedtimes, getting-up times. A few days more and there were clean shoes for indoors, clean boots for out. Not only that, but the silk dresses were cleaned, mended, made to fit and hung away for some mythical "best," and new dresses in navy and green cotton poplin with white sashes and collars appeared for everyday.

Emmeline thrived under the new regime. She was well fed at regular hours, allowed to play—under tight supervision—with Hester's shiny keys. She even developed a passion for baths. She struggled at first, yelled and kicked as Hester and the Missus stripped her and lowered her into the tub, but when she saw herself in the mirror afterward, saw herself clean and with her hair neatly braided and tied with a green bow, her mouth opened and she fell into another of her trances. She liked being shiny. Whenever Emmeline was in Hester's presence she used to study her face on the sly, on the lookout for a smile. When Hester did smile—it was not infrequent—Emmeline gazed at her face in delight. Before long she learned to smile back.

Other members of the household flourished, too. The Missus had her eyes examined by the doctor, and with much complaining was taken to a specialist. On her return she could see again. The Missus was so pleased at seeing the house in its new state of cleanliness that all the years she'd lived in a state of grayness fell away from her, and she was rejuvenated sufficiently to join Hester in this brave new world. Even John-the-dig, who obeyed Hester's orders morosely and kept his dark eyes always firmly averted from her bright, all-seeing ones, could not resist the positive effect of her energy in the household. Without a word to anyone, he took up his shears and entered the topiary garden for the first time since the catastrophe. There he joined his efforts to those already being made by nature to mend the violence of the past.

Charlie was less directly influenced. He kept out of her way and that suited both of them. She had no desire to do anything other than her job, and her job was us. Our minds, our bodies and our souls, yes, but our guardian was outside her jurisdiction, and so she left him alone. She was no Jane Eyre and he was no Mr. Rochester. In the face of her spruce energy he retreated to the old nursery rooms on the second floor behind a firmly locked door, where he and his memories festered together in squalor. For him the Hester effect was limited to an improvement in his diet and a firmer hand over his finances, which, under the honest but flimsy control of the Missus, had been plundered by unscrupulous traders and businesspeople. Neither of these changes for the good did he notice, and if he had noticed them I doubt he would have cared.

But Hester did keep the children under control and out of sight, and had he given it any thought he would have been grateful for this. Under Hester's reign there was no cause for hostile neighbors to come complaining about the twins, no imperative to visit the kitchen and have a sandwich made by the Missus, above all, no need to leave, even for a minute, that realm of the imagination that he inhabited with Isabelle, only with Isabelle, always with Isabelle. What he gave up in territory, he gained in freedom. He never heard Hester; he never saw her; the thought of her never once entered his head. She was entirely satisfactory.

Hester had triumphed. She might have looked like a potato, but there was nothing that girl couldn't do, once she put her mind to it.

❦

Miss Winter paused, her eyes set fixedly on the corner of the room, where her past presented itself to her with more reality than the present and me. At the corners of her mouth and eyes flickered half-expressions of sorrow and distress. Aware of the thinness of the thread that connected her to her past, I was anxious not to break it, but equally anxious for her not to stop her story.

203

The pause lengthened.

"And you?" I prompted softly. "What about you?"

"Me?" She blinked vaguely. "Oh, I liked her. That was the trouble."

"Trouble?"

She blinked again, shuffled in her seat and looked at me with a new, sharp gaze. She had cut the thread.

"I think that's enough for today. You can go now."

## THE BOX OF LIVES

With the story of Hester, I fell quickly back into my routine. In the mornings I listened to Miss Winter tell me her story, hardly bothering now with my notebook. Later in my room, with my reams of paper, my twelve red pencils and my trusty sharpener, I transcribed what I had memorized. As the words flowed from the point of my pencil onto the page, they conjured up Miss Winter's voice in my ear; later, when I read aloud what I had written, I felt my face rearranging itself into her expressions. My left hand rose and fell in mimicry of her emphatic gestures, while my right lay, as though maimed, in my lap. The words turned to pictures in my head. Hester, clean and neat and surrounded by a silvery gleam, an all-body halo that grew broader all the time, encompassing first her room, then the house, then its inhabitants. The Missus transformed from a slow-moving figure in darkness to one whose eyes darted about, bright with seeing. And Emmeline, under the spell of Hester's shiny aura, allowing herself to be changed from a dirty, malnourished vagabond into a clean, affectionate and plump little girl. Hester cast her light even into the topiary garden, where it shone onto the ravaged branches of the yews and brought forth fresh green growth. There was Charlie, of course, lumbering in the darkness outside the circle, heard but not seen. And John-the-dig, the strangely named gardener, brooding on its perimeter, reluctant to be drawn into the light. And Adeline, the mysterious and dark-hearted Adeline.

For all my biographical projects I have kept a box of lives. A box of index cards containing the details—name, occupation, dates, place of residence and any other piece of information that seems relevant—of all the significant people in the life of my subject. I never quite know what to make of my boxes of lives. Depending on my mood they either strike me as a memorial to gladden the dead ("Look!" I imagine them saying as they peer through the glass at me. "She's writing us down on her cards! And to think we've been dead two hundred years!") or, when the glass is very dark and I feel quite stranded and alone this side of it, they seem like little cardboard tombstones, inanimate and cold, and the box itself is as dead as the cemetery. Miss Winter's cast of characters was very small, and as I shuffled them in my hands their sparse flimsiness dismayed me. I was being given a story, but as far as information went, I was still far short of what I needed.

I took a blank card and began to write.

Hester Barrow
Governess
Angelfield House
Born: ?
Died: ?

I stopped. Thought. Did a few sums on my fingers. The girls had been only thirteen. And Hester was not old. With all that verve she couldn't be. Had she been thirty? What if she were only twenty-five? A mere twelve years older than the girls themselves. . . . Was it possible? I wondered. Miss Winter, in her seventies, was dying. But that didn't necessarily mean a person older than her would be dead. What were the chances?

There was only one thing to do.

I added another note to the card and underlined it.

<u>FIND HER</u>.

Was it because I had decided to look for Hester that I saw her that night in a dream?

A plain figure in a neatly belted dressing gown, on the galleried landing, shaking her head and pursing her lips at the fire-stained walls, the jagged, broken floorboards and the ivy winding its way up the stone staircase. In the middle of all this chaos, how lucid everything was close to her. How soothing. I approached, drawn to her like a moth. But when I entered her magic circle, nothing happened. I was still in darkness. Hester's quick eyes darted here and there, taking in everything, and came to rest on a figure standing behind my back. My twin, or so I understood in the dream. But when her eyes passed over me it was without seeing.

I woke, a familiar hot chill in my side, and reexamined the images from my dream to understand the source of my terror. There was nothing frightening in Hester herself. Nothing unnerving in the smooth passage of her eyes over and through my face. It was not what I *saw* in the dream but what I *was* that had me trembling in my bed. If Hester did not see me, then it must be because I was a ghost. And if I was a ghost, then I was dead. How could it be otherwise?

I rose and went into the bathroom to rinse my fear away. Avoiding the mirror, I looked instead at my hands in the water, but the sight filled me with horror. At the same time as they existed here, I knew they existed on the other side, too, where they were dead. And the eyes that saw them, my eyes, were dead in that other place, too. And my mind, which was thinking these thoughts . . . was it not also dead? A profound horror took hold of me. What kind of an unnatural creature was I? What abomination of nature is it that divides a person between two bodies before birth, and then kills one of them? And what am I that is left? Half-dead, exiled in the world of the living by day, while at night, my soul cleaves to its twin in a shadowy limbo.

I lit an early fire, made cocoa, then wrapped myself in dressing gown and blankets to write a letter to my father. How was the shop, and how was Mother, and how was he, and how, I wondered, would one go about finding someone? Did private detectives exist in reality or only in books? I told him what little I knew about Hester. Could a search be set in motion with so little information to go on? Would a private detective take on a job like the one I had in mind? If not, who might?

I reread the letter. Brisk and sensible, it betrayed nothing of my fear. Dawn was breaking. The trembling had stopped. Soon Judith would be here with breakfast.

## THE EYE IN THE YEW

There was nothing the new governess couldn't do if she put her mind to it.

That's how it seemed at first, anyway.

But after a time difficulties did begin to emerge. The first thing was her argument with the Missus. Hester, having tidied and cleaned rooms and left them locked behind her, was put out to discover them unlocked again. She called the Missus to her. "What need is there," she asked, "for rooms to be left open when they are not in use? You can see what happens: The girls go in as they please and make chaos where there was order before. It makes unnecessary work for you and for me."

The Missus seemed entirely to concur, and Hester left the interview quite satisfied. But a week later, once again, she found doors open that should have been locked, and with a frown called the Missus once again. This time she would accept no vague promises but was determined to get to the heart of the matter.

"It's the air," explained the Missus. "Without the air moving about, a house gets dreadful damp."

Hester gave the Missus a succinct lecture in simple terms about air circulation and damp and sent her away, certain that this time she had solved the difficulty.

A week later she noticed again that doors were unlocked. This time she did not call the Missus. Instead she reflected. There was more to this problem of door-locking than met the eye. She resolved that she would study the Missus, discover by observation what lay behind the unlocking of doors.

The second problem involved John-the-dig. His suspicion of her had not escaped her notice, but she was not put off. She was a stranger in the house, and it was up to her to demonstrate that she was there for the good of all and not to cause trouble. In time, she knew, she would win him over. Yet though he seemed to get used to her presence, his suspicion was unexpectedly slow to fade. And then one day suspicion flared into something else. She had approached him over something quite banal. In our garden she had seen, or so she maintained, a child from the village who should have been at school. "Who is the child?" she wanted to know, "Who are his parents?"

"Nothing to do with me," John told her, with a surliness that took her aback.

"I don't say it is," she responded calmly, "but the

child should be in school. I'm sure you'll agree with me on that. If you will just tell me who it is, then I will speak to the parents and the schoolmistress about it."

John-the-dig shrugged his shoulders and made to leave, but she was not a woman who would be put off in this manner. She darted around him, stood in front of him and repeated her demand. Why should she not? It was an entirely reasonable one and she was making it in a civil fashion. Whatever reason would the man have to refuse?

But refuse he did. "Children from the village do not come up here" was his only response.

"This one did," she went on.

"They stay away out of fear."

"That's ridiculous. Whatever do they have to be afraid of here? The child was in a wide-brimmed hat and a man's trousers cut down to fit. His appearance was quite distinctive. You must know who he is."

"I have seen no such child," came the answer, dismissively, and once again John made to leave.

Hester was nothing if not persistent. "But you *must* have seen him—"

"It takes a certain kind of mind, Miss, to see things that aren't there. Me, I'm a sensible fellow. Where there is nothing to see, I see nothing. If I were you, Miss, I would do the same. Good day to you."

With that he left, and this time Hester made no attempt to block him. She simply stood, shaking her head in bewilderment and wondering what on earth had got into the man. Angelfield, it seemed, was a house full of puzzles. Still, there was nothing she liked more than mental exercise. She would soon get to the bottom of things.

Hester's gifts of insight and intelligence were quite extraordinary. Yet counterbalancing these talents was the fact that she did not know quite who she was up against. Take for instance her habit of leaving the twins to their own devices for short periods while she followed her own agenda elsewhere. She watched the twins closely first, evaluating their moods, weighing up their fatigue, the closeness to mealtimes, their patterns of energy and rest. When the results of this analysis told her the twins were set for an hour of quiet indoor lolling, she would leave them unattended. On one of these occasions she had a special purpose in mind. The doctor had come and she wanted a particular word with him. A *private* word.

Foolish Hester. There is no privacy where there are children.

She met him at the front door. "It is a nice day. Shall we walk in the garden?"

They set off toward the topiary garden, unaware that they were being followed.

"You have worked a miracle, Miss Barrow," the doctor began. "Emmeline is transformed."

"No," said Hester.

"Yes, I assure you. My expectations have been more than fulfilled. I am very impressed."

Hester bowed her head and turned her body fractionally away from him. Taking her response for modesty, he fell silent, thinking her overwhelmed by his professions of esteem. The newly clipped yew gave him something to admire while the governess recovered her sangfroid. It's just as well he was engrossed in its geometric lines, else he might have caught her wry look and realized his error.

Her protesting "No" was far from being the feminine simpering that the doctor took it for. It was a straightforward statement of fact. Of course Emmeline was transformed. Given the presence of Hester, how could it have been otherwise? There was nothing miraculous about it. That is what she meant by her "No."

Yet she was not surprised by the condescension in the doctor's comment. It was not a world in which signs of genius were likely to be noticed in governesses, but nonetheless I think she was disappointed. The doctor was the one person at Angelfield, she thought, who *might* have understood her. But he did not understand her.

She turned toward the doctor and found herself facing his back. He stood, hands in pocket, the line of his shoulders straight, looking up to where the yew tree ended and the sky began. His neat hair was graying, and there was a perfect circle of pink scalp an inch and a half wide on the top of his head.

"John is making good the damage that the twins did," Hester said.

"What made them do it?"

"In Emmeline's case that is an easy question to

answer. Adeline made her do it. As for what made Adeline do it, that is a harder question altogether. I doubt she knows herself. Most of the time she is governed by impulses that appear to have no conscious element. Whatever the reason, the result was devastating for John. His family has tended this garden for generations."

"Heartless. All the more shocking coming from a child."

Unseen by the doctor, she pulled another face. Clearly he did not know much about children. "Heartless indeed. Though children are capable of great cruelty. Only we do not like to think it of them."

Slowly they began to walk between the topiary shapes, admiring the yews while speaking of Hester's work. Keeping a safe distance, but always within earshot, a little spy followed them, moving from the protection of one yew to another. Left and right they moved; sometimes they turned to double back on themselves; it was a game of angles, an elaborate dance.

"You are satisfied with the results of your efforts with Emmeline, I imagine, Miss Barrow?"

"Yes. With another year or so of my attention, I see no reason why Emmeline should not give up unruliness for good and become permanently the sweet girl she knows how to be at her best. She will not be clever, but still, I see no reason why she should not one day lead a satisfying life separately from her sister. Perhaps she might even marry. All men do not seek intelligence in a wife, and Emmeline is very affectionate."

"Good, good."

"With Adeline it is a different matter entirely."

They came to a standstill, next to a leafy obelisk with a gash cut into its side part of the way up. The governess peered at the brown inner branches and touched one of the new twigs with its bright green leaves that was growing from the old wood toward the light. She sighed.

"Adeline puzzles me, Dr. Maudsley. I would value your medical opinion."

The doctor gave a courteous half bow. "By all means. What is it that is troubling you?"

"I have never known such a confusing child." She paused. "Forgive my slowness, but there is no succinct way to explain the strangeness I have noticed in her."

"Then take your time. I am in no rush."

The doctor indicated a low bench, at the back of which a hedge of box had been trained into an elaborately curlicued arch, the kind that frequently forms the headboard of a highly crafted bedstead. They sat and found themselves facing the good side of one of the garden's largest geometrical pieces. "A dodecahedron, look."

Hester disregarded his comment and began her explanation.

"Adeline is a hostile and aggressive child. She resents my presence in the house and resists all my efforts to impose order. Her eating is erratic; she refuses food until she is half starving, and only then will she eat but the merest morsel. She has to be bathed by force, and, despite her thinness, it takes two people to hold her in the water. Any warmth I show her is met by utter indifference. She seems incapable of all the normal range of human emotion, and, I speak frankly to you, Dr. Maudsley, I have wondered whether she has it in her to return to the fold of common humanity."

"Is she intelligent?"

"She is wily. She is cunning. But she cannot be stimulated to take an interest in anything beyond the realm of her own wishes, desires and appetites."

"And in the classroom?"

"You appreciate of course that with girls like these the classroom is not what it might be for normal children. There is no arithmetic, no Latin, no geography. Still, in the interests of order and routine, the children are made to attend for two hours, twice a day, and I educate them by telling stories."

"Does she appreciate these lessons?"

"If only I knew how to answer that question! She is quite *wild*, Dr. Maudsley. She has to be trapped in the room by trickery, or sometimes I have to get John to bring her by force. She will do anything to avoid it, flailing her arms or else holding her whole body rigid to make it awkward to carry her through the door. Seating her behind a desk is practically impossible. More often than not John is obliged to simply leave her on the floor. She will neither look at me nor listen to me in the classroom, but retreats to some inner world of her own."

The doctor listened closely and nodded. "It is a difficult case. Her behavior causes you greater anxiety and you fear that the results of your efforts may be less successful than with her sister. And yet"—his smile was charming—"forgive me, Miss Barrow, if I do not see why you profess to be baffled by her. On the contrary, your account of her behavior and mental state is more coherent than many a medical student might make, given the same evidence."

She eyed him levelly. "I have not yet come to the confusing part."

"Ah."

"There are methods that have been successful with children like Adeline in the past. There are strategies of my own that I have some faith in and would not hesitate to put into action were it not that . . . ."

Hester hesitated, and this time the doctor was wise enough to wait for her to go on. When she spoke again it was slowly, and she weighed her words with care.

"It is as though there is a mist in Adeline, a mist that separates her not only from humanity but from herself. And sometimes the mist thins, and sometimes the mist clears, and another Adeline appears. And then the mist returns and she is as before."

Hester looked at the doctor, watching his reaction. He frowned, but above his frown, where his hair was receding, his skin was an unwrinkled pink. "What is she like during these periods?"

"The outward signs are very small. For several weeks I was not aware of the phenomenon, and even then I waited some time before being sure enough to come to you."

"I see."

"First of all there is her breathing. It changes sometimes, and I know that though she is pretending to be in a world of her own, she is listening to me. And her hands—"

"Her hands?"

"Usually they are splayed, tense, like this"—Hester demonstrated—"but then sometimes I notice they relax, like this"—and her own fingers relaxed into softness. "It is as if her involvement with the story has captured her attention and in doing so undermined her defenses, so that she relaxes and forgets her show of rejection and defiance. I have worked with a great many difficult children, Dr. Maudsley. I have considerable expertise. And what I have seen amounts to this: Against all the odds, there is a *fermentation* in her."

The doctor did not answer immediately but considered, and Hester seemed gratified at his application.

"Is there any pattern to the emergence of these signs?"

"Nothing I can be sure of as yet, but . . ."

He put his head on one side, encouraging her to go on.

"It's probably nothing, but certain stories . . ."

"Stories?"

"*Jane Eyre*, for instance. I told them a shortened version of the first part, over several days, and I certainly noticed it then. Dickens, too. The historical tales and the moral tales have never had the same effect."

The doctor frowned. "And is it consistent? Does reading *Jane Eyre* always bring about the changes you have described?"

"No. That is the difficulty."

"Hmm. So what do you mean to do?"

"There are methods for managing selfish and resistant children such as Adeline. A strict regime now might be enough to keep her out of an institution later in life. However, this regime, involving the imposition of strict routine and the removal of much that stimulates her, would be most detrimental to—"

"To the child we see through the gaps in the mist?"

"Precisely. In fact, for *that* child, nothing would be worse."

"And that child, the girl in the mist, what future could you foresee for her?"

"It is a premature question. Suffice it to say that I cannot at present countenance her being lost. Who knows what she might become?"

They sat in silence, gazing at the leafy geometry opposite and contemplating the problem Hester had set out while, unbeknownst to them, the problem itself, well concealed by topiary, stared back at them through the gaps in the branches.

Finally the doctor spoke. "There is no medical condition I know of that would cause mental effects of quite the kind you describe. However, that may be my own ignorance." He waited for her to protest; she didn't. "H-hum. It would be sensible for me to give the child a thorough examination in order to establish her overall state of health, both mental and physical, as a first step."

"That is just what I was thinking," Hester replied. "Now . . ."—she rummaged in her pocket—"here are my notes. You will find descriptions of each instance I have witnessed, together with some preliminary analysis. Perhaps after the medical you might stay for half an hour to give me your first thoughts? We can decide on the appropriate next step then."

He looked at her in some amazement. She had stepped out of her role as governess, was behaving as though she were some fellow expert!

Hester had caught herself out.

She hesitated. Could she backtrack? Was it too late? She made her resolution. In for a penny, in for a pound. "It's not a dodecahedron," she told him slyly. "It's a tetrahedron."

The doctor rose from the bench, stepped toward the topiary shape. One, two, three, four . . . His lips moved as he counted.

My heart stopped. Was he going to walk around the tree, making his tally of planes and corners? Was he going to trip over me?

But he reached six and stopped. He knew she was right.

Then there was a curious little moment when they just looked at each other. His face was uncertain. What was this woman? By what authority did she speak to him the way she did? She was just a dumpy, potato-faced, provincial governess. Wasn't she?

In silence she stared back at him, transfixed by the uncertainty glimmering in his face.

The world seemed to tilt a fraction on its axis, and they each looked awkwardly away.

"The medical," Hester began.

"Wednesday afternoon, perhaps?" proposed the doctor.

"Wednesday afternoon."

And the world returned to its proper axis.

They walked back toward the house, and at the turn in the path the doctor took his leave.

Behind the yew the little spy bit her nails and wondered.

## FIVE NOTES

A scratchy veil of fatigue irritated my eyes. My mind was paper thin. I had been working all day and half the night, and now I was afraid to go to sleep.

Was my mind playing tricks on me? It seemed that I could hear a tune. Well, hardly a tune. Just five lost notes. I opened the window to be sure. Yes. There was definitely sound coming from the garden.

*Words* I can understand. Give me a torn or damaged fragment of text and I can divine what must have come before and what must come after. Or if not, I can at least reduce the number of possibilities to the most likely option. But music is not my language. Were these five notes the opening of a lullaby? Or the dying fall of a lament? It was impossible to say. With no beginning and no ending to frame them, no melody to hold them in place, whatever it was that bound them together seemed precariously insecure. Every time the first note struck up its call, there was a moment of anxiety while it waited to find out whether its companion was still there, or had drifted off, lost for good, blown away by the wind. And so with the third and the fourth. And with the fifth, no resolution, only the feeling that sooner or later the fragile bonds that linked this random set of notes would give way as the links with the rest of the tune had given way, and even this last, empty fragment would be gone for good, scattered to the wind like the last leaves from a winter tree.

Stubbornly mute whenever my conscious mind called upon them to perform, the notes came to me out of nowhere when I was not thinking of them. Lost in my work in the evening, I would become aware that they had been repeating themselves in my mind for some time. Or else in bed, drifting between sleep and wakefulness, I would hear them in the distance, singing their indistinct, meaningless song to me.

But now I really heard it. A single note first, its companions drowned in the rain that rapped at the window. It was nothing, I told myself, and prepared to go back to sleep. But then, in a lull in the rainstorm, three notes raised themselves above the water.

The night was very thick. So black was the sky that only the sound of the rain allowed me to picture the garden. That percussion was the rain on the windows.

The soft, random squalls were fresh rain on the lawn. The trickling sound was water coming down gutters and into drains. Drip . . . drip . . . drip. Water falling from leaves to the ground. Behind all this, beneath it, between it, if I was not mad or dreaming, came the five notes. La la la la la.

I pulled on boots and a coat and went outside into the blackness.

I could not see my hand in front of my face. Nothing to hear but the squelch of my boots on the lawn. And then I caught a trace of it. A harsh, unmusical sound; not an instrument, but an atonal, discordant human voice.

Slowly and with frequent stops I tracked the notes. I went down the long borders and turned into the garden with the pond—at least I think that is where I went. Then I mistook my way, blundered across soft soil where I thought a path should be, and ended up not beside the yew as I expected, but in a patch of knee-high shrubs with thorns that caught at my clothes. From then on I gave up trying to work out where I was, took my bearings from my ears alone, followed the notes like Ariane's thread through a labyrinth I had ceased to recognize. It sounded at irregular intervals, and each time I would head toward it, until the silence stopped me and I paused, waiting for a new clue. How long did I stumble after it in the dark? Was it a quarter of an hour? Half an hour? All I know is that at the end of that time I found myself back at the very door by which I had left the house. I had come—or been led—full circle.

The silence was very final. The notes had died, and in their place, the rain started again.

Instead of going in, I sat on the bench, rested my head on my crossed arms, feeling the rain tap on my back, my neck, my hair.

It began to seem a foolish thing to have gone chasing about the garden after something so insubstantial, and I managed to persuade myself, almost, that I had heard nothing but the creation of my own imagination. Then my thoughts turned in other directions. I wondered when my father would send me advice about searching for Hester. I thought about Angelfield and frowned: What would Aurelius do when the house was demolished? Thinking about Angelfield made me think of the ghost, and that made me think of my own ghost, the photograph I had taken of her, lost in a blur of white. I made a resolution to telephone my mother the next day, but it was a safe resolution; no one can hold you to a decision made in the middle of the night.

And then my spine sent me an alarm.

*A presence. Here. Now. At my side.*

I jerked up and looked around.

The darkness was total. There was nothing and no one to see. Everything, even the great oak, had been swallowed up in the darkness, and the world had shrunk to the eyes that were watching me and the wild frenzy of my heart.

Not Miss Winter. Not here. Not at this time of night. Then who?

I felt it *before* I felt it. The touch against my side—the here and gone again—

It was the cat, Shadow.

Again he nudged me, another cheek rub against my ribs, and a meow, rather tardily, to announce himself. I reached out my hand and stroked him, while my heart attempted to find a rhythm. The cat purred.

"You're all wet," I told him. "Come on, silly. It's no night to be out."

He followed me to my room, licked himself dry while I wrapped my hair in a towel, and we fell asleep together on the bed. For once—perhaps it was the cat's protection—my dreams kept well away.

The next day was dull and gray. After my regular interview, I took myself for a walk in the garden. I tried in the dismal light of early afternoon to retrace the path I had taken by dead of night. The beginning was easy enough: down the long borders and into the garden with the pond. But after that I lost my track. My memory of stepping across the soft wet soil of a flower bed had me stumped, for every bed and border was pristinely raked and in order. Still, I made a few haphazard guesses, one or two random decisions, and took myself on a roughly circular route that might or might not have mirrored, in part at least, my nighttime stroll.

I saw nothing out of the ordinary. Unless you count the fact that I came across Maurice, and for once he spoke to me. He was kneeling over a section of churned-up soil, straightening and smoothing and putting right. He felt me come onto the lawn behind him and looked up. "Damn foxes," he growled. And turned back to his work.

I returned to the house and began transcribing the morning's interview.

## THE EXPERIMENT

The day of the medical examination came, and Dr. Maudsley presented himself at the house. As usual Charlie was not there to welcome the visitor. Hester had informed him of the doctor's visit in her usual way (a letter left outside his rooms on a tray), and having heard no more about it, assumed quite correctly that he took no interest in the matter.

The patient was in one of her sullen but unresisting moods. She allowed herself to be led into the room where the examination took place, and submitted to being poked and prodded. Invited to open her mouth and stick out her tongue, she would not, but at least when the doctor stuck his fingers in her mouth and physically separated upper from lower jaw to peer in, she did not bite him. Her eyes slid away from him and his instruments; she seemed scarcely aware of him and his examination. She could not be induced to speak a single word.

Dr. Maudsley found his patient to be underweight and to have lice; otherwise she was physically healthy in every respect. Her psychological state, however, was more difficult to determine. Was the child, as John-the-dig implied, mentally deficient? Or was the girl's behavior caused by parental neglect and lack of discipline? This was the view of the Missus, who, publicly at least, was inclined always to absolve the twins.

These were not the only opinions the doctor had in mind when he examined the wild twin. The previous night in his own house, pipe in mouth, hand on fireplace, he had been musing aloud about the case (he enjoyed having his wife listen to him; it inspired him to greater eloquence), enumerating the instances of misbehavior he had heard of. There had been the thieving from villagers' cottages, the destruction of the topiary garden, the violence wrought upon Emmeline, the fascination with matches. He had been pondering the possible explanations when the soft voice of his wife broke in. "You don't think she is simply wicked?"

For a moment he was too surprised at being interrupted to answer.

"It's only a suggestion," she said with a wave of her hand, as if to discount her words. She had spoken mildly, but that hardly mattered. The fact that she had spoken at all was enough to give her words an edge.

And then there was Hester.

"What you must bear in mind," she had told him, "is that in the absence of any strong parental attachment, and with no strong guidance from any other quarter, the child's development to date has been wholly shaped by the experience of twinness. Her sister is the one fixed and permanent point in her consciousness; therefore her entire worldview will have been formed through the prism of their relationship."

She was quite right, of course. He had no idea what book she had got it out of, but she must have read it closely, for she elaborated on the idea very sensibly. As he listened, he had been rather struck by her queer little voice. Despite its distinctively feminine pitch it had more than a little masculine authority about it. She was articulate. She had an amusing habit of expressing views of her own with the same measured command as when she was explaining a theory by some authority she had read. And when she paused for breath at the end of a sentence, she would give him a quick look—he had found it disconcerting the first time, though now he thought it rather droll—to let him know whether he was allowed to speak or whether she intended to go on speaking herself.

"I must do some more research," he told Hester when they met to discuss the patient after the examination. "And I shall certainly look very closely at the significance of her being a twin."

Hester nodded. "The way I look at it is this," she said. "In a number of ways, you could view the twins as having divided a set of characteristics between them. Where an ordinary, healthy person will feel a whole range of different emotions, display a great variety of behaviors, the twins, you might say, have divided the range of emotions and behaviors into two and taken one set each. One twin is wild and given to physical rages; the other is indolent and passive. One prefers cleanliness; the other craves dirt. One has an endless appetite for food, the other can starve herself for days. Now, if this polarity—we can argue later about how consciously it has been adopted—is crucial to Adeline's sense of identity, it is unsurprising, is it not, if she suppresses within herself everything that in her view falls on Emmeline's side of the boundary?" The question was rhetorical; she did not indicate to the doctor that he might speak, but drew in a measured breath and continued. "Now, consider the qualities in the girl in the mist. She listens to stories, is capable of understanding and being moved by a language that is not twin language. This suggests a willingness to engage with other people. But of the twins, which is it who has been allocated the job of engaging with others? Emmeline! And so Adeline must repress this part of her humanity."

Hester turned her head to the doctor and gave him the look that meant it was his turn to speak.

"It's a curious idea," he answered cautiously. "I should have thought the opposite, wouldn't you? That you could expect them to be more alike than dissimilar?"

"But we know from observation that that isn't the case," she countered briskly.

"Hmm."

She did not speak but let him consider. He stared at the empty wall, deep in thought, while she cast anxious glances in his direction, trying to divine the reception of her theory from his face. Then he was ready to make his pronouncement.

"While this idea of yours is an interesting one"—he put on a sympathetic smile to soften the effect of his discouragement—"I don't recall ever reading about such a division of character between twins in any of the authorities."

She ignored the smile and met his eyes levelly. "It isn't in the authorities, no. If it was going to be anywhere it would be in Lawson, and it isn't."

"You have read Lawson?"

"Of course. I would not dream of pronouncing an opinion on any subject without being sure of my references first."

"Oh."

"There is a reference to the Peruvian boy twins in Harwood that is suggestive, though he stops short of the full conclusion that might be drawn."

"I remember the example you mean . . ." He gave a little start. "Oh! I see the connection! Well, I wonder whether the Brasenby case study is of any relevance?"

"I haven't been able to obtain the full study. Can you lend it to me?"

So it began.

Impressed by the acuity of Hester's observations, the doctor lent her the Brasenby case study. When she returned it, there was a sheet of pithily expressed notes and questions attached. He, in the meantime, had obtained a number of other books and articles to complete his library on twins, recently published pieces, copies of work in progress from various specialists, foreign works. He found after a week or two

229

that he could save himself time by passing these to Hester first, and reading for himself just the concise and intelligent summaries she produced. When between them they had read everything it was possible to read, they returned to their own observations. Both of them had compiled notes, his medical, hers psychological; there were copious annotations in his handwriting in the margins of her manuscript, but she had made even more notes on his, and sometimes attached her own cogent essays on separate pieces of paper.

They read; they thought; they wrote; they met; they discussed. This went on until they knew everything there was to know about twins, but there was still one thing they did not know, and it was the one thing that mattered.

"All this work," the doctor said one evening in the library, "all this paper. And we are still no nearer." He ran his hand through his hair in an agitated manner. He had told his wife he would be back by half past seven, and he was going to be late. "Is it because of Emmeline that Adeline represses the girl in the mist? I think the answer to that question lies outside the bounds of current knowledge." He sighed and tossed his pencil onto the desk, half annoyed, half resigned.

"You are quite right. It does." You could forgive her for sounding testy—it had taken him four weeks to reach the conclusion she could have given him at the beginning if he had only been willing to listen.

He turned to her.

"There is only one way to find out," she said quietly.

He raised an eyebrow.

"My experience and observations have led me to believe that there is scope for an original research project here. Of course, as a mere governess, I would have difficulty in persuading the appropriate journal to publish anything I produced. They would take one look at my qualifications and think I was nothing but a silly woman with ideas beyond her competence." She shrugged and cast her eyes down. "Perhaps they are right, and I am. All the same"—slyly she glanced up again—"for a man with the right background and knowledge, I am sure there is a meaty project there."

The doctor looked at first surprised, then his eyes turned misty. Original research! The idea was not so very preposterous. It struck him that at this moment, at the culmination of all the reading he had done in recent months, he must surely be the best-read doctor in the country on the subject of twins! Who else knew what he knew? And more to the point, who else had the perfect case study under his nose? Original research? Whyever not?

She let him indulge himself for a few minutes, and when she saw that her suggestion had taken root in his heart, murmured, "Of course, if you needed an assistant, I'd be glad to help in any way I could."

"Very kind of you." He nodded. "Of course, you've worked with the girls . . . Practical experience . . . Invaluable . . . Quite invaluable."

He left the house and floated home on a cloud, where he failed to notice that his dinner was cold and his wife bad-tempered.

Hester gathered up the papers from the desk and left the room; her neat footsteps and firm closing of the door had the ring of satisfaction about them.

The library seemed empty, but it wasn't.

Lying full-length on top of the bookcases, a girl was biting her nails and thinking.

Original research.

*Is it because of Emmeline that Adeline represses the girl in the mist?*

Didn't take a genius to figure out what was going to happen next.

They did it at night.

Emmeline never stirred as they lifted her from her bed. She must have felt herself safe in Hester's arms; perhaps she recognized the smell of soap in her sleep as she was carried out of the room and along the corridor. Whatever the reason, she didn't realize that night what was happening. Her awakening to the truth was hours away.

It was different for Adeline. Quick and sharp, she awoke at once to her sister's absence. Darted to the door but found it locked already by Hester's swift hand. In a flash she knew it all, felt it all. Severance. She didn't shriek, she didn't fling her fists against the door, she didn't claw at the lock with her nails. All the fight went out of her. She sank to the floor, collapsed into a little heap against the door, and that is where she stayed all night. The bare boards bit into her jutting bones, but she didn't feel the pain. There was no fire and her night-dress was thin, but she didn't feel the cold. She felt nothing. She was broken.

When they came for her the next morning, she was deaf to the key in the lock, didn't react when the opening door shunted her out of its way. Her eyes were dead, her skin bloodless. How cold she was. She might have been a corpse, if it had not been for her lips that twitched ceaselessly, repeating a silent mantra that might have been *Emmeline, Emmeline, Emmeline*.

Hester lifted Adeline in her arms. Not difficult. The child was fourteen now, but she was skin and bones. All her strength was in her will, and when that was gone, the rest was insubstantial. They carried her down the stairs as easily as if she were a feather pillow going to be aired.

John drove. Silent. Approving, disapproving, it hardly mattered. Hester did the decision making.

They told Adeline she was going to see Emmeline; a lie they needn't have bothered with; they could have taken Adeline anywhere and she'd not have fought them. She was lost. Absent from herself. Without her sister, she was nothing and she was no one. It was just the shell of a person they took to the doctor's house. They left her there.

Back at home, they moved Emmeline from the bed in Hester's room back into her own without waking her.

233

She slept for another hour, and when she did open her eyes was mildly surprised to find her sister gone. As the morning drew on, her surprise grew, turning to anxiety in the afternoon. She searched the house. She searched the gardens. She went as far as she dared in the woods, the village.

At teatime Hester found her at the road's edge, staring in the direction that would have taken her, if she had followed it, to the door of the doctor's house. She had not dared follow it. Hester put a hand on Emmeline's shoulder and drew her close, then led her back to the house. From time to time, Emmeline stopped, hesitant, wanting to turn back, but Hester took her hand and guided her firmly in the direction of home. Emmeline followed with obedient but puzzled steps. After tea she stood by the window and looked out. She grew fearful as the light faded, but it was not until Hester locked the doors and began the routine of putting Emmeline to bed that she became distraught.

All night long she cried. Lonely sobs that seemed to go on forever. What had snapped in an instant in Adeline took an agonizing twenty-four hours to break in Emmeline. But when dawn came, she was quiet. She had wept and shuddered herself into oblivion.

The separation of twins is no ordinary separation. Imagine surviving an earthquake. When you come to, you find the world unrecognizable. The horizon is in a different place. The sun has changed color. Nothing remains of the terrain you know. As for you, you are alive. But it's not the same as living. It's no wonder the survivors of such disasters so often wish they had perished with the others.

❧❦

Miss Winter sat staring into space. Her famous copper tint had faded to a tender apricot. She had abandoned her hairspray and the solid coils and twists had given way to a soft, shapeless tangle. But her face was set hard and she held herself rigid, as though girding herself against a biting wind that only she could feel. Slowly she turned her eyes to mine.

"Are you all right?" she asked. "Judith says you don't eat very much."

"I've always been like that."

"But you look pale."

"A bit tired, maybe."

We finished early. Neither of us, I think, felt up to carrying on.

## DO YOU BELIEVE IN GHOSTS?

The next time I saw her, Miss Winter looked different. She closed her eyes wearily, and it took her longer than usual to conjure the past and begin to speak. While she gathered the threads, I watched her and noticed that she had left off her false eyelashes. There was the habitual purple eye shadow, the sweeping line of black. But without the spider lashes, she had the unexpected appearance of a child who had been playing in her mother's makeup box.

235

Things weren't as Hester and the doctor expected. They were prepared for an Adeline who would rant and rage and kick and fight. As for Emmeline, they were counting on her affection for Hester to reconcile her to her twin's sudden absence. They were expecting, in short, the same girls they had before, only separate where they had been together. And so, initially, they were surprised by the twins' collapse into a pair of lifeless rag dolls.

Not quite lifeless. The blood continued to circulate, sluggishly, in their veins. They swallowed the soup that was spooned into their mouths by in one house the Missus, in the other the doctor's wife. But swallowing is a reflex, and they had no appetite. Their eyes, open during the day, were unseeing, and at night, though their eyes closed, they had not the tranquillity of sleep. They were apart; they were alone; they were in a kind of limbo. They were like amputees, only it was not a limb they were missing, but their very souls.

Did the scientists doubt themselves? Stop and wonder whether they were doing the right thing? Did the lolling, unconscious figures of the twins cast a shadow over their beautiful project? They were not willfully cruel, you know. Only foolish. Misguided by their learning, their ambition, their own self-deceiving blindness.

The doctor carried out tests. Hester observed. And they met every day, to compare notes. To discuss what at first they optimistically called progress. Behind the doctor's desk, or in the Angelfield library, they sat together, heads bent over papers on which were recorded every detail of the girls' lives. Behavior, diet, sleep. They puzzled over absent appetites, the propensity to sleep all the time—that sleep which was not sleep. They proposed theories to account for the changes in the twins. The experiment was not going as well as they had expected, had begun in fact disastrously, but the two scientists skirted around the possibility that they might be doing harm, preferring to retain the belief that together they could work a miracle.

The doctor derived great satisfaction from the novelty of working for the first time in decades with a scientific mind of the highest order. He marveled at his protégée's ability to grasp a principle one minute and to apply it with professional originality and insight the next. Before long he admitted to himself that she was more a colleague than a protégée. And Hester was thrilled to find that at long last her mind was adequately nourished and challenged. She came out of their daily meetings aglow with excitement and pleasure. So their blindness was only natural. How could they be expected to understand that what was doing them such good could be doing such great harm to the children in their care? Unless perhaps, in the evenings, each sitting in solitude to write up the day's notes, they might individually have raised their eyes to the unmoving, dead-eyed child in a chair in the corner and felt a doubt cross their minds. Perhaps. But if they did, they did not record it in their notes, did not mention it to the other.

So dependent did the pair become on their joint undertaking that they quite failed to see that the grand project was making no progress at all. Emmeline and Adeline were all but catatonic, and the girl in the mist was nowhere to be seen. Undeterred by their lack of findings, the scientists continued their work: They made tables and charts, proposed theories and developed elaborate experiments to test them. With each failure they told themselves that they had eliminated something from the field of examination and went on to the next big idea.

The doctor's wife and the Missus were involved, but at one remove. The physical care of the girls was their responsibility. They spooned soup into the unresisting mouths of their charges three times a day. They dressed the twins, bathed them, did their laundry, brushed their hair. Each woman had her reasons for disapproving of the project; each had her reasons for keeping mum about her thoughts. As for John-the-dig, he was outside it all. His opinion was sought by no one, not that that stopped him making his daily pronouncement to the Missus in the kitchen: "No good will come of it. I'm telling you. No good at all."

There came a moment when they might have had to give up. All their plans had come to nothing, and though they racked their brains, they were lost for a new trick to try. At precisely this point Hester detected small signs of improvement in Emmeline. The girl had turned her head toward a window. She was found clutching some shiny bauble and would not be separated from it. By listening outside doors (which is not bad manners, incidentally, when it is done in the name of science) Hester discovered that when left alone the child was whispering to herself in the old twin language.

"She is soothing herself," she told the doctor, "by imagining the presence of her sister."

The doctor began a regime of leaving Adeline alone for periods of several hours and listening outside the door, notepad and pen in hand. He heard nothing.

Hester and the doctor advised themselves of the need for patience in the more severe case of Adeline, while they congratulated themselves on the improvements in Emmeline. Brightly they noted Emmeline's increased appetite, her willingness to sit up, the first few steps she took of her own accord. Soon she was wandering around the house and garden again with something of her old purposelessness. Oh yes, Hester and the doctor agreed, the experiment was really going somewhere now! Whether they stopped to consider that what they termed "improvements" were only Emmeline returning to the habits she already displayed before the experiment began is hard to judge.

It wasn't all plain sailing with Emmeline. There was a dreadful day when she followed her nose to the cupboard filled with the rags her sister used to wear. She held them to her face, inhaled the stale, animal odor and then, in delight, arrayed herself in them. It was awkward, but worse was to come. Dressed in this fashion, she caught sight of herself in a mirror and, taking her reflection for her sister, ran headlong into it. The crash was loud enough to bring the Missus running, and she found Emmeline weeping beside the mirror, crying not for her own pain but for her poor sister, who had broken into several pieces and was bleeding.

Hester took the clothes away from her and instructed John to burn them. As an extra precaution, she ordered the Missus to turn all the mirrors to the wall. Emmeline was perplexed, but there were no more incidents of the kind.

She would not speak. For all the solitary whispering that went on behind closed doors, always in the old twin language, Emmeline could not be induced to speak a single word of English to the Missus or to Hester. This was something to confer about. Hester and the doctor held a lengthy meeting in the library, at the end of which they concluded that there was no cause for worry. Emmeline could talk, and she would, given time. The refusal to speak, the incident with the mirror—they were disappointments, of course, but science has its disappointments. And look at the progress! Why, wasn't Emmeline strong enough to be allowed outside? And she spent less time these days loitering at the roadside, at the invisible boundary beyond which she dared not step, staring in the direction of the doctor's house. Things were going as well as could be expected.

Progress? It was not what they had hoped at the outset. It was not much at all compared to the results

Hester had achieved with the girl when she first arrived. But it was all they had and they made the most of it. Perhaps they were secretly relieved. For what would have been the result of a definitive success? It would have eliminated all reason for their continued collaboration. And though they were blind to the fact, they would not have wanted that.

They would never have ended the experiment of their own accord. Never. It was going to take something else, something external, to put a stop to it. Something that came quite out of the blue.

❧

"What was it?"

Though it was the end of our time, though she had the drawn, gray-white look that she got when the time for her medication grew near, though it was forbidden to ask questions, I couldn't help myself.

Despite her pain, there was a green gleam of mischief in her eyes as she leaned forward confidingly.

"Do you believe in ghosts, Margaret?"

Do I believe in ghosts? What could I say? I nodded.

Satisfied, Miss Winter sat back in her chair, and I had the not unfamiliar impression of having given away more than I thought.

"Hester didn't. Not scientific, you see. So, not believing in ghosts, she had a good deal of trouble when she saw one."

❧

It was like this:

One bright day Hester, having finished her duties in

241

plenty of time, left the house early and decided to take the long way round to the doctor's house. The sky was gloriously blue, the air fresh-smelling and clear, and she felt full of a powerful energy that she couldn't put a name to but that made her yearn for strenuous activity.

The path around the fields took her up a slight incline that, though not much of a hill, gave her a fine view of the fields and land around. She was about halfway to the doctor's, striding out vigorously, heartbeat raised but without the slightest sense of overexertion, feeling quite probably that she could fly if she just put her mind to it, when she saw something that stopped her dead.

In the distance, playing together in a field, were Emmeline and Adeline. Unmistakable. Two manes of red hair, two pairs of black shoes; one child in the navy poplin that the Missus had put Emmeline in that morning, the other in green.

It was impossible.

But no. Hester was scientific. She was seeing them, hence they were there. There must be an explanation. Adeline had escaped from the doctor's house. Her torpor had left her as suddenly as it had come and, taking advantage of an open window or a set of keys left unattended, she had escaped before anyone had noticed her recovery. That was it.

What to do? Running to the twins was pointless. She'd have had to approach them across a long stretch of open field, and they would see her and flee before she had covered half the distance. So she went to the doctor's house. At a run.

In no time she was there, hammering impatiently at the door. It was Mrs. Maudsley who opened it, tight-lipped at the racket, but Hester had more important things on her mind than apologies and pushed past her to the door of the surgery. She entered without knocking.

The doctor looked up, startled to see his collaborator's face flushed with exertion, her hair, normally so neat, flying free from its grips. She was out of breath. She wanted to speak but for the moment could not.

"Whatever is it?" he asked, rising from his seat and coming around the desk to put his hands on her shoulders.

"Adeline!" she gasped. "You've let her out!"

The doctor, puzzled, frowned. He turned Hester by the shoulders, until she was facing the other end of the room.

There was Adeline.

Hester spun back around to the doctor. "But I've just seen her! With Emmeline! On the edge of the woods beyond Oates's field . . ." She began vehemently enough, but her voice tailed off as she began to wonder.

"Calm yourself, sit down, here, take a sip of water," the doctor was saying.

"She must have run off. How could she have got out? And come back so quickly?" Hester tried to make sense of it.

"She has been here in this room this last two hours. Since breakfast. She has not been unsupervised in all that time." He looked into Hester's eyes, stirred by her emotion. "It must have been another child. From the village," he suggested, maintaining his doctorly decorum.

"But—" Hester shook her head. "It was Adeline's clothes. Adeline's hair."

Hester turned to look at Adeline again. Her open eyes were indifferent to the world. She was wearing not the green dress Hester had seen a few minutes before but a neat navy one, and her hair was not loose but braided.

The eyes Hester turned back to the doctor were full of bewilderment. Her breathing would not steady. There was no rational explanation for what she had seen. It was unscientific. And Hester knew the world was totally and profoundly scientific. There could be only one explanation. "I must be mad," she whispered. Her pupils dilated and her nostrils quivered. "I have seen a ghost!"

Her eyes filled with tears.

It produced a strange sensation in the doctor to see his collaborator reduced to such a state of disheveled emotion. And although it was the scientist in him that had first admired Hester for her cool head and reliable brain, it was the man, animal and instinctive, that responded to her disintegration by putting his arms around her and placing his lips firmly upon hers in a passionate embrace.

Hester did not resist.

Listening at doors is not bad manners when it is done in the name of science, and the doctor's wife was a keen scientist when it came to studying her own husband. The kiss that so startled the doctor and Hester came as no surprise at all to Mrs. Maudsley, who had been expecting something rather like it for some time.

She flung the door open and in a rush of outraged righteousness burst into the surgery.

"I will thank you to leave this house instantly," she said to Hester. "You can send John in the brougham for the child."

Then, to her husband, "I will speak to you later."

The experiment was over. So were many other things.

John fetched Adeline. He saw neither the doctor nor his wife at the house but learned from the maid about the events of the morning.

At home he put Adeline in her old bed, in the old room, and left the door ajar.

Emmeline, wandering in the woods, raised her head, sniffed the air and turned directly toward home. She came in the kitchen door, made straight for the stairs, went up two steps at a time and strode unhesitatingly to the old room. She closed the door behind her.

And Hester? No one saw her return to the house, and no one heard her leave. But when the Missus knocked on her door the next morning, she found the neat little room empty and Hester gone.

❧

I emerged from the spell of the story and into Miss Winter's glazed and mirrored library.

"Where did she go?" I wondered.

Miss Winter eyed me with a slight frown. "I've no idea. What does it matter?"

"She must have gone somewhere."

The storyteller gave me a sideways look. "Miss Lea, it doesn't do to get attached to these secondary characters. It's not their story. They come, they go, and when they go they're gone for good. That's all there is to it."

I slid my pencil into the spiral binding of my notebook and walked to the door, but when I got there, I turned back.

"Where did she come from, then?"

"For goodness' sake! She was only a governess! She is irrelevant, I tell you."

"She must have had references. A previous job. Or else a letter of application with a home address. Perhaps she came from an agency?"

Miss Winter closed her eyes and a long-suffering expression appeared on her face. "Mr. Lomax, the Angelfield family solicitor, will have all the details I'm sure. Not that they'll do you any good. It's my story. I should know. His office is in Market Street, Banbury. I will instruct him to answer any inquiries you choose to make."

I wrote to Mr. Lomax that night.

The next morning, when Judith came with my breakfast tray, I gave her the letter for Mr. Lomax, and she took a letter for me from her apron pocket. I recognized my father's handwriting.

My father's letters were always a comfort, and this one was no exception. He hoped I was well. Was my work progressing? He had read a very strange and delightful nineteenth-century Danish novel that he would tell me about when I returned. At auction he had come across a bundle of eighteenth-century letters no one seemed to want. Might I be interested? He had bought them in case. Private detectives? Well, perhaps, but would a genealogical researcher not do the job just as well or perhaps better? There was a fellow he knew who had all the right skills, and come to think of it, he owed Father a favor—he sometimes came into the shop to use the almanacs. In case I intended to pursue the matter, here was his address. Finally, as always, those well meant but desiccated four words: *Mother sends her love.*

Did she really say it? I wondered. Father mentioning, *I'll write to Margaret this afternoon,* and she—casually? warmly?—*Send her my love.*

No. I couldn't imagine it. It would be my father's addition. Written without her knowledge. Why did he bother? To please me? To make it true? Was it for me or for her that he made these thankless efforts to connect us? It was an impossible task. My mother and I were like two continents moving slowly but inexorably apart; my father, the bridge builder, constantly extending the fragile edifice he had constructed to connect us.

A letter had come for me at the shop; my father enclosed it with his own. It was from the law professor Father had recommended to me.

*Dear Miss Lea,*

*I was not aware Ivan Lea even had a daughter, but now I know he has one, I am pleased to make your acquaintance—and even more pleased to be of assistance. The legal decree of decease is just what you imagine it to be: a presumption in law of the death of a person whose whereabouts have been unknown for such a length of time and in such circumstances that death is the only reasonable assumption. Its main function is to enable the estate of a missing person to be passed into the hands of his inheritors.*

*I have undertaken the necessary researches and traced the documents relating to the case you are particularly interested in. Your Mr. Angelfield was apparently a man of reclusive habits, and the date and circumstances of his disappearance appear not to be known. However, the painstaking and sympathetic work carried out by one Mr. Lomax on behalf of the inheritors (two nieces) enabled the relevant formalities to be duly carried out. The estate was of some significant value, though diminished somewhat by a fire that left the house itself uninhabitable. But you will see all this for yourself in the copy I have made you of the relevant documents.*

*You will see that the solicitor himself has signed on behalf of one of the beneficiaries. This is common in situations where the beneficiary is unable for some reason (illness or other incapacity, for instance) to take care of his own affairs.*

*It was with a most particular attention that I noted the signature of the other beneficiary. It was almost illegible, but I managed to work it out in the end. Have I stumbled across one of the best-kept secrets of the day? But perhaps you knew it already? Is this what inspired your interest in the case?*

*Fear not! I am a man of the greatest discretion! Tell your father to give me a good discount on the* Justitiae Naturalis Principia, *and I will say not a word to anyone!*

*Your servant,*
*William Henry Cadwalladr*

I turned straight to the end of the neat copy Professor Cadwalladr had made. Here was space for the signatures of Charlie's nieces. As he said, Mr. Lomax had signed for Emmeline. That told me that she had survived the fire, at least. And on the second line, the name I had been hoping for. *Vida Winter.* And after it, in

249

brackets, the words, *formerly known as Adeline March*.

Proof.

Vida Winter was Adeline March.

She was telling the truth.

With this in mind, I went to my appointment in the library, and listened and scribbled in my little book as Miss Winter recounted the aftermath of Hester's departure.

❦

Adeline and Emmeline spent the first night and the first day in their room, in bed, arms wrapped around each other and gazing into each other's eyes. There was a tacit agreement between the Missus and John-the-dig to treat them as though they were convalescent, and, in a way, they were. An injury had been done to them. So they lay in bed, nose to nose, gazing cross-eyed at each other. Without a word. Without a smile. Blinking in unison. And with the transfusion that took place via that twenty-four-hour-long gaze, the connection that had been broken, healed. And like any wound that heals, it left its scar.

Meanwhile the Missus was in a state of confusion over what had happened to Hester. John, reluctant to disillusion her about the governess, said nothing, but his silence only encouraged her to wonder aloud. "I suppose she'll have told the doctor where she's gone," she concluded miserably. "I'll have to find out from him when she's coming back."

Then John had to speak, and he spoke roughly. "Don't you go asking him where she's gone! Don't ask him anything at all. Besides, we won't be seeing him around the place no more."

The Missus turned away from him, frowning. What was the matter with everyone? Why was Hester not there? Why was John all upset? And the doctor—he who had been the household's constant visitor—why should he not be coming anymore? Things were happening that were beyond her comprehension. More and more often these days, and for longer and longer periods, she had the sense that something had gone wrong with the world. More than once she seemed to wake up in her head to find that whole hours had passed by without leaving a trace in her memory. Things that clearly made sense to other people didn't always make sense to her. And when she asked questions to try and understand it, a queer look came into people's eyes, which they quickly covered up. Yes. Something odd was happening, and Hester's unexplained absence was only part of it.

John, though he regretted the unhappiness of the Missus, was relieved that Hester had gone. The departure of the governess seemed to take a great burden from him. He came more freely into the house, and in the evenings spent longer hours with the Missus in the kitchen. To his way of thinking, losing Hester was no loss at all. She had really made only one improvement to his life—by encouraging him to take up work again in the topiary garden—and she had done it so subtly, so discreetly, that it was a simple matter for him to reorganize his mind until it told him that the decision had been entirely his own. When it became clear that she had gone for good, he brought his boots from the shed and sat polishing them by the stove, legs up on the table, for who was there to stop him now?

In the nursery Charlie's rage and fury seemed to have deserted him, leaving in their place a woeful fatigue. You could sometimes hear his slow, dragging steps across the floor, and sometimes, ear to the door, you heard him crying with the exhausted sobs of a wretched two-year-old. Could it be that in some deeply mysterious though still scientific way, Hester had influenced him through locked doors and kept the worst of his despair at bay? It did not seem impossible.

It was not only people who reacted to Hester's absence. The house responded to it instantly. The first thing was the new quiet. There was no tap-tap-tap of Hester's feet trotting up and down stairs and along corridors. Then the thumps and knocks of the workmen on the roof came to a halt, too. The roofer, discovering that Hester was not there, had the well-founded suspicion that with no one to put his invoices under Charlie's nose, he would not be paid for his work. He packed up his tools and left, came back once for his ladders, was never seen again.

On the first day of silence, and as if nothing had ever happened to interrupt it, the house picked up again its long, slow project of decay. Small things first: Dirt began to seep from every crevice in every object in every room. Surfaces secreted dust. Windows covered themselves with the first fine layer of grime. All of

Hester's changes had been superficial. They required daily attention to be maintained. And as the Missus's cleaning schedules at first wavered, then crashed, the real, permanent nature of the house began to reassert itself. The time came when you couldn't pick anything up without feeling the old cling of grime on your fingers.

Objects, too, went quickly back to their old ways. The keys were first to go walkabout. Overnight they slipped themselves out of locks and off keyrings, then they gathered together in dusty companionship in the cavity beneath a loose floorboard. Silver candlesticks, while they still had their gleam of Hester's polish, made their way from the drawing room mantelpiece to Emmeline's stash of treasure under the bed. Books left their library shelves and took themselves upstairs, where they rested in corners and under sofas. Curtains took to drawing and closing themselves. Even the furniture made the most of the lack of supervision to move about. A sofa inched forward from its place against the wall, a chair shifted two feet to the left. All evidence of the house ghost reasserting herself.

A roof in the process of being repaired gets worse before it gets better. Some of the holes left by the roofer were larger than the ones he had been called in to mend. It was all right to lie on the floor of the attic and feel the sunshine on your face, but rain was another matter. The floorboards began to soften, then water dripped through into the rooms below. There were places you knew not to tread, where the floor sagged precariously beneath your feet. Soon it would collapse and you would be able to see straight through into the room below. And how long before that room's floor gave way and you would see into the library? And could the library floor give way? Would it one day be possible to stand in the cellars and look up through four floors of rooms to the sky?

Water, like God, moves in mysterious ways. Once inside a house, it obeys the force of gravity indirectly. Inside walls and under floors it finds secret gullies and runways; it seeps and trickles in unexpected directions; surfaces in the most unlikely places. All around the house were cloths to soak up the wet, but no one ever wrung them out; saucepans and bowls were placed here and there to catch drips, but they overflowed before anyone remembered to change them. The constant wetness brought the plaster off the walls and was eating into the mortar. In the attic, there were walls so unsteady that with one hand you could rock them like a loose tooth.

And the twins in all of this?

It was a serious wound that Hester and the doctor had inflicted. Of course things would never be the same again. The twins would always share a scar, and the effects of the separation would never be entirely eradicated. Yet they felt the scar differently. Adeline after all had fallen quickly into a state of fugue once she understood what Hester and the doctor were about. She lost herself almost at the moment she lost her twin and had no recollection of the time passed away from her. As far as she knew, the blackness that had been interposed between losing her twin and finding her again might have been a year or a second. Not that it mattered now. For it was over, and she had come to life again.

For Emmeline, things were different. She had not had the relief of amnesia. She had suffered longer, and she had suffered more. Each second was agony in the first weeks. She was like an amputee in the days before anesthesia, half crazed with pain, astounded that the human body could feel so much and not die of it. But slowly, cell by painful cell, she began to mend. There came a time when it was no longer her whole body that burned with pain but only her heart. And then there came a time when even her heart was able, for a time at least, to feel other emotions besides grief. In short, Emmeline adapted to her twin's absence. She learned how to exist apart.

Yet still they reconnected and were twins again. Though Emmeline was not the same twin as before, and this was something Adeline did not immediately know.

At the beginning there was only the delight of reunion. They were inseparable. Where one went, the other followed. In the topiary gardens they circled around the old trees, playing endless games of now-you-see-me-now-you-don't, a repetition of their recent experience of loss and rediscovery that Adeline never seemed to tire of. For Emmeline, the novelty began gradually to wear off. Some of the old antagonism crept in. Emmeline wanted to go one way, Adeline the other, so they fought. And as before, it was usually

Emmeline who gave in. In her new, secret self, she minded this.

Though Emmeline had once been fond of Hester, she didn't miss her now. During the experiment her affection had waned. She knew, after all, that it was Hester who had separated her from her sister. And not only that, but Hester had been so taken up with her reports and her scientific consultations that, perhaps without realizing it, she had neglected Emmeline. During that time, finding herself in unaccustomed solitude, Emmeline had found ways of distracting herself from her sorrow. She discovered amusements and entertainments that she grew to enjoy for their own sake. Games that she did not expect to give up just because her sister was back.

So it was that on the third day after the reunion, Emmeline abandoned the lost-and-found game in the topiary garden and wandered off to the billiards room, where she kept a pack of cards. Lying on her stomach in the middle of the baize table, she began her game. It was a version of solitaire, but the simplest, most childish kind. Emmeline won every time; the game was designed so that she couldn't fail. And every time she was delighted.

Halfway through a game, she tilted her head. She couldn't exactly hear it, but her inner ear, which was tuned constantly to her twin, told her Adeline was calling her. Emmeline ignored it. She was busy. She would see Adeline later. When she had finished her game.

An hour later, when Adeline came storming into the room, eyes screwed tight with rage, there was nothing Emmeline could do to defend herself. Adeline clambered onto the table and, hysterical with fury, launched herself at Emmeline.

Emmeline did not raise a finger to defend herself. Nor did she cry. She made not a sound, neither during the attack nor when it was all over.

When Adeline's rage was spent, she stood for a few minutes watching her sister. Blood was seeping into the green baize. Playing cards were scattered everywhere. Emmeline was curled into a ball, and her shoulders were jerkily rising and falling with her breath.

Adeline turned her back and walked away.

Emmeline remained where she was, on the table, until John came to find her hours later. He took her to the Missus, who washed the blood out of her hair, put a compress on her eye and treated her bruises with witch hazel.

"This wouldn't have happened when Hester was here," she commented. "I do wish I knew when she was coming back."

"She won't be coming back," John said, trying to contain his annoyance. He didn't like to see the child like this either.

"But I don't see why she would have gone like that. Without a word. Whatever can have happened? Some emergency, I suppose. With her family . . ."

John shook his head. He'd heard this a dozen times, this idea the Missus clung to, that Hester would be coming back. The whole village knew she would not come back. The Maudsleys' servant had heard everything. She professed to have seen it, too, and more besides, and by now it was impossible that there was a single adult in the village who did not know for a fact that the plain-faced governess had been carrying on an adulterous affair with the doctor.

It was inevitable that one day rumors of Hester's "behavior" (a village euphemism for misbehavior) should reach the ears of the Missus. At first she was scandalized. She refused to entertain the idea that Hester—*her* Hester—could have done such a thing. But when she reported angrily to John what was being said, he only confirmed it. He had been at the doctor's that day, he reminded her, collecting the child. He had heard it directly from the housemaid. On the very day it occurred. And besides, why would Hester have left so suddenly, without warning, if something out of the ordinary hadn't occurred?

"Her family," the Missus stammered, "an emergency. . . ."

"Where's the letter, then? She'd have written, wouldn't she, if she meant to come back? She'd have explained. Have you had a letter?"

The Missus shook her head.

"Well then," finished John, unable to keep the satisfaction from his voice, "she's done something that she didn't ought to, and she won't be coming back. She's gone for good. Take it from me."

The Missus went round and around it in her head. She

didn't know what to believe. The world had become a very confusing place.

## GONE!

Only Charlie was unaffected. There were changes, of course. The proper meals that under Hester's regime had been placed outside his door at breakfast, lunch and dinner became occasional sandwiches, a cold chop and a tomato, a bowl of congealed scrambled egg, appearing at unpredictable intervals, whenever the Missus remembered. It didn't make any difference to Charlie. If he felt hungry and it was there, he might eat a mouthful of yesterday's chop, or a dry end of bread, but if it wasn't there he wouldn't, and his hunger didn't bother him. He had a more powerful hunger to worry about. It was the essence of his life and something that Hester, in her arrival and in her departure, had not changed.

Yet change did come for Charlie, though it had nothing to do with Hester.

From time to time a letter would come to the house, and from time to time someone would open it. A few days after John-the-dig's comment about there having been no letter from Hester, the Missus, finding herself in the hall, noticed a small pile of letters gathering dust on the mat under the letter box. She opened them.

One from Charlie's banker: was he interested in an investment opportunity . . . ?

The second was an invoice from the builders for the work done on the roof.

Was the third from Hester?

No. The third was from the asylum. Isabelle was dead.

The Missus stared at the letter. Dead! Isabelle! Could it be true? Influenza, the letter said.

Charlie would have to be told, but the Missus quailed at the prospect. Better talk to Dig first, she resolved, putting the letters aside. But later, when John was sitting at his place at the kitchen table and she was topping up his cup with fresh tea, there remained no trace of the letter in her mind. It had joined those other, increasingly frequent, lost moments, lived and felt but unrecorded and then lost. Nevertheless, a few days later, passing through the hall with a tray of burnt toast and bacon, she mechanically put the letters on the tray with the food, though she had no memory at all of their contents.

And then the days passed and nothing seemed to happen at all, except that the dust got thicker, and the grime accumulated on the windowpanes, and the playing cards crept farther and farther from their box in the drawing room, and it became easier and easier to forget that there had ever been a Hester.

It was John-the-dig who realized in the silence of the days that something had happened.

He was an outdoors man and not domesticated. Nevertheless he knew that there comes a time when cups cannot be made to do for one more cup of tea without being first washed, and he knew moreover that a plate that has held raw meat cannot be used straight after for cooked. He saw how things were going with the Missus; he was no fool. So when the pile of dirty plates and cups piled up, he would set to and do the washing up. It was an odd thing to see him at the sink in his Wellington boots and his cap, so clumsy with the cloth and china where he was so adroit with his terra-cotta pots and tender plants. And it came to his attention that the number of cups and plates was diminishing. Soon there would not be enough. Where was the missing crockery? He thought instantly of the Missus making her haphazard way upstairs with a plate for Master Charlie. Had he ever seen her return an empty plate to the kitchen? No.

He went upstairs. Outside the locked door, plates and cups were arranged in a long queue. The food, untouched by Charlie, was providing a fine feast for the flies that buzzed over it, and there was a powerful, unpleasant smell. How many days had the Missus been leaving food here without noticing that the previous day's was still untouched? He toted up the number of plates and cups and frowned. That is when he knew.

He did not knock at the door. What was the point? He had to go to his shed for a piece of timber strong enough to use as a battering ram. The noise of it against the oak, the creaking and smashing as metal hinges tore away from wood, was enough to bring us all, even the Missus, to the door.

When the battered door fell open, half broken off its hinges, we could hear buzzing flies, and a terrible stench billowed out, knocking Emmeline and the Missus back a few steps. Even John put his hand to his mouth and turned a shade whiter. "Stay back," he ordered as he entered the room. A few paces behind, I followed him.

We stepped gingerly through the debris of rotting food on the floor of the old nursery, stirring clouds of flies up into the air as we passed. Charlie had been living like an animal. Dirty plates covered with mold were on the floor, on the mantelpiece, on chairs and on the table. The bedroom door was ajar. With the end of the battering ram he still had in his hand, John nudged the door cautiously, and a startled rat came scurrying out over our feet. It was a gruesome scene. More flies, more decomposing food and worse: The man had been ill. A pile of dried, fly-spotted vomit encrusted the rug on the floor. On the table by the bed was a heap of bloody handkerchiefs and the Missus's old darning needle.

The bed was empty. Just crumpled, filthy sheets stained with blood and other human vileness.

We did not speak. We tried not to breathe, and when, of necessity, we inhaled through our mouths, the sick, repugnant air caught in our throats and made us retch. Yet we had not had the worst of it. There was one more room. John had to steel himself to open the door to the bathroom. Even before the door was fully open, we sensed the horror of it. Before it snagged in my nostrils, my skin seemed to smell it, and a cold sweat bloomed all over my body. The toilet was bad enough. The lid was down but could not quite contain the overflowing mess it was supposed to cover. But that was nothing. For in the bath—John took a sharp step back and would have stepped on me if I had not, at the same moment, taken two steps back myself. In the bath was a dark swill of bodily effluence, the stink of which sent John and me racing to the door, back through the rat droppings and the flies, out into the corridor, down the stairs and out of doors.

I was sick. On the green grass, my pile of yellow vomit looked fresh and clean and sweet.

"All right," said John, and he patted my back with a hand that was still trembling.

The Missus, having followed at her own hurried shuffle, approached us across the lawn, questions all over her face. What could we tell her?

We had found Charlie's blood. We had found Charlie's shit, Charlie's piss and Charlie's vomit. But Charlie himself?

"He's not there," we told her. "He's gone."

❧

I returned to my room, thinking about the story. It was curious in more than one respect. There was Charlie's disappearance, of course, which was an interesting turn of events. It left me thinking about the almanacs and that curious abbreviation: ldd. But there was more. Did she know I had noticed? I had made no outward sign. But I *had* noticed. Today Miss Winter had said *I*.

❧

In my room, on a tray next to the ham sandwiches, I

found a large brown envelope.

Mr. Lomax, the solicitor, had replied to my letter by return of post. Attached to his brief but kindly note were copies of Hester's contract, which I glanced at and put aside, a letter of recommendation from a Lady Blake in Naples, who wrote positively of Hester's gifts, and, most interesting of all, a letter accepting the offer of employment, written by the miracle worker herself.

*Dear Dr. Maudsley,*

*Thank you for the offer of work you have kindly made to me.*

*I shall be pleased to take up the post at Angelfield on the 19th April as you suggest.*

*I have made inquiries and gather that the trains run only to Banbury. Perhaps you would advise me how I can best make my way to Angelfield from there. I shall arrive at Banbury Station at half past ten.*

*Yours sincerely,*
*Hester Barrow*

There was firmness in Hester's sturdy capitals, consistency in the slant of the letters, a sense of smooth flow in the moderate loops of the *g*'s and the *y*'s. The letter size was small enough for economy of ink and paper, yet large enough for clarity. There were no embellishments. No elaborate curls, flounces or flourishes. The beauty of the orthography came from the sense of order, balance and proportion that governed each and every letter. It was a good, clean hand. It was Hester herself, made word.

In the top right-hand corner was an address in London.

Good, I thought. I can find you now.

I reached for paper, and before I began my transcription, wrote a letter to the genealogist Father had recommended. It was a longish letter: I had to introduce myself, for he would doubtless be unaware Mr. Lea even had a daughter; I had to touch lightly on the matter of the almanacs to justify my claim on his time; I had to enumerate everything I knew about Hester: Naples, London, Angelfield. But the gist of my letter was simple: *Find her.*

## AFTER CHARLIE

Miss Winter did not comment on my communications with her solicitor, though I am certain she was informed, just as I am certain the documents I requested would never have been sent to me without her consent. I wondered whether she might consider it cheating, whether this was the "jumping about in the story" she so disapproved of, but on the day I received the set of letters from Mr. Lomax and sent my request for help to the genealogist, she said not a word but only picked up her story where she had left it, as though none of these postal exchanges of information were happening.

Charlie was the second loss. The third if you count Isabelle, though to all practical purposes we had lost her two years before, and so she hardly counts.

John was more affected by Charlie's disappearance than by Hester's. Charlie might have been a recluse, an eccentric, a hermit, but he *was* the master of the house. Four times a year, at the sixth or seventh time of asking, he would scrawl his mark on a paper and the bank would release funds to keep the household ticking over. And now he was gone. What would become of the household? What would they do for money?

John had a few dreadful days. He insisted on cleaning up the nursery quarters—"It'll make us all ill other-wise"—and when he could bear the smell no longer, he sat on the steps outside, drawing in the clean air like a man saved from drowning. In the evening he took long baths, using up a whole bar of soap, scrubbing his skin till it glowed pink. He even soaped the inside of his nostrils.

And he cooked. We'd noticed how the Missus lost track of herself halfway through preparing a meal. The vegetables would boil to a mush, then burn on the bottom of the pan. The house was never without the smell of carbonized food. Then one day we found John in the kitchen. The hands that we knew dirty, pulling potatoes from the ground, were now rinsing the yellow-skinned vegetables in water, peeling them, rattling pan lids at the stove. We ate good meat or fish with plenty of vegetables, drank strong, hot tea. The Missus sat in her chair in the corner of the kitchen, with no apparent sense that these used to be her tasks. After the washing up, when night fell, the two of them sat talking over the kitchen table. His concerns were always the same. What would they do? How could they survive? What would become of us all?

"Don't worry, he'll come out," the Missus said.

*Come out?* John sighed and shook his head. He'd heard this before. "He's not there, Missus. He's gone, have you forgotten already?"

"Gone!" She shook her head and laughed as if he'd made a joke.

At the moment she first learned the fact of Charlie's departure, it had brushed her consciousness momentarily but had not found a place to settle there. The passages, corridors and stairwells in her mind, that connected her thoughts but also held them apart, had been undermined. Picking up one end of a trail of thought, she followed it through holes in walls, slipped into tunnels that opened beneath her feet, came to vague, semi-puzzled halts: Wasn't there something . . . ? Hadn't she been . . . ? Thinking of Charlie locked in the nursery, crazed with grief for love of his dead sister, she fell through a trapdoor in time, without even realizing it, into the thought of his father, newly bereaved, locked in the library to grieve for his lost wife.

"I know how to get him out of there," she said with a wink. "I'll take the infant to him. That'll do the trick. In fact, I'll go and look in on the baby now."

John didn't explain to her again that Isabelle had died, for it would only bring on grief-stricken surprise and a demand to know how and why. "An asylum?" she would exclaim, astonished. "But why didn't anyone tell me Miss Isabelle was in an asylum? To think of the girl's poor father! How he dotes on her! It will be the death of him." And she would lose herself for hours in the shattered corridors of the past, grieving over tragedies long gone as though they had happened only yesterday, and heedless of today's sorrows. John had been through it half a dozen times and hadn't the heart to go through it again.

Slowly the Missus raised herself out of her chair and, putting one foot painfully in front of the other, shuffled out of the room to see to the baby who, in the years her memory had lost, had grown up, married, had twins and died. John didn't stop her. She would forget where she was going before she even reached the stairs. But behind her back he put his head in his hands and sighed.

What to do? About Charlie, about the Missus, about everything? It was John's constant preoccupation. At the end of a week, the nursery was clean and a plan of sorts had arisen out of the evenings of deliberation. No reports of Charlie had been received, from near or far. No one had seen him go, and no one outside the house knew he was gone. Given his hermitlike habits, no one was likely to discover his absence, either. Was he under any kind of obligation, John wondered, to inform anyone—the doctor? the solicitor?—of Charlie's disappearance? Over and over he turned the question in his mind, and each time he found the answer to be no. A man had the perfect right to leave his home if he so chose, and to go without telling his employees his destination. There was no benefit John could see in telling the doctor, whose previous intervention in the household had brought nothing but ill, and as for the solicitor . . .

Here John's thinking out loud grew slower and more complicated. For if Charlie did not return, who would authorize the withdrawals from the bank? John knew obscurely that the solicitor would have to be involved if Charlie's disappearance was prolonged, but yet . . . His reluctance was natural. At Angelfield they had lived with their backs to the world for years. Hester had been the one outsider to enter their world, and look what had happened there! Besides, he had an innate mistrust of solicitors. John had no specific charge against Mr. Lomax, who gave every appearance of being a decent, sensible chap, yet he could not find it in himself to confide the household's difficulty to a member of a profession that made its living from having its nose in other people's private affairs. And besides, if Charlie's absence became public knowledge, as his strangeness already was, would the solicitor be content to put his sign on Charlie's bank papers, just so that John and the Missus could continue to pay the grocery bills? No. He knew enough about solicitors to know that it would not be as simple as that. John frowned as he envisaged Mr. Lomax in the house, opening doors, rummaging through cupboards, casting his eye into every dark corner and carefully cultivated shadow of the Angelfield world. There would be no end to it.

And then the solicitor would need to come to the house only once to see the Missus wasn't right. He would insist on the doctor being called in. And the same would happen to the Missus as had happened to Isabelle. She would be taken away. How could that do any good?

No. They had just got rid of one outsider; it was no time to invite in another. Much safer to deal with private things privately. Which meant, now that things were as they were, by himself.

There was no urgency. The most recent withdrawal had been only a few weeks earlier, so they were not entirely without money. Also, Hester had gone without collecting her wages, so that cash was available if she did not write for it and things got desperate. There was no need to pay for a lot of food, since there were vegetables and fruit to feed an army in the garden, and the woods were full of grouse and pheasant. And if it came to it, if there was an emergency, a calamity (John hardly knew what he meant by this—was what they had already suffered not a calamity? Was it possible that worse should be in store? Somehow he thought so), then he knew someone who would have a few discreet cases of claret out of the cellar and give him a bob or two in return.

"We'll be all right for a bit," he told the Missus, over a cigarette, one night in the kitchen. "Probably manage four months if we're careful. Don't know what we'll do then. We'll have to see."

It was a self-comforting pretense at conversation; he'd given up expecting straightforward answers from the Missus. But the habit of talking to her was too long in him to be given up lightly. So he continued to sit across the table in the kitchen, sharing his thoughts, his dreams, his worries with her. And when she answered—random, rambling drifts of words—he puzzled over her pronouncements, trying to find the connection between her answer and his question. But the labyrinth inside her head was too complex for him to navigate, and the thread that led her from one word to the next had slipped through her fingers in the darkness.

He kept food coming from the kitchen garden. He cooked; he cut up meat on the Missus's plate and put tiny forkfuls in her mouth. He poured out her cold cups of tea and made fresh ones. He was no carpenter, but he nailed fresh boards over rotten ones here and there, kept the saucepans emptied in the main rooms and stood in the attic, looking at the holes in the roof and scratching his head. "We'll have to get that sorted," he would say with an air of decision, but it wasn't raining much, and it wasn't snowing, and it was a job that could wait. There was so much else to do. He washed sheets and clothes. They dried stiff and sticky with the residue of soap flakes. He skinned rabbits and plucked pheasants and roasted them. He did the washing up and cleaned the sink. He knew what needed to be done. He had seen the Missus do it a hundred times.

From time to time he spent half an hour in the topiary garden, but he could not enjoy it. The pleasure of being there was overshadowed by worry about what might be going on indoors, in his absence. And besides, to do it properly required more time than he was able to give it. In the end, the only part of the garden that he kept up was the kitchen garden and the rest he let go.

Once we got used to it, there was a certain comfort in our new existence. The wine cellar proved a substantial and discreet source of household finance, and as time went by, our way of life began to feel sustainable. Better really if Charlie were just to stay absent. Unfound and unreturning, neither dead nor alive, he could do no harm to anyone.

So I kept my knowledge to myself.

In the woods there was a hovel. Unused for a hundred years, overgrown with thorns and surrounded by nettles, it was where Charlie and Isabelle used to go. After Isabelle was taken to the asylum, Charlie went there still; I knew, because I had seen him there, sniveling, scratching love letters on his bones with that old needle.

It was the obvious place. So when he disappeared, I had gone there again. I squeezed through the brambles and hanging growth that masked the entrance into air sweet with rottenness, and there, in the gloom, I found him. Slumped in a corner, gun by his side, face half blown away. I recognized the other half, despite the maggots. It was Charlie, all right.

I backed out of the doorway, not caring about the nettles and the thorns. I couldn't wait to get away from the sight of him. But his image stayed with me and, though I ran, it seemed impossible to escape his hollow, one-eyed stare.

Where to find comfort?

There was a house I knew. A simple little house in the woods. I had stolen food there once or twice. That was where I went. By the window I hid, getting my breath back, knowing I was close to ordinary life. And when I had stopped gasping for air, I stood looking in, at a woman in her chair, knitting. Though she didn't know I was there, her presence soothed me, like a kind grandmother in a fairy tale. I watched her, cleansing my eyes, until the vision of Charlie's body had faded and my heartbeat returned to normal.

I walked back to Angelfield. And I didn't tell. We were better off as we were. And anyway, it couldn't make any difference to him, could it?

He was the first of my ghosts.

※

It seemed to me that the doctor's car was forever in Miss Winter's drive. When I first arrived in Yorkshire he would call every third day, then it became every other day, then every day and now he was coming to the house twice a day. I studied Miss Winter carefully. I knew the facts. Miss Winter was ill. Miss Winter was dying. All the same, when she was telling me her story she seemed to draw on a well of strength that was unaffected by age and illness. I explained the paradox by telling myself it was the very constancy of the doctor's attention that was sustaining her.

And yet in ways invisible to my eyes, she must have been weakening quite seriously. For what else could explain Judith's unexpected announcement one morning? Quite out of the blue she told me that Miss Winter was too unwell to meet me. That for a day or two she would be unable to engage in our interviews. That with nothing to do here, I may as well take a short holiday.

"A holiday? After the fuss she made about my going away last time, I would have thought the last thing she would do would be to send me on a holiday now. And with Christmas only a few weeks away, too!"

Though Judith blushed, she was not forthcoming with any more information. Something wasn't right. I was being shifted out of the way.

"I can pack a case for you, if it would help?" she offered. She smiled apologetically, knowing I knew she was hiding something.

"I can do my own packing." Annoyance made me curt.

"It's Maurice's day off, but Dr. Clifton will run you to the station."

Poor Judith. She hated deceit and was no good at sub-terfuge.

"And Miss Winter? I'd like a quick word with her. Before I go."

"Miss Winter? I'm afraid she . . . ."

"Won't see me?"

"*Can't* see you." Relief flooded her face and sincerity rang out in her voice as at last she was able to say something true. "Believe me, Miss Lea. She just *can't*."

Whatever it was that Judith knew, Dr. Clifton knew it, too.

"Whereabouts in Cambridge is your father's shop?" he wanted to know, and "Does he deal in medical history at all?" I answered him briefly, more concerned with my own questions than his, and after a time his attempts at small talk came to an end. As we drove into Harrowgate, the atmosphere in the car was heavy with Miss Winter's oppressive silence.

## ANGELFIELD AGAIN

The day before, on the train, I had imagined activity and noise: shouted instructions and arms sending messages in urgent semaphore; cranes, plangent and slow; stone crashing on stone. Instead, as I arrived at the lodge gates and looked toward the demolition site, everything was silent and still.

There was nothing to see; the mist that hung in the air made everything invisible that was more than a short distance away. Even the path was indistinct. My feet were there one moment, gone the next. Lifting my head, I walked blindly, tracing the path as I remembered it from my last visit, as I remembered it from Miss Winter's descriptions.

My mind map was accurate: I came to the garden

exactly when I expected to. The dark shapes of the yew stood like a hazily painted stage set, flattened into two dimensions by the blank background. Like ethereal bowler hats, a pair of domed forms floated on the cloudlike mist, the trunks that supported them fading into the whiteness beneath. Sixty years had left them overgrown and out of shape, but it was easy today to suppose that it was the mist that was softening the geometry of the forms, that when it lifted, it would reveal the garden as it was then, in all its mathematical perfection, set in the grounds not of a demolition site, nor of a ruin, but of a house intact.

Half a century, as insubstantial as the water suspended in this air, was ready to evaporate with the first ray of winter sun.

I brought my wrist close to my face and read the time. I had arranged to meet Aurelius, but how to find him in this mist? I could wander forever without seeing him, even if he passed within arm's reach.

I called out "Hello!" and a man's voice was carried back to me.

"Hello!"

Impossible to tell whether he was distant or close by. "Where are you?"

I pictured Aurelius staring into the mist looking for a landmark.

"I'm next to a tree." The words were muffled.

"So am I," I called back. "I don't think yours is the same tree as mine. You sound too far away."

"You sound quite near, though."

"Do I? Why don't you stay where you are and keep talking, and I'll find you!"

"Right you are! An excellent plan! Though I shall have to think of something to say, won't I? How hard it is to speak to order, when it seems so easy the rest of the time. . . . What dismal weather we're having. Never known murkiness like it."

And so Aurelius thought aloud, while I stepped into a cloud and followed the thread of his voice in the air.

That is when I saw it. A shadow that glided past me, pale in the watery light. I think I knew it was not Aurelius. I was suddenly conscious of the beating of my heart, and I stretched out my hand, half fearful, half hopeful. The figure eluded me and swam out of view.

"Aurelius?" My voice sounded shaky to my own ears.

"Yes?"

"Are you still there?"

"Of course I am."

His voice was in quite the wrong direction. What had I seen? It was not Aurelius. It must have been an effect of the mist. Afraid of what I might yet see if I waited, I stood still, staring into the aqueous air, willing the figure to appear again.

"Aha! There you are!" boomed a great voice behind me. Aurelius. He clasped my shoulders in his mittened hands as I turned to face him. "Goodness gracious, Margaret, you're as white as a sheet. Anyone would think you'd seen a ghost!"

We walked together in the garden. In his overcoat,

Aurelius seemed even taller and broader than he really was. Beside him, in my mist-gray raincoat, I felt insubstantial.

"How is your book going?"

"It's just notes at the moment. Interviews with Miss Winter. And research."

"Today is research, is it?"

"Yes."

"What do you need to know?"

"I just want to take some photographs. I don't think the weather is on my side, though."

"You'll get to see it properly within the hour. This mist won't last long."

We came to a kind of walkway, lined on each side with cones grown so wide that they almost made a hedge.

"Why do *you* come here, Aurelius?"

We strolled on to the end of the path, then into a space where there seemed to be nothing but mist. When we came to a wall of yew twice as high as Aurelius himself, we followed it. I noticed a sparkling in the grass and on the leaves: The sun had come out. The moisture in the air began to evaporate and the circle of visibility grew wider by the minute. Our wall of yew had led us full circle around an empty space; we had arrived back at the same walkway we had entered by.

When my question seemed so lost in time that I was not even sure I had asked it, Aurelius answered. "I was born here."

I stopped abruptly. Aurelius wandered on, unaware of

the effect his words had had on me. I half ran a few paces to catch up with him.

"Aurelius!" I took hold of the sleeve of his greatcoat. "Is it true? Were you really born here?"

"Yes."

"When?"

He gave a strange, sad smile. "On my birthday."

Unthinking, I insisted, "Yes, but when?"

"Sometime in January, probably. Possibly February. Possibly the end of December, even. Sixty years ago, roughly. I'm afraid I don't know any more than that."

I frowned, remembered what he had told me before about Mrs. Love and not having a mother. But in what circumstances would an adopted child know so little about his original circumstances that he does not even know his own birthday?

"Do you mean to tell me, Aurelius, that you are a foundling?"

"Yes. That is the word for what I am. A foundling."

I was lost for words.

"One does get used to it, I suppose," he said, and I regretted that he had to comfort me for his own loss.

"Do you really?"

He considered me with a curious expression, no doubt wondering how much to tell me. "No, actually," he said.

With the slow and heavy steps of invalids, we resumed our walking. The mist was almost gone. The magical shapes of the topiary had lost their charm and looked like the unkempt bushes and hedges they were.

"So it was Mrs. Love who . . ." I began.

". . . found me. Yes."

"And your parents . . ."

"No idea."

"But you know it was here? In this house?"

Aurelius shoved his hands into the depths of his pockets. His shoulders tightened. "I wouldn't expect other people to understand. I haven't got any proof. *But I do know.*" He sent me a quick glance, and I encouraged him, with my eyes, to continue.

"Sometimes you can know things. Things about yourself. Things from before you can remember. I can't explain it."

I nodded, and Aurelius went on.

"The night I was found there was a big fire here. Mrs. Love told me so, when I was nine. She thought she should, because of the smell of smoke on my clothes when she found me. Later I came over to have a look. And I've been coming ever since. Later I looked it up in the archives of the local paper. Anyway—"

His voice had the unmistakable lightness of someone telling something extremely important. A story so cherished it had to be dressed in casualness to disguise its significance in case the listener turned out to be unsympathetic.

"Anyway, the minute I got here I knew. *This is home,* I said to myself. *This is where I come from.* There was no doubt about it. I knew."

With his last words, Aurelius had let the lightness slip, allowed a fervor to creep in. He cleared his throat.

"Obviously I don't expect anyone to believe it. I've no evidence as such. Only a coincidence of dates, and Mrs. Love's vague memory of a smell of smoke—and my own conviction."

"I believe it," I said.

Aurelius bit his lip and sent me a wary sideways look.

His confidences, this mist, had led us unexpectedly onto a peninsula of intimacy, and I found myself on the brink of telling what I had never told anyone before. The words flew ready-formed into my head, organized themselves instantly into sentences, long strings of sentences, bursting with impatience to fly from my tongue. As if they had spent years planning for this moment.

"I believe you," I repeated, my tongue thick with all the waiting words. "I've had that feeling, too. Knowing things you can't know. From before you can remember."

And there it was again! A sudden movement in the corner of my eye, there and gone in the same instant.

"Did you see that, Aurelius?"

He followed my gaze to the topiary pyramids and beyond. "See what? No, I didn't see anything."

It had gone. Or else it had never been there at all.

I turned back to Aurelius, but I had lost my nerve. The moment for confidences was gone.

"Have *you* got a birthday?" Aurelius asked.

"Yes. I've got a birthday."

All my unsaid words went back to wherever they had been all these years.

"I'll make a note of it, shall I?" he said brightly. "Then I can send you a card."

I feigned a smile. "It's coming up soon, actually. "

Aurelius opened a little blue notebook divided into months.

"The nineteenth," I told him, and he wrote it down with a pencil so small it looked like a toothpick in his huge hand.

## MRS. LOVE TURNS A HEEL

When it started to rain we put our hoods up and made our way hurriedly to the shelter of the church. In the porch we did a little jig to drive the raindrops off our coats, and then went inside.

We sat in a pew near the altar and I stared up at the pale, vaulted ceiling until I made myself dizzy.

"Tell me about when you were found," I said. "What do you know about it?"

"I know what Mrs. Love told me," he answered. "I can tell you that. And of course there's always my inheritance."

"You have an inheritance?"

"Yes. It's nothing much. Not what people usually mean when they talk about an inheritance, but all the same . . . In fact, I could show it to you later."

"That would be nice."

"Yes . . . Because I was thinking, nine is a bit too adjacent to breakfast for cake, isn't it?" It was said with a reluctant grimace that turned into a gleam with his next words: "So I thought, Invite Margaret back for elevenses. Cake and coffee, how does that sound? You could do with feeding up. And I'll show you my inheritance at the same time. What little there is to see."

I accepted the invitation.

Aurelius took his glasses from his pocket and began to polish them absently with a handkerchief.

"Well now." Slowly he took a deep breath. Slowly he exhaled. "As it was told to me. Mrs. Love, and her story."

His face settled into passive neutrality, a sign that, in the way of all storytellers, he was disappearing to make way for the voice of the story itself. And then he recited, and from his very first words, at the heart of his voice, it was Mrs. Love I heard, conjured from the grave by the memory of her story.

Her story, and Aurelius's, and also, perhaps, Emmeline's.

There was a pitch-black sky that night, and a storm was brewing in it. In the treetops the wind was whistling, and it was raining fit to break the windows. I was knitting in this chair by the fire, a gray sock it was, the second one, and I was just turning the heel. Well, I felt a shiver. Not that I was cold, mind you. I'd a nice lot of firewood piled up in the log basket that I'd brought in from the shed that afternoon, and I'd only just put another log on. So I wasn't cold, not at all, but I thought to myself, What a night, I'm glad I'm not some poor soul caught outdoors away from home on a night like this, and it was thinking of that poor soul as made me shiver.

Everything was quiet indoors, only the crack of the fire every so often, and the click-click of the knitting needles, and my sighs. My sighs, you say? Well, yes, my sighs. Because I wasn't happy. I'd fallen into remembering, and that's a bad habit for a woman of fifty. I'd got a warm fire, a roof over my head and a cooked dinner inside me, but was I content? Not I. So there I sat sighing over my gray sock, while the rain kept coming. After a time I got up to fetch a slice of plum cake from the pantry, nice and mature, fed with brandy. Cheered me up no end. But when I came back and picked up my knitting, my heart quite turned over. Do you know why? I'd turned the heel of that sock twice!

Now that bothered me. It really bothered me, because I'm a careful knitter, not slapdash like my sister Kitty used to be, nor half blind like my poor old mother when she got near the end. I'd only made that mistake twice in my life.

The first time I turned a heel too often was when I was a young thing. A sunny afternoon. I was sitting by an open window, enjoying the smell of everything blooming in the garden. It was a blue sock then. For . . . well, for a young man. My young man. I won't tell you his name, there's no need. Well, I'd been daydreaming. Silly. White dresses and white cakes and a lot of nonsense like that. And all of a sudden I looked down and saw that I'd turned the heel twice. There it was, plain as day. A ribbed leg part, a heel, more ribbing for the foot and then—another heel. I laughed out loud. It didn't matter. Easy enough to undo it and put it right.

I'd already drawn the needles out when Kitty came running up the garden path. What's up with her? I thought, all of a hurry. I saw her face was greenish white, and then she stopped dead the minute she saw me through the window. That's when I knew it wasn't a trouble for her but for me. She opened her mouth but she couldn't even say my name. She was crying. And then out she came with it.

There'd been an accident. He'd been out with his brother, my young man. After some grouse. Where they didn't ought to have been. Someone saw them and they took fright. Ran off. Daniel, the brother, he got to the stile first and hopped over. My young man, he was too hasty. His gun got caught in the stile. He should have slowed down, taken his time. He heard footsteps coming after them and panicked. Yanked at the gun. I don't need to spell it out, do I? You can guess what happened.

I undid my knitting. All those little knots that you make one after another, row by row, to knit a sock, I undid them. It's easy. Take the needles out, a little tug and they just fall apart. One after another, row by row. I undid the extra heel and then I just kept going. The foot, the first heel, the ribbing of the leg. All those loops unraveling themselves as you pull the wool. Then there was nothing left to unravel, only a pile of crinkled blue wool in my lap.

It doesn't take long to knit a sock and it takes a lot less to undo it.

I expect I wound the blue wool into a ball to make something else. But I don't remember that.

The second time I turned a heel twice, I was beginning to get old. Kitty and me were sitting by the fireside here, together. It was a year since her husband had died, nearly a year since she'd come to live with me. She was getting so much better, I thought. She'd been smiling more. Taking an interest in things. She could hear his name without welling up. We sat here and I was knitting—a nice pair of bed socks it was, for Kitty, softest lambs' wool, pink to go with her dressing gown—and she had a book in her lap. She can't have been looking at it, though, because she said, "Joan, you've turned that heel twice."

I held up my work and she was right. "Well, I'm blowed," I said.

She said if it had been her knitting, she wouldn't be surprised. She was always turning heels twice, or else forgetting to turn at all. More than once she'd knitted a sock for her man with no heel, just a leg and a toe. We laughed. But she was surprised at me, she said. It wasn't like me to be so absentminded.

"Well," I said, "I have made this mistake before. Only the once." And I reminded her of what I've just told you. All about my young man. And while I was reminiscing aloud, I carefully undid the second heel and got started to put it right. Takes a bit of concentration, and the light was going. Well, I finished my story, and she didn't say anything, and I thought she was thinking about her husband. You know, me talking about my loss all those years ago, and hers so recent by comparison.

It was too dark to finish the toe properly, so I put it aside and looked up. "Kitty?" I said. "Kitty?" There was no answer. I did for a moment think she might be asleep. But she wasn't.

She looked so peaceful there. She had a smile on her face. As if she was happy to be back with him. Back with her husband. In the time I'd been peering at that bed sock in the dark, chattering away with my old story, she'd gone to him.

So it bothered me, that night of the pitch-black sky, to find that I'd knitted a second heel. Once I'd done it and lost my young man. Twice and I'd lost my sister. Now a third time. I had no one left to lose. There was only me now.

I looked at the sock. Gray wool. A plain thing. It was meant for me.

Perhaps it didn't matter, I told myself. Who was there to miss me? No one would suffer from my going. That was a blessing. After all, at least I'd *had* a life, not like my young man. And also I remembered the look on Kitty's face, that happy, peaceful look. Can't be so bad, I thought.

I set to unraveling the extra heel. What was the point of that, you might wonder. Well, I didn't want to be found with it. "Silly old woman," I imagined them saying. "They found her with her knitting in her lap, and guess what? She'd turned her heel twice." I didn't want them saying that. So I undid it. And as I worked I was readying myself to go, in my mind.

I don't know how long I sat there like that. But eventually a noise found its way into my ear. From out-of-doors. A cry, like some lost animal. I was away in my thoughts, not expecting anything to come now between me and my end, so at first I paid no notice. But I heard it again. It seemed to be calling me. For who else was going to hear it, stuck out here in the middle of nowhere? I thought perhaps it was a cat, lost its mother or something. And although I was preparing to meet my maker, the image of this little cat, with its wet fur, kept distracting me. And I thought, Just because I'm dying, that's no reason to deny one of God's creatures a bit of warmth and something to eat. And I might as well tell you, I didn't mind the thought of having some living creature by me right at that moment. So I went to the door.

And what did I find there?

Tucked in the porch, out of the rain, a baby! Swaddled in canvas, mewling like a kitten. Poor little mite. Cold and wet and hungry, you were. I could hardly believe my eyes. I bent down and picked you up, and the minute you saw me you stopped crying.

I didn't linger outdoors. You wanted feeding and some dry things. So no, I didn't stop long in the porch. Just a quick look. Nothing there. Nobody at all. Just the

wind rustling the trees at the edge of the wood, and—
odd this—smoke rising into the sky off toward
Angelfield?

I clutched you to me, came inside and closed the door.

Twice before I had knitted two heels into a sock, and
death had come close to me. The third time, and it was
life that came to the door. That taught me not to go
reading too much into coincidences. I had no time to be
thinking about death after that, anyway.

I had you to think about.

And we lived happily ever after.

❦

Aurelius swallowed. His voice had grown hoarse and
broken. The words had come out of him like an incantation; words that he had heard a thousand times as a
boy, repeated inside himself for decades as a man.

When the story was finished, we sat in silence, contemplating the altar. Outside the rain continued to fall,
unhurried. Aurelius was still as a statue by my side,
yet his thoughts, I suspected, were anything but quiet.

There were lots of things I might have said, but I said
nothing. I just waited for him to return to the present in
his own time. When he did, he spoke to me.

"The thing is, it's not my story, is it? I mean, I'm in it,
that's obvious, but it's not my story. It belongs to Mrs.
Love. The man she wanted to marry; her sister Kitty;
her knitting. Her baking. All that is her story. And then
just when she thinks it's all coming to an end, I arrive
and give the story a new start.

"But that doesn't make it my story, does it? Because

*before* she opened the door . . . *before* she heard the sound in the night . . . *before*—"

He halted, breathless, made a gesture to cut off his sentence and start again:

"Because for someone to *find* a baby like that, just *find* him, all alone like that in the rain, it means that *before* then, in order for it to happen, of necessity—"

Another frantic erasing gesture of the hands, eyes ranging wildly around the church ceiling as though somewhere he would spot the verb he needed that would allow him finally to anchor what it was he wanted to say:

"Because if Mrs. Love *found me,* it can only mean that before that happened, someone else, some other person, some *mother* must have—"

There it was. That verb.

His face froze into despair. His hands, halfway through an agitated gesture, were arrested in an attitude that suggested a plea or a prayer.

There are times when the human face and body can express the yearning of the heart so accurately that you can, as they say, read them like a book. I read Aurelius.

*Do not abandon me.*

I touched my hand to his, and the statue returned to life.

"There's no point waiting for the rain to stop," I whispered. "It's set in for the day. My photos can wait. We may as well go."

"Yes," he said, with a gruff edge in his throat. "We may as well."

It's a mile and a half direct," he said, pointing into the woods, "longer by road."

We crossed the deer park and had nearly reached the edge of the woods when we heard voices. It was a woman's voice that swam through the rain, up the gravel drive to her children and over the park as far as us. "I told you, Tom. It's too wet. They can't work when it's raining like this." The children had come to a halt in disappointment at seeing the stationary cranes and machinery. With their sou'westers over their blond heads, I could not tell them apart. The woman caught up with them, and the family huddled for a moment in a brief conference of mackintoshes.

Aurelius was rapt by the family tableau.

"I've seen them before," I said. "Do you know who they are?"

"They're a family. They live in The Street. The house with the swing. Karen looks after the deer here."

"Do they still hunt here?"

"No. She just looks after them. They're a nice family."

Enviously he gazed after them, then he broke his attention with a shake of his head. "Mrs. Love was very good to me," he said, "and I loved her. All this other stuff—" He made a dismissive gesture and turned toward the woods. "Come on. Let's go home."

The family in mackintoshes, turning back toward the

lodge gates, had clearly reached the same decision.

Aurelius and I walked through the woods in silent friendship.

There were no leaves to cut out the light and the branches, blackened by rain, reached dark across the watery sky. Stretching out an arm to push away low branches, Aurelius dislodged extra raindrops to add to those that fell on us from the sky. We came across a fallen tree and leaned over it, staring into the dark pool of rain in its hollow that had softened the rotting bark almost to fur.

Then, "Home," Aurelius pronounced.

It was a small stone cottage. Built for endurance rather than decoration, but attractive all the same, in its simple and solid lines. Aurelius led me around the side of the house. Was it a hundred years old or two hundred? It was hard to tell. It wasn't the kind of house that a hundred years made much difference to. Except that at the back there was a large new extension, almost as large as the house itself, and taken up entirely with a kitchen.

"My sanctuary," he said as he showed me in.

A massive stainless-steel oven, white walls, two vast fridges—it was a real kitchen for a real cook.

Aurelius pulled out a chair for me and I sat at a small table by a bookcase. The shelves were filled with cookbooks, in French, English, Italian. One book, unlike the others, was out on the table. It was a thick notebook, corners blunt with age, and covered in brown paper that had gone transparent after decades of being handled with buttery fingers. Someone had written *RECIPIES* on the front, in old-fashioned, school-formed capitals. Some years later the writer had crossed out the second *I*, using a different pen.

"May I?" I asked.

"Of course."

I opened the book and began to leaf through it. Victoria sponge, date and walnut loaf, scones, ginger cake, maids of honor, bakewell tart, rich fruit cake . . . the spelling and the handwriting improving as the pages turned.

Aurelius turned a dial on the oven, then, moving lightly, assembled his ingredients. After that everything was within reach, and he stretched out an arm for a sieve or a knife without looking. He moved in his kitchen the way drivers change gear in their cars: an arm reaching out smoothly, independently, knowing exactly what to do, while his eyes never left the fixed spot in front of him: the bowl in which he was combining his ingredients. He sieved flour, chopped butter into dice, zested an orange. It was as natural as breathing.

"You see that cupboard?" he said "There to your left? Would you open it?"

Thinking he wanted a piece of equipment, I opened the cupboard door.

"You'll find a bag hanging on a peg inside."

It was a kind of satchel. Old and curiously designed, its sides were not stitched but just tucked in. It fastened with a buckle, and a long, broad leather strap, attached with a rusty clasp at each side, allowed you presumably to wear it diagonally across your body. The leather was dry and cracked, and the canvas that might once have been khaki was now just the color of age.

"What is it?" I asked.

For a second he raised his eyes from the bowl to me.

"It's the bag I was found in."

He turned back to combining his ingredients.

*The bag he was found in?* My eyes moved slowly from the satchel to Aurelius. Even bent over his kneading he was over six feet tall. I had thought him a storybook giant when I first set eyes on him, I remembered. Today the strap wouldn't even go around his girth, yet sixty years ago he had been small enough to fit inside. Dizzy at the thought of what time can do, I sat down again. Who was it that had placed a baby in this satchel so long ago? Folded its canvas around him, fastened the buckle against the weather and placed the strap over her body to carry him, through the night, to Mrs. Love's? I ran my fingers over the places she had touched. Canvas, buckle, strap. Seeking some trace of her. A clue, in Braille or invisible ink or code, that my touch might reveal if only it knew how. It did not know how.

"It's exasperating, isn't it?" Aurelius said.

I heard him slide something into the oven and close the door, then I felt him behind me, looking over my shoulder.

"You open it—I've got flour on my hands."

I undid the buckle and opened the pleats of canvas. They unfolded into a flat circle in the center of which lay a tangle of paper and rag.

"My inheritance," he announced.

The things looked like a pile of discarded junk waiting to be swept into the bin, but he gazed at them with the intensity of a boy staring at a treasure trove. "These things are my story," he said. "These things tell me who I am. It's just a matter of . . . of *understanding* them." His bafflement was intent but resigned. "I've tried all my life to piece them together. I keep thinking, If only I could find the thread . . . it would all fall into place. Take that, for instance—"

It was a piece of cloth. Linen, once white, now yellow. I disentangled it from the other objects and smoothed it out. It was embroidered with a pattern of stars and flowers also in white; there were four dainty mother-of-pearl buttons; it was an infant's dress or nightgown. Aurelius's broad fingers hovered over the tiny garment, wanting to touch, not wanting to mark it with flour. The narrow sleeves would just fit over a finger now.

"It's what I was wearing," Aurelius explained.

"It's very old."

"As old as me, I suppose."

"Older than that, even."

"Do you think so?"

"Look at the stitching here—and here. It's been mended more than once. And this button doesn't match. Other babies wore this before you."

His eyes flitted from the scrap of linen to me and back to the cloth, hungry for knowledge.

"And there's this." He pointed at a page of print. It was torn from a book and riddled with creases. Taking it in my hands I started to read.

"*. . . not at first aware what was his intention; but when I saw him lift and poise the book and stand in act to hurl it, I instinctively started aside with a cry of alarm—*"

Aurelius took up the phrase and continued, reading not from the page but from memory: "*. . . not soon enough however; the volume was flung, it hit me, and I fell, striking my head against the door and cutting it.*"

Of course I recognized it. How could I not, for I had read it goodness knows how many times. "*Jane Eyre,*" I said wonderingly.

"You recognized it? Yes, it is. I asked a man in a library. It's by Charlotte someone. She had a lot of sisters, apparently."

"Have you read it?"

"Started to. It was about a little girl. She's lost her family, and so her aunt takes her in. I thought I was on to something with that. Nasty woman, the aunt, not like Mrs. Love at all. This is one of her cousins throwing the book at her, on this page. But later she goes to school, a terrible school, terrible food, but she does make a friend." He smiled, remembering his reading. "Only then the friend died." His face fell. "And after that . . . I seemed to lose interest. Didn't read the end. I couldn't see how it fitted after that." He shrugged off his puzzlement. "Have you read it? What happened to her in the end? Is it relevant?"

"She falls in love with her employer. His wife—she's mad, lives in the house but secretly—tries to burn the house down, and Jane goes away. When she comes back, the wife has died, and Mr. Rochester is blind, and Jane marries him."

"Ah." His forehead wrinkled as he tried to puzzle it all out. But he gave up. "No. It doesn't make sense, does it? The beginning, perhaps. The girl without the mother. But after that . . . I wish someone could tell me what it means. I wish there was someone who could just *tell me the truth.*"

He turned back to the torn-out page. "Probably it's not the book that's important at all. Perhaps it's just this page. Perhaps it has some secret meaning. Look here—"

Inside the back cover of his childhood recipe book were tightly packed columns and rows of numbers and letters written in a large, boyish hand. "I used to think it was a code," he explained. "I tried to decipher it. I tried the first letter of every word, the first of every line. Or the second. Then I tried replacing one letter for another." He pointed to his various trials, eyes feverish, as though there was still a chance he might see something that had escaped him before.

I knew it was hopeless.

"What about this?" I picked up the next object and couldn't help giving a shudder. Clearly it had been a feather once, but now it was a nasty, dirty-looking thing. Its oils dried up, the barbs had separated into stiff brown spikes along the cracked spine.

Aurelius shrugged his shoulders and shook his head in helpless ignorance, and I dropped the feather with relief.

And then there was just one more thing. "Now this . . ." Aurelius began, but he didn't finish. It was a scrap of paper, roughly torn, with a faded ink stain that might once have been a word. I peered at it closely.

"I think—" Aurelius stuttered, "well, Mrs. Love thought— We both agreed, in fact"—he looked at me in hope—"that it must be my name."

He pointed. "It got wet in the rain, but here, just here—" He led me to the window, gestured at me to hold the paper scrap up to the light. "Something like an *A* at the beginning. And then an *S*. Just here, toward the end. Of course, it's faded a bit, over the years; you have to look hard, but you *can* see it, can't you?"

I stared at the stain.

"*Can't* you?"

I made a vague motion with my head, neither nod nor shake.

"You see! It's obvious when you know what you're looking for, isn't it?"

I continued to look, but the phantom letters that he could see were invisible to my eye.

"And *that*," he was saying, "is how Mrs. Love settled on Aurelius. Though I might just as easily be Alphonse, I suppose."

He laughed at himself, sadly, uneasily, and turned

away. "The only other thing was the spoon. But you've seen that." He reached into his top pocket and took out the silver spoon I had seen at our first meeting, when we ate ginger cake while sitting on the giant cats flanking the steps of Angelfield House.

"And the bag itself," I wondered. "What kind of a bag is it?"

"Just a bag," he said vaguely. He lifted it to his face and sniffed it delicately. "It used to smell of smoke, but not anymore." He passed it to me, and I bent my nose to it. "You see? It's faded now."

Aurelius opened the oven door and took out a tray of pale gold biscuits that he set to cool. Then he filled the kettle and prepared a tray. Cups and saucers, a sugar bowl, a milk jug and little plates.

"You take this," he said, passing the tray to me. He opened a door that showed a glimpse of a sitting room, old comfy chairs and floral cushions. "Make yourself at home. I'll bring the rest in a minute." He kept his back to me, head bowed as he washed his hands. "I'll be with you when I've put these things away."

I went into Mrs. Love's front room and sat in a chair by the fireplace, leaving him to stow his inheritance— his invaluable, indecipherable inheritance—safely away.

※※

I left the house with something scratching at my mind. Was it something Aurelius had said? Yes. Some echo or connection had vaguely appealed for my attention but had been swept away by the rest of his story. It didn't matter. It would come back to me.

In the woods there is a clearing. Beneath it, the ground falls away steeply and is covered in patchy scrub before it levels out and there are trees again. Because of this, it provides an unexpected vantage point from which to view the house. It was in this clearing that I stopped, on my way back from Aurelius's cottage.

The scene was bleak. The house, or what remained of it, was ghostly. A smudge of gray against a gray sky. The upper stories on the left-hand side were all gone. The ground floor remained, the door frame demarcated by its dark stone lintel and the steps that led up to it, but the door itself was gone. It was not a day to be open to the elements, and I shivered for the half-dismantled house. Even the stone cats had abandoned it. Like the deer, they had taken themselves off out of the wet. The right-hand side of the building was still largely intact, though to judge by the position of the crane it would be next to go. Was all that machinery really necessary? I caught myself thinking. For it looked as if the walls were simply dissolving in the rain; those stones still standing, pale and insubstantial as rice paper, seemed ready to melt away under my very eyes if I just stood there long enough.

My camera was slung around my neck. I disentangled it from under my coat and raised it to my eyes. Was it possible to capture the evanescent appearance of the house through all this wetness? I doubted it but was willing to try.

I was adjusting the long-distance lens when I caught a slight movement at the edge of the frame. Not my ghost. The children were back. They had seen something in the grass, were bending over it excitedly. What was it? A hedgehog? A snake? Curious, I fine-tuned the focus to see more clearly.

One of the children reached into the long grass and lifted the discovery out of it. It was a yellow builder's hat. With a delighted smile he pushed back his sou'wester—I could see it was the boy now—and placed the hat on his head. Stiff as a soldier he stood, chest out, head up, arms by his side, face intent with concentration to keep the too-large hat from slipping.

Just as he struck his pose there came a small miracle. A shaft of sunlight found its way through a gap in the cloud and fell upon the boy, illuminating him in his moment of glory. I clicked the shutter and my photo was taken. The boy in the hat, over his left shoulder a yellow Keep Out sign, and to his right, in the background, the house, a dismal smudge of gray.

The sun disappeared, and I took my eye off the children to wind the film and tuck my camera away in the dry. When I looked back, the children were halfway down the drive. His left hand in her right, they were whirling around and around as they approached the lodge gates, equal stride, equal weight, each one a perfect counterbalance to the other. With the tails of their mackintoshes flaring behind them, feet barely skimming the ground, they looked as if they were about to lift into the air and fly.

When I went back to Yorkshire, I received no explanation for my banishment. Judith greeted me with a constrained smile. The grayness of the daylight had crept under her skin, collected in shadows under her eyes. She pulled the curtains back a few more inches in my sitting room, exposing a bit more window, but it made no difference to the gloom. "Blasted weather," she exclaimed, and I thought she seemed at the end of her tether.

Though it was only days, it felt like an eternity. Often night, but never quite day, the darkening effect of the heavy sky threw us all out of time. Miss Winter arrived late to one of our morning meetings. She, too, was pale-faced; I didn't know whether it was the memory of recent pain that put the darkness in her eyes or something else.

"I propose a more flexible timetable for our meetings," she said when she was settled in her circle of light.

"Of course." I knew of her bad nights from my interview with the doctor, could see when the medication she took to control her pain was wearing off or had not yet taken full effect. And so we agreed that instead of presenting myself at nine every morning, I would wait instead for a tap at my door.

At first the tap came always between nine and ten. Then it drifted to later. After the doctor altered her dosage, she took to asking for me early in the mornings, but our meetings were shorter; then we fell into a habit of meeting twice or three times a day, at random times. Sometimes she called me when she felt well and spoke at length, and in detail. At other times she called me when she was in pain. Then it was not so much the company she wanted as the anesthetic qualities of the storytelling itself.

The end of my nine o'clocks was another anchor in time gone. I listened to her story, I wrote the story, when I slept I dreamed the story, and when I was awake it was the story that formed the constant backdrop of my thoughts. It was like living entirely inside a book. I didn't even need to emerge to eat, for I could sit at my desk reading my transcript while I ate the meals that Judith brought to my room. Porridge meant it was morning. Soup and salad meant lunchtime. Steak and kidney pie was evening. I remember pondering for a long time over a dish of scrambled egg. What did it mean? It could mean anything. I ate a few mouthfuls and pushed the plate away.

In this long, undifferentiated lapse of time, there were a few incidents that stood out. I noted them at the time, separately from the story, and they are worth recalling here.

This is one.

I was in the library. I was looking for *Jane Eyre* and found almost a whole shelf of copies. It was the collection of a fanatic: There were cheap, modern copies, with no secondhand value; editions that came up so rarely on the market it would be hard to put a price to them; copies that fell at every point between these two extremes. The one I was looking for was an ordinary, though particular, edition from the turn of the century. While I was browsing, Judith brought Miss Winter in and settled her in her chair by the fire.

When Judith had gone, Miss Winter asked, "What are you looking for?"

"*Jane Eyre.*"

"Do you like *Jane Eyre*?" she asked.

"Very much. Do you?"

"Yes."

She shivered.

"Shall I stoke up the fire for you?"

She lowered her eyelids as if a wave of pain had come over her. "I suppose so."

Once the fire was burning strongly again, she said, "Do you have a moment? Sit down, Margaret."

And after a minute of silence she said this.

"Picture a conveyor belt, a huge conveyor belt, and at the end of it a massive furnace. And on the conveyor belt are books. Every copy in the world of every book you've ever loved. All lined up. *Jane Eyre. Villette. The Woman in White.*"

"*Middlemarch*," I supplied

"Thank you. *Middlemarch*. And imagine a lever with two labels, On and Off. At the moment the lever is off. And next to it is a human being, with his hand on the lever. About to turn it on. And you can stop it. You have a gun in your hand. All you have to do is pull the trigger. What do you do?"

"No, that's silly."

"He turns the lever to On. The conveyor belt has started."

"But it's too extreme, it's hypothetical."

"First of all, *Shirley* goes over the edge."

"I don't like games like this."

"Now George Sand starts to go up in flames."

I sighed and closed my eyes.

"*Wuthering Heights* coming up. Going to let that burn, are you?"

I couldn't help myself. I saw the books, saw their steady process to the mouth of the furnace, and flinched.

"Suit yourself. In it goes. Same for *Jane Eyre*?"

*Jane Eyre.* I was suddenly dry-mouthed.

"All you have to do is shoot. I won't tell. No one need ever know." She waited. "They've started to fall. Just the first few. But there are a lot of copies. You have a moment to make up your mind."

I rubbed my thumb nervously against a rough edge of nail on my middle finger.

"They're falling faster now."

She did not remove her gaze from me.

"Half of them gone. Think, Margaret. All of *Jane Eyre* will soon have disappeared forever. Think."

Miss Winter blinked.

"Two thirds gone. Just one person, Margaret. Just one tiny, insignificant little person."

I blinked.

"Still time, but only just. Remember, this person burns books. Does he really deserve to live?"

Blink. Blink.

"Last chance."

Blink. Blink. Blink.

*Jane Eyre* was no more.

*"Margaret!"* Miss Winter's face twisted in vexation as she spoke; she beat her left hand against the arm of her chair. Even the right hand, injured though it was, twitched in her lap.

Later, when I transcribed it, I thought it was the most spontaneous expression of feeling I had ever seen in Miss Winter. It was a surprising amount of feeling to invest in a mere game.

And my own feelings? Shame. For I had lied. Of course I loved books more than people. Of course I valued *Jane Eyre* over the anonymous stranger with his hand on the lever. Of course all of Shakespeare was worth more than a human life. Of course. Unlike Miss Winter, I had been ashamed to say so.

On my way out, I returned to the shelf of *Jane Eyre*s and took the one volume that met my criteria. Right age, right kind of paper, right typeface. In my room I turned the pages till I found the place.

*". . . not at first aware what was his intention; but when I saw him lift and poise the book and stand in act to hurl it, I instinctively started aside with a cry of alarm—not soon enough however; the volume was flung, it hit me, and I fell, striking my head against the door and cutting it."*

The book was intact. Not a single page was missing. This was not the volume Aurelius's page had been torn from. But in any case, why should it be? If his page had come from Angelfield—*if* it had—then it would have burned with the rest of the house.

For a time I sat doing nothing, only thinking of *Jane Eyre* and a library and a furnace and a house fire, but no matter how I combined and recombined them, I could not make sense of it.

The other thing I remember from this time was the incident of the photograph. A small parcel appeared with my breakfast tray one morning, addressed to me in my father's narrow handwriting. It was my photographs of Angelfield; I had sent him the canister of film, and he had had it developed for me. There were a few clear pictures from my first day: brambles growing through the wreckage of the library, ivy snaking its way up the stone staircase. I halted at the picture of the bedroom where I had come face-to-face with my ghost; over the old fireplace there was only the glare of a flashbulb reflected. Still, I took it out of the bundle and tucked it inside the cover of my book, to keep.

The rest of the photographs were from my second visit, when the weather had been against me. Most of them were nothing but puzzling compositions of murkiness. What I *remembered* was shades of gray overlaid with silver; the mist moving like a veil of gauze; my own breath at tipping point between air and water. But my camera had captured none of that, nor was it possible in the dark smudges that interrupted the gray to make out a stone, a wall, a tree or a forest. After half a dozen such pictures, I gave up looking. Stuffing the wad of photos in my cardigan pocket, I went downstairs to the library.

We were about halfway through the interview when I became aware of a silence. I was dreaming. Lost, as usual, in her world of childhood twinship. I replayed the sound track of her voice, recalled a changed tone, the fact that she had addressed me, but could not recall the words.

"What?" I said.

"Your pocket," she repeated. "You have something in your pocket."

"Oh . . . It's some photographs . . ." In that limbo state halfway between a story and your life, when you haven't caught up with your wits yet, I mumbled on. "Angelfield," I said.

By the time I returned to myself, the pictures were in her hands.

At first she looked closely at each one, straining through her glasses to make sense of the blurred shapes. As one indecipherable image followed another, she let out a small Vida Winter sigh, one that implied her low expectations had been amply fulfilled, and her mouth tightened into a critical line. With her good hand she began to flick through the pile of pictures more cursorily; to show that she no longer expected to find anything of interest, she tossed each one after the briefest glance onto the table at her side.

I was mesmerized by the discarded photos landing at

a regular rhythm on the table. They formed a messy sprawl on the surface, flopping on top of each other and gliding over each other's slippery surfaces with a sound like *useless, useless, useless.*

Then the rhythm came to a halt. Miss Winter was sitting with intent rigidity, holding up a single picture and studying it with a frown. She's seen a ghost, I thought. Then, after a long moment, pretending not to feel my gaze upon her, she tucked the photo behind the remaining dozen and looked at the rest, tossing them down just as before. When the one that had arrested her attention resurfaced, she barely glanced at it but added it to the others. "I wouldn't have been able to tell it was Angelfield, but if you say so . . ." she said icily, and then, in an apparently artless movement, she picked up the whole pile and, holding them toward me, dropped them.

"My hand. Do excuse me," she murmured as I bent down to retrieve the pictures, but I wasn't deceived.

And she picked up her story where she had left it.

Later I looked through the pictures again. For all that the dropping of the photos had muddled the order, it wasn't difficult to tell which one had struck her so forcefully. In the bundle of blurred gray images there was really only one that stood out from the rest. I sat on the edge of my bed, looking at the image, remembering the moment well. The thinning of the mist and the warming of the sun had combined at just the right time to allow a ray of light to fall onto a boy who posed stiffly for the camera, chin up, back straight, eyes betraying the anxious knowledge that at any minute his hard yellow hat was going to slip sideways on his head.

Why had she been so taken by that photograph? I scanned the background, but the house, half demolished already, was only a dismal smear of gray over the child's right shoulder. Closer to him, all that was visible was the grille of the safety barrier and the corner of the Keep Out sign.

Was it the boy himself who interested her?

I puzzled over the picture for half an hour, but by the time I came to put it away, I was no nearer an explanation. Because it perplexed me, I slipped it inside the cover of my book along with the picture of an absence in a mirror frame.

Apart from the photograph of the boy and the game of *Jane Eyre* and the furnace, not much else pierced the cloak the story had cast over me.

The cat, I remember. He took note of my unusual hours, came scratching at my door for a bit of fuss at random hours of the day and night. Finished up bits of egg or fish from my plate. He liked to sit on my piles of paper, watching me write. For hours I could sit scratching at my pages, wandering in the dark labyrinth of Miss Winter's story, but no matter how far I forgot myself, I never quite lost my sense of being watched over, and when I got particularly lost, it was the gaze of the cat that seemed to reach into my muddle and light my way back to my room, my notes, my pencils and my pencil sharpener. He even slept with me on my bed some nights, and I took to leaving my curtains open so that if he woke he could sit on my windowsill seeing things move in the dark that were invisible to the human eye.

And that is all. Apart from these things there was nothing else. Only the eternal twilight and the story.

## COLLAPSE

Isabelle had gone. Hester had gone. Charlie had gone. Now Miss Winter told me of further losses.

๑๑

Up in the attic I leaned with my back against the creaking wall. I pressed back to make it give, then released it. Over and over. I was tempting fate. What would happen, I wondered, if the wall came down? Would the roof cave in? Would the weight of it falling cause the floorboards to collapse? Would roof tiles and beams and stone come crashing through ceilings onto the beds and boxes as if there were an earthquake? And then what? Would it stop there? How far would it go? I rocked and rocked, taunting the wall, daring it to fall, but it didn't. Even under duress, it is astonishing just how long a dead wall will stay standing.

Then, in the middle of the night, I woke up, ears ajangle. The noise of it was finished already, but I could still feel it resounding in my eardrums and in my chest. I leaped out of bed and ran to the stairs, Emmeline at my heels.

We arrived on the galleried landing at the same time that John, who slept in the kitchen, arrived at the foot of the stairs, and we all stared. In the middle of the hallway the Missus was standing in her nightdress, staring upward. At her feet was a huge block of stone, and above her head, a jagged hole in the ceiling. The air was thick with gray dust. It rose and fell in the air, undecided where to settle. Fragments of plaster, mortar, wood were still falling from the floor above, with a sound like mice scattering, and from time to time I felt Emmeline jump as planks and bricks fell in the floors above.

The stone steps were cold, then splinters of wood and shards of plaster and mortar dug into my feet. In the center of all the detritus of our broken house, with the swirls of dust slowly settling around her, the Missus stood like a ghost. Dust-gray hair, dust-gray face and hands, dust-gray the folds of her long nightdress. She stood perfectly still and looked up. I came close to her and joined my stare to hers. We gazed through the hole in the ceiling, and beyond that another hole in another ceiling and then yet another hole in another ceiling. We saw the peony wallpaper in the bedroom above, the ivy trellis pattern in the room above that, and the pale gray walls of the little attic room. Above all of that, high above our heads, we saw the hole in the roof itself and the sky. There were no stars.

I took her hand. "Come on," I said. "It's no use looking up there."

I led her away, and she followed me like a little child.

"I'll put her to bed," I told John.

Ghost-white, he nodded. "Yes," he said, in a voice thick with dust. He could hardly bear to look at her. He made a slow gesture toward the destroyed ceiling. It was the slow motion of a drowning man dragged under by the current. "And I'll sort this out."

But an hour later, when the Missus was clean, and in a fresh nightdress, tucked up in bed and asleep, he was still there. Exactly as I had left him. Staring at the spot where she had been.

The next morning, when the Missus did not appear in the kitchen, it was I who went to wake her. She could not be woken. Her soul had departed through the hole in the roof, and she was gone.

"We've lost her," I told John in the kitchen. "She's dead."

His face didn't change. He continued to stare across the kitchen table as though he hadn't heard me. "Yes," he said eventually, in a voice that did not expect to be heard. "Yes."

It felt as if everything had come to an end. I had only one wish: to sit like John, immobile, staring into space and doing nothing. Yet time did not stop. I could still feel my heartbeat measuring out the seconds. I could feel hunger growing in my stomach and thirst in my throat. I was so sad I thought I would die, yet instead I was scandalously and absurdly alive—so alive I swear I could feel my hair and my fingernails growing.

For all the unbearable weight on my heart I could not, like John, give myself up to the misery. Hester was gone; Charlie was gone; the Missus was gone; John, in his own way, was gone, though I hoped he would find his way back. In the meantime the girl in the mist was going to have to come out of the shadows. It was time to stop playing and grow up.

"I'll put the kettle on, then," I said. "Make a cup of tea."

My voice was not my own. Some other girl, some sensible, capable, ordinary girl had found her way into my skin and taken me over. She seemed to know just what to do. I was only partly surprised. Hadn't I spent half my life watching people live their lives? Watching Hester, watching the Missus, watching the villagers?

I settled quietly inside myself while the capable girl boiled the kettle, measured out the tea leaves, stirred and poured. She put two sugars in John's tea, three in mine. When it was made, I drank it, and as the hot, sweet tea reached my stomach, at last I stopped trembling.

### THE SILVER GARDEN

Before I was quite awake I had the sense that something was different. And a moment later, before I even opened my eyes, I knew what it was. There was *light*.

Gone were the shadows that had lurked in my room since the beginning of the month; gone, too, the gloomy

314

corners and the air of mournfulness. The window was a pale rectangle, and from it there entered a shimmering paleness that illuminated every aspect of my room. It was so long since I had seen it that I felt a surge of joy, as though it weren't just a night that had ended but winter. It was as if spring had come.

The cat was on the window ledge, gazing intently into the garden. Hearing me stir, he immediately jumped down and pawed at the door to go out. I pulled my clothes and coat on, and we crept downstairs together, to the kitchen and the garden.

I realized my mistake the moment I stepped outdoors. It was not day. It was not the sun, but moonlight that shimmered in the garden, edging the leaves with silver and touching the outlines of the statuary figures. I stopped still and stared at the moon. It was a perfect circle, hanging palely in a clear sky. Mesmerized, I could have stood there till daybreak, but the cat, impatient, pressed my ankles for attention, and I bent to stroke him. No sooner had I touched him than he moved away, only to pause a few yards off and look over his shoulder.

I turned up the collar of my coat, shoved my cold hands in my pockets and followed.

He led me first down the grassy path between the long borders. On our left the yew hedge gleamed brightly; on the right the hedge was dark in the moon shadow. We turned into the rose garden where the pruned bushes appeared as piles of dead twigs, but the elaborate borders of box that surrounded them in sinuous Elizabethan patterns twisted in and out of the moonlight, showing here silver, there black. A dozen times I would have lingered—a single ivy leaf turned at an angle to catch the moonlight perfectly; a sudden view of the great oak tree, etched with inhuman clarity against the pale sky—but I could not stop. All the time, the cat stalked on ahead of me with a purposeful, even step, tail raised like a tour guide's umbrella signaling *this way, follow me.* In the walled garden he jumped up onto the wall that bordered the fountain pool and padded halfway around its perimeter, ignoring the moon's reflection that shone in the water like a bright coin at the bottom of the pool. And when he came level with the arched entrance to the winter garden, he jumped down and walked toward it.

Under the arch he paused. He looked left and right, intent. Saw something. And slunk off, out of sight, toward it.

Curious, I tiptoed forward to stand where he had, and look around.

A winter garden is colorful when you see it at the right time of day, at the right time of year. Largely it depends on daylight to bring it to life. The midnight visitor has to look harder to see its attractions. It was too dark to see the low, wide spread of hellebore leaves against the dark soil; too early in the season for the brightness of snowdrops; too cold for the daphne to release its fragrance. There was witch hazel, though; soon its branches would be decorated with trembling yellow and orange tassels, but for now it was the branches themselves that were the main attraction. Fine and leafless, they were delicately knotted, twisting randomly and with elegant restraint.

At its foot, hunched over the ground, was the rounded silhouette of a human figure.

I froze.

The figure heaved and shifted laboriously, releasing gasping puffs of breath and effortful grunts.

In a long, slow second my mind raced to explain the presence of another human being in Miss Winter's garden at night. Some things I knew instantly without needing even to think about them. For a start, it was not Maurice kneeling on the ground there. Though he was the least unlikely person to find in the garden, it never occurred to me to wonder whether it might be him. This was not his wiry frame, these not his measured movements. Equally it was not Judith. Neat, calm, Judith with her clean nails, perfect hair and polished shoes scrabbling about in the garden in the middle of the night? Impossible. I did not need to consider these two, and so I didn't.

Instead, in that second, my mind reeled to and fro a hundred times between two thoughts.

It was Miss Winter.

It couldn't be Miss Winter.

It was Miss Winter because . . . because it was. I could tell. I could sense it. It was her and I knew it.

It couldn't be her. Miss Winter was frail and ill. Miss Winter was always in her wheelchair. Miss Winter was too unwell to bend to pluck out a weed, let alone crouch on the cold ground disturbing the soil in this frantic fashion.

It wasn't Miss Winter.

But somehow, impossibly, despite everything, it was. That first second was long and confusing. The second, when it finally came, was sudden.

The figure froze . . . swiveled . . . rose . . . and I knew.

Miss Winter's eyes. Brilliant, supernatural green.

But not Miss Winter's face.

A patchwork of scarred and mottled flesh, criss-crossed by crevices deeper than age could make. Two uneven dumplings of cheeks. Lopsided lips, one half a perfect bow that told of former beauty, the other a twisted graft of white flesh.

*Emmeline! Miss Winter's twin! Alive, and living in this house!*

My mind was in turmoil; blood was pounding in my ears; shock paralyzed me. She stared at me unblinking, and I realized she was less startled than I was. But still, she seemed to be under the same spell as me. We were both cast into immobility.

She was the first to recover. In an urgent gesture she raised a dark, soil-covered hand toward me and, in a hoarse voice, rasped a string of senseless sounds.

Bewilderment slowed my responses; I could not even stammer her name before she turned and hurried away, leaning forward, shoulders hunched. From out of the shadows emerged the cat. He stretched calmly and, ignoring me, took himself off after her. They disappeared under the arch and I was alone. Me and a patch of churned-up soil.

Foxes indeed.

Once they were gone I might have been able to persuade myself that I had imagined it. That I had been sleepwalking, and that in my sleep I had dreamed that Adeline's twin appeared to me and hissed a secret, unintelligible message. But I knew it was real. And though she was no longer visible, I could hear her singing as she departed. That infuriating, tuneless five-note fragment. La la la la la.

I stood, listening, until it faded completely away.

Then, realizing that my feet and hands were freezing, I turned back to the house.

## PHONETIC ALPHABET

A great many years had passed since I learned the phonetic alphabet. It began with a chart in a linguistics book in father's shop. There was no reason for my interest at first, other than that I had nothing to do one weekend and was enamored of the signs and symbols it contained. There were familiar letters and foreign ones. There were capital *N*'s that weren't the same as little *n*'s and capital *Y*'s that weren't the same as little *y*'s. Other letters, *n*'s and *d*'s and *s*'s and *z*'s, had funny little tails and loops attached, and you could cross *h*'s and *i*'s and *u*'s as if they were *t*'s. I loved these wild and fanciful hybrids: I filled pages of paper with *m*'s that turned into *j*'s, and *v*'s that perched precariously on tiny *o*'s like performing dogs on balls at the circus. My father came across my pages of symbols and taught me the sounds that went with each. In the international phonetic alphabet, I discovered, you could write words that looked like math, words that looked like secret code, words that looked like lost languages.

I needed a lost language. One in which I could communicate with the lost. I used to write one special word over and over again. My sister's name. A talisman. I folded the word into elaborate miniature origami, kept my pleat of paper always close to me. In winter it lived in my coat pocket; in summer it tickled my ankle inside the fold of my sock. At night, I fell asleep clutching it in my hand. For all my care, I did not always keep track of these bits of paper. I lost them, made new ones, then came across the old ones. When my mother tried to prize one from my fingers, I swallowed it to thwart her, even though she wouldn't have been able to read it. But when I saw my father pick a grayed and fraying fold of paper out of the junk in the bottom of a drawer and unfold it, I did nothing to stop him. When he read the secret name, his face seemed to break, and his eyes, when they rose to me, were full of sorrow.

He would have spoken. He opened his mouth to speak but, raising my finger to my lips, I commanded his silence. I would not have him speak her name. Had he not tried to shut her away, in the dark? Had he not wanted to forget her? Had he not tried to keep her from me? He had no right to her now.

I prized the paper from his fingers. Without a word I left the room. On the window seat on the second floor I put the morsel of paper in my mouth, tasted its dry, woody tang, and swallowed. For ten years my parents had buried her name in silence, trying to forget. Now I would protect it in a silence of my own. And remember.

Alongside my mispronunciation of *hello, good-bye* and *sorry* in seventeen languages, and my ability to recite the Greek alphabet forward and backward (I who have never learned a word of Greek in my life), the phonetic alphabet was one of those secret, random wells of useless knowledge left over from my bookish childhood. I learned it only to amuse myself; its purpose in those days was merely private, so as the years passed I made no particular effort to practice it. That is why, when I came in from the garden and put pencil to paper to capture the sibilants and fricatives, the plosives and trills of Emmeline's urgent whisper, I had to make several attempts.

After three or four goes, I sat on the bed and looked at my line of squiggles and symbols and signs. Was it accurate? Doubts began to assail me. Had I remembered the sounds accurately after my five-minute journey back into the house? Was my recollection of the phonetic alphabet itself adequate? What if my first failed attempts had contaminated my memory?

I whispered what I had written on the paper. Whispered it again, urgently. Waited for the birth of some answering echo in my memory to tell me I had got it right. Nothing came. It was the travestied transcription of something misheard and then only half-remembered. It was useless.

I wrote the secret name instead. The spell, the charm, the talisman.

It had never worked. She never came. I was still alone.

I screwed the paper into a ball and kicked it into a corner.

## THE LADDER

M y story isn't boring you, is it, Miss Lea?" I endured a number of such comments the following day as, unable to suppress my yawns, I fidgeted and rubbed my eyes while listening to Miss Winter's narration.

"I'm sorry. I'm just tired."

"Tired!" she exclaimed. "You look like death warmed up! A proper meal would put you right. Whatever's the matter with you?"

I shrugged my shoulders. "Just tired. That's all."

She pursed her lips and regarded me sternly, but I said nothing more, and she took up her story.

For six months things went on. We sequestered ourselves in a handful of rooms: the kitchen, where John still slept at night, the drawing room and the library. We girls used the back stairs to get from the kitchen to the one bedroom that seemed secure. The mattresses we slept on were those we had dragged from the old room, the beds themselves being too heavy to move. The house had felt too big anyway, since the household had been so diminished in number. We survivors felt more at ease in the security, the manageability of our smaller accommodation. All the same, we could never quite forget the rest of the house, slowly festering behind closed doors, like a moribund limb.

Emmeline spent much of her time inventing card games. "Play with me. Oh, go on, do play," she would pester. Eventually I gave in and played. Obscure games with ever-shifting rules, games only she understood, and which she always won, which gave her constant delight. She took baths. She never lost her love of soap and hot water, spent hours luxuriating in the water I'd heated for the laundry and washing up. I didn't begrudge her. It was better if at least one of us could be happy.

Before we closed up the rooms, Emmeline had gone through cupboards belonging to Isabelle and taken dresses and scent bottles and shoes, which she hoarded in our campsite of a bedroom. It was like trying to sleep in a dressing-up box. Emmeline wore the dresses. Some were out of date by ten years, others—belonging to Isabelle's mother, I presume—were thirty and forty years old. Emmeline entertained us in the evenings by making dramatic entrances into the kitchen in the more extravagant outfits. The dresses made her look older than fifteen; they made her look womanly. I remembered Hester's conversation with the doctor in the garden—*There is no reason why Emmeline should not marry one day*—and I remembered what the Missus had told me about Isabelle and the picnics—*She was the kind of girl men can't look at without wanting to touch*—and I felt a sudden anxiety. But then she flopped down on a kitchen chair, took a pack of cards from a silk purse and said, all child, "Play cards with me, go on." I was half reassured, but still, I made sure she did not leave the house in her finery.

John was listless. He did rouse himself to do the unthinkable, though: He got a boy to help in the garden. "It'll be all right," he said. "It's only old Proctor's boy, Ambrose. He's a quiet lad. It won't be for long. Only till I get the house fixed up."

That, I knew, would take forever.

The boy came. He was taller than John and broader across the shoulders. They stood hands in pockets, the two of them, and discussed the day's work, and then the boy started. He had a measured, patient way of digging; the smooth, constant chime of spade on soil got on my nerves. "Why do we have to have him?" I wanted to know. "He's an outsider just like the others."

But for some reason, the boy wasn't an outsider to John. Perhaps because he came from John's world, the world of men, the world I didn't know.

"He's a good lad," John said time and time again in answer to my questions. "He's a hard worker. He doesn't ask too many questions, and he doesn't talk too much."

324

"He might not have a tongue, but he's got eyes in his head."

John shrugged and looked away, uneasy.

"I won't always be here," he said eventually. "Things can't go on forever like this." He sketched a vague gesture that took in the house, its inhabitants, the life we led in it. "One day things will have to change."

*"Change?"*

"You're growing up. It won't be the same, will it? It's one thing, being children, but when you're grown up. . . ."

But I was already gone. I didn't want to know what it was he had to say.

Emmeline was in the bedroom, picking sequins off an evening scarf for her treasure box. I sat down beside her. She was too absorbed in her task to look up when I came in. Her plump, tapered fingers picked relentlessly at a sequin until it came away, then dropped it into the box. It was slow work, but then Emmeline had all the time in the world. Her calm face never changed as she bent over the scarf. Lips together. Her gaze at once intent and dreamy. Every so often her eyelids descended, closing off the green irises, then, as soon as they had touched the lower lid, rising again to reveal the green unchanged.

Did I really look like that? I wondered. Oh, I knew what a good match my eyes were to hers in the mirror. And I knew we had the same sideways kink underneath the weight of red hair at the back of our necks. And I knew the impact we could make on the villagers on those rare occasions when we walked arm in arm down The Street in matching dresses. But still, I didn't look like Emmeline, did I? My face could not do that placid concentration. It would be screwed up in frustration. I would be biting my lip, pushing my hair angrily back over my shoulder and out of the way, huffing with impatience. I would not be tranquil like Emmeline. I would bite the sequins off with my teeth.

You won't leave me, will you? I wanted to say. Because I won't leave you. We'll stay here forever. Together. Whatever John-the-dig says.

"Why don't we play?"

She continued her silent work as though she hadn't heard me.

"Let's play getting married. You can be the bride. Go on. You can wear . . . this." I pulled a yellow piece of gauzy stuff from the pile of finery in the corner. "It's like a veil, look." She didn't look up, not even when I tossed it over her head. She just brushed it out of her eyes and carried on picking at her sequin.

And so I turned my attention to her treasure box. Hester's keys were still in there, still shiny, though Emmeline had, so far as one could tell, forgotten their previous keeper. There were bits and pieces of Isabelle's jewelry, the colored wrappers from the sweets Hester had given her one day, an alarming shard of glass from a broken green bottle, a length of ribbon with a gold edge that used to be mine, given to me by the Missus more years ago than I could remember. Underneath all the other junk there would still be the threads of silver she had worked out of the curtains the day Hester arrived. And half-hidden beneath the jumble of rubies, glass and junk, there was something that didn't seem to belong. Something leather. I put my head on one side to get a better view. Ah! That was why she wanted it! Gold lettering. *I A R*. What was *I A R?* Or who was *I A R?* Tilting my head the other way I caught sight of something else. A tiny lock. And a tiny key. No wonder it was in Emmeline's treasure box. Gold letters *and* a key. I should think it was her prize possession. And suddenly it struck me. *I A R!* Diary!

I reached out a hand.

Quick as a flash—her looks could be deceiving—Emmeline's hand came down like a vise on my wrist and stopped me from touching. Still she didn't look at me. She moved my hand away with a firm movement and brought the lid down on her box.

There were white pressure marks on my wrist where she had held me.

"I'm going to go away," I said experimentally. My voice didn't sound terribly convincing. "I am. And I'm going to leave you here. I'm going to grow up and live *on my own.*"

Then, full of dignified self-pity, I stood up and walked out of the room.

It wasn't until the end of the afternoon that she came to find me on the window seat in the library. I had drawn the curtain to hide me, but she came straight to the place and peered around. I heard her approaching steps, felt the curtain move when she lifted it. Forehead pressed against the glass, I was watching the drops of rain against the windowpane. The wind was making them shiver; they were constantly threatening to set off on one of their zigzag courses where they swallow up every droplet in their path and leave a brief silvery trail behind. She came to me and rested her head against my shoulder. I shrugged her off angrily. Would not turn and speak to her. She took my hand and slipped something onto my finger.

I waited for her to go before I looked. A ring. She had given me a ring.

I twisted the stone inward, to the palm side of my finger, and brought it close to the window. The light brought the stone to life. Green, like the color of my eyes. Green, like the color of Emmeline's eyes. She had given me a ring. I closed my fingers into my palm and made a tight fist with the stone at its heart.

John collected buckets of rainwater and emptied them; he peeled vegetables for the pot; he went to the farm and returned with milk and butter. But after every task, his slowly gathered energy seemed exhausted, and every time I wondered whether he would have the strength to heave his lean frame up from the table to get on with the next thing.

"Shall we go to the topiary garden?" I asked him. "You might show me what to do there."

He didn't reply. He hardly heard me, I think. For a few days I left it, then I asked again. And again. And again.

Eventually he went to the shed, where he sharpened the pruning shears with his old smooth rhythm. Then we lifted down the long ladders and carried them out-of-doors. "Like this," he said, reaching to show me the safety catch on the ladder. He extended the ladder against the solid garden wall. I practiced the safety catch a few times, then went up a few feet and down again. "It won't feel so secure when it's resting against yew," he told me. "It's safe enough, if you get it right. You have to get a feel for it."

And then we went to the topiary garden. He led me to a medium-size yew shape that had grown shaggy. I went to rest the ladder against it, but "No, no," he cried. "Too impatient." Three times he walked slowly around the tree. Then he sat down on the ground and lit a cigarette. I sat down and he lit one for me, too. "Never cut into the sun," he told me. And "Don't cut into your own shadow." He drew a few times on his cigarette. "Be wary of clouds. Don't let them skew your line when they blow about. Find something permanent in your line of vision. A roof or a fence. That's your anchor. And never be in a hurry. Three times as long in the looking as in the cutting." He never lifted his eye from the tree all the time he spoke, and neither did I. "You have to have a feeling for the back of the tree while you're trimming the front, and the other way around. And don't just cut with the shears. Use your whole arm. All the way up to your shoulder."

We finished the cigarettes and stubbed out the ends under the toes of our boots.

"And how you see it now, from a distance, keep that in your head when you're seeing it close up."

I was ready.

Three times he let me rest the ladder against the tree before he was satisfied it was safe. And then I took the shears and went up.

I worked for three hours. At first I was conscious of the height, kept looking down, had to force myself to go one more step up the ladder. And each time I moved the ladder, it took me several goes to get it safe. But gradually the task took me over. I hardly knew how high I was, so absorbed was my mind in the shape I was making. John stood by, mostly silent. Once in a while he made a comment—*Watch your shadow!* or *Think of the back!*—but mostly he just watched and smoked. It was only when I came down from the ladder for the last time, slipped the safety catch and telescoped it, that I realized how sore my hands were from the weight of the shears. But I didn't care.

I stood well back to study my work. I walked three times around the tree. My heart leaped. It was *good*.

John nodded. "Not bad," he pronounced. "You'll do."

I went to get the ladder from the shed to trim the big bowler hat, and the ladder was gone. The boy I didn't like was in the kitchen garden with the rake. I went up to him, scowling. "Where's the ladder?" It was the first time I had spoken to him.

He ignored my brusqueness and answered me politely. "Mr. Digence took it. He's around the front, fixing the roof."

I helped myself to one of the cigarettes John had left in the shed, and smoked it, sending mean looks to the boy, who eyed it enviously. Then I sharpened the pruning shears. Then, liking the sharpening, I sharpened the garden knife, taking my time, doing it well. All the time, behind the rhythm of the stone against the blade, was the rhythm of the boy's rake over the soil. Then I looked at the sun and thought it was getting late to be starting on the large bowler hat. *Then* I went to find John.

The ladder was lying on the ground. Its two sections made a crazy clock-hands angle; the metal channel that was supposed to hold them at a constant six o'clock had been wrenched from the wood, and great splinters protruded from the gash in the side rail. Beside the ladder lay John. He did not move when I touched his shoulder, but he was warm as the sun that touched his splayed limbs and his bloodied hair. He was staring straight up into the clear blue sky, but the blue of his eyes was strangely overcast.

The sensible girl deserted me. All of a sudden I was only myself, just a stupid child, almost nothing at all.

"What shall I do?" I whispered.

"What shall I *do?*" My voice frightened me.

Stretched out on the ground, with John's hand clutched in mine and shards of gravel digging into my temple, I watched time pass. The shadow of the library bay spread across the gravel and reached the farthest rungs of the ladder. Rung after rung it crept up the ladder toward us. It reached the safety catch.

*The safety catch.* Why had John not checked the safety catch? Surely he would have checked it? Of course he would. But if he *did* check it, then how . . . why . . . ?

It didn't bear thinking about.

Rung, after rung, after rung, the shadow of the bay crept nearer and nearer. It reached John's worsted trousers, then his green shirt, then his hair—how thin his hair had grown! Why had I not taken better care of him?

It didn't bear thinking about. Yet how not to think? While I was noticing the whiteness of John's hair, I noticed, too, the deep grooves cut into the earth by the feet of the ladder as it lurched away from under him. No other signs. Gravel is not sand or snow or even newly dug earth. It does not hold a footprint. No trace to show how someone might have come, how they might have loitered at the base of the ladder, how, when they had finished what they came for, they calmly walked away. For all the gravel could tell me, it might have been a ghost.

Everything was cold. The gravel, John's hand, my heart.

I stood up and left John without looking back. I went around the house to the kitchen garden. The boy was still there; he was putting the rake and the broom away. He stopped when he saw me approach, stared at me. And then, when I stopped—*Don't faint! Don't faint!* I told myself—he came running forward to catch me. I watched him as though from a long, long way away. And I didn't faint. Not quite. Instead, when he came close, I felt a voice rise up inside myself, words that I didn't choose to say, but which forced their way out of my strangled throat. "Why doesn't anybody *help* me?"

He grasped me under my arms; I slumped against him; he helped me gently down to the grass. "I'll help you," he said. "I will."

⁂

With the death of John-the-dig still fresh in my mind, the vision of Miss Winter's face, bereft, still dominating my memory, I barely noticed the letter that was waiting for me in my room.

I didn't open it until I had finished my transcription, and when I did, there wasn't much to it.

*Dear Miss Lea,*

*After all the assistance your father has given me over the years, may I say how glad I am to be able in some small way to return the favor to his daughter.*

*My initial researches in the United Kingdom have revealed no indication of the whereabouts of Miss Hester Barrow after her period of employment at Angelfield. I have found a certain number of documents relating to her life before that period, and I am compiling a report that you*

333

*should have within a few weeks.*

*My researches are by no means at an end. I have not yet exhausted my investigation of the Italian connection, and it is more than likely that some detail arising from the early years will throw up a new line of inquiry.*

*Do not despair! If your governess can be found, I will find her.*

> *Yours sincerely,*
> *Emmanuel Drake*

I put the letter away in a drawer, then pulled on my coat and gloves.

"Come on, then," I said to Shadow.

He followed me downstairs and outdoors, and we took the path along the side of the house. Here and there a shrub grown against the wall caused the path to drift; imperceptibly it led away from the wall, away from the house, to the mazelike enticements of the garden. I resisted its easy curve and continued straight on. Keeping the house wall always on my left meant squeezing behind an ever-widening thicket of densely grown, mature shrubs. Their gnarled stems caught my ankles; I had to wrap my scarf around my face to avoid being scratched. The cat accompanied me so far, then stopped, overwhelmed by the thickness of the under-growth.

I kept going. And I found what I was looking for. A window, almost overgrown with ivy, and with such a denseness of evergreen leaf between it and the garden that the glimmer of light escaping from it would never be noticed.

Directly inside the window, Miss Winter's sister sat at a table. Opposite her was Judith. She was spooning mouthfuls of soup between the invalid's raw, patched lips. Suddenly, midway between bowl and mouth, Judith paused and looked directly toward me. She couldn't see me; there was too much ivy. She must have felt the touch of my gaze. After a moment's pause, she turned back to her task and carried on. But not before I had noticed something strange about the spoon. It was a silver spoon with an elongated *A* in the form of a stylized angel ornamenting the handle.

I had seen a spoon like that before. *A*. Angel. Angelfield. Emmeline had a spoon like that, and so did Aurelius.

Keeping flat to the wall, and with the branches tangling in my hair, I wriggled back out of the shrubbery. The cat watched me as I brushed the bits of broken twig and dead leaves from my sleeves and shoulders.

"Inside?" I suggested, and he was more than happy to concur.

Mr. Drake hadn't been able to trace Hester for me. On the other hand, I had found Emmeline.

In my study I transcribed; in the garden I wandered; in my bedroom I stroked the cat and held off my nightmares by staying awake. The moonlit night when I had seen Emmeline appear in the garden seemed like a dream to me now, for the sky had closed in again, and we were immersed once more in the endless twilight.

With the deaths of the Missus and now John-the-dig, an additional chill crept into Miss Winter's story. Was it Emmeline—that alarming figure in the garden—who had tampered with the ladder? I could only wait and let the story reveal itself. Meanwhile, with December waxing, the shadow hovering at my window grew always more intense. Her closeness repelled me, her distance broke my heart, every sight of her evoked in me the familiar combination of fear and longing.

I got to the library in advance of Miss Winter— morning or afternoon or evening, I don't know, they were all the same by now—and stood by the window to wait. My pale sister pressed her fingers to mine, trapped me in her imploring gaze, misted the glass with her cool breath. I only had to break the glass, and I could join her.

"Whatever are you looking at?" came Miss Winter's voice behind me.

Slowly I turned.

"Sit down," she barked at me. Then, "Judith, put

another log on the fire, would you, and then bring this girl something to eat."

I sat down.

Judith brought cocoa and toast.

Miss Winter continued her story while I sipped at the hot cocoa.

❦

"I'll help you," he said. But what could he do? He was just a boy.

I got him out of the way. I sent him to fetch Dr. Maudsley, and while he was gone I made strong, sweet tea and drank a potful. I thought hard thoughts and I thought them quickly. By the time I was at the dregs, the prick of tears had quite retreated from my eyes. It was time for action.

By the time the boy returned with the doctor, I was ready. The moment I heard their steps approaching the house, I turned the corner to meet them.

"Emmeline, poor child!" the doctor exclaimed as he came near, hand outstretched in a sympathetic gesture, as though to embrace me.

I took a step back, and he halted. "Emmeline?" In his eyes, uncertainty flared. Adeline? It was not possible. It could not be. The name died on his lips. "Forgive me," he stammered. But still he did not know.

I did not help him out of his confusion. Instead I cried.

Not real tears. My real tears—and I had plenty of them, believe me—were all stored up. Sometime, tonight or tomorrow or sometime soon, I did not exactly know when, I would be alone and I would cry for hours. For John. For me. I would cry out loud, shrieking my tears, the way I used to cry as a little girl when only John could soothe me, stroking my hair with hands that smelled of tobacco and the garden. Hot, ugly tears they would be, and when the end came—if it came—my eyes would be so puffed up I would have only red-rimmed slits to see out of.

But those were private tears, and not for this man. The tears I gratified him with were fake ones. Ones to set off my green eyes the way diamonds set off emeralds. And it worked. If you dazzle a man with green eyes, he will be so hypnotized that he won't notice there is someone inside the eyes spying on him.

"I'm afraid there's nothing I can do for Mr. Digence," he said, rising from beside the body.

It was odd to hear John's real name.

"However did it happen?" He looked up at the balustrade where John had been working, then bent over the ladder. "Did the safety catch fail?"

I could look at the corpse without emotion, almost. "Might he have slipped?" I wondered aloud. "Did he grab at the ladder as he fell and bring it down after him?"

"No one saw him fall?"

"Our rooms are at the other side of the house, and the boy was in the vegetable garden." The boy stood slightly apart from us, looking away from the body.

"Hmm. There is no family, I seem to remember."

"He always lived quite alone."

"I see. And where is your uncle? Why is he not here to meet me?"

I had no idea what John had told the boy about our situation. I had to play it by ear.

With a sob to my voice, I told the doctor that my uncle had gone away.

"Away!" The doctor frowned.

The boy did not react. Nothing to surprise him so far, then. He stood looking at his feet so as not to look at the corpse, and I had time to think him a sissy before going on to say, "My uncle won't be back for a few days."

"How many days?"

"Oh! Now, when was it exactly he went away . . . ?" I frowned and made a little pretense of counting back the days. Then, allowing my eyes to rest on the corpse, I let my knees quiver.

The doctor and the boy both leaped to my side, taking an elbow each.

"All right. Later, my dear, later."

I permitted them to lead me around the house toward the kitchen door.

"I don't know exactly what to do!" I said as we rounded the corner.

"About what, exactly?"

"The funeral."

"You don't need to do anything. I will arrange the undertakers, and the vicar will take care of the rest."

"But what about the money?"

"Your uncle will settle that when he returns. Where is he, by the way?"

"But what if he should be delayed?"

"You think it likely he will be delayed?"

"He's an . . . unpredictable man."

"Indeed." The boy opened the kitchen door, and the doctor guided me in and pulled out a chair. I collapsed into it.

"The solicitor will sort out anything that needs doing, if it comes to it. Now, where is your sister? Does she know what's happened?"

I didn't bat an eyelid. "She is sleeping."

"Just as well. Let her sleep, perhaps, eh?"

I nodded.

"Now, who can look after you while you're on your own here, then?"

"Look after us?"

"You can hardly stay here on your own. . . . Not after this. It was rash of your uncle to leave you in the first place so soon after losing your housekeeper and without finding a replacement. Someone must come."

"Is it really necessary?" I was all tears and green eyes; Emmeline wasn't the only one who knew how to be womanly.

"Well, surely you—"

"It's just that the last time someone came to take care of us— You do remember our governess, don't you?" And I flashed him a look so mean and so quick he could hardly believe he'd seen it. He had the grace to blush and looked away. When he looked back, I was nothing but emeralds and diamonds again.

The boy cleared his throat. "My grandmother could

come and look in, sir. Not to stay like, but she could come every day, just for a bit."

Dr. Maudsley, disconcerted, considered. It was a way out, and he was looking for a way out.

"Well, Ambrose, I think that would be the ideal arrangement. In the short term, at least. And no doubt your uncle will be back in a very few days, in which case there will be no need, as you say, to, er, to—"

"Indeed." I rose smoothly from my chair. "So if you will see to the undertakers, I will see the vicar." I held out my hand. "Thank you for coming so quickly."

The man had lost his footing entirely. He rose to his feet at my prompt, and I felt the brief touch of his fingers in mine. They were sweaty.

Once again he searched in my face for my name. Adeline or Emmeline? Emmeline or Adeline? He took the only way out. "I'm sorry about Mr. Digence. Truly I am, Miss March."

"Thank you, Doctor." And I hid my smile behind a veil of tears.

Dr. Maudsley nodded at the boy on his way out and closed the door behind him.

Now for the boy himself.

I waited for the doctor to get away, then opened the door and invited the boy to go through it. "By the way," I said as he reached the threshold, in a voice that showed I was mistress of the house, "there's no need for your grandmother to come in."

He gave me a curious look. Here was one who saw the green eyes and the girl inside them.

341

"Just as well," he said with a casual touch to the brim of his cap, "since I haven't got a grandmother."

"I'll help you," he had said, but he was only a boy. He did know how to drive a car, though.

The next day he drove us to the solicitor in Banbury, I beside him and Emmeline behind. After a quarter of an hour waiting under the eye of a receptionist, we were finally asked into Mr. Lomax's office. He looked at Emmeline and he looked at me and he said, "No need to ask who you two are."

"We're in something of a quandary," I explained. "My uncle is absent, and our gardener has died. It was an accident. A tragic accident. Since he has no family and has worked for us forever, I do feel the family should pay for the funeral, only we are a little short . . ."

His eyes veered from me to Emmeline and back again.

"Please excuse my sister. She is not quite well." Emmeline did indeed look odd. I had let her dress in her outmoded finery, and her eyes were too full of beauty to leave room for anything so mundane as intelligence.

"Yes," said Mr. Lomax, and he lowered his voice a sympathetic half-tone. "I had heard something to that effect."

Responding to his kindness, I leaned over the desk and confided, "And of course, with my uncle—well, you've had dealings with him, so you'll know, won't you? Things are not always terribly easy there, either."

I offered him my most transparent stare. "In fact, it's a real treat to talk to someone sensible for a change!"

He turned the rumors he had heard over in his mind. One of the twins was not quite right, they said. Well, he concluded, clearly no flies on the other one.

"The pleasure is entirely mutual, Miss, er, forgive me, but what was your father's name again?"

"The name you are after is March. But we have become used to being known by our mother's name. The Angelfield twins, they call us in the village. No one remembers Mr. March, especially us. We never had the chance to meet him, you see. And we have no dealings at all with his family. I have often thought it would be better to change our names formally.

"Can be done. Why not? Simple matter, really."

"But that's for another day. Today's business . . ."

"Of course. Now let me put your mind at rest about this funeral. You don't know when your uncle will be back, I take it?"

"It may be quite some time," I said, which was not exactly a lie.

"It doesn't matter. Either he will be back in time to settle the expenses himself, or if he is not, then I will settle it on his behalf and sort things out when he comes home."

I turned my face into the picture of relief he was looking for, and while he was still warm with the pleasure of having been able to take the load off my mind, I plied him with a dozen questions about what would happen if a girl like me, having the responsibility of a sister like mine, should have the misfortune of mislaying her guardian for good. In a few words he explained the whole situation to me, and I saw clearly the steps I would have to take and how soon I would need to take them. "Not that any of this applies to you, in your position!" he concluded, as if he had quite run away with himself in painting this alarming scenario and wished he could take back three quarters of what he had said. "After all, your uncle will be back with you in a few short days."

"God willing!" I beamed at him.

We were at the door when Mr. Lomax remembered the essential thing.

"Incidentally, I don't suppose he left an address?"

"You know my uncle!"

"I thought as much. You do know approximately where he is, though?"

I liked Mr. Lomax, but it didn't stop me lying to him when I had to. Lying was second nature to a girl like me.

"Yes . . . that is, no."

He gave me a serious look. "Because if you don't know where he is . . ." His mind returned to all the legalities he had just enumerated for me.

"Well, I can tell you where he *said* he was going."

Mr. Lomax looked at me, eyebrows raised.

"He *said* he was going to Peru."

Mr. Lomax's rounded eyes bulged, and his mouth dropped open.

"But of course, we both know that's ridiculous, don't

we?" I finished. "He can't possibly be in Peru, can he?"

And with my most reassured, most pluckily capable smile, I closed the door behind me, leaving Mr. Lomax to worry on my behalf.

The day of the funeral came and still I hadn't had a chance to cry. Every day there had been something. First the vicar, then villagers arriving warily at the door, wanting to know about wreaths and flowers; even Mrs. Maudsley came, polite but cold, as though I were somehow tainted with Hester's crime. "Mrs. Proctor, the boy's grandmother, has been a marvel," I told her. "Do thank your husband for suggesting it."

Through it all I suspected that the Proctor boy was keeping an eye on me, though I could never quite catch him at it.

John's funeral wasn't the place to cry, either. It was the very last place. For I was Miss Angelfield, and who was he? Only the gardener.

At the end of the service, while the vicar was speaking kindly, uselessly, to Emmeline—Would she like to attend church more frequently? God's love was a blessing to all his creatures—I listened to Mr. Lomax and Dr. Maudsley, who thought themselves out of earshot behind my back.

"A competent girl," the solicitor said to the doctor. "I don't think she quite realizes the gravity of the situation; you realize no one knows where the uncle is? But when she does, I've no doubt she'll cope. I've put things in train to sort out the money side of things. She

345

was worried about paying for the gardener's funeral, of all things. A kind heart to go with the wise head on her shoulders."

"Yes," said the doctor weakly.

"I was always under the impression—don't know where it came from, mind you—that the two of them were . . . not quite right. But now I've met them it's plain as day that it's only the one of them afflicted. A mercy. Of course, you'll have known how it was all along, being their doctor."

The doctor murmured something I did not hear.

"What's that?" the solicitor asked. "Mist, did you say?"

There was no answer, then the solicitor asked another question. "Which one is which, though? I never did find out when they came to see me. What is the name of the one who is sensible?"

I turned just enough to be able to see them out of the corner of my eye. The doctor was looking at me with the same expression he had had in his eyes during the whole service. Where was the dull-minded child he had kept in his house for several months? The girl who could not lift a spoon to her lips or speak a word of English, let alone give instructions for a funeral and ask intelligent questions of a solicitor. I understood the source of his bafflement.

His eyes flickered from me to Emmeline, from Emmeline to me.

"I think it's Adeline." I saw his lips form the name, and I smiled as all his medical theories and experiments came tumbling down about his feet.

Catching his eye, I raised my hand to the pair of them. A gracious gesture of thanks to them for coming to the funeral of a man they hardly knew in order to be of service to me. That's what the solicitor took it for. The doctor may have taken it rather differently.

Later. Many hours later.

The funeral over, at last I could cry.

Except that I couldn't. My tears, kept in too long, had fossilized.

They would have to stay in forever now.

## FOSSILIZED TEARS

E xcuse me . . ." Judith began, and stopped. She pressed her lips tight, then with an uncharacteristic flutter of the hands, "The doctor is already out on a call—he won't be here for an hour. Please . . ."

I belted my dressing gown and followed; Judith was half running a few paces ahead. We went up and down flights of stairs, turned into passages and corridors, arrived back on the ground floor but in a part of the house I hadn't seen before. Finally we came to a series of rooms that I took to be Miss Winter's private suite. We paused before a closed door, and Judith gave me a troubled look. I well understood her anxiety. From behind the door there came deep, inhuman sounds, bellows of pain interrupted by jagged gasps for breath.

347

Judith opened the final door and we went in.

I was astonished. No wonder the noise reverberated so! Unlike the rest of the house, with its overstuffed upholstery, lavish drapes, baffled walls and tapestries, this was a spare and naked little room. The walls were bare plaster, the floor simple boards. A plain bookcase in the corner was stuffed with piles of yellowing paper, and in the corner stood a narrow bed with simple white covers. At the window a calico curtain hung limply each side of the panes, letting the night in. Slumped over a plain little school desk, with her back to me, was Miss Winter. Gone were her fiery orange and resplendent purple. She was dressed in a white long-sleeved chemise, and she was weeping.

A harsh, atonal scraping of air over vocal cords. Jarring wails that veered into frighteningly animal moans. Her shoulders heaved and crashed and her torso shuddered; the force traveled through her frail neck to her head, along her arms into her hands, which jolted against the desktop. Judith hurried to replace a cushion beneath Miss Winter's temple; Miss Winter, utterly possessed by the crisis, seemed not to know we were there.

"I've never seen her like this before," Judith said, fingers pressed to her lips. And with a rising note of panic, "I don't know what to do."

Miss Winter's mouth gaped and grimaced, contorted into wild, ugly shapes by the grief that was too big for it.

"It's all right," I said to Judith. It was an agony I

knew. I drew up a chair and sat down beside Miss Winter.

"Hush, hush, I know." I placed an arm across her shoulder, drew her two hands into mine. Shrouding her body with my own, I bent my ear close to her head and went on with the incantation. "It's all right. It will pass. Hush, child. You're not alone." I rocked her and soothed her and never stopped breathing the magic words. They were not my own words, but my father's. Words that I knew would work, because they had always worked for me. "Hush," I whispered. "I know. It will pass."

The convulsions did not stop, nor the cries become less painful, but they gradually became less violent. She had time between each new paroxysm to take in desperate, shuddering breaths of air.

"You're not alone. I'm with you."

Eventually she was quiet. The curve of her skull pressed into my cheek. Wisps of her hair touched my lips. Against my ribs I could feel her little flutters of breath, the tender convulsions in her lungs. Her hands were very cold in mine.

"There. There now."

We sat in silence for minutes. I pulled the shawl up and arranged it more warmly around her shoulders, and tried to rub some warmth into her hands. Her face was ravaged. She could scarcely see out of her swollen eyelids, and her lips were sore and cracked. The birth of a bruise marked the spot where her head had been shaken against the desk.

"He was a good man," I said. "A good man. And he loved you."

Slowly she nodded. Her mouth quivered. Had she tried to say something? Again her lips moved.

The safety catch? Was that what she had said?

"Was it your sister who interfered with the safety catch?" It seems a brutal question now, but at the time, with that flood of tears having swept all etiquette away, the directness did not feel out of place.

My question caused her one last spasm of pain, but when she spoke, she was unequivocal.

"Not Emmeline. Not her. Not her."

"Who, then?"

She squeezed her eyes shut, began to sway and shook her head from side to side. I have seen the same movement in animals in zoos when they have been driven mad by their captivity. Beginning to fear the renewal of her agony, I remembered what it was that my father used to do to console me when I was a child. Gently, tenderly, I stroked her hair until, soothed, she came to rest her head on my shoulder.

Finally she was quiet enough for Judith to be able to put her to bed. In a sleepy, childlike voice she asked for me to stay, and so I stayed with her, kneeling by her bedside and watching her fall asleep. From time to time a shiver disturbed her slumber and a look of fear came on her sleeping face; when this happened I smoothed her hair until her eyelids settled back into peace.

When was it that my father had consoled me like this? An incident rose out of the depths of my memory. I must have been twelve or so. It was Sunday; Father and I were eating sandwiches by the river when twins appeared. Two blond girls with their blond parents, day-trippers come to admire the architecture and enjoy the sunshine. Everyone noticed them; they must have been used to the stares of strangers. But not mine. I saw them and my heart leaped. It was like looking into a mirror and seeing myself complete. With what ardor I stared at them. With what hunger. Nervous, they turned away from the girl with the devouring stare and reached for their parents' hands. I saw their fear, and a hard hand squeezed my lungs until the sky went dark. Then later, in the shop. I on the window seat, between sleep and a nightmare; he, crouched on the floor, stroking my hair, murmuring his incantation, "Hush, it will pass. It's all right. You're not alone."

Sometime later, Dr. Clifton came. When I turned to see him in the doorway I got the feeling that he may have been there for some time already. I slipped past him on my way out, and there was something in his expression I did not know how to read.

## UNDERWATER CRYPTOGRAPHY

I returned to my own rooms, my feet moving as slowly as my thoughts. Nothing made sense. Why had John-the-dig died? Because someone had interfered with the safety catch on the ladder. It can't have been the boy. Miss Winter's story gave him a clear alibi: While John and his ladder were tumbling from the balustrade through the empty air to the ground, the boy was eyeing her cigarette, not daring to ask for a drag. Then surely it must have been Emmeline. Except that nothing in the story suggests that Emmeline would do such a thing. She was a harmless child, even Hester said so. And Miss Winter herself couldn't have been clearer. No. Not Emmeline. Then who? Isabelle was dead. Charlie was gone.

I came to my rooms, went in, stood by the window. It was too dark to see; there was only my reflection, a pale shadow you could see the night through. "Who?" I asked it.

At last I listened to the quiet, persistent voice in my head that I had been trying to ignore. *Adeline.*

No, I said.

*Yes,* it said. *Adeline.*

It was not possible. The cries of grief for John-the-dig were still fresh in my mind. No one could mourn a man like that if she had killed him, could she? No one could murder a man she loved enough to cry those tears for?

But the voice in my head recounted episode after episode from the story I knew so well. The violence in the topiary garden, each swipe of the shears a blow to John's heart. The attacks on Emmeline, the hair-pulling, the battering, the biting. The baby removed from the perambulator and left carelessly, to die or to be found. One of the twins was not quite right, they said in the village. I remembered and I wondered. Was it possible?

Had the tears I had just witnessed been tears of guilt? Tears of remorse? Was it a murderess I had held in my arms and comforted? Was this the secret Miss Winter had hidden from the world for so long? An unpleasant suspicion revealed itself to me. Was this the point of Miss Winter's story? To make me sympathize with her, exonerate her, forgive her? I shivered.

But one thing at least I was sure of. She had loved him. How could it be otherwise? I remembered holding her racked and tormented body against mine and knew that only broken love can cause such despair. I remembered the child Adeline reaching into John's loneliness after the death of the Missus, drawing him back to life by getting him to teach her to prune the topiary.

The topiary *she* had damaged.

Oh, perhaps I wasn't sure after all!

My eyes roamed over the darkness outside the window. Her fabulous garden. Was it her homage to John-the-dig? Her lifelong penitence for the damage she had wrought?

I rubbed my tired eyes and knew I ought to go to bed. But I was too tired to sleep. My thoughts, if I did nothing to stop them, would go round in circles all night long. I decided to have a bath.

While I waited for the tub to fill, I cast about for something to occupy my mind. A ball of paper half visible beneath the dressing table caught my attention. I unfolded it, flattened it out. A row of phonetic script.

In the bathroom, with the water thundering in the background, I made a few short-lived attempts at picking some kind of meaning out of my string of symbols. Always there was that undermining feeling that I hadn't captured Emmeline's utterance quite accurately. I pictured the moonlit garden, the contortions of the witch hazel, the grotesque, urgent face; I heard again the abruptness of Emmeline's voice. But however hard I tried, I could not recall the pronouncement itself.

I climbed into the bath, leaving the scrap of paper on the edge. The water, warm to my feet, legs, back, felt distinctly cooler against the macula on my side. Eyes closed, I slid right under the surface. Ears, nose, eyes, right to the top of my head. The water rang in my ears, my hair lifted from its roots.

I came up for air, then instantly plunged underwater again. More air, then water.

In a loose, underwater fashion, thoughts began to swim in my mind. I knew enough about twin language to know that it was never totally invented. In the case of Emmeline and Adeline, it would be based on English or French or could contain elements of both.

Air. Water.

Introduced distortions. In the intonation, maybe. Or the vowels. And sometimes extra bits, added to camouflage rather than to carry meaning.

Air. Water.

A puzzle. A secret code. A cryptograph. It wouldn't be as hard as the Egyptian hieroglyphs or Mycenaean Linear B. How would you have to go about it? Take each syllable separately. It could be a word or a part of a word. Remove the intonation first. Play with the stress. Experiment with lengthening, shortening, flattening the vowel sounds. Then what did the syllable suggest in English? In French? And what if you left it out and played with the syllables on either side instead? There would be a vast number of possible combinations. Thousands. But not an infinite number. A computing machine could do it. So could a human brain, given a year or two.

*The dead go underground.*

What? I sat bolt upright in shock. The words came to me out of nowhere.

They beat painfully in my chest. It was ridiculous. It couldn't be!

Trembling, I reached to the edge of the bath where I had left my jottings, and drew the paper near to me. Anxiously I scanned it. My notes, my symbols and signs, my squiggles and dots, were gone. They had been sitting in a pool of water and had drowned.

I tried once more to remember the sounds as they had come to me underwater. But they were wiped from my memory. All I could remember was her fraught, intent face and the five-note sequence she sang as she left.

*The dead go underground.* Words that had arrived fully formed in my mind, leaving no trail behind them. Where had they come from? What tricks had my mind been playing to come up with these words out of nowhere?

I didn't actually believe that this was what she had said to me, did I?

Come on, be sensible, I told myself.

I reached for the soap and resolved to put my under-water imaginings out of my mind.

## HAIR

At Miss Winter's house I never looked at the clock. For seconds I had words, minutes were lines of pencil script. Eleven words to the line, twenty-three lines to the page was my new chronometry. At regular intervals I stopped to turn the handle of the pencil sharpener and watch curls of lead-edged wood dangle their way to the wastepaper basket; these pauses marked my "hours."

I was so preoccupied by the story I was hearing, writing, that I had no wish for anything else. My own life, such as it was, had dwindled to nothing. My daytime thoughts and my nighttime dreams were peopled by figures not from my world but from Miss Winter's. It was Hester and Emmeline, Isabelle and Charlie, who wandered through my imagination, and the place to which my thoughts turned constantly was Angelfield.

In truth I was not unwilling to abdicate my own life. Plunging deep into Miss Winter's story was a way of turning my back on my own. Yet one cannot simply snuff oneself out in that fashion. For all my willed blindness, I could not escape the knowledge that it was December. In the back of my mind, on the edge of my sleep, in the margins of the pages I filled so frenetically with script, I was aware that December was counting down the days, and I felt the anniversary crawling closer all the time.

On the day after the night of the tears, I did not see Miss Winter. She stayed in bed, seeing only Judith and Dr. Clifton. This was convenient. I had not slept well myself. But the following day she asked for me. I went to her plain little room and found her in bed.

Her eyes seemed to have grown larger in her face. She wore not a trace of makeup. Perhaps her medication was at its peak of effectiveness, for there was a tranquillity about her that seemed new. She did not smile at me, but when she looked up as I entered, there was kindness in her eyes.

"You don't need your notebook and pencil," she said. "I want you to do something else for me today."

"What?"

Judith came in. She spread a sheet on the floor, then brought Miss Winter's chair in from the adjoining room and lifted her into it. In the center of the sheet she positioned the chair, angling it so that Miss Winter could see out of the window. Then she tucked a towel around Miss Winter's shoulders and spread her mass of orange hair over it.

Before she left she handed me a pair of scissors. "Good luck," she said with a smile.

"But what am I supposed to do?" I asked Miss Winter.

"Cut my hair, of course."

"Cut your hair?"

"Yes. Don't look like that. There's nothing to it."

"But I don't know how."

"Just take the scissors and cut." She sighed. "I don't care how you do it. I don't care what it looks like. Just get rid of it."

"But I—"

*"Please."*

Reluctantly I took up position behind her. After two days in bed, her hair was a tangle of orange, wiry threads. It was dry to the touch, so dry I almost expected it to crackle, and punctuated with gritty little knots.

"I'd better brush it first."

The knots were numerous. Though she spoke not a word of reproach, I felt her flinch at every brushstroke. I put the brush down; it would be kinder to simply cut the knots out.

Tentatively I made the first cut. A few inches off the ends, halfway down her back. The blades sheared cleanly through the hair, and the clippings fell to the sheet.

"Shorter than that," Miss Winter said mildly.

"To here?" I touched her shoulders.

"Shorter."

I took a lock of hair and snipped at it nervously. An orange snake slithered to my feet, and Miss Winter began to speak.

꩜

I remember a few days after the funeral, I was in Hester's old room. Not for any special reason. I was just standing there, by the window, staring at nothing. My fingers found a little ridge in the curtain. A tear that she had mended. Hester was a very neat needlewoman. But there was a bit of thread that had come loose at the end. And in an idle, rather absent sort of way, I began to worry at it. I had no intention of pulling it, I had no intention of any sort, really . . . But all of a sudden, there it was, loose in my fingers. The thread, the whole length of it, zigzagged with the memory of the stitches. And the hole in the curtain gaping open. Now it would start to fray.

John never liked having Hester at the house. He was glad she went. But the fact remained: If Hester had been there, John would not have been on the roof. If Hester had been there, no one would have meddled with the safety catch. If Hester had been there, that day would have dawned like any other day, and as on any other day, John would have gone about his business in the garden. When the bay window cast its afternoon shadow over the gravel, there would have been no ladder, no rungs, no John sprawled on the ground to be taken in by its chill. The day would have come and gone like any other, and at the end of it John would have gone to bed and slept soundly, without even a dream of falling through the empty air.

If Hester had been there.

I found that fraying hole in the curtain utterly unbearable.

※※

I had been snipping at Miss Winter's hair all the time

she was talking, and when it was level with her ear-lobes, I stopped.

She lifted a hand to her head and felt the length.

"Shorter," she said.

I picked up the scissors again and carried on.

☙❧

The boy still came every day. He dug and weeded and planted and mulched. I supposed he kept coming because of the money he was owed. But when the solicitor gave me some cash—"To keep you going till your uncle gets back"—and I paid the boy, he still kept coming. I watched him from the upstairs windows. More than once he looked up in my direction and I jumped out of view, but on one occasion he caught sight of me, and when he did, he waved. I did not wave back.

Every morning he brought vegetables to the kitchen door, sometimes with a skinned rabbit or a plucked hen, and every afternoon he came to collect the peelings for the compost. He lingered in the doorway, and now that I had paid him, more often than not he had a cigarette between his lips.

I had finished John's cigarettes, and it annoyed me that the boy could smoke and I couldn't. I never said a word about it, but one day, shoulder against the door frame, he caught me eyeing the pack of cigarettes in his breast pocket.

"Swap you one for a cup of tea," he said.

He came into the kitchen—it was the first time he had actually come in since the day John died—and sat in

John's chair, elbows on the table. I sat in the chair in the corner, where the Missus used to sit. We drank our tea in silence and exhaled cigarette smoke that rose upward toward the dingy ceiling in lazy clouds and spirals. When we had taken our last drag and stubbed the cigarettes out on our saucers, he rose without a word, walked out of the kitchen and returned to his work. But the next day, when he knocked with the vegetables, he walked straight in, sat in John's chair and tossed a cigarette across to me before I had even put the kettle on.

We never spoke. But we had our habits.

Emmeline, who never rose before lunchtime, sometimes spent the afternoons outdoors looking on as the boy did his work. I scolded her about it. "You're the daughter of the house. He's a gardener. For God's sake, Emmeline!" But it made no difference. She would smile her slow smile at anyone who caught her fancy. I watched them closely, mindful of what the Missus had told me about men who couldn't see Isabelle without wanting to touch her. But the boy showed no indication of wanting to touch Emmeline, though he spoke kindly to her and liked to make her laugh. I couldn't be easy in my mind about it, though.

Sometimes from an upstairs window I would watch the two of them together. One sunny day I saw her lolling on the grass, head on hand, supported by her elbow. It showed the rise from her waist to her hips. He turned his head to answer something she said and while he looked at her, she rolled onto her back, raised a hand and brushed a stray lock of hair from her forehead. It

361

was a languorous, sensuous movement that made me think she would not mind it if he did touch her.

But when the boy had finished what he was saying, he turned his back to Emmeline as though he hadn't seen and continued his work.

The next morning we were smoking in the kitchen. I broke our usual silence.

"Don't touch Emmeline," I told him.

He looked surprised. "I haven't touched Emmeline."

"Good. Well, don't."

I thought that was that. We both took another drag on our cigarettes and I prepared to lapse back into silence, but after exhaling, he spoke again. "I don't want to touch Emmeline."

I heard him. I heard what he said. That curious little intonation. I heard what he *meant*.

I took a drag of my cigarette and didn't look at him. Slowly I exhaled. I didn't look at him.

"She's kinder than you are," he said.

My cigarette wasn't even half finished, but I stubbed it out. I strode to the kitchen door and flung it open.

In the doorway he paused level with me. I stood stiffly, staring straight ahead at the buttons on his shirt.

His Adam's apple bobbed up and down as he swallowed. His voice was a murmur. "Be kind, Adeline."

Stung to anger I lifted my eyes up, meaning to fire daggers at him. But I was startled by the tenderness in his face. For a moment I was . . . confused.

He took advantage. Raised his hand. Was about to stroke my cheek.

But I was quicker. I raised my fist, lashed his hand away.

I didn't hurt him. I couldn't have hurt him. But he looked bewildered. Disappointed.

And then he was gone.

The kitchen was very empty after that. The Missus was gone. John was gone. Now even the boy was gone.

"I'll help you," he had said. But it was impossible. How could a boy like him help me? How could *anybody* help me?

❧❧

The sheet was covered in orange hair. I was walking on hair and hair was stuck to my shoes. All the old dye had been cut away; the sparse tufts that clung to Miss Winter's scalp were pure white.

I took the towel away and blew the stray bits of hair from the back of her neck.

"Give me the mirror," Miss Winter said.

I handed her the looking glass. With her hair shorn, she looked like a grizzled child.

She stared at the glass. Her eyes met her own, naked and somber, and she looked at herself for a long time. Then she put the mirror, glass side down, on the table.

"That is exactly what I wanted. Thank you, Margaret."

I left her, and when I went back to my room I thought about the boy. I thought about him and Adeline, and I thought about him and Emmeline. Then I thought about Aurelius, found as an infant, wearing an old-fashioned garment and wrapped in a satchel, with a spoon from

Angelfield and a page of *Jane Eyre*. I thought about it all at length, but for all my thinking, I did not arrive at any conclusion.

One thing did occur to me, though, in one of those unfathomable side steps of the mind. I remembered what it was Aurelius had said the last time I was at Angelfield: "I just wish there was someone to *tell me the truth*." And I found its echo: "Tell me the truth." The boy in the brown suit. Now, that would explain why the *Banbury Herald* had no record of the interview their young reporter had gone to Yorkshire for. He wasn't a reporter at all. It was Aurelius all along.

## RAIN AND CAKE

The next day I woke to it: today, today, today. A tolling bell only I could hear. The twilight seemed to have penetrated my soul; I felt an unearthly weariness. My birthday. My deathday.

Judith brought a card from my father with the breakfast tray. A picture of flowers, his habitual, vaguely worded greetings and a note. He hoped I was well. He was well. He had some books for me. Should he send them? My mother had not signed the card; he had signed it for both of them. *Love from Dad and Mother.* It was all wrong. I knew it and he knew it, but what could anyone do?

Judith came. "Miss Winter says would now . . . .?"

I slid the card under my pillow before she could see

364

it. "Now would be fine," I said, and picked up my pencil and pad.

"Have you been sleeping well?" Miss Winter wanted to know, and then, "You look a little pale. You don't eat enough."

"I'm fine," I assured her, though I wasn't.

All morning I struggled with the sensation of stray wisps of one world seeping through the cracks of another. Do you know the feeling when you start reading a new book before the membrane of the last one has had time to close behind you? You leave the previous book with ideas and themes—characters even— caught in the fibers of your clothes, and when you open the new book, they are still with you. Well, it was like that. All day I had been prey to distractions. Thoughts, memories, feelings, irrelevant fragments of my own life, playing havoc with my concentration.

Miss Winter was telling me about something when she interrupted herself. "Are you listening to me, Miss Lea?"

I jerked out of my reverie and fumbled for an answer. Had I been listening? I had no idea. At that moment I couldn't have told her what she had been saying, though I'm sure that somewhere in my mind there was a place where it was all recorded. But at the point when she jerked me out of myself, I was in a kind of no-man's-land, a place between places. The mind plays all sorts of tricks, gets up to all kinds of things while we ourselves are slumbering in a white zone that looks for all the world like inattention to the onlooker. Lost for words, I stared at her for a minute, while she grew more and more irritated, then I plucked at the first coherent sentence that presented itself to me.

"Have you ever had a child, Miss Winter?"

"Good Lord, what a question. Of course I haven't. Have you gone mad, girl?"

"Emmeline, then?"

"We have an agreement, do we not? No questions?" And then, changing her expression, she bent forward and scrutinized me closely. "Are you ill?"

"No, I don't think so."

"Well, you are clearly not in your right mind for work."

It was a dismissal.

Back in my room I spent an hour bored, unsettled, plagued by myself. I sat at my desk, pencil in hand, but did not write; felt cold and turned the radiator up, then, too hot, took my cardigan off. I'd have liked a bath, but there was no hot water. I made cocoa and put extra sugar in it; then the sweetness nauseated me. A book? Would that do it? In the library the shelves were lined with dead words. Nothing there could help me.

There came a dash of raindrops, scattering against the window, and my heart leaped. *Outside*. Yes, that was what I needed. And not just the garden. I needed to get away, right away. Onto the moors.

The main gate was kept locked, I knew, and I had no wish to ask Maurice to open it for me. Instead, I headed through the garden to the farthest point from the house, where there was a door in the wall. The door, over-grown with ivy, had not been opened for a long time, and I had to pull the foliage away with my hands before I could open the latch. When the door swung toward me, there was more ivy to be pushed aside before I could step, a little disheveled, outside.

I used to think that I loved rain, but in fact I hardly knew it. The rain I loved was genteel town rain, made soft by all the obstacles the skyline put in its path, and warmed by the rising heat of the town itself. On the moors, enraged by the wind and embittered by the chill, the rain was vicious. Needles of ice stung my face and, behind me, vessels of freezing water burst against my shoulders.

Happy birthday.

If I was at the shop, my father would produce a present from beneath the desk as I came down the stairs. There would be a book or books, purchased at auction and put aside during the year. And a record or perfume or a picture. He would have wrapped them in the shop, at the desk, some quiet afternoon when I was at the post office or the library. He would have gone out one lunchtime to choose a card, alone, and he would have written in it, *Love from Dad and Mother,* at the desk. Alone, quite alone. He would go to the bakery for a cake, and somewhere in the shop—I had never discovered where; it was one of the few secrets I had not fathomed—he kept a candle, which came out on this day every year, was lit, and which I blew out, with as good an impression of happiness as I could muster. Then we ate the cake, with tea, and settled down to quiet diges-tion and cataloging.

I knew how it was for him. It was easier now that I was grown up than when I was a child. How much harder birthdays had been in the house. Presents hidden overnight in the shed, not from me, but from my mother, who could not bear the sight of them. The inevitable headache was her jealously guarded rite of remembrance, one that made it impossible to invite other children in the house, impossible, too, to leave her for the treat of a visit to the zoo or the park. My birthday toys were always quiet ones. Cakes were never home-made, and the leftovers had to be divested of their can-dles and icing before they could be put in the tin for the next day.

*Happy birthday?* Father whispered the words, *Happy Birthday,* hilariously, right in my ear. We played silent card games where the winner pulled gleeful faces and the loser grimaced and slumped, and nothing, not a peep, not a splutter, could be heard in the room above our heads. In between games, up and down he went, my poor father, between the silent pain of the bedroom and the secret birthday downstairs, changing his face from jollity to sympathy, from sympathy back to jollity, in the stairwell.

Unhappy birthday. From the day I was born, grief was always present. It settled like dust upon the household. It covered everyone and everything; it invaded us with every breath we took. It shrouded us in our own sepa-rate miseries.

Only because I was so cold could I bear to contemplate these memories.

Why couldn't she love me? Why did my life mean less to her than my sister's death? Did she blame me for it? Perhaps she was right to. I was alive now only because my sister had died. Every sight of me was a reminder of her loss.

Would it have been easier for her if we had both died?

Stupefied, I walked. One foot in front of the other, again and again and again, mesmerized. No interest in where I was heading. Looking nowhere, seeing nothing, I stumbled on.

Then I bumped into something.

"Margaret! Margaret!"

I was too cold to be startled, too cold to make my face respond to the vast form that stood before me, shrouded in tentlike drapes of green rainproof fabric. It moved, and two hands came down on my shoulders and gave me a shake.

"Margaret!"

It was Aurelius.

"Look at you! You're blue with cold! Quick, come with me." He took my arm and led me briskly off. My feet stumbled over the ground behind him until we came to a road, a car. He bundled me in. There was a slamming of doors, the hum of an engine, and then a blast of warmth around my ankles and knees. Aurelius opened a Thermos flask and poured a mug of orange tea.

"Drink!"

I drank. The tea was hot and sweet.

"Eat!"

I bit into the sandwich he held out.

In the warmth of the car, drinking hot tea and eating chicken sandwiches, I felt colder than ever. My teeth started to chatter and I shivered uncontrollably.

"Goodness gracious!" Aurelius exclaimed softly as he passed me one dainty sandwich after another. "Dear me!"

The food seemed to bring me to my senses a little. "What are you doing here, Aurelius?"

"I came to give you this," he said, and he reached over to the back and lifted a cake tin through the gap between the seats.

Placing the tin on my lap, he beamed gloriously at me as he removed the lid.

Inside was a cake. A homemade cake. And on the cake, in curly icing letters, were three words: *Happy Birthday Margaret.*

I was too cold to cry. Instead the combination of cold and cake set me talking. Words emerged from me, randomly, like objects disgorged by glaciers as they thaw. Nocturnal singing, a garden with eyes, sisters, a baby, a spoon. "And she even knows the house," I babbled while Aurelius dried my hair with paper towels, "your house and Mrs. Love's. She looked through the window and thought Mrs. Love was like a fairy-tale grandmother. . . . Don't you see what it means? "

Aurelius shook his head. "But she told me—"

"She lied to you, Aurelius! When you came to see her in your brown suit, she lied. She has admitted it."

"Bless me!" exclaimed Aurelius. "However did you know about that brown suit of mine? I had to pretend to be a journalist, you know." But then, as what I was telling him began to sink in, "A spoon like mine, you say? And she knew the house?"

"She's your aunt, Aurelius. And Emmeline is your mother."

Aurelius stopped patting my hair, and for a long moment he stared out of the car window in the direction of the house. "My mother," he murmured, "there."

I nodded.

There was another silence, and then he turned to me. "Take me to her, Margaret."

I seemed to wake up. "The thing is, Aurelius, she's not well."

"Ill? Then you *must* take me to her. Without delay!"

"Not ill, exactly." How to explain? "She was injured in the fire, Aurelius. Not only her face. Her mind."

He absorbed this new information, added it to his store of loss and pain, and when he spoke again it was with a grave firmness of purpose. "Take me to her."

Was it illness that dictated my response? Was it the fact that it was my birthday? Was it my own motherlessness? These factors might have had something to do with it, but more significant than all of them was Aurelius's expression as he waited for my answer. There were a hundred and one reasons to say no to his demand, but faced with the ferocity of his need, they faded to nothing.

I said yes.

## REUNION

My bath went some way toward thawing me out, but did nothing to soothe the ache behind my eyes. I gave up all thoughts of working for the rest of the afternoon and crept into bed, pulling the extra covers well up over my ears. Inside I was still shivering. In a shallow sleep I saw strange visions. Hester and my father and the twins and my mother, visions in which everyone had someone else's face, in which everyone was someone else disguised, and even my own face was disturbing to me as it shifted and altered, sometimes myself, sometimes another. Then Aurelius's bright head appeared in my dream: himself, always himself, only himself, and he smiled and the phantoms were banished. Darkness closed over me like water, and I sank to the depths of sleep.

I awoke with a headache, aches in my limbs and my joints and my back. A tiredness that had nothing to do with exertion or lack of sleep weighed me down and slowed my thoughts. The darkness had thickened. Had I slept through the hour of my appointment with Aurelius? The thought nagged at me but only very distantly, and long minutes passed before I could rouse myself to look at my watch. For during my sleep, an obscure sentiment had formed within me—trepidation? nostalgia? excitement?—and it had given rise to a sense of expectation. The past was returning! My sister was near. There was no doubting it. I couldn't see her, couldn't smell her, but my inner ear, attuned always and only to her, had caught her vibration, and it filled me with a dark and soporific joy.

There was no need to put off Aurelius. My sister would find me, wherever I was. Was she not my twin? In fact, I had half an hour before I was due to meet him at the garden door. I dragged myself heavily from my bed and, too cold and weary to take off my pajamas before dressing, I pulled a thick skirt and sweater on over the top. Bundled up like a child on firework night, I went downstairs to the kitchen. Judith had left a cold meal for me, but I had no appetite and left the food untouched. For ten minutes I sat at the kitchen table, longing to close my eyes and not daring to, in case I gave in to the torpor that was inviting my head toward the hard tabletop.

With five minutes to spare, I opened the kitchen door and slipped into the garden.

No light from the house, no stars. I stumbled in the darkness; soft soil underfoot and the brush of leaves and branches told me when I had veered off the path. Out of nowhere a branch scratched my face and I closed my eyes to protect them. Inside my head was a half-painful, half-euphoric vibration. I understood entirely. It was her song. My sister was coming.

I reached the meeting point. The darkness stirred

itself. It was him. My hand bumped clumsily against him, then felt itself clasped.

"Are you all right?"

I heard the question, but distantly.

"Do you have a temperature?"

The words were there; it was curious that they had no meaning.

I'd have liked to tell him about the glorious vibrations, to tell him that my sister was coming, that she would be here with me any minute now. I knew it; I knew it from the heat radiating from her mark on my side. But the white sound of her stood between me and my words and made me dumb.

Aurelius let go of my hand to remove a glove, and I felt his palm, strangely cool in the hot night, on my forehead. "You should be in bed," he said.

I pulled at Aurelius's sleeve, a feeble tug, but enough. He followed me through the garden as smoothly as a statue on casters.

I have no memory of Judith's keys in my hand, though I must have taken them. We must have walked through the long corridors to Emmeline's apartment, but that, too, has been wiped from my mind. I do remember the door, but the picture that presents itself to my mind is that it swung open as we reached it, slowly and of its own accord, which I know to be quite impossible. I must have unlocked it, but this piece of reality has been lost and the image of the door opening by itself persists.

My memory of what happened in Emmeline's quarters that night is fragmented. Whole tracts of time have collapsed in on themselves, while other events seem in my recollection to have happened over and over again in rapid succession. Faces and expressions loom frighteningly large, then Emmeline and Aurelius appear as tiny marionettes a great distance away. As for myself, I was possessed, sleepy, chilled—and distracted during the whole affair by my own overwhelming preoccupation: my sister.

By a process of logic and reason, I have attempted to place into a meaningful sequence images that my mind recorded only incompletely and in random fashion, like events in a dream.

Aurelius and I entered Emmeline's rooms. Our step was soundless on the deep carpet. Through one doorway then another we stepped, until we came to a room with an open door giving onto the garden. Standing in the doorway with her back to us was a white-haired figure. She was humming. La-la-la-la-la. That broken piece of melody, without a beginning, without a resolution, that had haunted me ever since I came to the house. It wormed its way into my head, where it vied with the high-pitched vibration of my sister. At my side Aurelius waited for me to announce us to Emmeline. But I could not speak. The universe was reduced to an unbearable ululation in my head; time stretched into one eternal second; I was struck dumb. I brought my hands to my ears, desperate to ease the cacophony. Seeing my gesture, it was Aurelius who spoke. "Margaret!"

And hearing an unknown voice behind her, Emmeline turns.

Since she was taken by surprise, there is anguish in her green eyes. Her lipless mouth pulls into a distorted *O,* but the humming does not stop, only veers and lurches into a shrill wail, like a knife in my head.

Aurelius turns in shock from me to Emmeline and is transfixed by the broken face of the woman who is his mother. Like scissors, the sound from her lips slashes the air.

For a time I am both blinded and deafened. When I can see again, Emmeline is crouched on the floor, her keening fallen to a whimper. Aurelius kneels over her. Her hands scrabble at him, and I do not know whether she means to clasp him or to repel him, but he takes her hand in his and holds it.

Hand in hand. Blood with blood.

He is a monolith of sorrow.

Inside my head, still, a torment of bright white sound.

My sister— My sister—

The world retreats and I find myself alone in an agony of noise.

I know what happened next, even if I can't remember it. Aurelius releases Emmeline tenderly onto the floor as he hears steps in the hall. There is an exclamation as Judith realizes she does not have her keys. In the time it takes her to go and find a second set—Maurice's, probably—Aurelius darts toward the door and disappears into the garden. When Judith at last enters the room, she stares at Emmeline on the floor, then, with a cry of alarm, steps in my direction.

But at the time I know none of this. For the light that is my sister embraces me, possesses me, relieves me of consciousness.

At last.

## EVERYBODY HAS A STORY

Anxiety, sharp as one of Miss Winter's green gazes, needles me awake. What name have I pronounced in my sleep? Who undressed me and put me to bed? What will they have read into the sign on my skin? What has become of Aurelius? And what have I done to Emmeline? More than all the rest it is her distraught face that torments my conscience when it begins its slow ascent out of sleep.

When I wake I do not know what day or time it is. Judith is there; she sees me stir and holds a glass to my lips. I drink.

Before I can speak, sleep overwhelms me again.

The second time I woke up, Miss Winter was at my bedside, book in hand. Her chair was plump with velvet cushions, as always, but with her tufts of pale hair around her naked face, she looked like a naughty child who has climbed onto the queen's throne for a joke.

Hearing me move, she lifted her head from her reading.

"Dr. Clifton has been. You had a very high temperature."

I said nothing.

"We didn't know it was your birthday," she went on.
"We couldn't find a card. We don't go in much for
birthdays here. But we brought you some daphne from
the garden."

In the vase were dark branches, bare of leaf, but with
dainty purple flowers all along their length. They filled
the air with a sweet, heady fragrance.

"How did you know it was my birthday?"

"You told us. While you were sleeping. When are you
going to tell me *your* story, Margaret?"

"Me? I haven't got a story," I said.

"Of course you have. Everybody has a story."

"Not me." I shook my head. In my head I heard indistinct echoes of words I may have spoken in my sleep.

Miss Winter placed the ribbon at her page and closed
the book.

"Everybody has a story. It's like families. You might
not know who they are, might have lost them, but they
exist all the same. You might drift apart or you might
turn your back on them, but you can't say you haven't
got them. Same goes for stories. So," she concluded,
"everybody has a story. When are you going to tell me
yours?"

"I'm not."

She put her head to one side and waited for me to go
on.

"I've never told anyone my story. *If* I've got one, that

is. And I can't see any reason to change now."

"I see," she said softly, nodding her head as though she really did. "Well, it's your business, of course." She turned her hand in her lap and stared into her damaged palm. "You are at liberty to say nothing, if that is what you want. But silence is not a natural environment for stories. They need words. Without them they grow pale, sicken and die. And then they haunt you." Her eyes swiveled back to me. "Believe me, Margaret. I know."

For long stretches of time I slept, and whenever I woke, there was some invalid's meal by my bed, prepared by Judith. I ate a mouthful or two, no more. When Judith came to take the tray away she could not disguise her disappointment at seeing my leavings, yet she never mentioned it. I was in no pain—no headache, no chills, no sickness—unless you count profound weariness and a remorse that weighed heavily in my head and in my heart. What had I done to Emmeline? And Aurelius? In my waking hours I was tormented by the memory of that night; the guilt pursued me into sleep.

"How is Emmeline?" I asked Judith. "Is she all right?"

Her answers were indirect: Why should I be worried about Miss Emmeline when I was poorly myself? Miss Emmeline had not been right for a very long time. Miss Emmeline was getting on in years.

Her reluctance to spell it out told me everything I wanted to know. Emmeline was not well. It was my fault.

As for Aurelius, the only thing I could do was write. As soon as I was able, I had Judith bring me pen and paper and, propped up on a pillow, drafted a letter. Not satisfied, I attempted another and then another. Never had I had such difficulty with words. When my bedcover was so strewn with rejected versions that I despaired at myself, I selected one at random and made a neat copy:

> *Dear Aurelius,*
> *Are you all right?*
> *I'm so sorry about what happened. I never meant to hurt anyone. I was mad, wasn't I?*
> *When can I see you?*
> *Are we still friends?*
>
> *Margaret*

It would have to do.

Dr. Clifton came. He listened to my heart and asked me lots of questions. "Insomnia? Irregular sleep? Nightmares?"

I nodded three times.

"I thought so."

He took a thermometer and instructed me to place it under my tongue, then rose and strode to the window. With his back to me, he asked, "And what do you read?"

With the thermometer in my mouth I could not reply.

"*Wuthering Heights*—you've read that?"

"Mm-hmm."

"And *Jane Eyre*?"

"Mm."

"*Sense and Sensibility*?"

"Hm-m."

He turned and looked gravely at me. "And I suppose you've read these books more than once?"

I nodded and he frowned.

"Read and reread? Many times?"

Once more I nodded, and his frown deepened.

"Since childhood?"

I was baffled by his questions, but compelled by the gravity of his gaze, nodded once again.

Beneath his dark brow his eyes narrowed to slits. I could quite see how he might frighten his patients into getting well, just to be rid of him.

And then he leaned close to me to read the thermometer.

People look different from close up. A dark brow is still a dark brow, but you can see the individual hairs in it, how nearly they are aligned. The last few brow hairs, very fine, almost invisible, strayed off in the direction of his temple, pointed to the snail-coil of his ear. In the grain of his skin were closely arranged pinpricks of beard. There it was again: that almost imperceptible flaring of the nostrils, that twitch at the edge of the mouth. I had always taken it for severity, a clue that he thought little of me; but now, seeing it from so few inches away, it occurred to me that it might not be disapproval after all. Was it possible, I thought, that Dr.

Clifton was secretly *laughing* at me?

He removed the thermometer from my mouth, folded his arms and delivered his diagnosis. "You are suffering from an ailment that afflicts ladies of romantic imagination. Symptoms include fainting, weariness, loss of appetite, low spirits. While on one level the crisis can be ascribed to wandering about in freezing rain without the benefit of adequate water-proofing, the deeper cause is more likely to be found in some emotional trauma. However, unlike the hero-ines of your favorite novels, your constitution has not been weakened by the privations of life in earlier, harsher centuries. No tuberculosis, no childhood polio, no unhygienic living conditions. You'll sur-vive."

He looked me straight in the eyes, and I was unable to slide my gaze away when he said, "You don't eat enough."

"I have no appetite."

*"L'appétit vient en mangeant."*

"Appetite comes by eating," I translated.

"Exactly. Your appetite will come back. But you must meet it halfway. You must want it to come."

It was my turn to frown.

"Treatment is not complicated: eat, rest and take this . . ."—he made quick notes on a pad, tore out a page and placed it on my bedside table—"and the weakness and fatigue will be gone in a few days." Reaching for his case, he stowed his pen and paper. Then, rising to leave, he hesitated. "I'd like to ask you about these dreams of yours, but I suspect you wouldn't like to tell me . . ."

Stonily I regarded him. "I wouldn't."

His face fell. "Thought not."

From the door he saluted me and was gone.

I reached for the prescription. In a vigorous scrawl, he had inked: *Sir Arthur Conan Doyle,* The Case Book of Sherlock Holmes. *Take ten pages, twice a day, till end of course.*

## DECEMBER DAYS

Obeying Dr. Clifton's instructions, I spent two days in bed, eating and sleeping and reading Sherlock Holmes. I confess I overdosed on my pre-scribed treatment, gulping down one story after another. Before the end of the second day Judith had been down to the library and fetched another volume of Conan Doyle for me. She had grown suddenly kind toward me since my collapse. It was not the fact that she was sorry for me that altered her—though she *was* sorry—but the fact that now Emmeline's presence was no longer a secret in the house, she was at liberty to let her natural sympathies govern her exchanges with me, instead of maintaining a constantly guarded facade.

"And has she never said anything about the thirteenth tale?" she asked me wistfully one day.

"Not a word. And to you?"

She shook her head. "Never. It's strange, isn't it, after all she's written, that the most famous story of all is one that might not even exist. Just think, she could probably publish a book with *all* the stories missing and it would still sell like hotcakes." And then, with a shake of the head to clear her thoughts, and a new tone, "So what do you make of Dr. Clifton, then?"

When Dr. Clifton dropped by to see how I was doing, his eye alighted on the volumes by my bedside; he said nothing but his nostrils twitched.

On the third day, feeling as frail as a newborn, I got up. As I pulled the curtains apart, my room was flooded with a fresh, clean light. Outside, a brilliant, cloudless blue stretched from horizon to horizon, and beneath it the garden sparkled with frost. It was as if during those long overcast days the light had been accumulating behind the cloud, and now that the cloud was gone there was nothing to stop it flooding down, drenching us in a fortnight's worth of illumination at once. Blinking in the brilliance, I felt something like life begin to move sluggishly in my veins.

Before breakfast I went outdoors. Slowly and cautiously I stepped around the lawn with Shadow at my heels. It was crisp underfoot, and everywhere the sun sparkled on icy foliage. The frost-rimed grass held the imprint of my soles, but at my side Shadow stepped like a dainty ghost, leaving no prints. At first the cold, dry air was like a knife in my throat, but little by little it rejuvenated me, and I rejoiced in the exhilaration. Nevertheless, a few minutes were enough; cheeks tingling, pink-fingered and with aching toes, I was glad to come back in and Shadow was glad to follow. First breakfast, then the library sofa, the blazing fire, and something to read.

I could judge how much better I was by the fact that my thoughts turned not to the treasures of Miss Winter's library, but to her own story. Upstairs I retrieved my pile of paper, neglected since the day of my collapse, and brought it back to the warmth of the hearth where, with Shadow by my side, I spent the best part of the daylight hours reading. I read and I read and I read, discovering the story all over again, reminding myself of its puzzles, mysteries and secrets. But there were no revelations. At the end of it all I was as baffled as I had been before I started. Had someone tampered with John-the-dig's ladder? But who? And what was it that Hester had seen when she thought she saw a ghost? And, more inexplicable than all the rest, how had Adeline, that violent vagabond of a child, unable to communicate with anyone but her slow-witted sister and capable of heartbreaking acts of horticultural destruction, developed into Miss Winter, the self-disciplined author of dozens of best-selling novels and, furthermore, maker of an exquisite garden?

I pushed my pile of papers to one side, stroked Shadow and stared into the fire, longing for the comfort of a story where everything had been planned well in advance, where the confusion of the middle was invented only for my enjoyment, and where I could measure how far away the solution was by feeling the thickness of pages still to come. I had no idea how many pages it would take to complete the story of

Emmeline and Adeline, nor even whether there would be time to complete it.

Despite my absorption in my notes, I couldn't help wondering why I hadn't seen Miss Winter. Each time I asked after her Judith gave me the same reply: She is with Miss Emmeline. Until evening, when she came with a message from Miss Winter herself: Was I feeling well enough to read to her for a while before supper?

When I went to her I found a book—*Lady Audley's Secret*—on the table by Miss Winter's side. I opened it at the bookmark and read. But I had read only a chapter when I stopped, sensing that she wanted to talk to me.

"What *did* happen that night?" Miss Winter asked. "The night you fell ill?"

I was nervously glad to have an opportunity for explanation. "I already knew Emmeline was in the house. I had heard her at night. I had seen her in the garden. I found her rooms. Then on that particular night I brought someone to see her. Emmeline was startled. The last thing I intended was to frighten her. But she was taken by surprise when she saw us, and—" My voice caught in my throat.

"This is not your fault, you know. Don't alarm yourself. The wailing and the nervous collapse—it is something I and Judith and the doctor have seen many times before. If anyone is to blame, it is me, for not letting you know sooner that she was here. I have a tendency to be overprotective. I was foolish not to tell you." She paused. "Do you intend to tell me whom it was you brought with you?"

386

"Emmeline had a baby," I said. "That's the person who came with me. The man in the brown suit." And after I'd told what I knew, the questions I didn't know the answer to came rushing to my lips, as though my own frankness might encourage her to be candid in return. "What is it Emmeline was looking for in the garden? She was trying to dig something up when I saw her there. She often does it: Maurice says it's the work of foxes, but I know that is not the truth."

Miss Winter was silent and very still.

*"The dead go underground,"* I quoted. "That's what she told me. Who does she think is buried? Is it her child? Hester? Who is she looking for underground?"

Miss Winter uttered a murmur, and though it was faint, it instantly awakened the lost memory of the hoarse pronouncement launched at me by Emmeline in the garden. The very words! "Is that it?" added Miss Winter. "Is that what she said?"

I nodded.

"In twin language?"

I nodded again.

Miss Winter looked at me with interest. "You are doing very well, Margaret. Better than I thought. The trouble is, the timing of this story is getting rather out of hand. We are getting ahead of ourselves." She paused, staring into her palm, then looked straight at me. "I said I meant to tell you the truth, Margaret. And I do. But before I can tell you, something must happen first. It is going to happen. But it has not happened yet."

"What—?"

But before I could finish my question, she shook her head. "Let us return to Lady Audley and her secret, shall we?"

I read for another half hour or so, but my mind was not on the story, and I had the impression Miss Winter's attention was wandering, too. When Judith tapped at the door at suppertime, I closed the book and put it to one side, and as if there had been no interruption, as if it were a continuation of the discussion we had been having before, Miss Winter said, "If you are not too tired, why don't you come and see Emmeline this evening?"

## SISTERS

When it was time, I went to Emmeline's quarters. It was the first time I had been there as an invited guest, and the first thing I noticed, before I even entered the bedroom, was the thickness of the silence. I paused in the doorway—they had not noticed me yet—and realized it was their whispering. On the edge of inaudibility, the rub of breath over vocal cords made ripples in the air. Soft plosives that were gone before you could hear them, muffled sibilants that you might mistake for the sound of your own blood in your ears. Each time I thought it had stopped a hushed sussuration brushed against my ear like a moth alighting on my hair, then fluttered away again.

I cleared my throat.

"Margaret." Miss Winter, her wheelchair positioned next to her sister, gestured to a chair on the other side of the bed. "How good of you."

I looked at Emmeline's face on the pillow. The red and the white were the same red and white of scarring and burn damage that I had seen before; she had lost none of her well-fed plumpness; her hair was still the tangled skein of white. Listlessly her gaze wandered over the ceiling; she appeared indifferent to my presence. Where was the difference? For she *was* different. Some alteration had taken place in her, a change instantly visible to the eye, though too elusive to define. She had lost nothing of her strength, though. One arm extended outside the coverlet and in it she had Miss Winter's hand in a firm grip.

"How are you, Emmeline?" I asked nervously.

"She is not well," said Miss Winter.

Miss Winter, too, had changed in recent days. But in her disease was a distillation: The more it reduced her, the more it exposed her essence. Every time I saw her she seemed diminished: thinner, frailer, more transparent, and the weaker she grew, the more the steel at her center was revealed.

All the same, it was a very thin, weak hand that Emmeline was grasping in the clutch of her own heavy fist.

"Would you like me to read?" I asked.

"By all means."

I read a chapter. Then, "She's asleep," Miss Winter murmured. Emmeline's eyes were closed; her breathing was deep and regular. She had released her grip on her sister's hand, and Miss Winter was rubbing the life back into it. There were the beginnings of bruises on her fingers.

Seeing the direction of my gaze, she drew her hands into her shawl. "I'm sorry about this interruption to our work," she said. "I had to send you away once before when Emmeline was ill. And now, too, I must spend my time with her, and our project must wait. But it won't be long now. And there is Christmas coming. You will be wanting to leave us and be with your family. When you come back after the holiday we will see how things stand. I expect . . ."—it was the briefest of pauses—"we shall be able to work again by then."

I did not immediately understand her meaning. The words were ambiguous; it was her voice that gave it away. My eyes leaped to Emmeline's sleeping face.

"Do you mean . . . ?"

Miss Winter sighed. "Don't be taken in by the fact that she seems so strong. She has been ill for a very long time. For years I assumed that I would live to see her depart before me. Then, when I fell ill, I was not so sure. And now it seems we are in a race to the finish line."

So that's what we were waiting for. The event without which the story could not end.

Suddenly my throat was dry and my heart was frightened as a child's.

Dying. Emmeline was dying.

"Is it my fault?"

390

"Your fault? How should it be your fault?" Miss Winter shook her head. "That night had nothing to do with it."

She gave me one of her old, sharp looks that understood more than I meant to reveal. "Why does this upset you, Margaret? My sister is a stranger to you. And it is hardly compassion for me that distresses you so, is it? Tell me, Margaret, what is the matter?"

In part she was wrong. I did feel compassion for her. For I believed I knew what Miss Winter was going through. She was about to join me in the ranks of the amputees. Bereaved twins are half-souls. The line between life and death is narrow and dark, and a bereaved twin lives closer to it than most. Though she was often short-tempered and contrary, I had grown to like Miss Winter. In particular I liked the child she had once been, the child who emerged more and more frequently nowadays. With her cropped hair, her naked face, her frail hands denuded of their heavy stones, she seemed to grow more childlike every day. To my mind it was this child who was losing her sister, and this is where Miss Winter's sorrow met my own. Her drama was going to be played out here in this house, in the coming days, and it was the very same drama that had shaped my life, though it had taken place for me in the days before I could remember.

I watched Emmeline's face on the pillow. She was approaching the divide that already separated me from my sister. Soon she would cross it and be lost to us, a new arrival in that other place. I was filled with the absurd desire to whisper in her ear, a message for my sister, entrusted to one who might see her soon. Only what to say?

I felt Miss Winter's curious gaze upon my face. I restrained my folly.

"How long?" I asked.

"Days. A week, perhaps. Not long."

I sat up late that night with Miss Winter. I was there again at the side of Emmeline's bed the next day, too. We sat, reading aloud or in silence for long periods, with only Dr. Clifton coming to interrupt our vigil. He seemed to take my presence there as a natural thing, included me in the same grave smile he bestowed on Miss Winter as he spoke gently about Emmeline's decline. And sometimes then he sat with us for an hour or so, sharing our limbo, listening while I read. Books from any shelf, opened at any page, in which I would start and finish anywhere, mid-sentence sometimes. *Wuthering Heights* ran into *Emma,* which gave way to *The Eustace Diamonds,* which faded into *Hard Times,* which ceded to *The Woman in White.* Fragments. It didn't matter. Art, its completeness, its formedness, its finishedness, had no power to console. Words, on the other hand, were a lifeline. They left their hushed rhythm behind, a counter to the slow in and out of Emmeline's breathing.

Then the day faded and tomorrow would be Christmas Eve, the day of my departure. In a way I did not want to leave. The hush of this house, the splendid solitariness offered by its garden, were all I wanted of the world at present. The shop and my father seemed very small and far away, my mother, as ever, more distant still. As for Christmas . . . In our house the festive season followed too close upon my birthday for my mother to be able to bear the celebration of the birth of some other woman's child, no matter how long ago. I thought of my father, opening the Christmas cards from my parents' few friends, arranging over the fireplace the innocuous Santas, snow scenes and robins and putting aside the ones that showed the Madonna. Every year he collected a secret pile of them: jewel-colored images of the mother gazing in rapture at her single, complete, perfect infant; the infant gazing back at her; the two of them making a blissful circle of love and wholeness. Every year they went in the trash, the lot of them.

Miss Winter, I knew, would not object if I asked to stay. She might even be glad to have a companion in the days ahead. But I did not ask. I could not. I had seen Emmeline's decline. As she had weakened, so the hand on my heart had squeezed more tightly, and my growing anguish told me that the end was not far off. It was cowardly of me, but when Christmas came, it was an opportunity to escape, and I took it.

In the evening, I went to my room and did my packing, then went back to Emmeline's quarters to say good-bye to Miss Winter. All the sisters' whispers had fluttered away, the dimness hung heavier, stiller than before. Miss Winter had a book in her lap, but if she had been reading, she could see to read no longer; instead, her eyes watched in sadness her sister's face. In her bed, Emmeline lay immobile, the covers rising and falling gently with her breath. Her eyes were closed and she looked deeply asleep.

"Margaret," Miss Winter murmured, indicating a chair. She seemed pleased that I had come. Together we waited for the light to fade, listening to the tide of Emmeline's breath.

Between us, in the sickbed, Emmeline's breath rolled in and out, in a smooth, imperturbable rhythm, soothing like the sound of waves on a seashore.

Miss Winter did not speak, and I, too, was silent, composing in my mind impossible messages I might send to my sister via this imminent traveler to that other world. With every exhalation, the room seemed filled with a deeper and more enduring sorrow.

Against the window, a dark silhouette, Miss Winter stirred.

"You should have this," she said, and a movement in the darkness told me she was holding something out to me across the bed.

My fingers closed on a rectangular leather object with a metal lock. Some sort of book.

"From Emmeline's treasure box. It will not be needed anymore. Go away. Read it. When you come back we will talk."

Book in hand, I crossed the room to the door, feeling my way by the furniture in my path. Behind me was the tide of Emmeline's breath rolling in and out.

Hester's diary was damaged. The key was missing, the clasp so rusted that it left orange stains on your fingers. The first three pages were stuck together where the glue from the inner cover had melted into them. On every page the last word dissolved into a brownish tide mark, as if the diary had been exposed to dirt and damp together. A few pages had been torn; along the ripped edges was a tantalizing list of fragments: *abn, cr, ta, est.* Worst of all, it seemed that the diary had at some point been submerged in water. The pages undulated; when closed, the diary splayed to more than its intended thickness.

It was this submersion that was going to cause me the greatest difficulty. When one glanced at a page, it was clear that it was script. Not any old script, either, but Hester's. Here were her firm ascenders, her balanced, fluid loops; here were her comfortable slant, her economic yet functional gaps. But on a closer look, the words were blurred and faded. Was this line an *l* or a *t*? Was this curve an *a* or an *e*? Or an *s*, even? Was this configuration to be read as *bet* or *lost*?

It was going to be quite a puzzle. Although I subsequently made a transcript of the diary, on that day the holiday train was too crowded to permit pencil and paper. I hunched in my window seat, diary close to my nose, and pored over the pages, applying myself to the task of deciphering. I managed one word in three at first, then as I was drawn into the flow of her meaning, the words began to come halfway to meet me, rewarding my efforts with generous revelations, until I was able to turn the pages with something like the speed of reading. In that train, the day before Christmas, Hester came to life.

I will not test your patience by reproducing Hester's diary here as it came to me: fragmented and broken. In the spirit of Hester herself, I have mended and tidied and put in order. I have banished chaos and clutter. I have replaced doubt with certainty, shadows with clarity, lacunae with substance. In doing so, I may have occasionally put words into her page that she never wrote, but I can promise that if I have made mistakes, it is only in the small things; where it matters I have squinted and scrutinized until I am as sure as sure can be that I have distinguished her original meaning.

I do not give the entire diary, only an edited selection of passages. My choice has been dictated first by questions of relevance to my purpose, which is to tell the story of Miss Winter, and second by my desire to give an accurate impression of Hester's life at Angelfield.

❦

*Angelfield House is decent enough at a distance, although it faces the wrong way and the windows are badly positioned, but on approaching, one sees instantly the state of dilapidation it has been allowed to fall into. Sections of the stonework are dangerously weathered. Window frames are rotting. And it did look as though parts of the roof are storm-damaged. I shall make it a priority to check the ceilings in the attic rooms.*

*The housekeeper welcomed me at the door. Though she tries to hide it, I understood immediately that she has difficulty seeing and hearing. Given her great age, this is no surprise. It also explains the filthy state of the house, but I suppose the Angelfield family does not want to throw her out after a lifetime's service in the house. I can approve their loyalty, though I fail to see why she cannot be helped by younger, stronger hands.*

*Mrs. Dunne told me about the household. The family has been living here with what most would consider a greatly reduced staff for years now, and it has come to be accepted as part of the way of the house. Quite why it should be so, I have not yet ascertained, but what I do know is that there is, outside the family proper, only Mrs. Dunne and a gardener called John Digence. There are deer (though there is no hunting anymore), but the man who looks after them is never seen around the house; he takes instruction from the same solicitor who engaged me and who acts as a kind of estate manager—so far as there is any estate management. It is Mrs. Dunne herself who deals with the regular household finances. I supposed that Charles Angelfield looked over the books and the receipts each week, but Mrs. Dunne only laughed and asked if I thought she had the sight to go making lists of figures in a book. I cannot help but think this highly unorthodox. Not that I think Mrs. Dunne untrustworthy. From what I have seen she gives every indication of being a good-*

397

hearted, honest woman, and it is my hope that when I come to know her better I shall be able to ascribe her reticence entirely to deafness. I made a note to demonstrate to Mr. Angelfield the advantages of keeping accurate records and thought that I might offer to undertake the job myself if he was too busy to do it.

Pondering this, I began to think it time I met my employer, and could not have been more surprised when Mrs. Dunne told me he spends his entire day in the old nursery and that it is not his habit to leave it. After a great many questions I eventually ascertained that he is suffering from some kind of disorder of the mind. A great pity! Is there anything more sorrowful than a brain whose proper function has been disrupted?

Mrs. Dunne gave me tea (which I pretended to drink out of politeness, but later threw into the sink for I had no faith in the cleanliness of the teacup, having seen the state of the kitchen) and told me a little about herself. She is in her eighties, never married, and has lived here all her life. Naturally enough our talk then turned to the family. Mrs. Dunne knew the mother of the twins as a girl and young woman. She confirmed what I had already understood: that it is the recent departure of the mother to an asylum for the sick of mind that precipitated my engagement. She gave me such a contorted account of the events that precipitated the mother's committal that I could not make out whether the woman had or had not attacked the doctor's wife with a violin. It hardly matters; clearly there is a family history of dis-

*turbance in the brain, and I confess, my heart beat a little faster when I had it confirmed. What satisfaction is there, for a governess, in being given the direction of minds that already run in smooth and untrammeled lines? What challenge in maintaining ordered thinking in children whose minds are already neat and tidy? I am not only ready for this job, I have spent years longing for it. Here, I shall finally find out what my methods are worth!*

*I inquired after the father's family—for though Mr. March is deceased and the children never knew him, still, his blood is theirs and has an impact on their natures. Mrs. Dunne was able to tell me very little, though. Instead, she began a series of anecdotes about the mother and the uncle, which, if I am to read between the lines (as I'm sure she meant me to), contained hints of something scandalous. . . . Of course, what she suggests is not at all likely, not in England at least, and I suspect her of being somewhat fanciful. The imagination is a healthy thing, and a great many scientific discoveries could not have been made without it, but it needs to be harnessed to some serious object if it is to come to anything. Left to wander its own way, it tends to lead into silliness. Perhaps it is age that makes her mind wander, for she seems a kind thing in other ways, and not the sort to invent gossip for the sake of it. In any case, I immediately put the topic firmly from my mind.*

*As I write this I hear noises outside my room. The girls have come out of their hiding place and are creeping about the house. They have been done no* favors, allowed to suit themselves like this. They will benefit enormously from the regime of order, hygiene and discipline that I mean to instill in the house. I shall not go out to them. No doubt they will expect me to, and it will suit my purposes to disconcert them at this stage.

Mrs. Dunne showed me the rooms on the ground floor. There is filth everywhere, all the surfaces thick with dust, and curtains hanging in tatters, though she does not see it and thinks of them as they were years ago in the time of the twins' grandfather, when there was a full staff. There is a piano that may be beyond saving, but I will see what can be done, and a library that may be full of knowledge once the dust is wiped and one can see what is there.

The other floors I explored alone, not wanting to inflict too many stairs at once on Mrs. Dunne. On the first floor I became aware of a scuffling, a whispering and smothered giggling. I had found my charges. They had locked the door and fell silent when I tried the handle. I called their names once, then left them to their own devices and went on to the second floor. It is a cardinal rule that I do not chase my charges, but train them to come to me.

The second-floor rooms were in the most terrible disorder. Dirty, but I had come to expect that. Rainwater had come through the roof (I expected as much) and there were fungi growing in some of the rotting floorboards. This is a truly unhealthy environment in which to raise children. A number of floorboards were missing, looked as if they had been deliberately

400

removed. I shall have to see Mr. Angelfield about getting these repaired. I shall point out to him that someone could fall downstairs or at the very least twist an ankle. All the hinges need oiling, and all the door frames are warped. Wherever I went I was followed by a squeaking of doors swinging on their hinges, a creaking of floorboards, and drafts that set curtains fluttering, though it is impossible to tell exactly where they come from.

I returned to the kitchen as soon as I could. Mrs. Dunne was preparing our evening meal, and I had no inclination to eat food cooked in pots as unpleasant as the ones I had seen, so I got stuck into a great pile of washing up (after giving the sink the most thorough scrubbing it had seen for a decade) and kept a close eye on her with the preparation. She does her best.

The girls would not come down to eat. I called once and no more. Mrs. Dunne was all for calling and persuading, but I told her that I have my methods, and she must be on my side.

The doctor came to dine. As I had been led to expect, the head of the household did not appear. I had thought the doctor would be offended at this, but he seemed to find it entirely normal. So it was just the two of us, and Mrs. Dunne doing her best to wait at table, but needing much help from me.

The doctor is an intelligent, cultivated man. He has a sincere desire to see the twins improve and has been the prime mover in bringing me to Angelfield. He explained to me at great length the difficulties I am likely to face here, and I listened with as much politeness as I could muster. Any governess, after the few hours I have had in this house, would have a full and clear picture of the task awaiting her, but he is a man, hence cannot see how tiresome it is to have explained at length what one has already fully understood. My fidgeting and the slight sharpness of one or two of my answers entirely escaped his notice, and I fear that his energy and his analytical skills are not matched by his powers of observation. I do not criticize him unduly for expecting everyone he meets to be less able than himself. For he is a clever man, and more than that, he is a big fish in a small pond. He has adopted an air of quiet modesty, but I see through that easily enough, for I have disguised myself in exactly the same manner. However, I shall need his support in the project I have taken on, and shall work at making him my ally despite his shortcomings.

I hear sounds of an upset from downstairs. Presumably the girls have discovered the lock on the pantry door. They will be angry and frustrated, but how else can I train them to proper mealtimes? And without mealtimes, how can order be restored?

Tomorrow I will start by cleaning this bedroom. I have wiped the surfaces with a damp cloth this evening, and was tempted to clean the floor, but told myself no. It will only need doing again tomorrow when I scrub the walls and take down the curtains that are so thick with dirt. So tonight I sleep in dirt, but tomorrow I shall sleep in a bright clean room. It will be a good beginning. For I plan to restore order and discipline to this house, and to succeed in my aim must first of all make myself a clean room to think in. No one can think clearly and make progress if she is not surrounded by hygiene and order.

The twins are crying in the hall. It is time for me to meet my charges.

❦

I have been so busy organizing the house that I have had little time for my diary lately, but I must make the time, for it is chiefly in writing that I record and develop my methods.

Emmeline I have made good progress with, and my experience with her fits the pattern of behavior I have seen in other difficult children. She is not, I think, as badly disturbed as was reported, and with my influence will come to be a nice child. She is affectionate and sturdy, has learned to appreciate the benefits of hygiene, eats with a good appetite and can be made to obey instructions by kind coaxing and the promise of small treats. She will soon come to understand that goodness rewards by bringing the esteem of others in its wake, and then I will be able to reduce the bribery. She will never be clever, but then I know the limits of my methods. Whatever my strengths, I can only develop what is there to start with.

I am content with my work on Emmeline.

Her sister is a more difficult case. Violence I have seen before, and I am less shocked than Adeline thinks by her destructiveness. However, I am struck by one

403

thing: *In other children destructiveness is generally a side effect of rage and not its primary objective. The violent act, as I have observed it in other charges, is most frequently motivated by an excess of anger, and the outpouring of the anger is only incidentally damaging to people and property. Adeline's case does not fit this model. I have seen incidents myself, and been told of others, in which destruction seems to be Adeline's only motive, and rage something she has to tease out, stoke up in herself, in order to generate the energy to destroy. For she is a feeble little thing, skin and bone, and eats only crumbs. Mrs. Dunne has told me of one incident in the garden, when Adeline is known to have damaged a number of yews. If this is true, it is a great shame. The garden was clearly very beautiful. It could be put to rights, but John has lost heart over the matter, and it is not only the topiary but the garden in general that suffers from his lack of interest. I will find the time and a way to restore his pride. It will do much to improve the appearance and the atmosphere of the house if he can be made happy in his work and the garden made orderly again.*

*Talking of John and the garden reminds me—I must speak to him about the boy. Walking about the schoolroom this afternoon, I happened to come near the window. It was raining, and I wanted to close the window so as not to let any more damp in; the window ledge on the inside is already crumbling away. If I hadn't been so close to the window, nose almost pressed to the glass, in fact, I doubt I'd have seen him. But there*

404

he was: a boy, crouching in the flower bed, weeding. He was wearing a pair of men's trousers, cut off at the ankle and held up with a pair of braces. A wide-brimmed hat cast his face in shadow, and I was unable to get a clear impression of his age, though he might have been eleven or twelve. I know it is common practice in rural areas for children to engage in horticultural work, though I thought it was more commonly farmwork they did, and I appreciate the advantages of their learning their trade early, but I do not like to see any child out of school during school hours. I will speak to John about it and make sure he understands the boy must spend school hours in school.

But to return to my subject: Where Adeline's viciousness to her sister is concerned, she might be surprised to know it, but I have seen it all before. Jealousy and anger between siblings is commonplace, and in twins rivalries are frequently heightened. With time I will be able to minimize the aggression, but in the meantime constant vigilance is required to prevent Adeline hurting her sister, and this slows down progress on other fronts, which is a pity. Why Emmeline lets herself be beaten (and have her hair pulled out, and be chased by Adeline wielding the fire tongs in which she carries hot coals) I have yet to understand. She is twice the size of her sister and could defend herself more vigorously than she does. Perhaps she flinches from inflicting hurt on her sister; she is an affectionate soul.

❦

*My first judgment of Adeline in the early days was of a*

405

*child who might not ever come to live as independent and normal a life as her sister, but who could be brought to a point of balance, of stability, and whose rages could be contained by the imposition of a strict routine. I did not expect ever to bring her to understanding. The task I foresaw was greater than for her sister, but I expected far less thanks for it, for it would seem less in the eyes of the world.*

*But I have been startled into modifying that opinion by signs of a dark and clouded intelligence. This morning she came into the classroom dragging her feet, but without the worst displays of unwillingness, and once in her seat, rested her head on her arm just as I have seen before. I began the lesson. It was nothing more than the telling of a story, an adaptation I had made for the purpose of the opening chapters of* Jane Eyre, *a story loved by a great many girls. I was concentrating on Emmeline, encouraging her to follow the story by animating it as much as possible. I gave one voice to the heroine, another to the aunt, yet another to the cousin, and I accompanied the storytelling with such gestures and expressions as seemed to illustrate the emotions of the characters. Emmeline did not take her eyes off me, and I was pleased with my effect.*

*Out of the corner of my eye I caught a movement. Adeline had turned her head in my direction. Still her head rested on her arm, still her eyes appeared closed, yet I had the distinct impression she was listening to me. Even if the change of position was meaningless (and it was not; she has always turned away from me before), there is the alteration in the way she held herself. Where she normally slumps over her desk when she sleeps, in a state of animal unconsciousness, today her whole body seemed alert: the set of the shoulders, a certain tension. As if she was straining toward the story, yet still trying to give the impression of inert slumber.*

*I did not want her to see that I had noticed anything. I continued to look as if I was reading only to Emmeline. I maintained the animation of my face and voice. But all the time I was keeping an eye on Adeline. And she wasn't only listening. I caught a quiver of her lids. I had thought her eyes closed, but not at all—from between her lashes, she was watching me!*

*It is a most interesting development, and one that I foresee will be the centerpin of my project here.*

❦

*Then the most unexpected thing happened. The doctor's face changed. Yes, changed, before my very eyes. It was one of those moments when a face comes suddenly into new focus, when the features, all recognizably as they were before, are prone to a dizzying shift and present themselves in an unexpected new light. I would like to know what it is in a human mind that causes the faces of those we know to shift and dance about like that. I have ruled out optical effects, phenomena related to light and so on, and have arrived at the conclusion that the explanation is rooted in the psychology of the onlooker. Anyway, the sudden movement and rearrangement of his facial features caused me to stare at him for a few moments, which must have seemed very strange to him. When his features had ceased their jumping about, there was something odd in his expression, too, something I could not, cannot fathom. I do dislike what I cannot fathom.*

*We stared at each other for a few seconds, each as awkward as the other, then rather abruptly he left.*

❦

*I wish Mrs. Dunne would not move my books about. How many times shall I have to tell her that a book is not finished until it is finished? And if she must move it, why not put it back in the library whence it came? What is the point of leaving it on the staircase?*

❦

*I have had a curious conversation with John the gardener.*

*He is a good worker, more cheerful now that his topiary is mending, and a helpful presence generally in the house. He drinks tea and chats in the kitchen with Mrs. Dunne; sometimes I come across them talking in low voices, which makes me think she is not as deaf as she makes out. Were it not for her great age I would imagine some love affair going on, but since that is out of the question I am at a loss to explain what their secret is. I taxed Mrs. Dunne with it, unhappily, because she and I have a friendly understanding about things for the most part; I think she approves of my presence here—not that it would make any difference if she didn't—and she told me that they talk of nothing but household matters, chickens to be killed, potatoes to be*

408

dug and the like. "Why talk so low?" I insisted, and she told me it was not low at all, at least not particularly so. "But you don't hear me when I talk low," I said, and she answered that new voices are harder than the ones she is used to, and if she understands John when he talks low it is because she has known his voice for many years and mine for only a couple of months.

I had forgotten all about the low voices in the kitchen, until this new oddness with John. A few mornings ago I was taking a walk just before lunch in the garden when I saw again the boy who was weeding the flower bed beneath the schoolroom window. I glanced at my watch, and again it was in school hours. The boy did not see me, for I was hidden by the trees. I watched him for a moment or two; he was not working at all but sprawled across the lawn, engrossed in something on the grass, right under his nose. He wore the same floppy hat as before. I stepped toward him meaning to get his name and give him a lecture on the importance of education, but on seeing me he leaped to his feet, clamped his hat to his head with one hand and sprinted away faster than I have seen anyone move before. His alarm is proof enough of his guilt. The boy knew perfectly well he should be at school. As he ran off he appeared to have a book in his hand.

I went to John and told him just what I thought. I told him I would not allow children to work for him in school hours, that it was wrong to upset their education just for the few pence they earn, and that if the parents did not accept that, I would go and see them myself. I

409

told him if it was so necessary to have further hands working on the garden that I would see Mr. Angelfield and employ a man. I had already made this offer to get extra staff, both for the garden and the house, but John and Mrs. Dunne were both so against the idea I thought it better to wait until I was more acquainted with the running of things here.

John's response was to shake his head and deny all knowledge of the child. When I impressed upon him the evidence of my own eyes, he said it must be a village child just come wandering in, that it happened some-times, that he was not responsible for all the village truants who happened to be in the garden. I told him then that I had seen the child before, the day I arrived, and that the child was clearly working. He was tight-lipped, only repeated that he had no knowledge of a child, that anyone could weed his garden who wanted to, that there was no such child.

I told John, with a little anger that I cannot regret, that I intended to speak to the schoolmistress about it, and that I would go directly to the parents and sort the matter out with them. He simply waved his hand, as if to say it was nothing to do with him and I might do as I liked (and I certainly shall). I am sure he knows who the boy is, and I am shocked at his refusal to help me in my duty toward him. It seems out of character for him to be obstructive, but then I suppose he began his own apprenticeship as a child and thought it never did him any harm. These attitudes are slow to die out in rural areas.

• • •

I was engrossed in the diary. The barriers to legibility forced me to read slowly, puzzling out the difficulties, using all my experience, knowledge and imagination to flesh out the ghost words, yet the obstacles seemed not to impede me. On the contrary, the faded margins, the illegibilities, the blurred words seemed to pulse with meaning, vividly alive.

While I was reading in this absorbed fashion, in another part of my mind entirely a decision was forming. When the train drew in at the station where I was to descend for my connection, I found my mind made up. I was not going home after all. I was going to Angelfield.

The local line train to Banbury was too crowded with Christmas travelers to sit, and I never read standing up. With every jolt of the train, every jostle and stumble of my fellow passengers, I felt the rectangle of Hester's diary against my chest. I had read only half of it. The rest could wait.

What happened to you, Hester, I thought. Where on earth did you go?


DEMOLISHING THE PAST

The windows showed me his kitchen was empty, and when I walked back to the front of the cottage and knocked on the door, there was no answer.

Might he have gone away? It was a time of year when

people did go away. But they went to their families, surely, and so Aurelius, having no family, would stay here. Belatedly the reason for Aurelius's absence occurred to me: He would be out delivering cakes for Christmas parties. Where else would a caterer be, just before Christmas? I would have to come back later. I put the card I had bought through the mail slot and set off through the woods toward Angelfield House.

It was cold; cold enough for snow. Beneath my feet the ground was frost-hard and above the sky was dangerously white. I walked briskly. With my scarf wrapped around my face as high as my nose, I soon warmed up.

At the clearing, I stopped. In the distance, at the site, there was unusual activity. I frowned. What was going on? My camera was around my neck, beneath my coat; the cold crept in as I undid my buttons. Using my long lens, I watched. There was a police car on the drive. The builders' vehicles and machinery were all stationary, and the builders were standing in a loose cluster. They must have stopped working a little while ago, for they were slapping their hands together and stamping their feet to keep warm. Their hats were on the ground or else slung by the strap from their elbows. One man offered a pack of cigarettes. From time to time one of them addressed a comment to the others, but there was no conversation. I tried to make out the expression on their unsmiling faces. Bored? Worried? Curious? They stood turned away from the site, facing the woods and my lens, but from time to time one or another cast a glance over his shoulder to the scene behind them.

Behind the group of men, a white tent had been erected to cover part of the site. The house was gone, but judging from the coach house, the gravel approach, the church, I guessed the tent was where the library had been. Beside it, one of their colleagues and a man I took to be their boss were in conversation with another pair of men. These were dressed one in a suit and overcoat, the other in a police uniform. It was the boss who was speaking, rapidly and with explanatory nods and shakes of the head, but when the man in the overcoat asked a question, it was the builder he addressed it to, and when he answered, all three men watched him intently.

He seemed unaware of the cold. He spoke in short sentences; in his long and frequent pauses the others did not speak, but watched him with intense patience. At one point he raised a finger in the direction of the machine and mimed its jaw of jagged teeth biting into the ground. At last he gave a shrug, frowned and drew his hand over his eyes as though to wipe them clean of the image he had just conjured.

A flap opened in the side of the white tent. A fifth man stepped out of it and joined the group. There was a brief, unsmiling conference and at the end of it, the boss went over to his group of men and had a few words with them. They nodded, and as though what they had been told was entirely what they were expecting, began to gather together the hats and thermos flasks at their feet and make their way to their cars parked by the lodge gates. The policeman in uniform positioned him-

413

self at the entrance to the tent, back to the flap, and the other ushered the builder and his boss toward the police car.

I lowered the camera slowly but continued to gaze at the white tent. I knew the spot. I had been there myself. I remembered the desolation of that desecrated library. The fallen bookshelves, the beams that had come crashing to the floor. My thrill of fear as I had stumbled over burned and broken wood.

There had been a body in that room. Buried in scorched pages, with a bookcase for a coffin. A grave hidden and protected for decades by the beams that fell.

I couldn't help the thought. I had been looking for someone, and now it appeared that someone had been found. The symmetry was irresistible. How not to make the connection? Yet Hester had left the year before, hadn't she? Why would she have come back? And then it struck me, and it was the very simplicity of the idea that made me think it might be true.

*What if Hester had never left at all?*

When I came to the edge of the woods, I saw the two blond children coming disconsolately down the drive. They wobbled and stumbled as they walked; beneath their feet the ground was scarred with curving black channels where the builders' heavy vehicles had gouged into the earth, and they weren't looking where they were going. Instead, they looked back over their shoulders in the direction they had come from.

It was the girl who, losing her footing and almost

falling, turned her head and saw me first. She stopped. When her brother saw me he grew self-important with knowledge and spoke.

"You can't go up there. The policeman said. You have to stay away."

"I see."

"They've made a tent," the girl added shyly.

"I saw it," I told her.

In the arch of the lodge gates, their mother appeared. She was slightly breathless. "Are you two all right? I saw a police car in The Street." And then to me, "What's going on?"

It was the girl who answered her. "The policemen have made a tent. You're not allowed to go near. They said we have to go home."

The blond woman raised her eyes to the site, frowning at the white tent. "Isn't that what they do when . . . ?" She didn't complete her question in front of the children, but I knew what she meant.

"I believe that is what has happened," I said. I saw her desire to draw her children close for reassurance, but she merely adjusted the boy's scarf and brushed her daughter's hair out of her eyes.

"Come on," she told the children. "It's too cold to be outdoors, anyway. Let's go home and have cocoa."

The children darted through the lodge gates and raced into the Street. An invisible cord held them together, allowed them to swing around each other or dash in any direction, knowing the other would always be there, the length of the cord away.

I watched them and felt a horrible absence by my side.

Their mother lingered next to me. "You could do with some cocoa yourself, couldn't you? You're as white as a ghost."

We fell into step, following the children. "My name's Margaret," I told her. "I'm a friend of Aurelius Love."

She smiled. "I'm Karen. I look after the deer here."

"I know. Aurelius told me."

Ahead of us, the girl lunged at her brother; he veered out of reach, running into the road to escape her.

"Thomas Ambrose Proctor!" my companion shouted out. "Get back on the pavement!"

The name sent a jolt through me. "What did you say your son's name was?"

The boy's mother turned to me curiously.

"It's just— There was a man called Proctor who worked here years ago."

"My father, Ambrose Proctor."

I had to stop to think straight. "Ambrose Proctor . . . the boy who worked with John-the-dig—he was your *father*?"

"John-the-dig? Do you mean John Digence? Yes. That's who got my father the job there. It was a long time before I was born, though. My father was in his fifties when I was born."

Slowly I began walking again. "I'll accept that offer of cocoa, if you don't mind. And I've got something to show you."

I took my bookmark out of Hester's diary. Karen smiled the instant she set eyes on the photo. Her son's serious face, full of pride, beneath the brim of the helmet, his shoulders stiff, his back straight. "I remember the day he came home and said he'd put a yellow hat on. He'll be so pleased to have the picture."

"Your employer, Miss March, has she ever seen Tom?"

"Seen Tom? Of course not! There are two of them, you know, the Miss Marches. One of them was always a bit retarded, I understand, so it's the other one who runs the estate. Though she is a bit of a recluse. She hasn't been back to Angelfield since the fire. Even I've never seen her. The only contact we have is through her solicitors."

Karen stood at the stove, waiting for the milk to heat. Behind her, the view from the small window showed the garden, and beyond it, the fields where Adeline and Emmeline had once dragged Merrily's pram with the baby still in it. There could be few landscapes that had changed so little.

I needed to be careful not to say too much. Karen gave no sign of knowing that her Miss March of Angelfield was the same woman as the Miss Winter whose books I had spotted in the bookcase in the hall as I came in.

"It's just that I work for the Angelfield family," I explained. "I'm writing about their childhood here. And when I was showing your employer some photos of the house I got the impression she recognized him."

"She can't have. Unless . . ."

She reached for the photograph and looked at it again, then called to her son in the next room. "Tom? Tom, bring that picture from the mantelpiece, will you? The one in the silver frame."

Tom came in, carrying a photograph, his sister behind him.

"Look," Karen said to him, "the lady has got a photograph of you."

A smile of delighted surprise crept onto his face when he saw himself. "Can I keep it?"

"Yes," I said.

"Show Margaret the one of your granddad."

He came around to my side of the table and held the framed picture out to me, shyly.

It was an old photograph of a very young man. Barely more than a boy. Eighteen, perhaps, maybe younger. He was standing by a bench with clipped yew trees in the background. I recognized the setting instantly: the topiary garden. The boy had taken off his cap, was holding it in his hand, and in my mind's eye I saw the movement he had made, sweeping his cap off with one hand, and wiping his forehead against the forearm of the other. He was tilting his head back slightly. Trying not to squint in the sun, and succeeding almost. His shirt-sleeves were rolled up above the elbow, and the top button of his shirt was open, but the creases in his trousers were neatly pressed, and he had cleaned his heavy garden boots for the photo.

"Was he working there when they had the fire?"

Karen put the mugs of cocoa on the table and the children came and sat to drink it. "I think he might have gone into the army by then. He was away from Angelfield for a long time. Nearly fifteen years."

I looked closely through the grainy age of the picture to the boy's face, struck by the similarity with his grandson. He looked *nice.*

"You know, he never spoke much about his early days. He was a reticent man. But there are things I wish I knew. Like why he married so late. He was in his late forties when he married my mother. I can't help thinking there must have been something in his past—a heartbreak, perhaps? But you don't think to ask those questions when you're a child, and by the time I'd grown up . . ." She shrugged sadly. "He was a lovely man to have as a father. Patient. Kind. He'd always help me with anything. And yet now I'm an adult, I sometimes have the feeling I never really *knew* him."

There was another detail in the photograph that caught my eye.

"What's this?" I asked.

She leaned to look. "It's a bag. For carrying game. Pheasants mainly. You can open it flat on the ground to lay them in, and then you fasten it up around them. I don't know why it's in the picture. He was never a gamekeeper, I'm sure."

"He used to bring the twins a rabbit or a pheasant when they wanted one," I said and she looked pleased

419

to have this fragment of her father's early life restored to her.

I thought of Aurelius and his inheritance. The bag he'd been carried in was a game bag. Of course there was a feather in it—it was used for carrying pheasants. And I thought of the scrap of paper. "Something like an *A* at the beginning," I remembered Aurelius saying as he held the blur of blue up to the window. "And then an *S.* Just here, toward the end. Of course, it's faded a bit, over the years, you have to look hard, but you *can* see it, can't you?" I hadn't been able to see it, but perhaps he really had. What if it was not his own name on the scrap of paper, but his father's? *Ambrose.*

From Karen's house I got a taxi to the solicitor's office in Banbury. I knew the address from the correspondence I had exchanged with him relating to Hester; now it was Hester again who took me to him.

The receptionist did not want to disturb Mr. Lomax when she learned I didn't have an appointment. "It is Christmas Eve, you know."

But I insisted. "Tell him it's Margaret Lea, regarding Angelfield House and Miss March."

With an air that said *It will make no difference,* she took the message into the office; when she came out it was to tell me, rather reluctantly, to go straight in.

The young Mr. Lomax was not very young at all. He was probably about the age the old Mr. Lomax was when the twins turned up at his office wanting money for John-the-dig's funeral. He shook my hand, a curious

420

gleam in his eye, a half-smile on his lips, and I under-stood that to him we were conspirators. For years he had been the only person to know the other identity of his client Miss March; he had inherited the secret from his father along with the cherry desk, the filing cabinets and the pictures on the wall. Now, after all the years of secrecy, there came another person who knew what he knew.

"Glad to meet you, Miss Lea. What can I do to help?"

"I've come from Angelfield. From the site. The police are there. They've found a body."

"Oh. Oh, goodness!"

"Will the police want to speak to Miss Winter, do you suppose?"

At my mention of the name, his eyes flickered dis-creetly to the door, checking that we could not be over-heard.

"They would want to speak to the owner of the prop-erty as a matter of routine."

"I thought so." I hurried on. "The thing is, not only is she ill—I suppose you know that?"

He nodded.

"—but also, her sister is dying."

He nodded, gravely, and did not interrupt.

"It would be better, given her fragility and the state of her sister's health, if she did not receive the news about the discovery too abruptly. She should not hear it from a stranger. And she should not be alone when the infor-mation reaches her."

"What do you suggest?"

"I can go back to Yorkshire today. If I can get to the station in the next hour, I can be there this evening. The police will have to come through you to contact her, won't they?"

"Yes. But I can delay things by a few hours. Enough time for you to get there. I can also drive you to the station, if you like."

At that moment the telephone rang. We exchanged an anxious look as he picked it up.

"Bones? I see . . . She is the owner of the property, yes . . . An elderly person and in poor health . . . A sister, gravely ill . . . Some likelihood of an imminent bereavement . . . It might be better . . . Given the circumstances . . . I happen to know of someone who is going there in person this very evening . . . Eminently trustworthy . . . Quite . . . Indeed . . . By all means."

He made a note on a pad and pushed it across the desk to me. A name and a telephone number.

"He would like you to telephone him when you get there to let him know how things stand with the lady. If she is able to, he will talk to her then; if not, it can wait. The remains, it seems, are not recent. Now, what time is your train? We should be going."

Seeing that I was deep in thought, the not-so-very-young Mr. Lomax drove in silence. Nevertheless a quiet excitement seemed to be eating away at him, and eventually, turning in to the road where the station was, he could contain himself no longer. "The thirteenth tale . . ." he said. "I don't suppose . . . ?"

"I wish I knew," I told him. "I'm sorry."

He pulled a disappointed face.

As the station loomed into sight, I asked a question of my own. "Do you happen to know Aurelius Love?"

"The caterer! Yes, I know him. The man's a culinary genius!"

"How long have you known him?"

He answered without thinking—"Actually, I was at school with him"—and in the middle of the sentence a curious quiver entered his voice, as though he had just realized the implications of my inquiry. My next question did not surprise him.

"When did you learn that Miss March was Miss Winter? Was it when you took over your father's business?"

He swallowed. "No." Blinked. "It was before. I was still at school. She came to the house one day. To see my father. It was more private than the office. They had some business to sort out and, without going into confidential details, it became clear during the course of their conversation that Miss March and Miss Winter were the same person. I was not eavesdropping, you understand. That is to say, not deliberately. I was already under the dining room table when they came in—there was a tablecloth that draped and made it into a sort of tent, you see—and I didn't want to embarrass my father by emerging suddenly, so I just stayed quiet."

What was it Miss Winter had told me? *There can be no secrets in a house where there are children.*

We had come to a stop in front of the station, and the young Mr. Lomax turned his stricken eyes toward me.

"I told Aurelius. The day he told me he had been found on the night of the fire. I told him that Miss Adeline Angelfield and Miss Vida Winter were one and the same person. I'm sorry."

"Don't worry about it. It doesn't matter now, anyway. I only wondered."

"Does she know I told Aurelius who she was?"

I thought about the letter Miss Winter had sent me right at the beginning, and about Aurelius in his brown suit, seeking the story of his origins. "If she guessed, it was decades ago. If she knows, I think you can presume she doesn't care."

The shadow cleared from his brow.

"Thanks for the lift."

And I ran for the train.

## HESTER'S DIARY II

From the station I made a phone call to the book-shop. My father could not hide his disappointment when I told him I would not be coming home. "Your mother will be sorry," he said.

"Will she?"

"Of course she will."

"I have to go back. I think I might have found Hester."

"Where?"

"They have found bones at Angelfield."

"Bones?"

"One of the builders discovered them when he was excavating the library today."

"Gracious."

"They are bound to get in touch with Miss Winter to ask her about it. And her sister is dying. I can't leave her on her own up there. She needs me."

"I see." His voice was serious.

"Don't tell Mother," I warned him, "but Miss Winter and her sister are twins."

He was silent. Then he just said, "You will take care, won't you, Margaret?"

A quarter of an hour later I had settled into my seat next to the window and was taking Hester's diary out of my pocket.

*I should like to understand a great deal more about optics. Sitting with Mrs. Dunne in the drawing room going over meal plans for the week, I caught sight of a sudden movement in the mirror. "Emmeline!" I exclaimed, irritated, for she was not supposed to be in the house at all, but outside, getting her daily exercise and fresh air. It was my own mistake, of course, for I had only to look out of the window to see that she was outside, and her sister, too, playing nicely for once. What I had seen, caught a misleading glimpse of, to be precise, must have been a flash of sunlight come in the window and reflected in the mirror.*

*On reflection (On reflection! An unintended drollery!), it is the psychology of seeing that caused my misapprehension, as much as any strangeness in the workings of the optical world. For being used to seeing the twins wandering about the house in places I would not expect them to be, and at times when I would expect them to be elsewhere, I have fallen into the habit of interpreting every movement out of the corner of my eye as evidence of their presence. Hence a flash of sunlight reflected in a mirror presents itself in a very convincing manner to the mind as a girl in a white dress. To guard against errors such as this, one would have to teach oneself to view everything without preconception, to abandon all habitual modes of thought. There is much to be said in favor of such an attitude in principle. The freshness of mind! The virginal response to the world! So much science has at its root the ability to see afresh what has been seen and thought to be understood for centuries. However, in ordinary life, one cannot live by such principles. Imagine the time it would take if every aspect of experience had to be scrutinized afresh every minute of every day. No; in order to free ourselves from the mundane it is essential that we delegate much of our interpretation of the world to that lower area of the mind that deals with the presumed, the assumed, the probable. Even though it sometimes leads us astray and causes us to misinterpret a flash of sunlight as a girl in a white dress, when these two things are as unlike as two things can be.*

*Mrs. Dunne's mind does wander sometimes. I fear she took in very little of our conversation about meal plans, and we shall have to go over the whole thing again tomorrow.*

✵

*I have a little plan regarding my activities here and the doctor.*

*I have told him at great length of my belief that Adeline demonstrates a type of mental disturbance that I have neither encountered nor read about before. I mentioned the papers I have been reading about twins and the associated developmental problems, and I saw his face approve my reading. I think he has a clearer understanding now of my abilities and talent. One book I spoke of, he did not know and I was able to give him a summary of the arguments and evidence in the book. I went on to point out the few significant inconsistencies that I had noticed in it, and to suggest how, if it were my book, I would have altered my conclusions and recommendations.*

*The doctor smiled at me at the end of my speech and said lightly, "Perhaps you should write your own book." This gave me exactly the opportunity I have been seeking for some time.*

*I pointed out to him that the perfect case study for such a book was at hand here in Angelfield House. That I could devote a few hours every day to working on writing up my observations. I sketched out a number of trials and experiments that could be undertaken to test my hypothesis. And I touched briefly on the value that the finished book would have in the eyes of the medical establishment. After this I lamented the fact that for all my experience, my formal qualifications are not grand enough to tempt a publisher, and finally I confessed that, as a woman, I was not entirely confident of being able to bring off such an ambitious project. A man, if only there were a man, intelligent and resourceful, sensitive and scientific, having access to my experience and my case study, would be sure to make a better job of it.*

҉

*And in such a manner it was decided. We are to work together!*

҉

*I fear Mrs. Dunne is not well. I lock doors and she opens them. I open curtains and she closes them. And still my books will not stay in their place! She tries to avoid responsibility for her actions by maintaining that the house is haunted.*

*Quite by chance, her talk of ghosts comes on the very day the book I am in the middle of reading has completely disappeared, only to be replaced by a novella by Henry James. I hardly suspect Mrs. Dunne of the substitution. She scarcely knows how to read herself and is not given to practical jokes. Obviously it was one of the girls. What makes it noteworthy is that a striking coincidence has made it a cleverer trick than they could have known. For the book is a rather silly story about a governess and two haunted children. I am afraid that in it Mr. James exposes the extent of his ignorance. He knows little about children and nothing at all about governesses.*

*It is done. The experiment has begun.*

*The separation was painful, and if I did not know the good that is to come of it, I should have thought myself cruel for inflicting it upon them. Emmeline sobs fit to break her heart. How is it for Adeline? For she is the one who is to be the most altered by the experience of independent life. I shall know tomorrow when we have our first meeting.*

*There is no time for anything but research, but I have managed to do one additional useful thing. I fell into conversation today with the schoolteacher outside the post office. I told her that I had spoken to John about the truant and that she should come to me if the boy is absent again without reason. She says she is used to teaching half a class at harvesttime when the children go spud-hucking with their parents in the fields. But it is not harvesttime, and the child was weeding the parterres, I told her. She asked me which child it was, and I felt foolish at not being able to tell her. The distinctive hat is no help at all in identifying him, since children do not wear hats in class. I could go back to John but doubt he will give me more information than last time.*

*I am not writing my diary much lately. I find that after the writing, late at night, of the reports I prepare every day about Emmeline's progress, I am frequently too tired to keep up with my own record of my activities. And I do want to keep a record of these days and weeks, for I am engaged, with the doctor, on very important research, and in years to come, when I have gone away and left this place, I may wish to look back and remember. Perhaps my efforts with the doctor will open some door for me into further work of this kind, for I find the scientific and intellectual work more engrossing and more satisfying than anything I have ever done. This morning for instance, Dr. Maudsley and I had the most stimulating conversation on the subject of Emmeline's use of pronouns. She is showing an ever-greater inclination to speak to me, and her ability to communicate improves every day. Yet the one aspect of her speech that is resistant to development is the persistence of the first person plural. "We went to the woods," she will say, and always I correct her: "I went to the woods." Like a little parrot she will repeat "I" after me, but in the very next sentence, "We saw a kitten in the garden," or some such thing.*

*The doctor and I are much intrigued by this peculiarity. Is it simply an ingrained habit of speech carried over from her twin language into English, a habit that will in time right itself? Or does the twinness go so deep in her that even in her language she is resistant to the idea of having a separate identity from that of her sister? I told the doctor about imaginary friends that so many disturbed children invent, and together we explored the implications of this. What if the child's dependence on her twin is so great that the separation causes a mental trauma such that the damaged mind provides solace by the creation of an imaginary twin, a fantasy companion? We arrived at no satisfactory conclusion but parted with the satisfaction of having located another area of future study: linguistics.*

꘍

*What with Emmeline, and the research, and the general housekeeping that needs to be done, I find I am sleeping too little, and despite my reserves of energy, which I maintain by healthy diet and exercise, I can distinguish the symptoms of sleep deprivation. I irritate myself by putting things down and forgetting where I have left them. And when I pick up my book at night, my bookmark tells me that the previous night I must have turned the pages blindly, for I have no recollection at all of the events on the page or the one before. These small annoyances and my constant tiredness are the price I pay for the luxury of working alongside the doctor on our project.*

*However, that is not what I wanted to write about. I meant to write about our work. Not our findings, which are documented thoroughly in our papers, but the pattern of our minds, the fluency with which we understand each other, the way in which our instant understanding permits us almost to do without words. When we are both engaged in plotting the changes in sleep patterns of our separate subjects, for instance, he may want to draw my attention to something, and he does not need to speak, for I can feel his eyes on me, his mind calling to me, and I raise my head from my work, quite ready for him to point out whatever it is.*

*Skeptics might consider this pure coincidence, or sus-pect me of magnifying a chance incidence into a habitual occurrence by imagination, but I have come to see that when two people work closely together on a joint project—two intelligent people, I mean to say—a bond of communication develops between them that can enhance their work. All the while they are jointly engaged on a task, they are aware of, acutely sensitive to, each other's tiniest movements, and can interpret them accordingly. This, even without seeing the infini-tesimal movements. And it is no distraction from the work. On the contrary, it enhances it, for our speed of understanding is quickened. Let me add one simple example, small in itself but standing in for countless others. This morning, I was intent upon some notes, trying to see a pattern of behavior emerging from his jottings on Adeline. Reaching for a pencil to make an annotation in the margin, I felt the doctor's hand brush mine and he passed the pencil I sought into it. I looked up to thank him, but he was deeply engrossed in his own papers, quite unconscious of what had happened. In such a way we work together: minds, hands, always in conjunction, always anticipating the other's needs and thoughts. And when we are apart, which we are for most of the day, we are always thinking of small details relating to the project, or else observations about the broader aspects of life and science, and even this shows how well suited we are for this joint undertaking.*

*But I am sleepy, and though I could write at length of*

the joys of coauthoring a research paper, it is really
time to go to bed.

*I have not written for nearly a week and do not offer my
usual excuses. My diary disappeared.*

*I spoke to Emmeline about it—kindly, severely, with
offers of chocolate and threats of punishment (and yes,
my methods have broken down, but frankly, losing a
diary touches one most personally)—but she continues
to deny everything. Her denials were consistent and
showed many signs of good faith. Anyone not knowing
the circumstances would have believed her. Knowing
her as I do, I found the theft unexpected myself and find
it hard to explain it within the general progress she has
made. She cannot read and has no interest in other
people's thoughts and inner lives, other than so far as
they affect her directly. Why should she want it? Presumably it is the shine of the lock that tempted her—her
passion for shiny things is undiminished, and I do not
try to reduce it; it is usually harmless enough. But I am
disappointed in her.*

*If I were to judge by her denials and her character
alone, I would conclude that she was innocent of the
theft. But the fact remains that it cannot have been
anyone else.*

*John? Mrs. Dunne? Even supposing that the servants
should have wanted to steal my diary, which I don't
believe for a minute, I remember clearly that they were
busy elsewhere in the house when it went missing. In
case I was wrong about this, I brought the conversation*

433

around to their activities, and John confirms that Mrs. Dunne was in the kitchen all morning ("making a right racket, too," he told me). She confirms that John was at the coach house mending the car ("noisy old job"). It cannot have been either of them.

And so, having eliminated all the other suspects I am obliged to believe that it was Emmeline.

And yet I cannot shake off my misgivings. Even now I can picture her face—so innocent in appearance, so distressed at being accused—and I am forced to wonder, is there some additional factor at play here that I have failed to take into account? When I view the matter in this light it gives rise to an uneasiness in me: I am suddenly overwhelmed by the presentiment that none of my plans is destined to come to fruition. Something has been against me ever since I came to this house! Something that wants to thwart me and frustrate me in every project I undertake! I have checked and rechecked my thinking, retraced every step in my logic, I can find no flaw, yet still I find myself beset by doubt. . . . What is it that I am failing to see?

Reading over this last paragraph I am struck by the most uncharacteristic lack of confidence in my tone. It is surely only tiredness that makes me think thus. An unrested mind is prone to wander into unfruitful avenues; it is nothing that a good night's sleep cannot cure.

Besides, it is all over now. Here I am, writing in the missing diary. I locked Emmeline in her room for four hours, the next day for six, and she knew the day after, *it would be eight. On the second day, shortly after I came down from unlocking her door I found the diary on my desk in the schoolroom. She must have slipped down very quietly to put it there; I did not see her go past the library door to the schoolroom even though I left the door open deliberately. But it was returned. So there is no room for doubt, is there?*

〰〰

*I am so tired and yet I cannot sleep. I hear steps in the night, but when I go to my door and look into the corridor there is no one there.*

〰〰

*I confess it made me uneasy—makes me uneasy still— to think that this little book was out of my possession even for two days. The thought of another person reading my words is most discomforting. I cannot help but think how another person would interpret certain things I have written, for when I write for myself only, and know perfectly well the truth of what I write, I am perhaps less careful of my expression, and writing at speed, may sometimes express myself in a way that could be misinterpreted by another who would not have my insight into what I really mean. Thinking over some of the things I have written (the doctor and the pencil— such an insignificant event—hardly worth writing about at all really), I can see that they might appear to a stranger in a light rather different from what I intended, and I wonder whether I should tear out these pages and destroy them. Only I do not want to, for these are the pages that I most want to keep, to read later, when I am old and gone from here, and think back to the happiness of my work and the challenge of our great project.*

*Why should a scientific friendship not be a source of joy? It is no less scientific for that, is it?*

*But perhaps the answer is to stop writing altogether, for when I do write, even now as I write this very sentence, this very word, I am aware of a ghost reader who leans over my shoulder watching my pen, who twists my words and perverts my meaning, and makes me uncomfortable in the privacy of my own thoughts.*

*It is very aggravating to be presented to oneself in a light so different from the familiar one, even when it is clearly a false light.*

*I will not write any more.*

# Endings

## THE GHOST IN THE TALE

Thoughtfully I lifted my eyes from the final page of Hester's diary. A number of things had struck my attention as I had been reading it, and now that I had finished, I had the leisure to consider them more methodically.

Oh, I thought.

*Oh.*

And then, *OH!*

How to describe my eureka? It began as a stray *what if,* a wild conjecture, an implausible notion. It was, well, not impossible perhaps, but *absurd!* For a start—

About to begin marshaling the sensible counterarguments, I stopped dead in my tracks. For my mind, racing ahead of itself in a momentous act of premonition, had already submitted to this revised version of events. In a single moment, a moment of vertiginous, kaleidoscopic bedazzlement, the story Miss Winter had told me unmade and remade itself, in every event identical, in every detail the same—yet entirely, profoundly different. Like those images that reveal a young bride if you hold the page one way, and an old crone if you hold it the other. Like the sheets of random dots that disguise teapots or clown faces or Rouen cathedrals if you can only learn to see them. The truth had been there all along, only now had I seen it.

There followed a long hour of musing. One element at a time, taking all the different angles separately, I reviewed everything I knew. Everything I had been told and everything I had discovered. *Yes,* I thought. And *yes,* again. That, and that, and that, too. My new knowledge blew life into the story. It began to breathe. And as it did so, it began to mend. The jagged edges smoothed themselves. The gaps filled themselves in. The missing parts were regenerated. Puzzles explained themselves, and mysteries were mysteries no longer.

At last, after all the tale telling and all the yarn spinning, after the smoke screens and the trick mirrors and the double bluffs, *I knew.*

<figure>⚜</figure>

I knew what Hester saw that day she thought she saw a ghost.

I knew the identity of the boy in the garden.

I knew who attacked Mrs. Maudsley with a violin.

I knew who killed John-the-dig.

I knew who Emmeline was looking for underground.

Details fell into place. Emmeline talking to herself behind a closed door, when her sister was at the doctor's house. *Jane Eyre,* the book that appears and reappears in the story, like a silver thread in a tapestry. I understood the mysteries of Hester's wandering bookmark, the appearance of *The Turn of the Screw* and the disappearance of her diary. I understood the strangeness of John-the-dig's decision to teach the girl who had once desecrated his garden how to tend it.

I understood the girl in the mist, and how and why she came out of it. I understood how it was that a girl like Adeline could melt away and leave Miss Winter in her place.

"I am going to tell you a story about twins," Miss Winter had called after me that first evening in the library, when I was on the verge of leaving. Words that with their unexpected echo of my own story attached me irresistibly to hers.

*Once upon a time there were two baby girls* . . .

Except that now I knew better.

She had pointed me in the right direction that very first night, if I had only known how to listen.

"Do you believe in ghosts, Miss Lea?" she had asked me. "I am going to tell you a ghost story."

And I had told her, "Some other time."

But she *had* told me a ghost story.

Once upon a time there were two baby girls . . .

Or alternatively: Once upon a time there were *three*.

Once upon a time there was a house and the house was haunted.

The ghost was, in the usual way of ghosts, mostly invisible, and yet not quite invisible. There was the closing of doors that had been left open, and the opening of doors left shut. The flash of movement in a mirror that made you glance up. The shimmer of a draft behind a curtain when there was no window open. The little ghost was there in the unexpected movement of books from one room to another, and in the mysterious movement of bookmark from page to page. It was her hand that lifted a diary from one place and hid it in another, her hand that replaced it later. If, as you turned into a corridor, the curious idea occurred to you that you had just missed seeing the sole of a shoe disappearing around the far corner, then the little ghost was not far away. And when, surprised by the back of the neck feeling as if someone has their eye on you, you raised your head to find the room empty, then you could be sure that the little ghost was hiding in the emptiness somewhere.

Her presence could be divined in any number of ways by those who had eyes to see. Yet she was not seen.

She haunted softly. On tiptoe, in bare feet, she made never a sound; and yet she recognized the footfall of every inhabitant of the house, knew every creaking board and every squeaky door. Every dark corner of the house was familiar to her, every nook and every cranny. She knew the gaps behind cupboards and between sets of shelves, she knew the backs of sofas and the underneath of chairs. The house, to her mind, was a hundred and one hiding places, and she knew how to move among them invisibly.

Isabelle and Charlie never saw the ghost. Living as they did, outside logic, outside reason, they were not the sort to be perplexed by the inexplicable. Losses and breakages and the mislaying of random items seemed to them part of the natural universe. A shadow that fell across a carpet where a shadow ought not to be did not cause them to stop and reflect; such mysteries seemed only a natural extension of the shadows in their hearts and minds. The little ghost was the movement in their peripheral vision, the unacknowledged puzzle in the back of their minds, the permanent shadow attached, without their knowing it, to their lives. She scavenged for leftovers in their pantry like a mouse, warmed herself at the embers of their fires after they had gone to bed, disappeared into the recesses of their dilapidation the instant anyone appeared.

She was the secret of the house.

Like all secrets, she had her guardians.

The housekeeper saw the little ghost as plain as day, despite her failing eyesight. A good thing, too. Without her collaboration there would never have been enough scraps in the pantry, enough crumbs from the breakfast loaf, to sustain the little ghost. For it would be a mistake to think that the ghost was one of those incorporeal, ethereal specters. No. She had a stomach, and when it was empty it had to be filled.

But she earned her keep. For as much as she ate, she also provided. The other person who had the knack of seeing ghosts, you see, was the gardener, and he was glad of an extra pair of hands. She wore a wide-brimmed hat and an old pair of John's trousers, cut off at the ankle and held up with braces, and her haunting of the garden was fruitful. In the soil potatoes grew swollen under her care; aboveground the fruit bushes flourished, producing clusters of berries that her hands

441

sought out under low leaves. Not only did she have a magic touch for fruit and vegetables, but the roses bloomed as they had never bloomed before. Later, she learned the secret desire of box and yew to become geometry. At her bidding leaves and branches grew corners and angles, curves and mathematically straight lines.

In the garden and in the kitchen the little ghost did not need to hide. The housekeeper and the gardener were her protectors, her guardians. They taught her the ways of the house and how to be safe in it. They fed her. They watched over her. When a stranger came to live in the house, with sharper eyes than most, with a desire to banish shadows and lock doors, they worried about her.

More than anything else, they loved her.

But where did she come from? What was her story? For ghosts do not appear at random. They come only to where they know they are at home. And the little ghost was at home in this house. At home in this family. Though she had no name, though she was no one, still the gardener and the housekeeper knew who she was all right. Her story was written in her copper hair and her emerald eyes.

For here is the most curious thing about the whole story. The ghost bore the most uncanny resemblance to the twins already living in the house. How else could she have lived there unsuspected for so long? Three girls with copper hair that fell in a mass down their backs. Three girls with striking emerald eyes. Odd, don't you think, the resemblance they both bore to the little ghost and she to them?

"When I was born," Miss Winter told me, "I was no more than a subplot." So she began the story in which Isabelle went to a picnic, met Roland and eventually ran away to marry him, escaping her brother's dark, unbrotherly passion. Charlie, neglected by his sister, went on a rampage, venting his rage, his passion, his jealousy on others. The daughters of earls or of shop-keepers, of bankers or of chimney sweeps; to him it did not really matter who they were. With or without their consent, he threw himself upon them in his desperation for oblivion.

Isabelle gave birth to her twins in a London hospital. Two girls with nothing of their mother's husband about them. Copper hair—just like their uncle. Green eyes—just like their uncle.

Here is the subplot: At about the same time, in some barn or dim cottage bedroom, another woman gave birth. Not the daughter of an earl, I think. Or a banker. The well-off have ways of dealing with trouble. She must have been some anonymous, ordinary, powerless woman. Her child was a girl, too. Copper hair. Emerald eyes.

Child of rage. Child of rape. *Charlie's child.*

Once upon a time there was a house called Angelfield.

Once upon a time there were twins.

Once upon a time there came to Angelfield a cousin. More likely a half sister.

As I sat in the train with Hester's diary closed in my lap, the great rush of sympathy I was beginning to feel for Miss Winter was curtailed when another illegitimate child came to mind. Aurelius. And my sympathy turned to anger. Why was he separated from his mother? Why abandoned? Why left to fend for himself in the world without knowing his own story?

I thought, too, of the white tent and the remains beneath it that I now knew not to be Hester's.

It all boiled down to the night of the fire. Arson, murder, abandonment of a baby.

When the train arrived in Harrogate and I stepped out onto the platform, I was surprised to find it ankle-deep in snow. For although I had been staring out the window of the train for the last hour, I had seen nothing of the view outside.

I thought I knew it all, when I had my moment of elucidation.

I thought, when I realized that there were not two girls at Angelfield but three, that I had the key to the whole story in my hand.

At the end of my cogitations I realized that until I knew what happened on the night of the fire, I knew nothing.

# BONES

It was Christmas Eve; it was late; it was snowing hard. The first taxi driver and the second refused to take me so far out of town on such a night, but the third, indifferent of expression, must have been moved by the ardor of my request, for he shrugged his shoulders and let me in. "We'll give it a go," he warned gruffly.

We drove out of town and the snow continued to fall, piling up meticulously, flake by flake, on every inch of earth, every hedge top, every bough. After the last village, the last farmhouse, we found ourselves in a white landscape, the road indistinguishable at times from the flat land all about, and I shrank into my seat, expecting at any moment that the driver would give up and turn back. Only my clear directions reassured him that we were in fact on a road. I got out myself to open the first gate, then we found ourselves at the second set, the main gates of the house.

"I hope you'll find your way back all right," I said.

"Me? I'll be all right," he said with another shrug.

As I expected, the gates were locked. Not wanting the driver to think I was some kind of thief, I pretended to be looking for my keys in my bag while he turned the car. Only when he was some distance away did I grab hold of the bars of the gate and clamber over.

The kitchen door was not locked. I pulled off my boots, shook the snow off my coat and hung it up. I walked through the empty kitchen and made my way to

445

Emmeline's quarters, where I knew Miss Winter would be. Full of accusations, full of questions, I stoked my rage; it was for Aurelius and for the woman whose bones had lain for sixty years in the burned-out ruins of Angelfield's library. For all my inward storming, my approach was silent; the carpet drank in the fury of my tread.

I did not knock but pushed the door open and went straight in.

The curtains were still closed. At Emmeline's bedside Miss Winter was sitting quietly. Startled by my entrance, she stared at me, an extraordinary shimmer in her eyes.

*"Bones!"* I hissed at her. "They have found *bones* at Angelfield!"

I was all eyes, all ears, waiting on tenterhooks for an admission to emerge from her. Whether it was in word or expression or gesture did not matter. She would make it, and I would read it.

Except that there was something in the room trying to distract me from my scrutiny.

"Bones?" said Miss Winter. She was paper-white and there was an ocean in her eyes, vast enough to drown all my fury.

"Oh," she said.

*Oh.* What richness of vibration a single syllable can contain. Fear. Despair. Sorrow and resignation. Relief, of a dark, unconsoling kind. And grief, deep and ancient.

And then the nagging distraction in the room swelled

so urgently in my mind that there was no room for any-thing else. What was it? Something extraneous to my drama of the bones. Something that preceded my intru-sion. For a faltering second I was confused, then all the insignificant things I had noticed without noticing came together. The atmosphere in the room. The closed cur-tains. The aqueous transparency of Miss Winter's eyes. The fact that the steel core that had always been her essence seemed to have simply gone from her.

My attention narrowed to one thing: Where was the slow tide of Emmeline's breath? No sound came to my ears.

"No! She's—"

I fell to my knees by the bed and stared.

"Yes," Miss Winter said softly. "She's gone. It was a few minutes ago."

I gazed at Emmeline's empty face. Nothing really had changed. Her scars were still angrily red; her lips had the same sideways slant; her eyes were still green. I touched her twisted patchwork hand, and her skin was warm. Was it true that she was gone? Absolutely, irrev-ocably gone? It seemed impossible that it should be so. Surely she had not deserted us completely? Surely there was something of her left behind to console us? Was there no spell, no talisman, no magic that would bring her back? Was there nothing I could say that would reach her?

It was the warmth in her hand that persuaded me she could hear me. It was the warmth in her hand that brought all the words into my chest, falling over each other in their impatience to fly into Emmeline's ear.

"Find my sister, Emmeline. Please find her. Tell her I'm waiting for her. Tell her—" My throat was too narrow for all the words and they broke against each other as they rose, choking, out of me. "Tell her I miss her! Tell her I'm lonely!" The words launched themselves impetuously, urgently from my lips. With fervor they flew across the space between us, chasing Emmeline. "Tell her I can't wait any longer! Tell her to *come!*"

But I was too late. The divide had come down. Invisible. Irrevocable. Implacable.

My words flew like birds into a pane of glass.

"Oh, my poor child." I felt the touch of Miss Winter's hand on my shoulder, and while I cried over the corpses of my broken words, her hand remained there, lightly.

Eventually I dried my eyes. There were only a few words left. Rattling around loose without their old companions. "She was my twin," I said. "She was here. Look."

I pulled at the jumper tucked into my skirt, revealed my torso to the light.

My scar. My half-moon. Pale silver-pink, a nacreous translucence. The line that divides.

"This is where she was. We were joined here. And they separated us. And she died. She couldn't live without me."

I felt the flutter of Miss Winter's fingers tracing the crescent on my skin, saw the tender sympathy in her face.

"The thing is—" (the final words, the very last words, after this I need never say anything, ever again) "I don't think I can live without *her*."

"Child." Miss Winter looked at me. Held me suspended in the compassion of her eyes.

I thought nothing. The surface of my mind was perfectly still. But under the surface there was a shifting and a stirring. I felt the great swell of the undercurrent. For years a wreck had sat in the depths, a rusting vessel with its cargo of bones. Now it shifted. I had disturbed it, and it created a turbulence that lifted clouds of sand from the seabed, motes of grit swirling wildly in the dark disturbed water.

All the time Miss Winter held me in her long green gaze.

Then slowly, slowly, the sand resettled and the water returned to its quietness, slowly, slowly. And the bones resettled in the rusting hold.

"You asked me once for my story," I said.

"And you told me you didn't have one."

"Now you know, I do have one."

"I never doubted it." She smiled a poor regretful smile. "When I invited you here I thought I knew your story already. I had read your essay about the Landier brothers. Such a good essay, it was. You knew so much about siblings. Insider knowledge, I thought. And the more I looked at your essay, the more I thought you must have a twin. And so I fixed upon you to be my biographer. Because if after all these years of tale telling I was tempted to lie to you, you would find me out."

"I *have* found you out."

She nodded, tranquil, sad, unsurprised. "About time, too. How much do you know?"

"What you told me. Only a subplot, is how you put it. You told me the story of Isabelle and her twins, and I wasn't paying attention. The subplot was Charlie and his rampages. You kept pointing me in the direction of *Jane Eyre*. The book about the outsider in the family. The motherless cousin. I don't know who your mother was. And how you came to be at Angelfield without her."

Sadly she shook her head. "Anyone who might have known the answer to those questions is dead, Margaret."

"Can't you remember?"

"I am human. Like all humans, I do not remember my birth. By the time we wake up to ourselves, we are little children, and our advent is something that happened an eternity ago, at the beginning of time. We live like latecomers at the theater; we must catch up as best we can, divining the beginning from the shape of later events. How many times have I gone back to the border of memory and peered into the darkness beyond? But it is not only memories that hover on the border. There are all sorts of phantasmagoria that inhabit that realm. The nightmares of a lonely child. Fairy tales appropriated by a mind hungry for story. The fantasies of an imaginative little girl anxious to explain to herself the inexplicable. Whatever story I may have discovered on the frontier of forgetting, I do

450

not pretend to myself that it is the truth."

*"All children mythologize their birth."*

"Quite. The only thing I can be sure of is what John-the-dig told me."

"And what did he tell you?"

"That I appeared like a weed between two strawberries."

She told me the story.

⁂

Someone was getting at the strawberries. Not birds, because they pecked and left pitted berries. And not the twins, because they trampled the plants and left footprints all over the plot. No, some light-footed thief was taking a berry here and a berry there. Neatly, without disturbing a thing. Another gardener wouldn't even have noticed. The same day John noticed a pool of water under his garden tap. The tap was dripping. He gave it a turn, tightened it up. He scratched his head, and went about his business. But he kept an eye out.

The next day he saw a figure in the strawberries. A little scarecrow, barely knee-high, in an overlarge hat that drooped down over its face. It ran off when it saw him. But the day after it was so determined to get its fruit that he had to yell and wave his arms to chase it off. Afterward he thought he couldn't put a name to it. Who in the village had a mite that size, small and underfed? Who around here would let their child go stealing fruit from other people's gardens? He was stumped for an answer.

*And* someone had been in the potting shed. He hadn't left the old newspapers in that state, had he? And those crates—they'd been put away tidy; he knew they had.

For once he put on the padlock before he went home.

Passing by the garden tap, he noticed it dripping again. Gave it a firm half turn without even thinking about it. Then, putting his weight into it, another quarter turn. That should do it.

In the night he awoke, uneasy in his mind for reasons he couldn't account for. Where would you sleep, he found himself wondering, if you couldn't get into the potting shed and make yourself a bed with newspapers in a crate? And where would you get water if the tap was turned off so tight you couldn't move it? Chiding himself for his midnight foolishness, he opened the window to feel the temperature. Too late for frosts. Cool for the time of year, though. And how much colder if you were hungry? And how much darker if you were a child?

He shook his head and closed the window. No one would abandon a child in his garden, would they? Of course they wouldn't. Nevertheless, before five he was up and out of bed. He took his walk around the garden early, surveying his vegetables, the topiary garden, planning his work for the day. All morning he kept an eye out for a floppy hat in the fruit bushes. But there was nothing to be seen.

"What's the matter with you?" said the Missus when he sat in silence at her kitchen table drinking a cup of coffee.

"Nothing," he said.

He drained his cup and went back to the garden. He stood and scanned the fruit bushes with anxious eyes.

Nothing.

At lunchtime he ate half a sandwich, discovered he had no appetite and left the other half on an upturned flowerpot by the garden tap. Telling himself he was a fool, he put a biscuit next to it. He turned the tap on. It took quite an effort even for him. He let the water fall, noisily, into a tin watering can, emptied it into the nearest bed and refilled it. The thunder of splashing water resounded around the vegetable garden. He took care not to look up and around.

Then he took himself a little way off, knelt on the grass, his back to the tap, and started brushing off some old pots. It was an important job; it had to be done; you could spread disease if you didn't clean your pots properly between planting.

Behind him, the squeak of the tap.

He didn't turn instantly. He finished the pot he was doing, brush, brush, brush.

*Then* he was quick. On his feet, over to the tap, faster than a fox.

But there was no need for such haste.

The child, frightened, tried to flee but stumbled. Picking itself up, it limped on a few more steps, then stumbled again. John caught it up, lifted it—the weight of a cat, no more—turned it to face him, and the hat fell off.

Little chap was a bag of bones. Starving. Eyes gone

crusty, hair black with dirt, and smelly. Two hot red spots for cheeks. He put a hand to the child's forehead and it was burning up. Back in the potting shed he saw its feet. No shoes, scabby and swollen, pus oozing through the dirt. A thorn or something, deep inside. The child trembled. Fever, pain, starvation, fear. If he found an animal in that state, John thought, he'd get his gun and put it out of its misery.

He locked it in the shed and went to fetch the Missus. She came. She peered, right up close, got a whiff and stepped back.

"No, no, I don't know whose he is. Perhaps if we cleaned him up a bit?"

"Dunk him in the water butt, you mean?"

"Water butt indeed! I'll go and fill the tub in the kitchen."

They peeled the stinking rags away from the child. "They're for the bonfire," the Missus said, and tossed them out into the yard. The dirt went all the way down to the skin; the child was encrusted. The first tub of water turned instantly black. In order to empty and refill the tub, they lifted the child out, and it stood, wavering, on its better foot. Naked and dripping, streaked with rivulets of gray-brown water, all ribs and elbows.

They looked at the child; at each other; at the child again.

"John, I may be poor of sight, but tell me, are you not seeing what I'm not seeing?"

"Aye."

"Little chap indeed! It's a little maid."

They boiled kettle after kettle, scrubbed at skin and hair with soap, brushed hardened dirt out from under the nails. Once she was clean they sterilized tweezers, pulled the thorn from the foot—she flinched but didn't cry out—and they dressed and bandaged the wound. They gently rubbed warmed castor oil into the crust around the eyes. They put calamine lotion onto the flea bites, petroleum jelly onto the chapped, split lips. They combed tangles out of long, matted hair. They pressed cool flannels against her forehead and her burning cheeks. At last they wrapped her in a clean towel and sat her at the kitchen table, where the Missus spooned soup into her mouth and John peeled her an apple.

Gulping down the soup, grabbing at the apple slices, she couldn't get it down fast enough. The Missus cut a slice of bread and spread it with butter. The child ate it ravenously.

They watched her. The eyes, cleared of their crust, were slivers of emerald green. The hair was drying to a bright red-gold. The cheekbones jutted wide and sharp in the hungry face.

"Are you thinking what I'm thinking?" said John.

"Aye."

"Will we tell him?"

"No."

"But she does belong here."

"Aye."

They thought for a moment or two.

"What about a doctor?"

The pink spots in the child's face were not so bright.

The Missus put a hand to the forehead. Still hot, but better.

"We'll see how she goes tonight. Get the doctor in the morning."

"If needs be."

"Aye. If needs be."

⚜

"And so it was settled," Miss Winter said. "I stayed."

"What was your name?"

"The Missus tried to call me Mary, but it didn't stick. John called me Shadow, because I stuck to him like a shadow. He taught me to read, you know, with seed catalogs in the shed, but I soon discovered the library. Emmeline didn't call me anything. She didn't need to, for I was always there. You only need names for the absent."

I thought about it all for a while in silence. The ghost child. No mother. No name. The child whose very existence was a secret. It was impossible not to feel compassion. And yet . . .

"What about Aurelius? You knew what it was like to grow up without a mother! Why did he have to be abandoned? The bones they found at Angelfield . . . I know it must have been Adeline who killed John-the-dig, but what happened to her afterward? Tell me, what happened the night of the fire?"

We were talking in the dark, and I couldn't see the expression on Miss Winter's face, but she seemed to shiver as she glanced at the figure in the bed.

"Pull the sheet over her face, would you? I will tell

you about the baby. I will tell you about the fire. But first, perhaps you could call Judith? She does not know yet. She will need to call Dr. Clifton. There are things that need to be done."

When she came, Judith's first care was for the living. She took one look at Miss Winter's pallor and insisted on putting her to bed and seeing to her medication before anything. Together we wheeled her to her rooms; Judith helped her into her nightgown; I made a hot-water bottle and folded the bed down.

"I'll telephone Dr. Clifton now," Judith said. "Will you stay with Miss Winter?" But it was only a few minutes later that she reappeared in the bedroom doorway and beckoned me into the anteroom.

"I couldn't speak to him," she told me in a whisper. "It's the telephone. The snow has brought the line down."

We were cut off.

I thought of the policeman's telephone number on the piece of paper in my bag and was relieved.

We arranged that I would stay with Miss Winter for the first shift, so that Judith could go to Emmeline's room and do what needed to be done there. She would relieve me later, when Miss Winter's next medication was due.

It was going to be a long night.

I n Miss Winter's narrow bed, her frame was marked by only the smallest rise and fall in the bedclothes. Warily she stole each breath, as though she expected to be ambushed at any minute. The light from the lamp sought out her skeleton: It caught her pale cheekbone and illuminated the white arc of her brow; it sank her eye in a deep pool of shadow.

Over the back of my chair lay a gold silk shawl. I draped it over the shade so that it might diffuse the light, warm it, make it fall less brutally upon Miss Winter's face.

Quietly I sat, quietly I watched, and when she spoke I barely heard her whisper.

"The truth? Let me see . . ."

The words drifted from her lips into the air; they hung there trembling, then found their way and began their journey.

I was not kind to Ambrose. I could have been. In another world, I might have been. It wouldn't have been so very hard: He was tall and strong and his hair was gold in the sun. I knew he liked me and I was not indifferent. But I hardened my heart. I was bound to Emmeline.

"Am I not good enough for you?" he asked me one day. He came straight out with it, like that.

I pretended not to hear, but he insisted.

"If I'm not good enough, you tell me so to my face!"

"You can't read," I said, "and you can't write!"

He smiled. Took my pencil from the kitchen windowsill and began to scratch letters onto a piece of paper. He was slow. The letters were uneven. But it was clear enough. *Ambrose.* He wrote his name and when he had done it, he took the paper and held it out to show me.

I snatched it out of his hand, screwed it into a ball and tossed it to the floor.

He stopped coming into the kitchen for his tea break. I drank my tea in the Missus's chair, missing my cigarette, while I listened for the sound of his step or the ring of his spade. When he came to the house with the meat, he passed the bag without a word, eyes averted, face frozen. He had given up. Later, cleaning the kitchen, I came across the piece of paper with his name on it. I felt ashamed of myself and put the paper in his game bag hanging behind the kitchen door, so it would be out of sight.

When did I realize Emmeline was pregnant? A few months after the boy stopped coming for tea. I knew it before she knew herself; she was hardly one to notice the changes in her body, or to realize the consequences. I questioned her about Ambrose. It was hard to make her understand the sense of my questions, and she quite failed to see why I was angry. "He was so sad" was all she would tell me. "You were too unkind." She spoke very gently, full of compassion for the boy, velveting her reproach for me.

I could have shaken her.

"You do realize that you're going to have a baby now, don't you?"

Mild astonishment passed across her face, then left it tranquil as before. Nothing, it seemed, could disturb her serenity.

I dismissed Ambrose. I gave him his pay till the end of the week and sent him away. I didn't look at him while I spoke to him. I didn't give him any reasons. He didn't ask any questions. "You may as well go immediately," I told him, but that wasn't his way. He finished the row of planting I had interrupted, cleaned the tools scrupulously, the way John had taught him, and put them back in the garden shed, leaving everything neat and tidy. Then he knocked at the kitchen door.

"What will you do for meat? Do you know how to kill a chicken at least?"

I shook my head.

"Come on."

He jerked his head in the direction of the pen, and I followed him.

"Don't waste any time," he instructed me. "Clean and quick is the way. No second thoughts."

He swooped on one of the copper-feathered birds pecking about our feet and held its body firmly. He mimed the action that would break its neck. "See?"

I nodded.

"Go on then."

He released the bird and it flurried to the ground

where its round back was soon indistinguishable from its neighbors.

"Now?"

"What else are you going to eat tonight?"

The sun was gleaming on the feathers of the hens as they pecked for seeds. I reached for a bird, but it scuttled away. The second one slipped through my fingers in the same way. Grabbing for a third, this time, clumsily, I held on to it. It squawked and tried to beat its wings in its panic to escape, and I wondered how the boy had held his so easily. As I struggled to keep it still under my arm and get my hands around its neck at the same time, I felt the boy's severe eye upon me.

"Clean and quick," he reminded me. He doubted me, I could tell from his voice.

I was going to kill the bird. I had decided to kill the bird. So, gripping the bird's neck, I squeezed. But my hands would only half obey me. A strangled cry of alarm flew from the bird's throat, and for a second I hesitated. With a muscular twist and a flap, the bird slipped from under my arm. It was only because I was struck by the paralysis of panic that I still had it by the neck. Wings beating, claws flailing wildly at the air, almost it lurched away from me.

Swiftly, powerfully, the boy took the bird out of my grasp and in a single movement he had done it.

He held the body out to me; I forced myself to take it. Warm, heavy, still.

The sun shone on his hair as he looked at me. His look was worse than the claws, worse than the beating wings. Worse than the limp body in my hands.

Without a word he turned his back and walked away.

What good was the boy to me? My heart was not mine to give; it belonged to another, and always had.

I loved Emmeline.

I believe that Emmeline loved me, too. Only she loved Adeline more.

It is a painful thing to love a twin. When Adeline was there, Emmeline's heart was full. She had no need of me, and I was left on the outside, a cast-off, a superfluity, a mere observer of the twins and their twinness.

Only when Adeline went roaming alone was there space in Emmeline's heart for another. Then her sorrow was my joy. Little by little I coaxed her away from her loneliness, offering gifts of silver thread and shiny baubles, until she almost forgot she had been abandoned and gave herself over to the friendship and companionship I could offer. By a fire we played cards, sang, talked. Together we were happy.

Until Adeline came back. Furious with cold and hunger, she would come raging into the house, and the instant she was there, our world of two came to an end, and I was on the outside again.

It wasn't fair. Though Adeline beat her and pulled her hair, Emmeline loved her. Though Adeline abandoned her, Emmeline loved her. Whatever Adeline did, it altered nothing, for Emmeline's love was total. And me? My hair was copper like Adeline's. My eyes were green like Adeline's. In the absence of Adeline, I could fool anyone. But I never fooled Emmeline. Her heart knew the truth.

Emmeline had her baby in January.

No one knew. As she had grown bigger, so she had grown lazier; it was no hardship for her to keep to the confines of the house. She was content to stay inside, yawning in the library, the kitchen, her bedroom. Her retreat was not noticed. Why should it have been? The only visitor to the house was Mr. Lomax; he came on regular days at regular hours. Easy as pie to have her out of the way by the time he knocked on the door.

Our contact with other people was slight. For meat and vegetables we were self-sufficient—I never learned to like killing chickens, but I learned to do it. As for other provisions, I went to the farm in person to collect cheese and milk, and when once a week the shop sent a boy on a bicycle with our other requirements, I met him on the drive and carried the basket to the house myself. I thought it would be a sensible precaution to have another twin seen by someone at least from time to time. Once, when Adeline seemed calm enough, I gave her the coin and sent her to meet the boy on the bicycle. "It was the other one today," I imagined him saying, back at the shop. "The weird one." And I wondered what the doctor would make of it if the boy's account reached his ears. But it soon grew impossible to use Adeline like this again. Emmeline's pregnancy affected her twin curiously: For the first time in her life she discovered an appetite. From being a scrawny bag of bones, she developed plump curves and full breasts. There were times—in half-light, from certain angles—when for a moment even I could not tell them apart. So from time to time on a Wednesday morning, I would be Adeline. I would mess my hair, grime my nails, set my face into a tight, agitated mask and go down the drive to meet the boy on the bicycle. Seeing the speed of my gait as I came down the gravel drive to meet him, he would know it was *the other one*. I could see his fingers curl anxiously around his handlebars. Watching me surreptitiously, he handed over the basket, then he pocketed his tip and was glad to bicycle away. The following week, when he was met by me as myself, his smile had a touch of relief in it.

Hiding the pregnancy was not difficult. But I was troubled during those months of waiting about the birth itself. I knew what the dangers of labor might be. Isabelle's mother had not survived her second labor, and I could not put this thought out of my head for more than a few hours at a time. That Emmeline should suffer, that her life should be put in danger—this was unthinkable. On the other hand, the doctor had been no friend of ours and I did not want him at the house. He had seen Isabelle and taken her away. That could not be allowed to happen to Emmeline. He had separated Emmeline and Adeline. That could not be allowed to happen to Emmeline and *me*. Besides, how could he come without there being immediate complications? And although he had been persuaded, though he did not understand it, that the girl in the mist had broken

464

through the carapace of the mute rag-doll Adeline who had once spent several months with him, if he were once to realize that there were *three* girls at Angelfield House, he would immediately see the truth of the affair. For a single visit, for the birth itself, I could lock Adeline in the old nursery, and we might get away with it. But once it was known there was a baby in the house, there would be no end of visits. It would be impossible to keep our secret.

I was well aware of the fragility of my position. *I* knew I belonged here, *I* knew it was my place. I had no home but Angelfield, no love but Emmeline, no life but this one here, yet I was under no illusions about how tenuous my claim would seem to others. What friends did I have? The doctor could hardly be expected to speak up for me, and though Mr. Lomax was kind to me now, once he knew I had impersonated Adeline, it was inevitable that his attitude would alter. Emmeline's affection for me and mine for her would count as nothing.

Emmeline herself, ignorant and placid, let the days of her confinement pass by untroubled. For me the time was spent in an agony of indecision. How to keep Emmeline safe? How to keep myself safe? Every day I put off the decision to the next. During the first months I felt sure the solution would come to me in time. Had I not resolved everything else, against the odds? Then this, too, could be arranged. But as the time grew nearer, the problem grew more urgent and I was no nearer a decision. I veered in the space of a minute between grabbing my coat to go to the doctor's house, there and then, to tell him everything, and the contrary thought: that to do so was to reveal myself, and that to reveal myself could only lead to my banishment. Tomorrow, I told myself, as I replaced my coat on the hook. I will think of something tomorrow.

But then it was too late for tomorrow.

I woke to a cry. *Emmeline!*

But it was not Emmeline. Emmeline was huffing and panting; like a beast she snorted and sweated; her eyes bulged and she showed her teeth, but she did not cry out. She ate her pain and it turned to strength inside her. The cry that had woken me, and the cries that continued to resound all around the house, were not hers but Adeline's, and they did not cease till morning, when Emmeline's infant, a boy, was delivered.

It was the seventh of January.

Emmeline slept; she smiled in her sleep.

I bathed the baby. He opened his eyes and goggled, astounded by the touch of the warm water.

The sun rose.

The time for decisions had come and gone, and no decision had been made, yet here we were, on the other side of disaster, and we were safe.

My life could go on.

Miss Winter seemed to sense the arrival of Judith, for when the housekeeper looked around the edge of the door, she found us in silence. She had brought me cocoa on a tray but also offered to replace me if I wanted to sleep. I shook my head. "I'm all right, thanks."

Miss Winter also refused when Judith reminded her she could take more of the white tablets if she needed them.

When Judith was gone, Miss Winter closed her eyes again.

"How is the wolf?" I asked.

"Quiet in the corner," she said. "Why shouldn't he be? He is certain of his victory. So he's content to bide his time. He knows I'm not going to make a fuss. We've agreed to terms."

"What terms?"

"He is going to let me finish my story, and then I am going to let him finish me."

She told me the story of the fire, while the wolf counted down the words.

※

I had never given a great deal of thought to the baby before he arrived. I had considered the practical aspects of hiding a baby in the house, certainly, and I had a plan for his future. If we could keep him secret for a time, my intention was to allow his presence to be known later. Though it would no doubt be whispered about, he could be introduced as the orphan child of a distant member of the family, and if people chose to wonder about his exact parentage, they were free to do so; nothing they could do would force us to reveal the truth. When making these plans, I had envisaged the baby as a difficulty that needed to be resolved. I had not taken into account that he was my flesh and blood. I had not expected to love him.

He was Emmeline's, that was reason enough. He was Ambrose's. That was a subject I did not dwell on. But he was also mine. I marveled at his pearly skin, at the pink jut of his lips, at the tentative movements of his tiny hands. The ferocity of my desire to protect him overwhelmed me: I wanted to protect him for Emmeline's sake, to protect her for his sake, to protect the two of them for myself. Watching him and Emmeline together, I could not drag my eyes away. They were beautiful. My one desire was to keep them safe. And I soon learned that they needed a guardian to keep them safe.

Adeline was jealous of the baby. More jealous than she had been of Hester, more jealous than of me. It was only to be expected: Emmeline had been fond of Hester, she loved me, but neither of these affections had touched the supremacy of her feeling for Adeline. But the baby . . . ah, the baby was different. The baby usurped all.

I should not have been surprised at the extent of Adeline's hatred. I knew how ugly her anger could be, had witnessed the extent of her violence. Yet the day I first understood the lengths she might go to, I could scarcely believe it. Passing Emmeline's bedroom, I silently pushed the door open to see if she was still sleeping. I found Adeline in the room, leaning over the crib by the bed, and something in her posture alarmed me. Hearing my step, she started, then turned and rushed past me out of the room. In her hands she clutched a small cushion.

I felt compelled to dash to the cot. The infant was sleeping soundly, hand curled by his ear, breathing his light, delicate baby breath.

Safe!

Until next time.

I began to spy on Adeline. My old days of haunting came in useful again as from behind curtains and yew trees I watched her. There was a randomness in her actions; indoors or outdoors, taking no notice of the time of day or the weather, she engaged in meaningless, repeated actions. She was obeying dictates that were outside my understanding. But gradually one activity came particularly to my attention. Once, twice, three times a day, she came to the coach house and left it again, carrying a can of petrol with her each time. She took the can to the drawing room, or the library or the garden. Then she would seem to lose interest. She knew what she was doing, but distantly, half forgetful. When she wasn't looking I took the cans away. Whatever did she make of the disappearing cans? She must have thought they had some animus of their own, that they could move about at will. Or perhaps she took her memories of moving them for dreams or plans yet to be realized. Whatever the reason, she did not seem to find it strange that they were not where she had left them. Yet despite the waywardness of the petrol cans, she persisted in fetching them from the coach house, and secreting them in various places around the house.

I seemed to spend half my day returning the cans to the coach house. But one day, not wanting to leave Emmeline and the baby asleep and unprotected, I put one instead in the library. Out of sight, behind the books, on an upper shelf. And it occurred to me that perhaps this was a better place. Because, by always returning them to the coach house, all I was doing was ensuring that it would go on forever. A merry-go-round. By removing them from the circuit altogether, perhaps I might put an end to the rigmarole.

Watching her tired me out, but *she*! She never tired. A little sleep went a long way with her. She could be up and about at any hour of the night. And I was getting sleepy. One day, in the early evening, Emmeline went to bed. The boy was in his cot in her room. He'd been colicky, awake and wailing all day, but now, feeling better, he slept soundly.

I drew the curtains.

It was time to go and check on Adeline. I was tired of always being vigilant. Watching Emmeline and her child while they slept, watching Adeline while they were awake, I hardly slept at all. How peaceful it was in the room. Emmeline's breathing, slowing me down, relaxing me. And alongside it, the light touch of air that was the baby breathing. I remember listening to them, the harmony of it, thinking how tranquil it was, thinking of a way of describing it—that was how I always entertained myself, the putting into words of things I saw and heard—and I thought I would have to describe how the breathing seemed to penetrate me, take over my breath, as though we were all part of the same thing, me and Emmeline and our baby, all three one breath. It took hold of me, this idea, and I felt myself drifting off with them, into sleep.

Something woke me. Like a cat I was alert before I ever had my eyes open. I didn't move, kept my breathing regular, and watched Adeline from between my lashes.

She bent over the cot, lifted the baby and was on her way out of the room. I could have called out to stop her. But I didn't. If I had cried out, she would have postponed her plan, whereas by letting her go on with it, I could find out what she intended and put a stop to it once and for all. The baby stirred in her arms. He was thinking about waking up. He didn't like to be in anyone's arms but Emmeline's, and a baby is not taken in by a twin.

I followed her downstairs to the library and peeped through the door that she had left ajar. The baby was on the desk, next to the pile of books that were never reshelved because I reread them so frequently. Next to their neat rectangle I saw movement in the folds of the baby's blanket. I heard his muffled half grunts. He was awake.

471

Kneeling by the fireside was Adeline. She took coals from the scuttle, logs from their place by the hearth, and deposited them haphazardly in the fireplace. She did not know how to make a proper fire. I had learned from the Missus the correct arrangement of paper, kindling, coals and logs; Adeline's fires were wild and random affairs that ought not to burn at all.

The realization of what she intended slowly unfolded in me.

She would not succeed, would she? There was only a shadow of warmth in the ashes, not enough to relight coals or logs, and I never left kindling or matches in reach. Hers was a mad fire; it couldn't catch; I knew it couldn't. But I could not reassure myself. Her desire for flames was all the kindling she needed. All she had to do was look at something for it to spark. The incendiary magic she possessed was so strong she could set fire to water if she wanted to badly enough.

In horror I watched her place the baby on the coals, still wrapped in his blanket.

Then she looked about the room. What was she after?

When she made for the door and opened it, I jumped back into the shadows. But she had not discovered my spying. It was something else she was after. She turned into the passage under the stairs and disappeared.

I ran to the fireplace and removed the baby from the pyre. I wrapped his blanket quickly around a moth-eaten bolster from the chaise longue and put it on the coals in his place. But there was no time to flee. I heard steps on the stone flags, a dragging noise that was the

472

sound of a petrol can scraping on the floor, and the door opened just as I stepped back into one of the library bays.

Hush, I prayed silently, don't cry now, and I held the infant close to my body so he would not miss the warmth of his blanket.

Back at the fireplace, head on one side, Adeline surveyed her fire. What was wrong? Had she noticed the change? But it appeared not. She looked around the room. What was it she wanted?

The baby stirred, a jerk of the arms, a kick of the legs, a tensing of the backbone that is so often the precursor to a wail. I resettled him, head heavy on my shoulder; I felt his breath on my neck. Don't cry. Please don't cry.

He was still again, and I watched.

My books. On the desk. The ones I couldn't pass without opening at random, for the pleasure of a few words, a quick hello. How incongruous to see them in her hands. Adeline and books? It looked all wrong. Even when she opened the cover, I thought for one long, bizarre moment that she was going to *read*—

She tore out pages by the fistful. She scattered them all over the desk; some slid off, onto the floor. When she had done with the ripping, she grabbed handfuls of them and screwed them into loose balls. Fast! She was a whirlwind! My neat little volumes, suddenly a paper mountain. To think a book could have so much paper in it! I wanted to cry out, but what? All the words, the beautiful words, pulled apart and crumpled up, and I, in the shadows, speechless.

473

She gathered an armful and released it onto the top of the white blanket in the fireplace. Three times I watched her turn from the desk to the fireplace, her arms full of pages, until the hearth was heaped high with torn-up books. *Jane Eyre, Wuthering Heights, The Woman in White* . . . Balls of paper toppled from the height of the pyre, some rolled as far as the carpet, joining those that she had dropped en route.

One came to a stop at my feet, and silently I dropped down to retrieve it.

Oh! The outrageous sensation of crumpled paper; words gone wild, flying in all directions, senseless. My heart broke.

Anger swept me up; it carried me like a piece of flotsam, unable to see or breathe; it roared like an ocean in my head. I might have cried out, leaped like a mad thing from my hiding place and struck her, but I had Emmeline's treasure in my arms, and so I stood by and watched, trembling, weeping in silence, as her sister desecrated the treasure that was mine.

At last she was satisfied with her pyre. Yet whichever way you looked at it, the mountain in the hearth was madness itself. It's all upside down, the Missus would have said; it'll never light—you want the paper at the bottom. But even if she had built it properly, it would make no difference. She couldn't light it: She had no matches. And even if she had been able to obtain matches, still she would not achieve her purpose, for the boy, her intended victim, was in my arms. And the greatest madness of all: Supposing I hadn't been there to stop her? Supposing I hadn't rescued the infant and she had burned him alive? How could she ever imagine that burning her sister's child would restore her sister to her?

It was the fire of a madwoman.

In my arms the baby stirred and opened his mouth to mewl. What to do? Behind Adeline's back I softly retreated, then fled to the kitchen.

I must get the baby to a place of safety, then deal with Adeline later. My mind was working furiously, proposing plan after plan. Emmeline will have no love left for her sister when she realizes what she tried to do. It will be she and I now. We will tell the police that Adeline killed John-the-dig, and they will take her away. No! We will tell Adeline that unless she leaves Angelfield we will tell the police . . . No! And then suddenly I have it! *We* will leave Angelfield. Yes! Emmeline and I will leave, with the baby, and we will start a new life, without Adeline, without Angelfield, but together.

And it all seems so simple I wonder I never thought of it before.

With the future glowing so brightly it seems realer than the present, I put the page from *Jane Eyre* in the game bag as well, for safekeeping, and a spoon that is on the kitchen table. We will need that, en route to our new life.

Now where? Somewhere not far from the house, where there is nothing to hurt him, where he will be warm enough for the few minutes it will take me to

come back to the house and fetch Emmeline and persuade her to follow . . .

Not the coach house. Adeline sometimes goes there.
The church. That is a place she never goes.

I run down the drive, through the lych-gate and into
the church. In the front rows are small tapestry cushions
for kneeling. I arrange them into a bed and lay the baby
on them in his canvas papoose.

Now, back to the house.

I am almost there when my future shatters. Shards of
glass flying through the air, one breaking window then
another, and a sinister, living light prowling in the
library. The empty window frame shows me liquid fire
spraying the room, petrol cans bursting in the heat. And
*two* figures.

*Emmeline!*

I run. The odor of fire catches my nostrils even in the
entrance hall, though the stone floor and walls are
cool—the fire has no hold here. But at the door of the
library I stop. Flames chase each other up the curtains;
bookshelves are ablaze; the fireplace itself is an inferno.
In the center of the room, the twins. For a moment, in
all the noise and heat of the fire, I stop dead. Amazed.
For Emmeline, the passive, docile Emmeline, is
returning blow for blow, kick for kick, bite for bite. She
has never retaliated against her sister before, but now
she is doing it. For her child.

Around them, above their heads, one burst of light
after another as the petrol cans explode and fire rains
down upon the room.

I open my mouth to call to Emmeline that the baby is safe, but the first breath I draw in is nothing but heat, and I choke.

I hop over fire, step around it, dodge the fire that falls on me from above, brush fire away with my hands, beat out the fire that grows in my clothes. When I reach the sisters I cannot see them, but reach blindly through the smoke. My touch startles them and they draw apart instantly. There is a moment when I see Emmeline, see her clearly, and she sees me. I grip her hand and pull her, through the flames, through the fire, and we reach the door. But when she realizes what I am doing— leading her away from the fire to safety—she stops. I tug at her.

"He's safe." My words come in a croak, but they are clear enough.

Why doesn't she understand?

I try again. "The baby. I have saved him."

Surely she has heard me? Inexplicably she resists my tug, and her hand slips from mine. Where is she? I can see only blackness.

I stumble forward into the flames, collide with her form, grasp her and pull.

Still she won't stay with me, turns once more into the room.

Why?

She is bound to her sister.

She is bound.

Blind and with my lungs burning, I follow her into the smoke.

I will break the bond.

Eyes closed against the heat, I plunge into the library, arms ahead of me, searching. When my hands reach her in the smoke, I do not let her go. I will *not* have her die. I *will* save her. And though she resists, I drag her ferociously to the door and out of it.

The door is made of oak. It is heavy. It doesn't burn easily. I push it shut behind us, and the latch engages.

Beside me, she steps forward, about to open it again. It is something stronger than fire that pulls her into that room.

The key that sits in the lock, unused since the days of Hester, is hot. It burns my palm as I turn it. Nothing else hurts me that night, but the key sears my palm and I smell my flesh as it chars. Emmeline puts out a hand to clutch the key and open it again. The metal burns her, and as she feels the shock of it, I pull her hand away.

A great cry fills my head. Is it human? Or is it the sound of the fire itself? I don't even know whether it is coming from inside the room or outside with me. From a guttural start it gathers strength as it rises, reaches a shrill peak of intensity, and when I think it must be at the end of its breath, it continues, impossibly low, impossibly long, a boundless sound that fills the world and engulfs it and contains it.

And then the sound is gone and there is only the roar of the fire.

Outdoors. Rain. The grass is soaked. We sink to the ground; we roll on the wet grass to damp our smoldering clothes and hair, feel the cool wet on our scorched flesh. On our backs we rest there, flat against the earth. I open my mouth and drink the rain. It falls on my face, cools my eyes, and I can see again. Never has there been a sky like it, deep indigo with fast-moving slate-black clouds, the rain coming down in blade edges of silver, and every so often a plume, a spray of bright orange from the house, a fountain of fire. A bolt of lightning cracks the sky in two, then again, and again.

The baby. I must tell Emmeline about the baby. She will be happy that I have saved him. It will make things all right.

I turn to her and open my mouth to speak. Her face—

Her poor beautiful face is black and red, all smoke and blood and fire.

Her eyes, her green gaze, ravaged, unseeing, unknowing.

I look at her face and cannot find my beloved in it.

"Emmeline?" I whisper. "Emmeline?"

She does not reply.

I feel my heart die. What have I done? Have I . . . ? Is it possible that . . . ?

I cannot bear to know.

I cannot bear not to know.

"Adeline?" My voice is a broken thing.

But she—this person, this someone, this one or the other, this might or might not be, this darling, this monster, this I don't know who she is—does not reply.

People are coming. Running up the drive, voices calling urgently in the night.

I rise to a crouch and scuttle away. Keeping low.

Hiding. They reach the girl on the grass, and when I am sure they have found her I leave them to it. In the church I put the satchel over my shoulder, clutching the baby in his papoose to my side, and set off.

It is quiet in the woods. The rain, slowed by the canopy of leaves, falls softly on the undergrowth. The child whimpers, then sleeps. My feet carry me to a small house on the other edge of the woods. I know the house. I have seen it often during my haunting years. A woman lives there, alone. Spying her through the window knitting or baking, I have always thought she looks nice, and when I read about kindly grandmothers and fairy godmothers in my books, I supply them with her face.

I take the baby to her. I glance in at the window, as I have before, see her in her usual place by the fire, knitting. Thoughtful and quiet. She is undoing her knitting. Just sitting there pulling the stitches out, with the needles on the table beside her. There is a dry place in the porch for the baby. I settle him there and wait behind a tree.

She opens the door. Takes him up. I know when I see her expression that he will be safe with her. She looks up and around. In my direction. As if she's seen something. Have I rustled the leaves, betrayed my presence? It crosses my mind to step forward. Surely she would befriend me? I hesitate, and the wind changes direction. I smell the fire at the same moment she does. She turns away, looks to the sky, gasps at the smoke that rises over the spot where Angelfield House stands. And then puzzlement shows in her face. She holds the baby close to her nose and sniffs. The smell of fire is on him, transferred from my clothes. One more glance at the smoke and she steps firmly back into her house and closes the door.

I am alone.

No name.

No home.

No family.

I am nothing.

I have nowhere to go.

I have no one who belongs to me.

I stare at my burned palm but cannot feel the pain.

What kind of a thing am I? Am I even alive?

I could go anywhere, but I walk back to Angelfield. It is the only place I know.

Emerging from the trees, I approach the scene. A fire engine. Villagers with their buckets, standing back, dazed and with smoke-blackened faces, watching the professionals do battle with the flames. Women, mesmerized by smoke rising into the black sky. An ambulance. Dr. Maudsley kneeling over a figure on the grass.

No one sees me.

On the edge of all the activity I stand, invisible. Perhaps I really am nothing. Perhaps no one can see me at all. Perhaps I died in the fire and haven't realized it yet. Perhaps I am finally what I have always been: a ghost.

Then one of the women looks in my direction.

"Look," she cries, pointing. "She's here!" and people turn. Stare. One of the women runs to alert the men.

They turn from the fire and look, too. "Thank God!" someone says.

I open my mouth to say . . . I don't know what. But I say nothing. Just stand there, making shapes with my mouth, no voice, and no words.

"Don't try to speak." Dr. Maudsley is by my side now.

I stare at the girl on the lawn. "She'll survive," says the doctor.

I look at the house.

The flames. My books. I don't think I can bear it. I remember the page of *Jane Eyre*, the ball of words I saved from the pyre. I have left it behind with the baby.

I begin to weep.

"She's in shock," says the doctor to one of the women. "Keep her warm and stay with her, while we put the sister in the ambulance."

A woman comes to me, clucking her concern. She takes off her coat and wraps it around me, tenderly, as though dressing a baby, and she murmurs, "Don't worry, you'll be all right, your sister's all right, oh, my poor dear."

They lift the girl from the grass and place her on the bed in the ambulance. Then they help me in. Sit me down opposite. And they drive us to the hospital.

*She* stares into space. Eyes open, empty. After the first moment I don't look. The ambulance man bends over her, assures himself that she is breathing, then turns to me.

"What about that hand, eh?"

I am clutching my right hand in my left, unconscious of the pain in my mind, but my body giving the secret away.

He takes my hand, and I let him unfold my fingers. A mark is burned deep into my palm. The key.

"That'll heal up," he tells me. "Don't worry. Now, are you Adeline or are you Emmeline?"

He gestures to the other one. "Is this Emmeline?"

I can't answer, can't feel myself, can't move.

"Not to worry," he said. "All in good time."

He gives up on making me understand him. Mutters for his own benefit, "Still, we've got to call you something. Adeline, Emmeline, Emmeline, Adeline. Fifty-fifty, isn't it? It'll all come out in the wash."

The hospital. Opening the ambulance doors. All noise and bustle. Voices speaking fast. The stretcher, lifted onto a trolley and wheeled away at speed. A wheelchair. Hands on my shoulders. "Sit down, dear." The chair moving. A voice behind my back. "Don't worry, child. We'll take care of you and your sister. You're safe now, Adeline."

❧

Miss Winter slept.

I saw the tender slackness of her open mouth, the tuft of unruly hair that did not lay straight from her temple, and in her sleep she seemed very, very old and very, very young. With every breath she took the bedclothes rose and fell over her thin shoulders, and at each sinking the ribboned edge of the blanket brushed against her face. She seemed unaware of it, but all the same, I bent over her to fold the covers back and smooth the curl of pale hair back into place.

She did not stir. Was she really asleep, I wondered, or was this unconsciousness already?

I can't say how long I watched her after that. There was a clock, but the movements of its hands were as meaningless as a map of the surface of the sea. Wave after wave of time lapped over me as I sat with my eyes closed, not sleeping, but with the vigilance of a mother for the breathing of her child.

I hardly know what to say about the next thing. Is it possible that I hallucinated in my tiredness? Did I fall asleep and dream? Or did Miss Winter really speak one last time?

*I will give your message to your sister.*

I jerked my eyes open, but hers were closed. She seemed to be sleeping as deeply as before.

I did not see the wolf when he came. I did not hear him. There was only this: A little before dawn I became aware of a hush, and I realized that the only breathing to be heard in the room was my own.

# *Beginnings*

## SNOW

**M**iss Winter died and the snow kept falling.
When Judith came she stood with me for a
time at the window, and we watched the eerie illumination of the night sky. Then, when an alteration in the
whiteness told us it was morning, she sent me to bed.

I awoke at the end of the afternoon.

The snow that had already deadened the telephone
now reached the window ledges and drifted halfway up
the doors. It separated us from the rest of the world as
effectively as a prison key. Miss Winter had escaped; so
had the woman Judith referred to as Emmeline, and
whom I avoided naming. The rest of us, Judith, Maurice and I, were trapped.

The cat was restless. It was the snow that put him out;
he did not like this change in the appearance of his universe. He went from one windowsill to another in
search of his lost world, and meowed urgently at Judith,
Maurice and me, as though its restoration was in our
hands. In comparison, the loss of his mistresses was a
small matter that, if he noticed it at all, left him fundamentally undisturbed.

The snow had blockaded us into a sideways extension
of time, and we each found our own way of enduring it.

Judith, imperturbable, made vegetable soup, cleaned the kitchen cupboards out and, when she ran out of jobs, manicured her nails and did a face pack. Maurice, chafing at the confinement and the inactivity, played endless games of solitaire, but when he had to drink his tea black for lack of milk, Judith played rummy with him to distract him from the bitterness.

As for me, I spent two days writing up my final notes, but when that was done, I found I could not settle to reading. Even Sherlock Holmes could not reach me in the snowlocked landscape. Alone in my room I spent an hour examining my melancholy, trying to name what I thought was a new element in it. I realized that I missed Miss Winter. So, hopeful of human company, I made my way to the kitchen. Maurice was glad to play cards with me, even though I knew only children's games. Then, when Judith's nails were drying, I made the cocoa and tea with no milk, and later let Judith file and polish my own nails.

In this way, we three and the cat sat out the days, locked in with our dead, and with the old year seeming to linger on past its time.

On the fifth day I allowed myself to be overcome by a vast sorrow.

I had done the washing up, and Maurice had dried while Judith played solitaire at the table. We were all glad of a change. And when the washing up was done, I took myself away from their company to the drawing room. The window looked out onto the part of the garden that was in the lee of the house. Here the snow did not drift so high. I opened a window, climbed out into the whiteness and walked across the snow. All the grief I had kept at bay for years by means of books and bookcases approached me now. On a bench sheltered by a tall hedge of yew I abandoned myself to a sorrow that was wide and deep as the snow itself, and as untainted. I cried for Miss Winter, for her ghost, for Adeline and Emmeline. For my sister, my mother and my father. Mostly, and most terribly, I cried for myself. My grief was that of the infant, newly severed from her other half; of the child bent over an old tin, making sudden, shocking sense of a few pieces of paper; and of a grown woman, sitting crying on a bench in the hallucinatory light and silence of the snow.

When I came to myself Dr. Clifton was there. He put an arm around me. "I know," he said. "I know."

He didn't know, of course. Not really. And yet that was what he said, and I was soothed to hear it. For I knew what he meant. We all have our sorrows, and although the exact delineaments, weight and dimensions of grief are different for everyone, the color of grief is common to us all. "I know," he said, because he was human, and therefore, in a way, he did.

He led me inside, to warmth.

"Oh dear," said Judith. "Shall I bring cocoa?"

"With a touch of brandy in it, I think," he said.

Maurice pulled out a chair for me and began to stoke the fire.

I sipped the cocoa slowly. There was milk—the

doctor had brought it when he came with the farmer on the tractor.

Judith tucked a shawl around me, then started peeling potatoes for dinner. She and Maurice and the doctor made the occasional comment—what we could have for supper, whether the snow was lighter now, how long it would be before the telephone line was restored—and in making them, took it upon themselves to start the laborious process of cranking up life again after death had stopped us all in its tracks.

Little by little the comments melded together and became a conversation.

I listened to their voices and, after a time, joined in.

## HAPPY BIRTHDAY

I went home.
To the bookshop.

"Miss Winter is dead," I told my father.

"And you? How are you?" he asked.

"Alive."

He smiled.

"Tell me about Mum," I said to him. "Why is she the way she is?"

He told me. "She was very ill when you were born. She never saw you before you were taken away. She never saw your sister. She nearly died. By the time she came around, your operation had already taken place and your sister . . ."

"My sister had died."

"Yes. There was no knowing how it would go with you. I went from her bedside to yours. . . . I thought I was going to lose all three of you. I prayed to every God I had ever heard of to save you. And my prayers were answered. In part. You survived. Your mother never really came back."

There was one other thing I needed to know.

"Why didn't you tell me? About being a twin?"

The face he turned to me was devastated. He swallowed, and when he spoke his voice was hoarse. "The story of your birth is a sad one. Your mother thought it too heavy for a child to bear. At least that's what your mother said. I would have borne it for you, Margaret, if I could. I would have done anything to spare you."

We sat in silence. I thought of all the other questions I might have asked, but now that the moment had come I didn't need to.

I reached for my father's hand at the same moment as he reached for mine.

I attended three funerals in as many days.

Miss Winter's mourners were many. The nation grieved for its favorite storyteller, and thousands of readers turned out to pay their respects. I came away as soon as I could, having said my good-byes already.

The second was a quiet affair. There were only Judith, Maurice, the doctor and me to mourn the woman referred to throughout the service as Emmeline. Afterward we said brief farewells and parted.

The third was lonelier still. In a crematorium in Banbury I was the only person in attendance when a bland-faced clergyman oversaw the passing into God's hands of a set of bones, identity unknown. Into God's hands, except that it was me who collected the urn later, "on behalf of the Angelfield family."

There were snowdrops in Angelfield. At least the first signs of them, boring their way through the frozen ground and showing their points, green and fresh, above the snow.

As I stood up I heard a sound. It was Aurelius, arriving at the lych-gate. Snow had settled on his shoulders and he was carrying flowers.

"Aurelius!" How could he have grown so sad? So pale? "You've changed," I said.

"I have worn myself out on a wild-goose chase." His eyes, always mild, had lightened to the same washed-out blue as the January sky; you could see straight through their transparency to his disappointed heart. "All my life I have wanted to find my family. I wanted to know who I was. And lately I have felt hopeful. I thought there might be some chance of restoration. Now I fear I was mistaken."

We walked along the grass path between the graves and cleared the snow from the bench and sat down before more could fall. Aurelius delved into his pocket and unwrapped two pieces of cake. Absently he handed one to me and dug his teeth into the other.

"Is that what you have for me?" he asked, looking at

the casket. "Is that the rest of my story?"

I handed him the casket.

"Isn't it light? Light as air. And yet . . ." His hand veered to his heart; he sought a gesture to show how heavy his heart was; not finding it, he put down the casket and took another bite of cake.

When he had finished the last morsel he spoke. "If she was my mother, why was I not with her? Why did I not die with her, in this place? Why would she take me away to Mrs. Love's house and then come back here to a house on fire? Why? It doesn't make sense."

I followed him as he stepped off the central path and made his way into the maze of narrow borders between the graves. He stopped at a grave I had looked at before and laid down his flowers. The stone was a simple one.

JOAN MARY LOVE
NEVER FORGOTTEN

Poor Aurelius. He was so very weary. He hardly seemed to notice as I slipped my arm through his. But then he turned to face me fully. "Perhaps it's better not to have a story at all, rather than have one that keeps changing. I have spent my whole life chasing after my story and never quite catching it. Running after my story when I had Mrs. Love all along. She loved me, you know."

"I never doubted it." She had been a good mother to him. Better than either of the twins could have been.

"Perhaps it's better not to know," I suggested.

He looked from the gravestone to the white sky. "Do *you* think so?"

"No."

"Then why suggest it?"

I slid my arm from his and tucked my cold hands under the arms of my coat. "It's what my mother would say. She thinks a weightless story is better than one that's too heavy."

"So. My story is a heavy one."

I said nothing, and when the silence grew long, I told him not his story but my own.

"I had a sister," I began. "A twin."

He turned to face me. His shoulders were solid and wide against the sky and he listened gravely to the story I poured out to him.

"We were joined. Here—" and I brushed my hand down my left side. "She couldn't live without me. She needed my heart to beat for her. But I couldn't live with her. She was draining my strength. They separated us, and she died."

My other hand joined the first over my scar, and I pressed hard.

"My mother never told me. She thought it was better for me not to know."

"A weightless story."

"Yes."

"But you do know."

I pressed harder. "I found out by accident."

"I am sorry," he said.

492

I felt my hands taken by his, and he enclosed both of them into one great fist. Then, with his other arm, he drew me to him. Through layers of coats I felt the softness of his belly, and a rush of noise came to my ear. It is the beating of his heart, I thought. A human heart. By my side. So this is what it's like. I listened.

Then we drew apart.

"And is it better to know?" he asked me.

"I can't tell you. But once you know, it's impossible to go back."

"And you know my story."

"Yes."

"My true story."

"Yes."

He barely hesitated. Just took a breath and seemed to grow a little bigger.

"You had better tell me, then," he said.

I told. And while I told we walked, and when I finished telling we were standing at the place where the snowdrops were pointing through the whiteness of the snow.

With the casket in his hands, Aurelius hesitated. "I have a feeling this is against the rules."

I thought it was, too. "But what else can we do?"

"The rules don't work for this case, do they?"

"Nothing else would be right."

"Come on, then."

We used the cake knife to gouge a hollow in the frozen earth above the coffin of the woman I knew as

493

Emmeline. Aurelius tipped the ashes into it, and we replaced the earth to cover them. Aurelius pressed down with all his weight, and then we rearranged the flowers to hide the disturbance.

"It will level out with the melting of the snow," he said. And he brushed the snow from his trouser legs.

"Aurelius, there is more to your story."

I led him to another part of the churchyard. "You know about your mother now. But you had a father, too." I indicated Ambrose's gravestone. "The *A* and the *S* on the piece of paper you showed me. It was *his* name. His bag, too. It was used for carrying game. That explains the feather."

I paused. It was a lot for Aurelius to take in. When after a long moment he nodded, I went on. "He was a good man. You are very like him."

Aurelius stared. Dazed. More knowledge. More loss. "He is dead. I see."

"That's not all," I said softly. He turned his eyes slowly to mine, and I read in them the fear that there was to be no end to the story of his abandonment.

I took his hand. I smiled at him.

"After you were born, Ambrose married. He had another child."

It took a moment for him to realize what it meant, and when he did, a jolt of excitement brought his frame to life. "You mean . . . I have . . . And she . . . he . . . she—"

"Yes! A sister!"

The smile grew broad on his face.

I went on. "And she has her own children in turn. A boy and a girl!"

"A niece! And a nephew!"

I took his hands into mine to stop them shaking. "A *family,* Aurelius. *Your* family. You know them already. And they are expecting you."

I could hardly keep up with him as we passed through the lych-gate and strode down the avenue to the white gatehouse. Aurelius never looked back. Only at the gatehouse did we pause, and that was because of me.

"Aurelius! I almost forgot to give you this."

He took the white envelope and opened it, distracted by joy. He drew out the card and gave me a look. "What? Not really?"

"Yes. Really."

"Today?"

"Today!" Something possessed me at that moment. I did something I have never done in my life before and never expected to do, either. I opened my mouth and shouted at the top of my voice, *"HAPPY BIRTHDAY!"*

I must have been a bit mad. In any case, I felt embarrassed. Not that Aurelius cared. He was standing motionless, arms stretched out on either side of him, eyes closed and face turned skyward. All the happiness in the world was falling on him with the snow.

In Karen's garden the snow bore the prints of chase games, small footprints and smaller ones following one another in broad circles. The children were nowhere to be seen, but as we got nearer we heard their voices coming from the niche in the yew tree.

"Let's play Snow White."

"That's a girls' story."

"What story do you want to play?"

"A story about rockets."

"I don't want to be a rocket. Let's be boats."

"We were boats yesterday."

Hearing the latch of the gate, they peered out of the tree, and with their hoods hiding their hair, you could hardly tell brother from sister.

"It's the cake man!"

Karen stepped out of the house and came across the lawn. "Shall I tell you who this is?" she asked the children as she smiled shyly at Aurelius. "This is your uncle."

Aurelius looked from Karen to the children and back to Karen, his eyes scarcely big enough to take in everything he wanted to. He was lost for words, but Karen reached out a tentative hand, and he took it in his.

"It's all a bit . . ." he began.

"Isn't it?" she agreed. "But we'll get used to it, won't we?"

He nodded.

The children were staring with curiosity at the adult scene.

"What are you playing?" Karen asked, to distract them.

"We don't know," the girl said.

"We can't decide," said her brother.

"Do you know any stories?" Emma asked Aurelius.

"Only one," he told her.

"Only one?" She was astounded. "Has it got any frogs in it?"

"No."

"Dinosaurs?"

"No."

"Secret passages?"

"No."

The children looked at each other. It wasn't much of a story, clearly.

"We know loads of stories," Tom said.

"Loads," she echoed dreamily. "Princesses, frogs, magic castles, fairy godmothers—"

"Caterpillars, rabbits, elephants—"

"All sorts of animals."

"All sorts."

They fell into silence, absorbed in shared contemplation of countless different worlds.

Aurelius watched them as though they were a miracle.

Then they returned to the real world. "Millions of stories," the boy said.

"Shall I tell *you* a story?" the girl asked.

I thought perhaps Aurelius had had enough stories for one day, but he nodded his head.

She picked up an imaginary object and placed it in the palm of her right hand. With her left she mimed the opening of a book cover. She glanced up to be sure she had the full attention of her companions. Then her eyes returned to the book in her hand, and she began.

"Once upon a time . . ."

Karen and Tom and Aurelius: three sets of eyes all resting on Emma and her storytelling. They would be all right together.

Unnoticed, I stepped back from the gate and slipped away along the street.


## THE THIRTEENTH TALE

I will not publish the biography of Vida Winter. The world may well be agog for the story, but it is not mine to tell. Adeline and Emmeline, the fire and the ghost, these are stories that belong to Aurelius now. The graves in the churchyard are his; so is the birthday that he can mark as he chooses. The truth is heavy enough without the additional weight of the world's scrutiny on his shoulders. Left to their own devices, he and Karen can turn the page, start afresh.

But time passes. One day Aurelius will be no more; one day Karen, too, will leave this world. The children, Tom and Emma, are already more distant from the events I have told here than their uncle. With the help of their mother they have begun to forge their own stories; stories that are strong and solid and true. The day will come when Isabelle and Charlie, Adeline and Emmeline, the Missus and John-the-dig, the girl without a name, will be so far in the past that their old bones will have no power to cause fear or pain. They will be nothing but an old story, unable to do any harm to anyone. And when that day comes—I will be old myself by then—I shall give Tom and Emma this document. To read and, if they choose, to publish.

I hope that they will publish. For until they do, the spirit of that ghost-child will haunt me. She will roam in my thoughts, linger in my dreams, my memory her only playground. It is not much, this posthumous life of hers, but it is not oblivion. It will be enough, until the day when Tom and Emma release this manuscript and she will be able to exist more fully after death than she ever lived before it.

And so the story of the ghost girl is not to be published for many years, if at all. That does not mean, however, that I have nothing to give the world immediately to satisfy its curiosity about Vida Winter. For there is something. At the end of my last meeting with Mr. Lomax, I was about to leave when he stopped me. "Just one more thing." And he opened his desk and took out an envelope.

I had that envelope with me when I slipped unremarked out of Karen's garden and turned my steps back toward the lodge gates. The ground for the new hotel had been flattened, and when I tried to remember the old house, I could find only photographs in my memory. But then it came to me how it always seemed to face the wrong way. It had been twisted. The new building was going to be much better. It would face straight toward you.

I diverged from the gravel pathway to cross the snow-covered lawn toward the old deer park and the woods. The dark branches were heavy with snow, which sometimes fell in soft swathes at my passing. I came at last to the vantage point on the slope. You can see everything from there. The church and its graveyard, the wreaths of flowers bright against the snow. The lodge gates, chalk-white against the blue sky. The coach house, denuded of its shroud of thorns. Only the house had gone, and it had gone completely. The men in their yellow hats had reduced the past to a blank page. We had reached tipping point. It was no longer possible to call it a demolition site. Tomorrow, today perhaps, the workers would return and it would become a construction site. The past demolished, it was time for them to start building the future.

I took the envelope from my bag. I had been waiting. For the right time. The right place.

The letters on the envelope were curiously misformed. The uneven strokes either faded into nothing or else were engraved into the paper. There was no sense of flow: Each letter gave the impression of having been completed individually, at great cost, the next undertaken as a new and daunting enterprise. It was like the hand of a child or a very old person. It was addressed to Miss Margaret Lea.

I slit open the flap. I drew out the contents. And I sat on a felled tree to read it, because I never read standing up.

*Dear Margaret,*
*Here is the piece I told you about.*
*I have tried to finish it, and find that I cannot. And*

*so this story that the world has made so much fuss about must do as it is. It is a flimsy thing: something of nothing. Do with it what you will.*

*As for titles, the one that springs to my mind is "Cinderella's Child," but I know quite enough about readers to understand that whatever I might choose to call it, it will only ever go by one title in the world, and it won't be mine.*

There was no signature. No name.

But there was a story.

It was the story of Cinderella, like I'd never read it before. Laconic, hard and angry. Miss Winter's sentences were shards of glass, brilliant and lethal.

*Picture this,* the story begins. *A boy and a girl; one rich, one poor. Most often it's the girl who's got no gold and that's how it is in the story I'm telling. There didn't have to be a ball. A walk in the woods was enough for these two to stumble into each other's paths. Once upon a time there was a fairy godmother, but the rest of the time there was none. This story is about one of those other times. Our girl's pumpkin is just a pumpkin, and she crawls home after midnight, blood on her petticoats, violated. There will be no footman at the door with moleskin slippers tomorrow. She knows that already. She's not stupid. She is pregnant, though.*

In the rest of the story, Cinderella gives birth to a girl, raises her in poverty and filth, abandons her after a few years in the grounds of the house owned by her violator. The story ends abruptly.

*Halfway along a path in a garden she has never been to before, cold and hungry, the child suddenly realizes she is alone. Behind her is the garden door that leads into the forest. It remains ajar. Is her mother behind it still? Ahead of her is a shed that, to her child's mind, has the look of a little house. A place she might shelter. Who knows, there might even be something to eat.*

*The garden door? Or the little house?*

*Door? Or house?*

*The child hesitates.*

*She hesitates . . .*

And the story ends there.

Miss Winter's earliest memory? Or just a story? The story invented by an imaginative child to fill the space where her mother ought to have been?

The thirteenth tale. The final, the famous, the unfinished story.

I read the story and grieved.

Gradually my thoughts turned away from Miss Winter and to myself. She might not be perfect, but at least I had a mother. Was it too late to make something of ourselves? But that was another story.

I put the envelope in my bag, stood up and brushed the bark dust from my trousers before heading back to the road.

I was engaged to write the story of Miss Winter's life, and I have done it. There is really nothing more I need do in order to fulfill the terms of the contract. One copy of this document is to be deposited with Mr. Lomax, who will store it in a bank vault and then arrange for a large amount of money to be paid to me. Apparently he doesn't even have to check that the pages I give him are not blank.

"She trusted you," he told me.

Clearly she did trust me. Her intentions in the contract that I never read or signed are quite unmistakable. She wanted to tell me the story before she died; she wanted me to make a record of it. What I did with it after that was my business. I have told the solicitor about my intentions regarding Tom and Emma, and we have made an appointment to formalize my wishes in a will just in case. And that ought to be the end of it.

But I don't feel I am quite done. I don't know who or how many people will eventually read this, but no matter how few they are, no matter how distant in time from this moment, I feel a responsibility toward them. And although I have told them all there is to know about Adeline and Emmeline and the ghost-child, I realize that for some that will not be quite enough. I know what it is like to finish a book and find oneself wondering, a day or a week later, what happened to the butcher or who got the diamonds, or whether or not the dowager was ever reconciled with her niece. I can imagine readers pondering what became of Judith and Maurice, whether anyone kept up the glorious garden, who came to live in the house.

And so, in case you are wondering, let me tell you. Judith and Maurice stayed on. The house was not sold; provision had been made in Miss Winter's will for the house and garden to be converted into a kind of literary museum. Of course it is the garden that has real value ("an unsuspected gem," an early horticultural review has called it), but Miss Winter realized that it was her reputation for storytelling more than her gardening skill that would draw the crowds. And so there are to be tours of the rooms, a teashop, and a bookshop. Coaches that bring tourists to the Brontë museum can come afterward to "Vida Winter's Secret Garden." Judith will continue as housekeeper, and Maurice as head gardener. Their first job, before the conversion can begin, is to clear Emmeline's rooms. These will not be visited, for there will be nothing to see.

And Hester. Now, this will surprise you; it certainly surprised me. I had a letter from Emmanuel Drake. To tell you the truth, I'd forgotten all about him. Slowly and methodically he continued his searches, and against all odds, late in the day, he found her. "It was the Italian connection that threw me off track," his letter explained, "when your governess had gone the other way entirely—to America!" For three years Hester had worked as clerical assistant to an academic neurologist, and when the time was up, guess who came to join her? Dr. Maudsley! His wife died (nothing more sinister than the flu, I did check), and within days of the funeral he was on the boat. It was love. They are both deceased now, but after a long and happy life together. They had four children, one of whom has written to me, and I have sent the original of his mother's diary to him to keep. I doubt he will be able to make out much more than one word in ten; if he asks me for elucidation, I will tell him that his mother knew his father here in England, during the time of his father's first marriage, but if he does not ask, I will keep my silence. In his letter to me, he enclosed a list of his parents' joint publications. They researched and wrote dozens of highly regarded articles (none on twins, I think they knew when to call it a day) and published them jointly: Dr. E. and Mrs. H. J. Maudsley.

H. J.? Hester had a middle name: *Josephine.*

What else will you want to know? Who looked after the cat? Well, Shadow came to live with me at the bookshop. He sits on the shelves, anywhere he can find a space between the books, and when customers come across him there, he returns their stares with placid equanimity. From time to time he will sit in the window, but not for long. He is baffled by the street, the vehicles, the passersby, the buildings opposite. I have shown him the shortcut via the alley to the river, but he scorns to use it.

"What do you expect?" my father says. "A river is no use to a Yorkshire cat. It is the moors he is looking for."

I think he is right. Full of expectation, Shadow jumps up to the window, looks out, then turns on me a long, disappointed stare.

I don't like to think that he is homesick.

Dr. Clifton came to my father's shop—he happened to be visiting the town, he said, and remembering that my father had a bookshop here, he thought it worthwhile to call in, though it was something of a long shot, to see if we had a particular volume on eighteenth-century medicine he was interested in. As it happened, we *did* have one, and he and my father chatted amiably about it at length, until well after closing time. To make up for keeping us so late he invited us out for a meal. It was very pleasant, and since he was still in town for another night, my father invited him the next evening for a meal with the family. In the kitchen my mother told me he was "a very nice man, Margaret. Very nice." The next afternoon was his last. We went for a walk by the river, but this time it was just the two of us, Father being too busy writing letters to be able to accompany us. I told him the story of the ghost of Angelfield. He listened closely, and when I had finished, we continued to walk, slowly and in silence.

"I remember seeing that treasure box," he said eventually. "How did it come to escape the fire?"

I stopped in my tracks, wondering. "You know, I never thought to ask."

"You'll never know now, will you?"

He took my arm and we walked on.

Anyway, returning to my subject, which is Shadow and his homesickness, when Dr. Clifton visited my father's shop and saw the cat's sadness he proposed to give Shadow a home with him. Shadow would be very happy back in Yorkshire, I have no doubt. But this offer, kind as it is, has plunged me into a state of painful perplexity. For I am not sure I can bear to be parted from him. He, I am sure, would bear my absence with the same composure with which he accepts Miss Winter's disappearance, for he is a cat; but being human, I have grown fond of him and would prefer if at all possible to keep him near me.

In a letter I betrayed something of these thoughts to Dr. Clifton; he replies that perhaps we might *both* go and stay, Shadow and I, for a holiday. He invites us for a month, in the spring. Anything, he says, may happen in a month, and by the end of it he thinks it possible that we may have thought of some way out of the dilemma that suits us all. I cannot help but think Shadow will get his happy ending yet.

And that is all.

## POSTSCRIPTUM

O r nearly all. One thinks something is finished, and then suddenly it isn't, quite.

I have had a visitor.

It was Shadow who was first to notice. I was humming as I packed for our holiday, suitcase open on the bed. Shadow was stepping in and out of it, toying with the idea of making himself a nest on my socks and cardigans, when suddenly he stopped, all intent, and stared toward the door behind me.

She came not as a golden angel, nor as the cloaked specter of death. She was like me: a tallish, thin, brown-haired woman you would not notice if she passed you in the street.

There were a hundred, a thousand things I thought I

would want to ask her, but I was so overcome I could hardly even speak her name. She stepped toward me, put her arms around me and pressed me to her side.

"Moira," I managed to whisper, "I was beginning to think you weren't real."

But she was real. Her cheek against mine, her arm across my shoulders, my hand at her waist. Scar to scar we touched, and all my questions faded as I felt her blood flow with mine, her heart beat with mine. It was a moment of wonderment, great and calm; and I knew that I *remembered* this feeling. It had been locked in me, closed away, and now she had come and released it. This blissful circuitry. This oneness that had once been ordinary and was today, now that I had recovered it, miraculous.

She came and we were together.

I understood that she had come to say good-bye. That next time we met it would be me who went to her. But this next meeting wouldn't be for a very long time. There was no rush. She could wait and so could I.

I felt the touch of her fingers on my face as I brushed away her tears, then, in joy, our fingers found each other and entwined. Her breath on my cheek, her face in my hair, I buried my nose in the crook of her neck and inhaled her sweetness.

Such joy.

No matter that she could not stay. She had come. She had come.

I'm not sure how or when she left. I simply realized that she was no longer there. I sat on the bed, quite calm, quite happy. I felt the curious sensation of my blood rerouting itself, of my heart recalibrating its beat for me alone. Touching my scar, she had brought it alive; now, gradually, it cooled until it felt no different from the rest of my body.

She had come and she had gone. I would not see her again this side of the grave. My life was my own.

In the suitcase, Shadow was asleep. I put out my hand to stroke him. He opened a cool green eye, regarded me for a moment, then closed it again.

# ACKNOWLEDGMENTS

With thanks to Jo Anson, Gaia Banks, Martyn Bedford, Emily Bestler, Paula Catley, Ross and Colin Catley, Jim Crace, Penny Dolan, Marianne Downie, Mandy Franklin, Anna and Nathan Franklin, Vivien Green, Douglas Gurr, Jenny Jacobs, Caroline le Marechal, Pauline and Jeffrey Setterfield, Christina Shingler, Janet and Bill Whittall, John Wilkes and Jane Wood.

With special thanks to Owen Staley, who has been a friend to this book from the very beginning, and Peter Whittall, to whom *The Thirteenth Tale* owes its title and a good deal more besides.

**Center Point Publishing**
600 Brooks Road ● PO Box 1
Thorndike ME 04986-0001 USA

(207) 568-3717

US & Canada:
1 800 929-9108